THE

FIRST

TASTE

JESSICA
HAWKINS

Editing by Elizabeth London Editing
Proofreading by Underline This Editing
Cover Design © Shanoff Formats.
Cover Photo © Wander Aguiar Photography

THE FIRST TASTE

ISBN: 0-9978691-0-0
ISBN-13: 978-0-9978691-0-1

TITLES BY
JESSICA HAWKINS
LEARN MORE AT JESSICAHAWKINS.NET/BOOKS

SLIP OF THE TONGUE
THE FIRST TASTE
YOURS TO BARE

THE CITYSCAPE SERIES
COME UNDONE
COME ALIVE
COME TOGETHER

EXPLICITLY YOURS SERIES
POSSESSION
DOMINATION
PROVOCATION
OBSESSION

STRICTLY OFF LIMITS

ONE
ANDREW

From the moment I left the house, I've been tempted to turn around and call the whole thing off. Tonight will be the first I've spent away from Bell since we've been on our own. Before her, I wouldn't have thought twice about that. Before her, I didn't think twice about much. One thing's for sure—my definition of a sleepover has changed drastically since I became a father.

"We'll roast marshmallows on the stove for s'mores and have girl talk." My six-year-old lists the ways her aunt has enticed her to come for the weekend as we fight our way through Penn Station. "She has a doll for me that wears diapers and everything."

"Diapers? Fascinating." Sadie will have no problem parenting if she's managed to trick Bell into thinking changing diapers is fun.

Bell tries to take her hand from my grip, but I tighten mine around hers and adjust her overnight bag on my shoulder. "Stay with me."

"Look." She points to the 1 train. "There it is!"

"Yeah," I say, my tone decidedly less enthusiastic. We get passes and board. Bell's nearly bouncing with excitement just from being on the subway. She didn't get her fascination with New York City from me. Each time I bring her, part of me hopes the city'll lose its appeal.

When we come up from the station into Times Square, though, I see that won't be happening anytime soon. "Can we go to M&M World?" she asks before pulling me in another direction. "Can I get a dress from the Disney store?"

"No," I say and repeat the same answer to all her demands. "I thought we were here to see Aunt Sadie, not buy a bunch of crap we don't need."

"We should bring Aunt Sadie a gift, though," she says. "I remember she loves M&Ms."

If I were younger, dumber, and greener, I'd praise my little girl for her selflessness. In fact, she'd pour "Aunt Sadie's M&Ms" into her mouth first chance she got.

I steer her away from the flashing screens and bright lights, and in the direction of Bryant Park. Parking, boarding the train to Penn Station, switching to the subway, walking to Sadie's office building—it's a fuck of a lot of trouble for something I don't even want to be doing.

We take the elevator to the seventh floor. The receptionist looks up from his computer when we walk in. With his gray button down and silver tie, he fits in perfectly with the neutral walls and glossy white desk of Amelia Van Ecken Communications, or *avec*.

"Look, Daddy," Bell says, running to a chair in the foyer to touch it. "Blue suede—like Elvis."

"That's velvet," I say.

She loses interest quickly and strides alongside me to the front desk. The lacquered surface reflects and distorts us as we approach, highlighting our height disparity, making our black hair even shinier.

The receptionist looks from me to Bell and back. "We don't take walk-ins. Models need to make advance appointments or wait for casting calls."

I straighten a little, feeling suddenly on display. It's not my first time being mistaken for someone in the entertainment industry when visiting the city, but it hasn't happened since my twenties. It's always uncomfortable. "I'm not a model." I show him a smudged hand. "Not unless it's a commercial for car grease."

"I was talking about her," he says, raising one pruned eyebrow in Bell's direction. "One of our clients designs a children's line, and we occasionally hire kids to model the clothing during events."

"Oh. Yeah, I figured." I rub the back of my neck. Bell's hair hasn't been brushed since this morning, and she's got Go-Gurt stains on her top but whatever. "I was joking."

"No worries." He trails his eyes down my body. "I can understand why you'd make that mistake."

"We're here to see Sadie Hunt," I say before we stumble into any more misunderstandings.

"Regarding?"

"She's my aunt," Bell says.

"Oh. Of course." He lifts a corner of his mouth and motions at a woman passing by. "Mindy—this is Sadie's niece. Will you take them back?"

She stops mid-stride, her brown ponytail swinging as she gazes at me, wide-eyed. "Sadie?" she asks.

"Yes, you know, the woman who's been training you the last month," he says. "The only other brunette on the floor. Your point person on the IncrediBlast campaign."

"Oh. Right. *Sadie.*" She blinks down to Bell's hand in mine and then to her face. "You must be Bell."

Bell squeezes my hand, rolling onto the balls of her feet. "You know me?"

"Sure." She smiles. "Sadie talks about you all the time. Come on, I'll take you to her desk."

Mindy takes us left into the next room, a sunlit, open space with large windows—not that it needs them, given there's a *massive* chandelier. Posh as hell

4

and the opposite of my taste. Long desks create a labyrinth of rows, each person's workspace separated by Mac desktops, colorful supplies, bedazzled picture frames. Nobody looks up from his or her computer. Sadie's dark hair pops against the white walls and gold-accented furniture. She stands, and Bell skips ahead to meet her, but Mindy walks me all the way to the desk.

"Thanks, Mindy," Sadie says before turning to me. "Did you meet Mindy? She just started here."

"Yes, I did." I smile politely. Mindy's a pretty girl with what I presume is good taste; I wouldn't know, but this is a fashion and beauty PR firm. If I weren't anxious about being apart from Bell this weekend, I might indulge in a little flirting. That's the furthest thing from my mind right now, though. "Can you give us a minute, Mindy?"

"Oh." She nods quickly. "Of course. It was nice to meet you."

"Andrew," Sadie scolds when we're alone. "That was rude."

"Was it?" I ask. "So about tonight—"

"She's cute," Sadie continues. "Don't you think?"

"Yeah." Bell has already taken over Sadie's desk, organizing her office supplies into piles. I squint past the pyramid of ballpoint pens and mess of metallic binder clips as I shake my head. "Is that stapler made of gold?" I ask.

"It's gold-*plated*," Sadie says, as if gold and gold-plated are in two completely different realms. She

5

glances at Bell and then moves closer to me. "What're your plans this weekend?"

"Not sure yet."

"You have two whole nights to yourself," she points out.

"I'm aware."

"It might not be a bad idea to . . . you know."

I know where she's going with this, and in my experience, it's best if we change topics. Once Sadie gets going about the reasons I need to start dating again, I tend to tune her out pretty quickly. "What?" I ask. "Masturbate?"

"Ugh—*gross*." She makes a face but undeterred, she nods in the direction Mindy just went. "Why don't you go talk to Mindy? She's single. I bet she'd be up for grabbing dinner tonight."

I roll my eyes. Sadie assumes that because I don't take women out, I don't get laid. She forgets I'm a man, and that nothing, not even fatherhood, can take me out of the game for good. "Anyway," I say. "About this weekend—"

"Don't worry," she says with an exasperated sigh. "We've got this. Nathan can't wait. He already bought a bunch of crap for Bell to play with."

"Why? It's just a weekend."

"I know. I told him." She touches her stomach so lightly, I doubt she even realizes she's doing it. "He says we'll need toys anyway."

"How're you feeling?"

"Better than the last time we talked. Now I'm mostly dealing with heartburn." She says it cheerfully, as if heartburn is something she'd been hoping to get.

"Have you felt the baby move yet?"

"I'm not sure. Maybe?" She makes a face. "Is it terrible that I don't know?"

"Nah. It can be hard to detect when it's your first one. You'll know when the baby really gets active."

At the word *baby*, Bell perks up, swiveling in Sadie's office chair. "Can I touch?"

Sadie smiles. "You don't have to ask."

"At nineteen weeks, barely anything there," I say. "Just looks like you have a small gut."

Sadie's smile fades into a scowl. "At least *I* have an excuse."

"Nice try." I pat my six-pack. "Hard as a rock, no matter what I eat."

She blatantly ignores me, because she knows it's true and her joke sucked.

Bell cradles her aunt's stomach like it's a bubble at risk of popping. "I think I can feel it," Bell says.

"Aww." Sadie smiles. "That's just gas, honey."

I rub the bridge of my nose as memories of my ex's pregnancy hit me. Not just a magical time, but also a gastrointestinal one.

Sadie runs a hand through Bell's dark hair. They look so much alike they could be mother and daughter. "You could've dropped her off at our place if you'd waited another hour," Sadie says. "I'm about to leave for the day."

"Bell's obsessed with riding the subway." I raise my palms. "Don't ask me why—I think she saw it in a movie. I've done my best to instill in her what a rotten place this city is, but she seems to like it." I lean in a little. "Just don't mention that Brooklyn isn't technically Manhattan. She'll throw a fit."

Sadie laughs. "She takes after her aunt."

"Not anymore, she doesn't. I thought you were liking it?"

"I am. Brooklyn's taken some getting used to," she says slowly, "but our neighborhood's great. We have friends close by and more space for what we were paying in Gramercy Park."

Six months ago, Sadie moved to Brooklyn with Nate to save a marriage she'd nearly wrecked. Can't say I blame her for trying to sabotage it, what with my parents and myself as relationship examples. "Things are still good, though, right?" I ask.

She nods. "We're working on it every day, but we're as happy as we've ever been."

I look down at her stomach. "Hard to imagine it any other way with that bundle of joy on the way."

"Oh, God." She rolls her eyes. "You sound like Nathan. You guys are so sappy. I don't know what's so joyous about having to use the ladies' room every hour or craving things I wouldn't normally touch with a pole."

I smile. All that'll leave her memory as soon as the nurse hands her the baby. It didn't exactly happen that way for Shana, who never forgot how much she hated being pregnant, but I know a lot of moms. They start talking about the next one pretty quickly. "You need anything at all and Nathan's not around, you call me. Seriously."

"Count on it."

"Speaking of the can," I say, "I need to take a leak."

"Charming."

"It took us almost an hour to get here because of the time of day." I slump Bell's duffel on the ground. "Nature calls."

"Go back the way you came," she says, pointing behind me. "Bathroom's right before reception."

I head through the maze of desks until I find a corridor with one door, but there's an out-of-order sign plastered to it.

I'm about to go in anyway when a woman speaks, her tone clear but edged with impatience. "*Finally*," she says. "Do you have any idea how long I've been waiting for you?"

I turn around and meet a pair of dusk-blue eyes. My gaze instantly drifts south. She's a leggy blonde in a colorful blouse and tight navy skirt that hugs her very slight curves. The cream parts of her top are sheer, so of course I notice the dark, lacy bra underneath.

She puts her hands on her hips, and I look up again. Her eyes sparkle like she's happy to see me, but the way she's frowning, I get the feeling that's not the case.

9

I glance from side to side, but we're alone in the hall. "If that was an attempt at a pick-up line, you need to work on your delivery."

She purses her red lips, forming them into a near-perfect heart. "There are *seven* women on this floor, *four* men, and one bathroom. You said you'd be here hours ago. Did you flush your work ethic down the toilet at your last job?"

I reel back, crossing my arms over my chest. That's a whole lot of attitude for so few words, and nobody but Bell gives me attitude. "I don't know what the hell you're talking about. I'm here to see my sister, not get yelled at."

She furrows her brows with a tilt of her head. "Aren't you with the plumbing company?"

My first instinct is to laugh, but I *think* she's just insulted me. I could see why she'd assume that if I were still in my coveralls from the garage, but I've showered and changed since leaving work. In jeans and a clean t-shirt, I'm not exactly King of England, but it's not like my ass crack is showing. "You've got the wrong guy."

"Then what're you doing in my agency?" she asks. "And why are you wasting my time?"

Sadie saves me. "I'm sorry, Amelia," she says, hurrying over. "This is my brother."

The woman—Amelia—stares at me, but I give it right back to her. I hold out my hand. "Andrew Beckwith, brother, father, non-plumber."

She looks at my hand, then at Sadie.

"He's just dropping off my niece for the weekend," Sadie explains.

The corners of Amelia's mouth droop. "There's a child in here?"

Sadie nods. "Yes, but I'm taking her home right now. She won't even have time to make a mess."

Spurned, I drop my hand back to my side and suck my front teeth. Typical New York City girl. Not a single blonde hair on her head is out of place. She's tall and thin, with a small but defined nose and almond-shaped, stunningly blue eyes. My first thought is that she's definitely not Shana. Black-haired, petite, tattooed and pierced ex-girlfriends used to be my type. Now, it's a woman who's anything but. This one may look like a sexy Barbie, but she's arrogant as hell. I don't think it's any coincidence every entitled chick I've come across in my thirty-five years hails from or is heading to the city.

If I'm expecting an apology from this woman, it's clear I'm not going to get one. But I still have to piss, and now that I'm aware of it, the situation's getting serious.

"If the repairman isn't here in the next ten minutes," Amelia announces, "I'll have to fix the toilet myself, and getting dirty in expensive clothes makes me very, very cranky."

Pretty sure I'd like to see her in her stuffy outfit on the bathroom floor getting *dirty*.

A few people groan.

I open my mouth to ask how much crankier she can get, maybe even lighten the mood with a joke, but Sadie shakes her head quickly, warning me off.

Instead, I ask, "Didn't you say there were four men on this floor?"

"Yes."

"Why can't one of them fix it?"

Amelia throws back her head and laughs, but it sounds more controlled than carefree. "Has hell frozen over? These boys wouldn't know a wrench if I knocked them upside the head with one. And believe me, I've considered it."

I check my watch, though I'm not sure why. I've got nowhere to be—except, hopefully, the toilet. "You got tools here? I'll take a look."

"Andrew's extremely handy," Sadie says.

Amelia doesn't miss a beat. She motions for me to follow her. "Right this way, handyman."

The pitter-patter of feet follows us as we continue down the short hallway. "Can I help?" Bell yells after me.

Amelia glances over her shoulder at me. "Is that your child?" she asks, as if she's accusing me of something.

"Yeah. There a problem?"

"No." She shrugs a shoulder before opening a door to a closet. On the floor sits an impressive steel caddy. "But why does she want to help fix a toilet?"

"Because like her old man, she knows the way to get shit done is to do it yourself. Maybe if you knew how, you wouldn't be in this situation."

"Oh, I know how," she says, glancing back at me. "I just choose to have others do it for me."

Before I can stop the image, I picture Amelia in the bathroom again, this time bent over, her skirt riding up the backs of her thighs. I shake the thought away, not even sure where it came from. If anything, she embraces a lot of what I avoid in women. Her clothes are all class, her hair and makeup perfect, and she seems more delighted than apologetic about mistaking me for a plumber. I'm either insulted or impressed that she's got me doing her bitch work within minutes of meeting me.

Ignoring her last comment, I turn and squat to Bell's level. "I got this, kid. Go wait with Aunt Sadie."

Her eyebrows vault together. "But I want to help," she whines. "You said I'm good with tools."

"Honey," Amelia says from above us, "when a man offers to do your dirty work, let him. Always."

I look to Sadie for help, who seems to notice my irritation and immediately calls Bell back.

When Bell's out of earshot, I stand and turn to Amelia. "Do not put that kind of bullshit in my kid's head," I warn.

Once again, an apology doesn't even seem to occur to her. Two dimples dent her cheeks as if she's holding in a smile. "How is that bullshit?"

13

"I'm not raising an entitled, spoiled brat. Bell's toilet needs fixing, she'll know how to do it herself."

"Are you calling me an entitled, spoiled brat?"

I look her over. It's hard to ignore the way her skirt accentuates her small waist and comes right up under her tits. She does have one thing in common with Shana, and that's a great rack. I return my eyes to her face. "If the skirt fits . . ."

Amelia glances down at her outfit quickly and then points to the tools. "Well, I won't try to change your mind," she says. "Now, how about that toilet?"

TWO

Downstairs, I walk Sadie and Bell to their subway station. "Maybe we should get dinner before you go," I say. "Bell hasn't eaten since . . ."

"Since?" Sadie prompts.

"The ride here."

She narrows her eyes at me. "I've already got a meal planned at home. Nathan and I went grocery shopping last night."

I open my mouth.

"And no," she cuts me off, "you can't come."

I'm not ready to say goodbye, but I can't figure out how to score an invite without sounding desperate.

"What'd you think of Mindy?" Sadie asks.

"Who?"

"The new girl. The one you *just* met upstairs not thirty minutes ago? She showed you to my desk?"

"Oh." I glance sidelong at Sadie. "I think all your colleagues will be happy they have a functioning toilet thanks to the handsome stranger."

Sadie elbows me. "*Andrew.*"

"Could we not talk about this in front of the kid?" I ask.

"We're not talking about anything," Sadie says.

I glance down at Bell, who hasn't said a word since we left Sadie's office. She walks between us, watching the sidewalk, completely oblivious to her surroundings. "You're quiet, Bluebell."

She looks up at me and smiles with her mouth closed—a telltale sign she's nervous. I'm not exactly at ease, either, but she doesn't need to know that. I ruffle her hair. "Looking forward to your sleepover?"

"Yes," she says.

I wait for her to launch like the rocket she is into all the things they're going to do tonight. One-word answers are a rarity with her.

"Ginger's excited to see you," Sadie offers.

Bell just takes my hand and says, "She's a dog. She doesn't know I'm coming."

I exchange a glance with Sadie. "Maybe this is a bad idea," I say under my breath.

"Relax. This is good for everyone. You need a break, and she needs to try something without you. You're always bragging about how independent she is, but she isn't when it comes to you."

I look at my shoes. That's because I want Bell to be independent—just not from me. That might be the last thing in the world I want. She's still my baby. I'm not sure how I'll sleep knowing she isn't under my roof where I can protect her. "What about you?"

"It's good for Nathan and me." Sadie smiles. "Practice."

My bad mood eases a little. In about four months, Bell will no longer be the baby of the family. As hard as it was, especially with Shana dragging her feet as a new mom, I miss baby Bell. She was as fussy then as she is now, and I didn't realize it at the time, but it was the start of the best years of my life.

We stop at the subway, and I pass Sadie Bell's overnight bag as I squat. "I'll pick you up Sunday. You can call me anytime if you need anything."

"How?"

"With Aunt Sadie's phone."

"But . . ." She looks up at Sadie and back to me. "Maybe you can come too?"

"Dad's are no fun at sleepovers," Sadie says. "I'm not even sure we'll let Uncle Nathan stay."

Bell swallows, and her eyes water. "I don't want to go."

"Aw, come on, kid," I say, smiling, even though her words tear my heart in half like it's straight up rice paper. "You've been excited about this all week."

"I changed my mind."

"You're a big girl, Bell," I say. "No tears. What do you always tell me about crying?"

She inhales a shaky breath but after a moment, her shoulders drop a few inches. "It's for little boys."

"There we go." I nod. "Now, go with Aunt Sadie, and give Ginger a kiss for me."

Her cheeks, pink from holding in tears, round with a small smile. "What about Uncle Nathan?"

"When have you ever seen me kiss Uncle Nathan?"

She giggles, and I peck her forehead before standing again. I want her to be tough. To speak her mind and stand up for herself. I also want her to stop growing up so fast. It's a war in me that never seems to end—raise a smart, mature, confident girl while keeping her my baby. Sometimes I worry I'm doing a shit job of all of it.

"What're you going to do now?" Sadie asks.

Normally at this time, I'd be prepping dinner. Maybe grocery shopping with Bell or listening to her day as I chop vegetables. It's too early for a drink, or I'd go to Timber Tavern, my local watering hole. "Head home, I guess."

She holds open her arms. "But you're in New York City. Why not do something fun? Live a little."

"I've hated this place since we were kids. It's full of superficial snobs, present company included."

She smirks, used to my teasing. "I'm just saying. You're a bachelor for forty-eight hours. Use them wisely."

"I'm also a thirty-five-year-old dad," I say, deadpan. "I'm hardly about to go on a bender."

"Then I suggest you do the thirties version of a bender and binge on good food. There's a place around the corner that has amazing pizza. Seriously. You'd die for it."

Sadie has a weird habit of saying she'd die for a meal. "I happen to like my life," I say. "But I'll think about it."

"Ready?" Sadie asks Bell, taking her hand.

We say goodnight, and the two most important women in my world descend down the steps without me.

I shove my hands in my pockets, watching long after they're gone. It's a fifteen-minute walk back to Penn Station, but at the thought of going home to an empty house, I slow to a crawl. I'll be on my own for an entire weekend—the first time since Bell's mom left almost four years ago. I have an open invitation to go out with the guys at my shop, but most of the time I prefer to stay home with Bell. And on the rare occasion I get a sitter, at least I know I'm coming home to find Bell safe in her bed. Two nights without that comfort feels like the loss of a limb.

As I approach Sadie's office on my way back to the train, my sight snags on the smoking-hot blonde coming out of the building before I realize who it is. Digging through her purse with one hand, Sadie's boss, Amelia, stops a few feet in front of me. She's carrying a small package, plus a laptop bag and purse over her shoulder, and both crooks of her arms are occupied by manila folders, magazines, and a coffee thermos.

I walk until I'm standing right in front of her. "Need some help?"

She keeps her head down. "No."

I cross my arms at her curtness. "Just trying to be friendly."

"Right," she snorts. "In this city? Friendly means—" She glances up and squints at me. "Oh. You're the plumber."

"For the last time, I'm *not* a plumber," I say. "I'm Sadie's brother."

The corner of her red mouth twitches as if she's going to smirk, but she manages to contain it, which is almost worse. "Of course. My mistake."

The thermos wedged in her elbow clatters on the ground. "Shit," she says, trying to balance everything and go after it.

"Let me give you a hand," I say, scooping it up. "Where are you headed?"

"I'm fine." She takes it from me. Some papers slide out of the folder, dangerously close to falling out. "Just because you fixed my toilet doesn't make me helpless."

"I wasn't implying you were." Since my help isn't wanted, I have to ball my hands under my pits to stop myself from saving the papers slipping through the folder. I glance at them, pages ripped from a yellow legal pad, hoping she'll get the hint. The handwriting—hers, I assume—is messy, but I still make out the words *assets* and *alimony.*

"If you're going to stare at my breasts, try not to be so obvious about it."

"I wasn't, actually," I say and let my gaze drift a few inches over. Unless she's wearing a bionic push-up bra, she's got more to work with than her slight frame suggests. "But I am now."

Amelia covers herself with the stack in her arms and one by one, papers start to flutter from her folder. "Goddamn it," she says, dropping the magazines to the sidewalk with a smack. A breeze scatters the scribble-covered pages away.

I keep my arms over my chest, watching her scurry around in an attempt to recover everything. "Well, don't just stand there," she snaps, barely glancing up. "This stuff is important."

I shake my head, chuckling to myself, and jog past her to retrieve the ones that skittered the farthest. I manage to grab them all, but not before a suit on legs with a cell attached to his ear walks right over them. "Hey, asshole," I say loud enough for him to hear. He doesn't bother to respond.

When I turn back, I'm greeted with a startling and welcome sight. Amelia's bent over, piling the contents of the folder on top of the magazines. The chick has barely an ounce fat on her, but she's got an ass like a couple of cantaloupes and I'm suddenly the kind of hungry that can't be satisfied with pizza. There's definitely enough for me to get a handful— and it's giving her rack a run for its money.

I let my eyes travel down her sculpted calves—is she a runner?—to her thin ankles and high, high black heels. The sleeping giant in me wakes, as if my body knows I finally have a weekend with nowhere to be— a rare couple days without the all-consuming responsibility of raising a six-year-old. My mood morphs. Curiosity gives way to intrigue. I stalk back toward her, and when she's gathered herself and is upright again, I hold out the stack I managed to collect. There's a footprint smudge on top of a paper printed with paragraphs of terms and conditions. She looks at it, blinks, and starts to laugh.

I grin, caught off guard by her sudden openness. "That's one way to get the message across," I say.

"It certainly is." She wipes the corner of one eye and pauses. "Wait, to who?"

"Your husband."

Her face freezes. She goes to take the papers, but she has a thermos in one hand and the package in the other. She extends her elbow a little bit, just enough for me to slip the pages in. I don't.

"That's what this is, isn't it?" I ask, looking them over, noting the copious notes in the margin. "Divorce agreement or something?"

Her expression cools, and even though she's done nothing but boss me around and attempt to belittle me since we met, I feel instantly bad about ruining her good mood. She doesn't seem the type to laugh easily.

"Never mind." I straighten the papers in my pile, sticking the handwritten notes on the bottom before grabbing more pages out of her hands.

"What are you—"

"You said they're important." I check the page numbers and start getting the contract back in order while she watches.

"They don't know we're still married," she says.

I glance up at her quickly before returning to my project. "Who?"

"Anyone. I told everyone it was done months ago when it was supposed to be, but it's not yet. So please don't mention it to your sister."

"Why not?"

"It's . . . complicated, and I don't want them to worry about—"

"No," I cut her off. I have no reason to mention it to Sadie, and it's Amelia's prerogative to keep it private. "I meant, why isn't it done?"

"Oh." Her eyes dart away. "Like I said. It's complicated."

"What isn't?"

"Not much these days, I guess." She glances at the pages between us. "I should go."

I don't give them to her. I'm not ready to say goodbye just yet. In the four years I've been single, I've had plenty of opportunities with eager women. I can't remember one who treated me like such a nuisance, though. It's almost nice, the change of pace, and since I've got nowhere to be, I might as well see where it leads. I nod behind her. "So this is your business?"

She looks up the building toward her floor and nods. "And no, my dad didn't give me the capital to start it."

This girl is feisty, but the more annoyed she seems, the more I want to needle her. "So your mom then?"

She sets her jaw. "Actually, no. I worked through college and then my twenties, saving every dollar I could. I have an investor, but that doesn't mean I didn't bust my ass to get here."

"Relax. I'm teasing you. I own a business too."

She shifts on her feet, her eyes bouncing from the papers I won't give her to my face. "Look, I don't date. So whatever you're doing, you can stop. I'm not interested."

I lift my chin. I'd be impressed with her candor if my attention hadn't snagged on what she'd said. "Don't date what?" I ask. "Plumbers? Outside the tri-state area?"

"No, I just don't date. Anyone. Period."

I lean in a little and catch a whiff of her perfume. It's dense, sophisticated, so different from the citrus-scented lotion of the girls I know at home. "Because you're married?"

"No."

"Something to do with the soon-to-be ex?"

She holds my gaze. "It doesn't take a genius."

"Well, then you'll be happy to hear I don't date, either. Not cute biker chicks in tight jeans, even though they're my type, and not prissy city girls, who are most definitely *not*."

She reels back as if I've slapped her, but takes a beat before she speaks. And in those few seconds, understanding crosses her face. "You have an ex too."

"I do."

"Being called a prissy city girl doesn't bother me."

"I didn't think it would." The more I stand here, the more I think Amelia might be just what I need this weekend. I have no complaints about my life, but before Bell came along, I was a lot more spontaneous. Sometimes I even thought about getting out of New Jersey. But the truth is, Jersey is my home. I wouldn't have lasted long before coming back. It's certainly more my speed than the city, but it's been a while since I spent an evening somewhere other than Timber Tavern, the only bar I've hit up since Bell was born. It's also been a while since I got to flirt with someone who wasn't a high school classmate, or a friend of one, or a friend of a friend of one . . .

On a whim, I hide her divorce papers behind my back. "What're your plans tonight?"

She scoffs. "It's Friday night. What *aren't* my plans? I have drinks with friends in an hour, then a late dinner, and who knows after that."

"Cancel them."

She gapes at me. "Cancel my plans? Why would I?"

"Come out with me. Sadie says there's a place around here with great pizza."

She laughs, tilting her head and exposing the smooth column of her throat. "First, I don't eat carbs, so there's no way you're getting me to do anything with the promise of pizza. Second, I just told you—I don't date."

"And neither do I."

"Then why are you asking me out?"

"Because despite what you may think, I'm a gentleman, and it's only good manners to buy you dinner first."

"First?" she asks, wrinkling her nose. "What's second?"

We stare at each other. I let her figure it out on her own. It's rare to meet a woman who, like me, truly has no interest in finding a partner. I've heard that claim from enough girls to know when they're bullshitting me, and unless Amelia is a Grade-A con artist, she definitely isn't looking to get serious.

When she understands, the wrinkles on her forehead ease, and she parts her lips. I answer with a knowing smile. Suggesting sex within half an hour of meeting someone might normally get me slapped, but I get the feeling Amelia appreciates a more direct approach.

"I don't date," I say, "but I'm still a man with eyes."

She makes no secret of looking me up and down. "You're not my type either," she warns. "I like men who carry a briefcase and see a barber regularly."

I run my hand through my black hair, which I know is too long. "How's that working out for you?"

She narrows her eyes. "Fine. Perfect."

"I have some tattoos too," I say. "And own a motorcycle. Since that's normally how I get most girls, I suppose those are turn-offs for you."

"They are," she says immediately, straightening her shoulders. "I've never understood the appeal of a bad boy."

"Then tonight, we're a match made in heaven, aren't we? It shouldn't be hard for either of us to say goodbye afterward."

She bats her eyelashes a few times, not because she's flirting but because she's thinking. Considering. Which means it's basically a done deal. I've never gotten this far with a girl only to have her walk away. "Why even bother with dinner?" she asks.

I take a moment to study her, her shoulder-length, perfectly coifed blonde hair. Her defined red lips that look like a heart when pursed, which is often. Yeah, based on the fact that I'm noticing details—something I try not to do anymore—I know I'm feeling her tonight. Most guys would jump at the opportunity to skip the small talk, but that doesn't really appeal to me. I like women, always have. Just because Shana fucked me in the head doesn't mean I don't appreciate them. Doesn't mean I don't want to spend time around them—just so long's it's surface stuff.

I don't want to scare her off by suggesting I might want to have a conversation with her, so I just shrug. "Because I'm starving."

"I'm not hungry."

"Indulge me then. I need my energy."

"For what?" she asks.

I arch an eyebrow at her. I'll definitely need sustenance to handle her for a night.

She reads my expression, and her cheeks redden. "Oh."

I mentally high-five myself for making this obviously composed woman both laugh and blush in such a short timespan.

She squints over my shoulder and after a few seconds, shakes her head. "No. It's a bad idea. I'm sorry."

Huh. I expected some pushback, but not a hard no. "What's bad about it?"

"I just haven't been with anybody since—" She focuses behind me, as if there's something holding her attention. I know there isn't. She doesn't want to refuse me, but it's easier if she pretends not to see me. "So, I wouldn't be . . . it's been a while since I did it."

"Did what?" I ask. I know what she's getting at, but she seems to value her façade, and that only makes me curious about what's beneath it.

She looks back at me. "Sex."

"Oh, don't worry about that." I grin. With a breeze, a few pieces of her hair break away from the mold and stick to her lipstick. There's not much she can do about it since her hands are full, so I reach up and clear the strands away, letting my fingertips graze her cheek. For such a hard exterior, her skin is surprisingly smooth. She flinches, but I push my luck and tuck the hair behind her ear. "It'll come back to you," I say. "I'll make sure of it."

"But—"

"Look at me."

She does, and whatever's holding her back dims. "Just so we're on the same page, you want to have a one-night stand. Sex only."

My stomach tightens at the image her bluntness conjures—her, naked beneath me, tits high, perfect blonde hair tangled from my hands, red lipstick smeared from my mouth. In no time at all, I could have this beauty's long, toned legs wrapped around my waist. She's everything I normally avoid—uptight, snobby, self-possessed—and I can't seem to walk away. Maybe dinner was a bad idea after all. I'm tempted to skip ahead to the good part.

"Yeah," I say. "Just sex."

"Completely casual. No strings. Just tonight."

I nod. "That's all I have to give."

"Same here."

"So let's start with dinner. See how we get on." Since I'm confident in my ability to seduce her, I add,

"If you change your mind, we'll go our separate ways."

"Okay." She steps back. "I know of a great dinner spot around here."

"Is there pizza?"

"No. I told you, I don't eat carbs."

"I don't understand that sentence." I nod for her to follow me. "Come on."

"I'm not getting pizza."

I keep walking, listening for the click of her heels behind me. "You don't like it?"

"Nope."

"Well, I don't like the city, but here I am, spending the evening here. We're changing things up tonight."

She huffs but doesn't protest any more. After a second, she catches up with me. "If you want to win me over, you should know, I don't take orders well."

I glance sidelong at her, containing my smile. "You will once I'm through with you."

She gapes. "What does that mean?"

"Means I never met a challenge I didn't accept, and you just gave me a very enticing one. We'll see later on how long you last resisting my orders."

She looks skeptical. "Have it your way, then. I was just trying to help you seduce me, but if you'd rather make more work for yourself . . ."

"So you're saying you aren't a sure thing tonight?" A young guy with music blasting from his phone dances jerkily toward us. I put an arm around

Amelia and steer her out of the way. "Because I don't mind," I continue. "Like I said, I'm up for the challenge."

"Good," she says, tossing her hair over one shoulder. "So am I."

"Then I hate to disappoint you, but I *am* a sure thing."

She raises an eyebrow up at me. "Well, you *are* a man."

"It's not that." It's more refreshing than I realized to be able to be straight with a woman. "I just find you attractive, and there's almost nothing you can say to change my mind at this point."

The guy has passed us, but Amelia doesn't pull away at first. When she does, I'm tempted to keep her close. I can see I'll have to give her a little longer to loosen up, though.

"Nothing at all?" she asks.

I groan. "Why do I think you're going to take that as a challenge to drive me away?"

"I wouldn't do that," she says, but I hear the teasing in her voice. She might. But I'm horny, and she's hot, so I'm up for a little game of cat and mouse. Besides, it's not as if I have anywhere to be tonight.

THREE

The pizza place has a line out the door, and as Amelia and I walk up, it becomes obvious it's more of a kiosk than a restaurant. Standing room only, people loiter outside with their slices.

"I didn't realize we couldn't sit down," I tell Amelia before I even notice her scowl. "Should we go somewhere else?"

"Somewhere without pizza?"

I chuckle. "No. There will be pizza."

"Then no." She smiles thinly and adjusts the things in her arms. "This is fine. Not much of a first date, but—"

"Whoa—hang on. If this is a date, I'll take you somewhere entirely different. I'll romance the shit out of you."

She looks amused. "It was a joke. Obviously, I prefer we leave romance out of it."

"Oh." I rub the back of my neck, surprised my mind went immediately to romance. There's a girl back in Jersey, Denise, a friend from high school. She gets my situation—I'm not emotionally available. Still, when Denise and I hook up, she always tries to squeeze some romance out of me, either with dinner or by asking about Bell. That hasn't been my thing since Shana left. "So what was his name?"

Amelia blinks and looks up at me. We take a step forward in line together. "Who?"

"The ex."

"Does it matter?"

"I guess not." I put my hands in my pockets. "Would you rather talk about the weather?"

Her shoulders lower just a bit. "Reggie. He works downtown. Finance."

"That still your type? Suits?"

"I don't know if I have a type anymore. I've considered becoming a lesbian, but . . ."

I roll my lips together and smile. She'd look good curled around another woman. Or around me. And since I know where she's headed with this, I'd love nothing more than for her to finish her sentence. "But?"

She looks me in the eye. "But I can't."

"Why not?"

"I'd miss . . ."

I egg her on. "You'd miss . . .?"

"A man," she says quickly. "The way it feels to be touched by a man."

It takes great effort to hold her gaze and not let my eyes travel down. Her skirt is tight, and I'd like to peel it away and see what's underneath. No doubt her ass is firm and round. My mind flashes to later, when her legs will be all mine—the insides of her thighs, the backs of her knees, the arches of her feet. I clear my throat. "Hot as it would be, I'm glad you aren't a lesbian."

"What about you?" she asks.

"I have nothing against lesbians," I say, raising the corner of my mouth. "Personally, I'm a fan."

A hint of a smile crosses her lips. "I mean, you've made it clear I'm not your type. Was your ex the 'biker chick' you referred to earlier?"

I glance down. It's been nearly four years, so I can finally think about Shana without getting too worked up. Still, she's far from my favorite topic. "Yeah."

"That's it?" Amelia asks. "Yeah? You're the one who brought exes up."

Her eyes sparkle. She knows exactly what she's doing, and that I'd rather not talk about it. But there's something appealing about the fact that Amelia knows nothing about me or Shana, unlike everyone else in my life. And if we're only spending one night together, what's the harm in making conversation? I blow out a sigh. "Even though she hurt me, I generally stick to that type of girl. Present company excluded."

She tilts her head. "Why me then?"

"Couldn't tell you," I say with a wink. I like that I can tease her without worrying how she'll react. To offend her, she'd have to care what I think, and she clearly doesn't.

She half-smirks. "What's her name?"

"Shana."

"Is she the mother of the girl with you earlier?"

"You mean my daughter? Yeah." I laugh. She's clearly uncomfortable with me having a kid. We take a few steps forward, nearing the counter. "Shana walked half a mile to my garage because of an empty tank, so I drove her back to her car, filled her up, and the rest is history. We were dating a few weeks when she got pregnant. Around Bell's third birthday, Shana left. The end."

Amelia jerks her head toward me. "The end? That's it?"

I look forward. I may have learned to accept how Shana left, but the pity in people's eyes never gets any easier to swallow. "It was almost four years ago. We get on fine without her. Better, even."

"I can understand why you don't date. I wouldn't either." She looks up at me. Her eyes are slightly too big for her face, and she looks deceivingly innocent. "Will you ever marry again?"

"Doubt it. You?"

"Never."

The abruptness of her answer shouldn't surprise me, but I cock my head. "Just like that? What if you fall in love?"

"I won't if I can help it."

I open my mouth to tell her that's a shame—even though she's given me nothing but shit, there are undoubtedly men out there who'd happily do the bidding of a sharp-witted, gorgeous blonde. But that'd make me a hypocrite. I'd be a fool to fall in love after the way I was burned, and I sure as hell don't plan on being a fool twice. "I think you and I are going to make great friends," I say.

"If we're going to eat pizza, have sex, and then get back to our own lives, then you might be my best friend in the world."

I grin. "Does this mean you'll have a slice?"

"Not a chance in hell."

"Next," a man behind the counter calls. We step up.

Before I can open my mouth, Amelia orders. "I'll have a salad, no cheese, dressing on the side."

"All we got is a side salad," the man says, punching the register. "Not exactly our specialty, though."

"That's fine. I'm not that hungry." She thumps her magazines, folders, thermos and package on the counter to rifle through one of her bags.

"I've got this," I tell her.

She ignores me, handing a five-dollar bill to the cashier.

I don't mind playing the boyfriend for a night, because I know this isn't real, but she seems to want to keep things separate. If there weren't a long line behind us, I'd argue with her.

"I'll take two slices of the Meat Lover's," I say, "and one cheese. You can put the cheese from her salad on that."

Amelia gapes at me. "*Three* slices? With extra cheese? They're the size of your head."

"Lay off." I rub my stomach. "I haven't eaten since lunch."

"It's six o'clock."

I shrug and pay for my pizza. She picks up all her things again, balancing the plastic salad container on top. Each of my slices is the size of the paper plate it's on, so I stack them. Since our hands are ridiculously full, I grab a plastic bag from the cashier.

"You have too much shit." I put my food on the seat of a chained-up bicycle and toss her thermos in the bag along with her divorce papers, magazines, the package, and anything else I can fit. "What do you need all this for?"

"It's work."

I hook the bag on my elbow and get my plates. "Damn. I forgot to order a drink."

"I'm not waiting in line again."

"It's fine. These places charge double what a bodega does. Let's walk."

As we head down the block, I take an enormous bite of the first slice, chewing as Amelia picks out a few rogue pieces of feta. Finally, she drizzles dressing on the lettuce and eats a forkful.

"That's disgusting," I say.

She widens her eyes. "*Salad?* Do you have any idea how many calories are in one of those slices, let alone three?"

"Are you calling me fat?"

"Hardly. You must find ways to burn it off."

"I do," I say, leaning toward her a little. "And I love to get creative about it."

I'm trying to get her to blush again, but to her credit, she doesn't. "So do I," she says. "I've been doing yoga for years, but sometimes nothing hits the spot like a few hours of straight-up, hardcore, sweaty cardio."

I don't know where to start with that. First, I'm picturing Amelia in naked downward dog, the only yoga position I know. She's not even bent over a second before I'm coming up behind her to cash in on that *sweaty, hardcore* cardio. I forget all about my pizza, and a slice slides over the edge. I fumble, barely catching it before it hits the ground.

Amelia doesn't even pretend to hide her laugh. "Smooth."

Christ, I need to get this woman in bed STAT. I can't decide if I want her to be this sassy between the sheets, or if I want her to drop the façade and submit. A little of both. This might be an all-nighter. "I hope you don't have an early morning planned," I say.

"I might, but it won't affect tonight."

God. Damn. I'm dangerously close to skipping ahead and booking us the nearest hotel. Luckily, we reach a bodega before I can Google where that might be. I run inside to grab beer and, with a bolt of lightning genius, condoms, just in case she doesn't have any. I stick two beers under my arm and return to Amelia, who's still picking at her salad. I can see by her figure she was telling the truth about yoga. She's thin and fit, but despite her ample breasts and ass, she could use some more meat on her bones. I snatch the salad from her hands.

"Hey," she squeals, leaping toward me.

I toss it in a nearby trashcan. "That was fine as an appetizer, but now you need to eat. I offer her the cheese slice from the bottom of my pizza tower. "Here."

"That's yours."

"I ordered it for you."

"But I told you—"

"You don't eat carbs, I know. Can you make an exception for me? I got you a beer too."

"You're insane," she says. "I haven't had beer since college. I only drink whisky."

"Whisky?" My pants get tight with a single word. "Let me get this straight . . . you don't get clingy, you're a yoga goddess, and you exclusively drink whisky? You just keep getting hotter."

"And I intend to stay that way." She takes a step back, raising her palms. "Thanks but no thanks."

She's fun to mess with, but it hits me that she might really take her diet too seriously. "Amelia, come on. I ordered this for you, and I'd like you to eat it."

She shakes her head. "I don't like pizza."

"I don't believe that. It's fucking cheese and bread. Nobody on this planet doesn't like cheese and bread."

"Then I must be from another planet."

"I'm beginning to think you are." I shove it toward her. "Just take a bite. I won't tell anyone."

"Listen . . ." She pauses with her mouth open. A flush creeps up her chest to her neck, and it takes me a moment to realize why.

"You don't remember my name," I say.

"I can't remember something you never told me."

"Sadie introduced us in your office."

She waves a hand. "I'm positive she didn't."

This woman has pretty much agreed to sleep with me without even knowing my name. What the fuck. I should be annoyed, but now I've got some leverage. "I'll tell you if you take a bite."

"I'm okay not knowing. We're only spending one night together."

Now I'm annoyed. I may have committed to a lifetime of casual sex, but that doesn't mean I think women are interchangeable or disposable. Is that what she thinks of me? I lower the pizza and step closer until we're toe to toe. "I'm not okay with it," I say slowly, "because I intend to spend the night doing everything I can to get you to *scream* my name. How'll that work if you don't even know it?"

She swallows, and I love that her cheeks are now as red as her neck. "I'm going to be naked in front of you," she says. "Do you really want me to have pizza and beer before that?"

"Yes." There's no way she'd look anything other than svelte, and even if she did, I know myself—I wouldn't care. Once the clothes come off, it's game on. "You're a beautiful woman, and I'm keeping my hands to myself because we're in public." A runner passes us, throwing a look over his shoulder at Amelia. I don't blame him. "And yeah," I go on, "I was staring at your tits earlier. But I'm finding you sexier by the minute, and it doesn't have as much to do with your body as you might think."

Amelia shakes her head but I'm doing something right, because she finally takes the plate. "Pizza? Really?"

I open a can, hold it out to her, and grin. "And beer. There's literally no better match in the world."

FOUR

Amelia moans a little with each bite. Eating pizza shouldn't be sexy, especially considering she has tomato sauce on her cheek. But she's enjoying it almost as much as I'm enjoying watching her, which is a lot.

"Thanks for forcing me to do this," she says, licking the corner of her mouth as we wander through the city.

"You missed," I say. "A little higher."

She sticks her tongue to the side and tries unsuccessfully to get the glob.

Containing a laugh, I lean over and suck it off her cheek.

She stops walking. "What was that?"

"There was no other way." I hold up my hands, which, like hers, are full of food and drink.

"Well, that was—"

"Sexy?" I ask right as she says, "Disappointing."

My mouth falls open. "*Disappointing*? Why?"

"For a first kiss—"

"That wasn't a kiss. It was . . . a taste."

"I'm just saying, as far as first kisses go, that ranks pretty low."

Though we're in the middle of a crowded sidewalk on Broadway, I set my beer and pizza on the ground along with her bag o' shit.

"What are you doing?"

"It wasn't a kiss," I say, taking her beer and pizza from her to place them next to mine, "and certainly not our first one."

"Okay, I was just teasing," she says. "You don't need to—"

I wrap one arm around her waist and the other around her shoulders, dip her, and plant a hard kiss on her lips. She doesn't respond. I don't fault her that. I've never kissed a woman in public this theatrically, but there's no way she isn't melting in my arms right now. People *ooh* and *ahh* around us. I draw my head back and look at her. "Now *that* was a kiss."

"Put me back," she says, and I realize her entire body is tense.

"Not until you admit that was good," I say. "I work out, Amelia—I can hold you like this all night."

She looks from side to side and lowers her voice as if she doesn't want anyone to hear. "Fine. As far as second kisses go, that ranks pretty highly."

I inhale a deep breath. "Not *second* kiss. First."

44

She wriggles in my arms, but I tighten my hold. While she's looking for an escape, I kiss her again, and this time, I go for the tongue. She stops squirming. Her mouth tastes like every man's dream—pizza, beer, and a promise of what's to come later.

"I'll keep going," I whisper against her mouth.

She rolls her eyes, but her body relaxes just a hint. Again, I wonder how she'll be once I strip her down and have her at my mercy. Will she keep up this futile struggle for control? I look forward to finding out.

"All right," she concedes. "You've won me over. What an *amazing* first kiss. Put me back."

"Not yet. Ask me my name like you're dying to know it."

"I told you, I don't take orders from anyone."

"Neither do I."

We engage in a full-on stare down. Suddenly, she sighs and slides her arms around my neck. "If we're going to do this, let's do it right." She shocks me with a slow, sensual kiss, the kind reserved for long-lost lovers recently reunited. Her back arches, and her tits press against my chest, right over my heart as it starts to pound. My cock nudges against my fly. With a groan, my arms go to jelly, and I slide a hand down her lower back, toward her sweet, sweet—

She shoves me off, leaping back. "Ha!" Her expression is smug. "Getting you to cave was easier than I thought it'd be. Who's in charge now?"

Empty-handed, out of breath, and sporting a tent for pants, I narrow my eyes on her. "All right," I say to appease her. I'll prove her wrong later, but first I need to get her in bed. "You're in charge."

"Thank you."

As I retrieve our things off the ground, she mumbles something.

"What was that?" I ask, standing.

"The *first* first kiss?" she says. "I lied. It was pretty up there too."

I let my grin happen slowly, just to make her squirm. "So you were tricking me into a real kiss."

"I don't play games." She takes her food from me and continues walking. Over her shoulder, she throws, "When I want something, I go after it."

With a few long strides, I'm at her side again. "It's Andrew, by the way."

She looks over at me. "I guess that's more convenient than calling you Sadie's brother."

Shit. Sadie! She and Bell should be at her apartment by now. I toss my empty beer to get out my phone, but I have no missed calls, no texts. Nothing.

"Is that Sadie?" Amelia asks, assuming I have a call.

"No, sorry." I put my cell away, even though I'd like to check in with them. I can wait a little longer. Can't I? It's barely been an hour. That's a whole hour without thinking about my daughter, and I'm not sure how to feel about it. Even when I'm working at the garage, I still wonder what she's up to at school.

"Tonight stays under wraps," she says.

I return my attention to Amelia. "Sorry?"

"This." She nods between us. "I don't want Sadie to know. I'm not only her boss—she also knows a lot about my history with Reggie."

"Oh." I rub my eyebrow as my mind shifts gears again, but not without some creaking. I've been at Bell's beck and call for almost four years straight, ever since her mom left. Doesn't that earn me a night off? I'm not sure it does, or that I even want one. "I don't really keep things from Sadie," I say.

I finish off my pizza and trash the plates. Then again, Sadie gave me about six months after Shana left before she got on my case about dating, even though I've repeatedly told her I'm done with relationships. For that reason, I don't want her to know about Amelia, or she'll make something out of nothing. "But yeah. I agree. That'd be best."

"Thanks."

"What does your history with Reggie have to do with it, though?"

Amelia shrugs. "I've confided in Sadie a lot. She knows how I feel about men."

"Not good, I'm guessing."

"I may have said some things about your gender, but nothing you didn't deserve. I doubt she wants me anywhere near you."

"Good thing I'm a grown man and can decide for myself."

She bumps me with her shoulder and holds up her beer. "Want the rest?"

"You sure?"

She nods. "I've proven myself, haven't I?"

I take her beer, swig the rest down, and throw out all our trash. "Dessert?" I ask.

She groans. "Give me a break."

I laugh. "Come on."

"I have something else in mind for dessert," she says. "And besides—we're here."

I furrow my eyebrows. "Where?"

"My apartment." She stops and looks up, so I follow her gaze up the high-rise.

"I didn't know we had a destination. I thought we were just wandering."

"I don't wander." She opens her purse and gets out a key fob. When she holds it up to a black pad, it beeps, and the door unlatches. She looks back at me. "Coming?"

I glance into the building. A uniformed man behind a desk reads *The New Yorker*. The marble floor is shiny enough that I can see my reflection from where I stand. I don't exactly live in a palace, but I like my familiar, comfortable home that's a little too worn in, a little too kid-friendly. "This is exactly the kind of place I pictured you in," I say.

"All right." She shrugs. "So?"

I put my hands in my pockets. I've been out of the game awhile, and aside from the girls I meet in bars, this is easier than I remember. "So nothing. We just go up and do it?"

She gives me a funny look. "Isn't that what you want?"

"Yes. I just want to make sure it's what you want."

"It is. Don't worry. I'd tell you if it wasn't."

I believe her. "Should we at least pick up some wine or something?"

She takes the plastic bag of things from me and nods toward the door. "I've got it covered. Come on."

I get the door for her. "By the way, isn't this his job?" I ask, nodding at the man in the lobby.

"It is absolutely his job," she says, not bothering to lower her voice. "Isn't it, Frank?"

Frank looks up, widens his eyes, and jumps out of his seat. "Miss Van Ecken. I didn't hear you come in."

"It's too late now. We're already inside." Her heels echo in the lobby as she strides toward his desk. She stops in front of him and waits. "Well?"

He looks to me, and I shrug. "I'm sorry?" he asks.

"I should've had a dress delivered today," she says.

"Oh. Of course." He fumbles the magazine, drops it, goes to pick it up, but decides to leave it.

"One moment." He hustles over to a door, opens it, and pulls out a long garment bag. "Here you are," he says, shuffling back toward us. As he does, his shoe catches the bottom of the dress, and he stumbles.

"Careful," she reprimands. "This is *Givenchy*, and it's worth, well—more than you are."

I cough into my fist to hide my amusement. This guy is more my crowd, and maybe that means I should interfere, but I don't need Amelia turning her wrath on me. Not when I'm this close to getting in. Slowly, he passes her the bag. Through a small plastic window, I see a flash of red. It's my favorite color on a woman, and I wonder where she plans to wear it. She drapes it over her elbow. "Thank you. You might as well get back to your job reading a magazine."

She pivots on her heel and walks away. The doorman—Frank—gives me a sympathetic look before I turn and follow. I try to reach the elevator before her, but she beats me to it and hits the call button.

"I don't get it," I say, when we're out of earshot. "You want him to get the door for you, but you won't let me pay for your four-dollar salad?"

With her back straight, she waits by the elevator, watching the digital numbers tick down.

"Do you want to be your own woman, or do you want men to do things for you?"

She looks abruptly at me, as if I've voiced some unspoken understanding between her and the universe. "I don't need you to get me, just like I don't need anyone to do anything for me. The beauty of being independent is I get to decide what I want from whom. Is that wrong?"

I consider it. Without being a mind reader, it could potentially be difficult to make someone like her happy. "I guess not, as long as you get what you need. How do I know what you want, though?"

"I'll tell you."

A woman who tells me outright what she wants and needs—it's unlikely. If one existed, though, Amelia might be her.

"Don't you do the same?" she asks. "Why shouldn't everyone do what's best for them?"

"Some of us have others to consider," I say.

"And you always put them first?"

"Bell, yes. Obviously. Sadie and Nate too when I can." Sadie's my baby sister, and I've always been protective of her, especially considering we grew up with an alcoholic father who liked to pick fights. As an extension of her, and one of the few men I get along with, Nathan's pretty much a brother to me.

"What about work?" she presses. "What about sex?"

Automatically, I think of Shana. It would be easy to say I had always put her first, but it wouldn't be true. She made it hard. "*You don't understand*" she would say, or "*You never listen,*" or "*You don't care about anyone but yourself.*" She pushed back for no other reason than to irritate me. I may not have always understood, but I listened, and I cared. She knew it too.

I push Shana out of my mind. She and Amelia are opposites in physicality, personality, and purpose. I loved Shana. I want to fuck Amelia. That's where *my* need overpowers my sense. If I could stay away from women completely, I would. I'm not fool enough to think Bell doesn't move me around like a pawn, but that right is reserved for my little girl.

Amelia boards the elevator first. "What happens if you and I want different things?" I ask.

The elevator takes off smoothly, but she grabs a railing, steadying herself. "What? No. We have an agreement—tonight only. If you're having second thoughts, we have to stop this right now."

If I'd had any doubt about her intentions tonight, they'd have vanished with the look on her face. One thing remains true—the fact that she's so composed makes her fun to mess with. I reach for the elevator's emergency-stop button. "Right *now*?"

"No—" She can't do anything. She has the dress in one hand, the key to the building in the other, plus two bags and her purse. "Are you insane? I'm talking about *us*. *We* need to stop."

I chuckle, dropping my arm back to my side.

"This can't ever continue past tomorrow," she says.

My smile fades, and I deepen my voice. "I'm not talking about tomorrow. I'm talking about tonight."

The elevator ride is calm, effortless. It doesn't rattle or sound like it's working hard to ascend. "I don't understand," she says.

I stalk toward her, and she backs up into one corner. "I'm asking what happens if we disagree tonight," I say, licking my lips. "What if I want to fuck you one way, and you want it another?"

She sucks in a breath. Mission accomplished. There's no rush quite like catching her off guard. Getting her up here has been easy, but part of me is looking forward to the fight I know she has in her. The elevator dings. The doors open. Neither of us moves.

"Well?" I ask.

"I guess we'll find out."

"I think we will," I say, stepping aside to let her pass.

I follow her down a white hallway to her apartment. If I'm not mistaken, she's hobbling a little bit. She runs a hand over her hair, patting it into place. When we reach the door to apartment 11D, she turns and faces me. "You sure you want to do this? You're not going to fall in love with me?"

"I won't if you don't."

She shakes her head firmly. "I won't. I'm serious, Andrew."

I drop my eyes to her lips. Most of her lipstick has rubbed off, and I look forward to kissing away the rest. Now that I'm this close to her, I see the perfect, smooth black lines of her eye makeup. The gunk on her lashes. Shana wore a lot of make up too, but never this neatly. Sometimes it smudged under her eyes. Sometimes she wore dark lipstick to shock people. I liked her best completely nude. I don't want to be thinking about Shana-fucking-Lanzo right now, but this is the most turned on I've been since she left. Left—and never looked back.

I lean in and drop the act so Amelia knows I'm serious. "I won't. If you have even the tiniest hope that I will, I'll leave. I like you. I don't want to hurt you."

"I have no hope," she says without hesitation. I hear the dryness of her throat, the determination in her voice. She wants nothing from me as badly as I want nothing from her. We're a perfect match.

"Then let me in," I say.

She does.

FIVE

Amelia's apartment is clean, and not just tidy. The walls are so white I wonder if they were recently painted. There aren't any marks on the blonde wood flooring. She has two great windows, but because this isn't one of the top floors, the view is mostly of the apartments across the street. As dusk settles, lights flicker on in neighboring buildings.

"Drink?" she asks from the kitchen.

"Sure." I stick my hands in my pockets and look around. The Upper West Side apartment is bigger than any I've been to in the city, but still significantly smaller than my house. From where I stand in the living room, I can see into the kitchen and her bedroom at the same time. She makes good use of the space with a large mirror propped against one wall, and a slim, gray couch that faces an empty space on the wall. I might've guessed she wouldn't have a television. She doesn't seem like the type to embrace guilty pleasures.

"Nice place," I say.

"Still think I'm a prissy city girl?" she asks.

"More than ever."

"Good."

In the center of the coffee table sits three glass globes of varying sizes. I lean closer for a better look. The bottom halves are sloping layers of white rock and soil. They're topped with green, blooming succulents edged in purple and pink. Each vessel has an opening large enough for a hand. I have space for a garden in my backyard but no interest in cultivating it. Bell has asked for roses, not that she understands anything beyond the fact that they're pretty.

"Where'd you get these plants?" I ask.

"They're terrariums. I make them."

I raise my eyebrows, watching as she moves around the kitchen. "Yeah?"

She nods. "I don't really do hobbies, but I guess if I had one, they would be it. There are more in my bedroom and my office."

"You're talented."

She sets two empty tumblers on the counter. "And you're far away."

I take the invitation and round the breakfast bar separating the two rooms. The countertops are smooth and shiny, and my first thought is that I'd like to fuck her on one, but my second is that they're legit marble, and Amelia could be quite wealthy. "How long have you lived here?"

"You're wondering how I afford it." She bends to open another cabinet. "Reggie bought it when we got married. He'd dumped a bunch of stock right before the market crashed in 2008. Then, with the fortune he'd saved, he bought it all back at a discount. Most of it multiplied in value."

The market collapsed before I was in any position to own stock, but I knew some people burned by it—and by assholes who cheated the system. What I know of Amelia's ex doesn't make him look good. "Sounds shady."

"It is," she says, pushing heavy-sounding glass around the wood cabinet. "When we met, he spun it to make himself seem clever. He didn't go to college, which had been a source of embarrassment for him until he became rich. Then he wore it like a badge of pride—filthy rich on a high school education. I eventually realized he'd been tipped off about the market, which is the complete opposite of cleverness."

She stands with a bottle and unscrews the cap. When I notice the label, I raise my eyebrows. I don't think I would've been more turned on if she'd taken off her top. "Glenlivet?" I ask, inching closer to her.

"It's my drink."

It's Cellar Collection, and expensive as fuck. "Do you serve that to all your guests?"

"No." She glances at me from under her lashes. "Just the ones I want to fuck."

I hum, my chest vibrating, my stomach dropping. Her light perfume mixes with the whisky's spice. She smells and looks good enough to devour.

She pours each drink carefully. "I hope neat is okay," she says, and she isn't asking.

"Perfect."

She hands me one, and we clink glasses. "To tonight," she says.

We each take a sip, and the liquor goes right down. It's been a while since I indulged like this. With the change in my priorities came a change in how money's spent.

"So," she says, glancing into her glass, "how do we start?"

"How?" As satisfying as the whisky is, it's no match for the taste of a woman. I set my tumbler on the counter and close the space between us. For once, she goes still and quiet. Perhaps I *can* flap the unflappable. I take her waist in my hands. "We can start like this." I run my thumbs up her flat stomach. She inhales through her nose. "Or this." I kiss her once on the lips before moving to the corner of her mouth. I brush her hair off her neck and make my way along her jaw. Already, her wispy breaths are bordering on soft moans.

"I'll get a condom," she says.

"I have one."

"Let's move to the bedroom."

Her skin is smooth under my lips. I take her earlobe between my teeth. "No."

"Why not?"

"I've got this, Amelia." I place one hand under her skirt, caressing the inside of her thigh to hopefully turn those moans audible. "Just relax."

"It's been a while."

"You said that already." I pull back a little but squeeze her knee. "Are you having second thoughts?"

"No," she says quickly.

My urge to have her, especially since it's been some time for both of us, simmers close to the surface—but she has to be comfortable. "How long's it been?"

"Reggie was the last . . ." She looks away. "That was a year ago, and even then, it was few and far between."

"Ah." A year. Good god. My dick stirs at the thought of how she'll come apart under my undivided attention tonight. Just for the amount of time she's waited, she deserves a ride to the moon and back. "Why me?"

"What?"

"Why'd you choose me? To be the first. I know you've had plenty of opportunities."

She smiles a little. "Not really. I work a lot, and the divorce takes up any free time."

"Bull." I hold eye contact. "You could have anyone."

She looks amused. "I thought I wasn't your type."

"You aren't, but I'm not deaf, dumb, or blind." Amelia surprised me tonight. I'm not used to such a direct woman, even if she is somewhat guarded. There's no room for misunderstandings here, and I'm discovering, probably due to my unstable dating history, that's a turn on for me. "You're smart," I tell her. "Upfront. Sarcastic. Beautiful, which goes without saying. I think all that's sexy. But best of all, you know it is."

She tilts her head at me, a smirk playing on her lips, her self-assurance back intact. "I'm not backing out," she says. "You don't have to woo me."

"I'm not." I wouldn't be able to go a year without burying myself in a woman—not just fucking, but enveloping myself in her scent, the feel of her skin, her mouth. Amelia needs this. I need this. "I could've easily gone home tonight," I say. "Something about you kept me in the city. I want to be here with you."

She lifts one angular shoulder. "Eh. I could take it or leave it."

I narrow my eyes at her, and she allows herself a small laugh. When I run my hand up the back of her thigh and take a handful of her firm, ample ass, her laughter vanishes. "I've been wanting to do that all night," I say.

"By 'all night' you mean the last couple hours?"

I lift her onto the counter by her waist, satisfied with the way her lips pop open for a gasp. She remembers her cool just as quickly and closes her mouth.

"You have a lot to say," I tell her.

"That surprises you?" she asks.

"No. You've been talking since the moment I met you." I lean in, nab her bottom lip between my teeth, and let it go. "You don't have to stop talking, but there are other things I'd like to hear you say."

"Such as?"

"'Oh, God.'"

"*Oh*," she repeats in a moan, "*God*."

I try again. "How about 'oh, Andrew'?"

"*Andrew*," she says, drawing out my name like she's begging for something.

My mouth goes desert-dry, as I've forgotten to swallow. The burn of desire scorches my patience. I slide her ass to the edge of the counter, push her skirt high enough to part her knees, and fit myself between them.

"Here?" she asks. The counter is the only thing separating the kitchen from the living room. I can see out her sizeable windows into the night, into the city that never sleeps, into the windows and lives of other New Yorkers. The kitchen lights are on, and if someone were to look in, they'd see us.

"Here," I say. "For round one."

"All right then, handyman." She leans back on one arm and picks up her drink. "Just how handy are you?"

"Allow me to demonstrate." I slide both palms up her thighs until my fingertips brush lace. I peek under her skirt. "You sure you weren't planning on getting lucky tonight?"

"Definitely not."

"You're wearing black lace underwear and your legs are as smooth as glass."

She smirks. "They aren't the only part of me that's smooth."

My cock, already awake, springs to attention. I dig my fingertips into the soft skin of her thighs, imagining what I'll find when I peel her underwear away. "You just happen to be ready for me?"

She takes a long sip of her drink, sets it down, and sits forward to take my face in her hands. "I didn't do it for you."

Maybe I should feel threatened, but I don't. She's made it clear there's no one else, and if there were, as worked up as I'm getting, I could run laps around him. If fucking were running, that is. "Who's it for then?"

"Me. I wear expensive lingerie and wax myself because it makes me feel good. Not because I hope it'll get me a man."

I arch one eyebrow and suddenly, it's clear as day: this is what drew me to Amelia from the start. Her amazing figure and her sweet red lips didn't hurt, but with confidence like hers, I can't help wondering where it comes from. I'm about to reach the source of it, my hands creeping higher. "You don't need a man to feel sexy."

"Does that scare you off?" she asks.

"No, but thanks for trying."

I tease the skin under the band of her panties where her thigh and hip meet. She bites her lip. I want inside that mouth. I want inside her walls tonight, even though they're high. It's been so long since I was this attracted to someone. "It's fine if you don't need me," I say, "but I need you."

She wiggles under my feather-light touch, smiling a little. "No you don't."

"Yeah. I do." I slide my finger down the elastic. "I need you tonight. Will you let me in?"

She wraps her hand around my wrist to hold me still, spreads her legs a little wider, and rolls her hips once. I don't need more invitation than that. I touch her gently with the pads of two fingers. It isn't fair for me to ask for more than this, especially because I'll be gone in the morning, and I won't look back. But I'm old enough to know there are two kinds of sex. You can see the person you're inside of, or you can do everything in your power not to. The sex I've had lately is the latter. It has to be. That doesn't mean I like it that way. I miss connecting with my partner when we're intimate.

No, it isn't fair to ask to be let in, but I need something with Amelia, even if it's small. "Don't hold back," I say. "Promise me."

"I think it's been too long for me to try and control myself," she says, her voice already tenuous, hinting at the passion building beneath the surface. "I'm likely to fall apart in your hands right now."

My heart thumps. It isn't what I meant, far more physical than emotional, but the thought of her dissolving for me gets me going. I want to undo her, mess up her perfect hair, chase away the tension in her muscles, smear her makeup. I swallow dryly and realize I'm breathing through my mouth again.

"Are you all right?" she asks.

"Yeah." Patience gone, I push her panties aside and really feel her. Her chest rises and falls a little faster, her forehead creases as she draws her eyebrows together. We maintain eye contact despite the rawness of the moment. She's hot against the tips of my fingers, but not as wet as I'd like. I tease her, watching her expression. She sucks her bottom lip into her mouth as I press into her warmth—her armor's not as impenetrable as I thought. Because of her hard shell, it feels like a win.

With my other hand at the back of her head, I pull her mouth to me. I taste the whisky on her tongue and push a finger inside her. She slickens around me. I add another, feeling her from the inside. Though our lips are mashed together, we don't kiss, simply breathing together and finding a rhythm, her grinding on my fingers as I flick them inside her. I want to fuck—*I* don't need any more convincing. She's got to be good and ready for me, though. If it's been a while for her, I have to make sure she enjoys this.

With my free hand, I search the back of her skirt. "How do I get this off?"

"Unzip it," she moans.

I feel nothing but fabric and impatiently pull on the waistband. "Where? What zipper?"

"What?" Her eyes slit open, a lusty, drunken gaze. "Oh. Side."

Side? What? I circle around her waist, searching, and she closes her eyes again, absolutely no help. "Please don't stop," she says.

I would chuckle over her sudden descent into arousal if I weren't so hot to get the fucking skirt off. It takes a few more seconds of one-handed struggling to locate a side zipper, get the skirt all the way around her waist and untuck her blouse. I stop fingering her long enough to remove them both, along with her underwear, and not a moment more. I want her sopping when I enter her.

I pop her bra with one hand, and her tits spill out. They're too big for her small frame, and her tiny, pebbled nipples beg for my mouth. I start with her neck, nibbling the thin skin under her jaw before making my way down. She arches for me, falling back onto her elbows, groaning. I take a nipple between my teeth as I continue to work her into a frenzy. She shudders against me, spurring me to thrust faster, harder. Her wetness makes my fingers slippery, and the sucking sound turns my cock to stone. I move to the other breast, feeling ravenous, mouthing her with fervor normally reserved for eating pussy.

Which I also plan to do—later.

I reach into my back pocket with my free hand and get a condom. Looking down her body, then into her eyes, I tear the wrapper with my teeth. "I'm going to fuck you now," I tell her.

She nods hard. "*Right* now."

"So give me back my hand," I tease as she writhes on my fingers, "or open my pants for me."

She pushes off her elbows and yanks me forward by the waist of my jeans. She unbuttons them deftly, sliding my zipper down. When she reaches in my underwear and wraps her hand around me, it's all I can do not to growl. She isn't timid. She holds me like a woman, her hand soft but firm, unafraid.

"You're hard," she says, stroking me once.

I stroke her too, curling my fingers inside her. "What'd you expect?"

"That you'd be hard." She circles the tip with her palm, spreading pre-cum over my head.

I grit my teeth.

"You're big," she adds.

I hold her gaze. I like where this dirty talk is going. "What'd you expect?"

"That you'd be big. That's two out of three things I was right about."

"What's the third?"

"I'll let you know." She pushes my pants down so they pool around my feet. Taking the condom from me, she positions it over my crown. Her fingers are long, but her hands are small, making me look even bigger as she rolls on the condom.

I love that she wants this as badly as I do. I love that she didn't ask me to turn out the lights, that it didn't even occur to her. I can see every part of her, the pinch of her eyebrows as she focuses, the pink flush of her chest, the swell of her nipples.

When she finishes, I kiss her hard, moving so my thighs press against the counter's cabinets. I take my dick in my free hand, position it, and spread my fingers inside her, opening her up for me.

And then, she tenses up so tightly, she constricts around my fingers. She stops kissing me. I pull back a little to look her in the face. "What's wrong?"

"Nothing." She pulls me back by my collar, and as quickly as she went taut, she's jelly again. "I'm good."

We both watch as I press my crown in. I don't remove my hand from between her legs right away. I want some part of me inside her at all times. When I've begun inching my way in, I remove my fingers to thrust deep, anchoring myself to the hilt.

Her uninhibited groan is music to my ears, undoing me just a little. I slide out and dive back in. She's hot, tight, but she takes all of me with each thrust. As I go harder, I reach up to touch her face, but she catches my wrist. She brings my hand to her mouth. I widen my eyes as she wraps her lips around my fingers and sucks herself off them.

Fuck me. The sensation of being suckled is enough to have me grinding into her but knowing she's not shy makes my balls ache in the best way. I wrap one arm around her waist, lift her, and hold in her place as I fuck up into her. She releases my fingers, drops her head back, and silently cries up at the ceiling. Her tits jiggle in my face. With my other hand, I grab the nape of her neck and bounce her harder onto me.

"Give me a drink," I command, my voice foreign and rough.

She rights her head, looking down at me a moment. Since my hands are full, she grabs my glass and tilts it over my mouth. She drips a little onto my tongue, but because I'm still fucking her, it trickles, and she laps it off my bottom lip. I try to capture her tongue, but she arches back, allowing me a deeper angle. She drips Glenlivet onto her chest, and it rivers between her breasts and down her stomach. I suck it off her, following its path, as if her skin isn't just covered in whisky but soaked in it.

"God, Andrew," she moans. "You can fuck. Just as I expected."

"Three for three?" I ask, panting.

She answers by swiveling her hips. My stomach tightens, my balls pulsing. I want to come. She hasn't yet, but I need my hands to get her there, and I don't want to put her down. I like holding her up, stealing any control she might try to keep.

"Touch yourself. Help me get you off."

She wraps one arm around my neck and puts a hand between us to circle her clit. "Like that?" she asks, batting her lashes at me.

"Just like that, you perfect tease." A growl rises in my chest as every muscle in my body tenses. "Come on, baby. I need to feel you grabbing my cock. I won't finish until you do."

She goes at herself harder, using her own juices to lube herself. Though the sight of her getting off with her own hand is something I'll be picturing for a long time to come, I raise my eyes. I need to see her face. By the way she's squeezing her eyes shut and gasping up at the ceiling, I can tell she's close. But she isn't there, not yet.

"Amelia. Look at me."

She blinks a few times. Her skin is flushed, her blue eyes murky with desire as they meet mine.

"Good girl." I want to watch her fall apart. Nothing will push me over the edge faster. "You wanted to fuck me in your office, didn't you?" I provoke her. "Even though I was just the plumber."

She bites her lip. "No."

"Don't lie. Wanted me to take you up against the wall. Fuck you like *I* was the boss, not you. Punish you for how you treated me."

"And-*rew*," she implores, using the same tone that nearly undid me earlier while digging her fingernails into my back.

The pinch of pain spurs me toward the finish line. "You're so fucking sexy when you're close. I knew you'd be."

Her eyes roll back in her head and she moans, "I'm coming. Oh, God, Jesus, Andrew—*fuck me*."

I drop her ass onto the counter, take her hips in a firm grip, and finally let go. I pound into her, fucking with a singular need to get off, knowing she's taken care of. She clenches around me over and over. Her hands find their way into my hair and pull. I growl and thrust and take until it feels like I'm going to explode on the spot. When I finally do, it's pure relief, like I've been working toward this all night, and nothing else would satisfy me. I stare up at the ceiling as I finish, my chest heaving. Her hands are still in my hair. I shut my eyes and continue milking myself with her sweet pussy until I've calmed. Sweat trickles down my temple. Somehow, I'm still wearing my t-shirt, and it sticks to my skin. I blow out a breath and finally look back at her.

Her face is red, her mascara smeared under one eye. There's a darkening spot on her chest from where I sucked whisky off. Her hair is the only thing that's still practically untouched, and I make a note to mess it up good next time.

With a shudder, she starts to tremble.

"Shit," I murmur, surprised at how breathless I am. For fuck's sake, I lift three days a week and get in cardio however I can. "You okay? Did I hurt you?"

"Am I okay?" she repeats. To my relief, the corner of her mouth lifts. "No. Absolutely terrible."

"I'm serious." I inhale a deep breath, trying to pull myself together, even though a wave of exhaustion overcomes me. Suddenly, I want a pillow, a bed, a warm body. I want to pass out, if only for a minute. I release her hips to take her face, pecking her forehead, then her cheek and finally, her mouth. I linger there, stroking my tongue over her bottom lip. Slipping my arm around her back, I hug her to me. A year is a long time to go without anyone's touch. "How do you feel?"

This time, her voice is a murmur. Unguarded. "Good."

"Good." I squeeze her shoulder, massaging it a little, trying to bring her down. She's no longer shaking, but she shudders a couple times. "Was it too much?"

"No. Just what I needed."

We stay like that a moment. My eyelids sag, but I doubt it's even nine. She's been a lot of work, and I have zero complaints. It's nice to put effort in for once.

"You can go," she says. "You don't have to do this part."

My drooping eyelids fling back open as I straighten up. "*Go?*" I jerk back to see her better.

"Are you kidding? This is my night off. That was just the warm up."

She scrunches her nose and, I think, almost giggles. "Oh. Really?"

"I don't know about your exes, but I've got a bit more stamina than that. Morning is a long ways off." I pull out of her. "I'll be ready again soon, and I have plans for you."

Her skepticism melts away into an easy smile. "I like how you think you're in charge. It's cute."

"Wasn't so cute a few minutes ago, was it?"

I think she's going to blush again, but I don't get the satisfaction. Instead, she hops off the counter, shaking her head. "Okay. I'll give you that one. But next time, we do it my way."

"All right, boss," I concede, knowing if she's naked and I'm horny, there's no way she'll be ordering me around. "What're we going to do until round two? I might need a power nap."

She laughs, and her gorgeous, full breasts bounce a little. "You're tired?"

"Exhausted. Aren't you?"

"Not at all."

"Hmm. Then a nap won't work." I look down, pinch the tip of the condom, and slide it off. "Trash?"

"Under the sink."

I toss it. This is usually the time I leave unless I'm horny enough to stick around for another go. Coincidentally, or not, it's also usually when the chick gets clingy, but Amelia seems to be at ease. Thank

God. I like her, and I want to keep hanging out, but I don't want her to turn into what I'm used to. Denise always tries to get me to stay the night, or worse, take a goddamn bubble bath. Apparently, it feels pretty good after sex. Eases the tension, according to her.

So fucking girly and romantic.

But, I'll admit, now that I'm thinking about it, easing the tension might be what I need. I just used muscles I haven't in months, even with my most thorough workouts. And I'll need them again shortly. A bath sounds oddly . . . perfect. After screwing like animals, is there a better way to come down? "Maybe we should clean up," I suggest.

"Bathroom's through my bedroom," she says.

"What about you?"

"I feel okay."

"Oh." I nod slowly. "I thought maybe you'd want to clean up with me."

"A shower?" she asks, dipping her head playfully. "I could do that."

"Yeah, or . . . you know, not a shower."

She blinks a few times. "What?"

I look around the kitchen. Since I'm not a teenage girl, I can't exactly suggest we take a bath and certainly not one that involves bubbles. I sniff, pushing out my chest. "Never mind. You have any broken appliances that need to be fixed?"

"No," she says drawing out the word, possibly suppressing a laugh. "Everything works fine. Sink. Toilet. Bathtub."

I look back at her. "Bathtub?"

"Yep." She leans against the counter. "It's huge. One of the reasons we picked this apartment."

"Cool." We stare at each other. *Shit*. Soaking myself in hot water with a beautiful woman is sounding better by the second. Fuck it. "We should use it."

"Use what?"

"The . . . tub."

"You want to take a bath?" she asks, pursing her lips. Her cheeks round as her face reddens. "With or without bubbles?"

"Without, obviously." I squint at the ceiling, pretending to check for cracks. Cracks could indicate a bad foundation, and I'd hate for her to be living somewhere dangerous. "Or with," I add. "That would be fine too."

"Oh my God." She bursts into laughter. "*Not a shower*," she mimics.

"You knew that's what I was getting at, didn't you?" I accuse.

"I just had to hear you say it. You're awfully handsome for such a girly girl."

I grunt, then startle her by scooping one arm under her legs and hoisting her into my arms. "I guess you think you're pretty clever. Now, where the hell do you keep the bubble bath?"

SIX
AMELIA

As I fill the tub, I decide a bubble bath isn't romantic when it's simply a follow-up to an intense workout. That's exactly what Andrew and I just did: worked the shit out of each other.

I drip liquid bath soak into the water, watching bubbles foam and rise. They're harmless, bubbles and baths. Our rules are still in place, and a little intimacy won't make us forget our pasts.

Andrew comes into the bathroom with drink refills. "Sorry it took me a minute," he says. "I called to say goodnight to my daughter."

"Oh." I take my glass. I'd almost forgotten about her, but apparently he hasn't. Why would he? He seems like a good dad, yet surprisingly well put together for a man with a young child. There're no

stains—markers or spit-up or whatever it is kids do—
on his clothing. He doesn't wear the defeated look
some of my girlfriends do. Maybe it's different for
men. But I don't want to think of him that way, as a
father. Tonight, he's just a man who crossed my path
at the right time. I wipe beads of sweat from my
temple.

"Smells good in here," he remarks, walking
farther into the bathroom. He picks up the bubble
bath and reads, "Apricot cream with Tahitian vanilla
extract. What the . . .?"

"What?" I ask.

"They couldn't find any American vanilla? And
they spelled cream wrong for fuck's sake."

I laugh. "It's *crème*," I say. "You know, French?
Like crème de la crème."

He removes the cap and takes a whiff. "God,
that's good. How much did this cost?"

"Not sure. Probably around seventy-five
dollars—"

"For *bubble bath*?"

"It was a gift," I say, holding up my palms. "I get
things like that delivered to the office all the time
from clients."

"No shit? Well, in that case . . ." He reaches
behind me and tips half the bottle into the water.
"You can never have too many bubbles."

I shake my head. "That's at least thirty bucks
down the drain."

"Worth it," he says.

My face aches from all the smiles I've been suppressing. It's nice to be in such a good mood for a change. As soon as the thought occurs to me, it's a damp cloth on my joy. Good moods lift you up—and leave a longer way to fall.

I take a sip, looking at him over the rim, remembering how he sucked whisky off my chest earlier. The man's a machine. I've never been held up and fucked at the same time. The thought of doing it again makes me shudder.

"Cold?" Andrew asks, setting down his drink.

"A little," I lie.

"Good thing the bath's almost ready. For the record, this was your idea."

"All right," I agree. "It'll be good incentive for you to keep your mouth shut. If I find out you told Sadie about tonight, the gloves come off. The whole world will know what a girl you are."

"Deal."

I like Sadie. She works hard, aims to please, and has smart, innovative ideas. She can't know about this, though. If I had a brother, I wouldn't want him sleeping with me, a woman who bashes men like it's her job. Sadie understands how I got this way—she's heard enough about my personal life to know how messed up I am.

I turn off the faucet when the bath is nearly full and cross the bathroom to dim the lights. "For ambiance," I explain, so he doesn't think I'm trying to be romantic. "You can't take a bath with all the lights on."

"Agree." Andrew peels off his t-shirt. How he managed to get this far in clothing is beyond me. Beyond me or not, any thoughts fly out of my head when I see all of him. Colorful ink paints his chest and upper arms. One tattoo wraps over his left shoulder and a hint of one peeks out from the side of his ribs.

"Wow," I say.

He tilts his head. "Good wow?" he asks, but by the cocky grin on his face, he seems to think he has me pegged.

His strength was evident when he held me, but now I'm faced with the cut and carve of muscles just beneath the skin. He picks up both our drinks and comes toward me, ink rippling over his olive-toned skin.

"You said you had *some* tattoos."

"Did I? More than some."

I put a hand up to stop him from getting in the bath, suddenly and strangely fascinated by this new body.

"What?" he asks, following my gaze to his chest. "Do they bother you? They're just pictures."

"No. I don't know." The words come out raspy. Despite his warning, I didn't imagine him to look like a piece of *art*. I didn't expect to uncover a new layer. "Can I touch?"

He laughs. "Of course."

I run my fingertips over the most vivid one, a bunch of flowers on his pec. They're the same purple-blue color of his eyes. I've never been with a man who looked like this. The tattoos are new to me. As are such defined muscles. He looks as though he spends all his free time at the gym. I don't think he does, though. As beautiful as they are, I'm not sure how I feel about the tattoos. They're loud. Permanent. I can't decide until I know what they mean, but I'm not about to ask. That's too personal.

"Keep touching me like that," he dares. "See where it leads."

I pull my hand back fast, as if his skin burns. Not because I'm afraid of where it'll lead, but because I zoned out for a second admiring them. I forgot where I was, and I always make a point to be aware of my surroundings.

I take the drinks from him. Andrew gets in the bath and sinks down. "Fuck," he groans, setting his head back against the lip and closing his eyes. "Really? I can't believe I never do this."

My insides tighten. He looks masculine as ever, even up to his neck in bubbles. I'm already getting hot for him again. I went a year without sex, and suddenly I don't want to wait minutes for it.

He opens his eyes and reaches a long arm over the side to stroke the outside of my thigh. "Coming?" he asks.

"I'm waiting for it to cool a little."

"But it's perfect now." He eyes me up and down. "Turn around. You have the best ass I've ever seen."

I'm sure it's an exaggeration, but nonetheless, my body warms under his approval. I do as he says and face the bathroom.

"Incredible," he says.

Suddenly, I'm alone again, and I don't want to be. "Okay. I'm ready."

"Get in here," he says. "Put that sweet ass in my lap."

I move a little slower than him, but soon I'm submerged. He pulls me back against his chest. I'd prefer to sit opposite him, the less intimate of the two options, but his arms are already strong around me. I'm not used to this much affection, especially from a one-night stand. I don't mind it, but it takes a little extra effort to remind myself every few minutes it's not real.

Tentatively, I lay my head back against his shoulder. "Is it everything you dreamed it would be?" I ask.

"And more," he says. "Between work, exercise, and having a daughter who thinks I'm a tree she can climb, I can be hard on my body. Sometimes I forget to slow down."

I shift in his grip. With two sentences he's painted me a picture of what he has—a full life—but also what he doesn't—someone to remind him to take care of himself. Like a puzzle, pieces of him are falling into place. I might prefer our conversations weren't so personal, but I hadn't even realized what was happening. We're getting to know each other.

Silence stretches between us. It's comfortable, but soon, comfortable silence begins to feel more intimate than casual conversation. "What do you do?" I ask.

"I own an auto shop. Car and bike repairs mostly. Some restoration of classic cars."

"I've never dated a mechanic," I say. Andrew's vastly different from anyone I've been with, but not just because of what he does.

"I'm more than a mechanic," he says.

"Oh, I know." My face, already warm from the temperature, gets hot. For the first time, I wonder if it's uncomfortable for him to be in another man's apartment, especially one as nice as this one. "I didn't mean to suggest you weren't."

"It's okay. You probably don't even own a vehicle."

"I don't."

"It's not your world."

"Not really." I scoop some bubbles into my palm. "So you like cars? And motorcycles?"

"Since I was a kid. Got it from my grandpa. You ever been on a bike?"

"No." I can have fun without risking my life and my hairstyle. "It's not for me."

"Is it a hair thing?"

I start to laugh but stop so I don't give myself away. Am I that easy to read? "No," I lie with enthusiasm. "I just don't see the appeal."

"So you have no issue getting your hair messy?"

"Of course not. It's just hair."

"Good," he says, ruffling the top of my head, sending bubbles down my nose.

Instinctively, I reach up and bat his wet hands away. "Hey!"

"That's better. It didn't even look like we just fucked," he says. "Not good for my ego."

"Your *ego?*" I ask, smoothing my long bob into obedience. "I'm beginning to wonder if girls with unkempt hair and beer guts do it for you."

He laughs, bouncing my body, then hugs me closer. "You always been this uptight?"

I mock-gasp. He's teasing me, but he speaks the truth, so I can't really be mad. "Pretty much," I admit. "I like things a certain way. I'm not sorry about it. I wouldn't be where I am otherwise."

"And where's that?"

"A successful entrepreneur by the age of—" I pause. "Of the age I am."

"Which would be?"

"It's not polite to ask a woman her age, Andrew." For women, age can be an enemy, especially in New York City. There's always someone younger looking to take over. At thirty-two, I don't need to worry—yet—but I won't always be thirty-two. I prefer not to expose my weaknesses, past, present, or future.

"All right," he says hesitantly. "You *are* from a different world."

"Why? I assure you, the girls you normally sleep with care about their ages too, even if they're young."

"How many girls do you think I'm with?"

I lift a shoulder. "One plus one equals two. You're sexy and single. You must have women falling all over you."

"A few . . ." he says. I appreciate his honesty, even if it's a little disappointing. No woman wants to hear about who else is screwing the man she's sleeping with, no matter how detached she is. Or wants be. It's only when he admits it that I realize I wish I *were* the only one. "There's one regular," he continues, "and once in a while when I get a night out, I might meet a woman. It's mostly the one, though. Denise."

I close my eyes at the name. *Fuck.* There's a girl, of course there's a girl, and she has a name—why? Why couldn't he have left the name out? If I'm at all jealous, it's eradicated by a deeper fear that immediately picks up on his subtext. "A regular one . . .? Jesus, Andrew. Please don't tell me she's your—"

"Girlfriend? No. I told you, I don't date."

Dread knots in my chest. I want to believe him, which is rare. Looking back, Reggie had tells—an inability to look me in the eye when he was being vague, or the way he made me feel foolish for acting suspicious, even though I had a right to be. I don't see those signs with Andrew, and my gut tells me he's genuine, but I've been wrong before. I could press him for details, try to catch him in a lie, but in the end, it wouldn't matter. I've known enough men to lie about it that I'd never completely believe him, no matter how sincere he sounded.

He seems like a good man, but even good men have weaknesses.

Even good men cheat.

"I'm sorry," Andrew says, "but I thought we were on the same page. I was pretty clear earlier."

I frown. "About what?"

"The fact that I don't date. I didn't mean it to come out so harsh. I mean, I'm having a good time, and I like you, I just—"

"Ohh," I say when I understand what he means. "No, it's not that."

"You sighed, then got quiet. I believe in woman-speak, that means you didn't like my answer."

"I was thinking about something else entirely."

"What?"

I'm reluctant to go down this path with Andrew, but I've backed myself into a corner. I try to think of a polite way to put it. "It's just that I don't know if I believe you. About Denise. I would never, ever want to hurt another woman the way I was . . ."

"Did your ex cheat on you?" he asks.

I look down into the bubbles. Reggie's infidelity is no secret, but there's no room for it in this tub. It's too heavy, too much, for a fling. For a vanilla bubble bath. For Andrew to take on when it isn't his problem. I shake my head. I mean that I don't want to talk about it, but if he misunderstands, I won't correct him.

"You said you're getting a divorce, but you didn't say why. If that's not the reason, what is?"

"Andrew, please. We're having a nice time."

"What kind of husband was he?"

I sigh, frustrated. Normally, I'll take any chance to bash Reggie, but this feels less like a defense mechanism and more like opening up. I'm already naked at his mercy as it is. "The distracted kind."

Finally, Andrew shuts up. I don't know what I expected him to say, just that I expected him to say *something*. When I tell women about Reggie's affair, they react different ways. Some apologize, as if we've done something wrong just by being women. Some launch into their personal experiences with cheating—that usually comes with anger. I'm the second type—I launch and rage.

Men, though, are different. They usually gloss over it when I bring it up, an anecdote they didn't ask for.

"Let's not talk about it," I say. "It's okay."

"Distracted," Andrew says after a few seconds, as if he's still registering the word. "Meaning . . .?"

"It's okay," I say. "Let's change the subject."

"Maybe it is okay, maybe it's not. When you say distracted," he presses, "you mean by other women?"

I bend my knees, breaching the scalding water in an attempt to cool off a little. It doesn't help. It's not that I don't want to talk about it, but everything so far tonight has been just right. I don't want Reggie to ruin it. I don't want Andrew's *reaction* to ruin it by disappointing me. "He cheated on me," I say. "With one woman that I know of. But it went on for almost a year."

"A *year?*" Andrew raises his voice, startling me. "Are you kidding?"

"Kidding . . .?" I ask, unsure what he means. "It was an affair."

He tightens his hold, tension cording his forearms. "An affair. For a year. Asshole."

"Yes, he is."

"*Coward.*"

I try to look back at him, confused, but I can't see his expression. His reaction isn't just unexpected; it's intense. His body changes under mine, curling around me like a shield. Is he telling me what I want to hear? If so, why bother? "Reggie's insecure, yes. It makes him weak, and it's the source of his mistakes." In business, in relationships, in life, Reggie always takes the shortcut, never puts all his cards on the table. He doesn't give if he doesn't think he can get. "How'd you know?"

"What other explanation is there?" Andrew asks. "He was scared. On some level, he knew he didn't deserve you. Right?"

"I'm not sure if it runs as deep as that for him."

"He hurt you before you could hurt him. It's the only explanation," he says again.

"It is?" I wrinkle my nose. In a way, it makes sense. Reggie doesn't like to lose. He once secretly slandered a colleague who'd been up for the same promotion as him—and had never been caught. It is possible, whether he knew it or not, Reggie was threatened by the distance that'd been growing between us before he'd strayed. "Have you been cheated on?" I ask. "You seem to know a lot about it."

"No, but what other reason is there? Clearly he didn't find anyone better."

I allow myself a small smile. "That's sweet of you to say. Really."

"It pisses me off," he says, as if he didn't hear me. "I don't have personal experience with cheating, but people close to me do."

Most likely, Andrew thinks because I'm Sadie's boss, I don't know her situation. Sadie continues to insist her husband never cheated on her, but I've heard that same thing from friends who later came crying back to me when they finally saw the truth. "You mean Sadie," I say.

"You know about that?"

"Yes. Well, not the details, but I know a woman who's been broken by a man when I see one, and that's what Sadie was six months ago. She was a wreck. I don't know how they got through his infidelity." I shake my head. "How do you stay civil with him? Don't you want to wring his neck?"

Andrew snorts. "You've got it all wrong, babe."

"I don't think so." Is Nathan really such a good liar that he has Andrew convinced as well? When Sadie announced her pregnancy, I nearly keeled over. She seems happy, but can it last after how Nathan betrayed her? "Cheating often comes with a degree of brainwashing, although I don't typically see it carry over to family members—"

"Wrong," Andrew repeats. "It's not my story to tell, but sometimes, things aren't what they seem, Amelia."

I let his words settle in. Up until now, I was confident I had Sadie's situation nailed. That I knew all the details of all my friends' relationships, whether or not they'd been divulged to me. Jennifer's boyfriend went to Vegas for a weekend to attend a bachelor party? Cheater. Suzanne found an ink-smudged napkin in her husband's briefcase? Adulterer. That's just how it is. That's life, especially in this city. The fact that I might be wrong makes me curious about the truth behind Nathan and Sadie.

"So that's why you don't date," Andrew states. "Ex-husband was a cheater."

It sounds like a limerick:

Amelia's husband was a cheater,
A dirty, dirty pussy eater.
Between someone else's legs he fell,
And several lies he did tell,

Then came home to his wife, and without telling her why, apologized with a bag from Chanel.

"When someone cheats on you, it—it puts all these ideas in your head, you know?"

"Like what?" he asks.

"We really don't have to talk about this."

"I want to. What ideas does it put in your head?"

I could ask why he cares or, if I really wanted, shut down the conversation. Andrew actually seems interested in what I have to say, though. When I talk about this with friends, it sometimes becomes a pissing contest. Who was hurt worst? Which of our ex-husband's girlfriends is the youngest, prettiest, thinnest? How many times did we just miss catching them together? We're making ourselves feel worse by pretending to help each other. I don't know if they know it, but I do, and yet, I still participate.

Andrew's concern might not be genuine, but it's nice to talk to a man who doesn't seem to blame me for Reggie's affair. "Why wasn't I enough?" I ask. "That's the one my therapist, Dianne, likes to focus on, but what I can't stop wondering is . . . if he was able to cheat on me for that long, what else did I miss? What am I still missing that's right in front of me? He made me feel crazy for my suspicions, and now I . . ."

"And now?" he prompts.

"I don't trust myself anymore." It's the first time I admit it outside of Dianne's office. "I don't trust my judgment. That's what he took away. My faith in others and in myself."

Andrew rakes some hair back from my face. "I get it," he says against my temple. "I think it's a shame, but I get it."

"Did you have a similar experience when your ex left?"

"Yeah."

I wait for him to continue, but he doesn't.

"Is he with her now?" he asks.

My answering laugh is forced. "I don't know. He came crawling back two weeks after I kicked him out, claiming he'd made a mistake. Slamming the door in his face was *almost* worth all the suffering."

"And that was the last time you spoke to him?"

"Unfortunately not. He stops by sometimes. Says they're not together, but I can't believe a word he says about anything. Most of our interaction lately is through our lawyers."

"He comes by here?"

"It's his apartment, but I don't let him in."

"Hmm."

"What?" I ask, sensing his *hmm* is more than just a *hmm*.

"Have you thought about moving out?"

"And give him the satisfaction?" I shake my head. "He loves this place—it was his first seven-figure purchase. But he claimed to love me too."

"Don't you want to be free of him?"

"Of course. It's more complicated than that, though. He's an investor in *avec*. My PR firm. He dumped a large sum into it. I thought it was a blessing at the time, but now I know it was a power play to control me."

"Control you how?"

"He owns a larger share than I do."

"Shit," Andrew mutters. "That's not good."

"I was financially able to buy him out a while ago, but he always made up excuses to deny me. Then came the divorce, and he continues to fight me on it. Until he agrees to give up *avec*, I won't leave."

"Why do you like it here so much?"

"I don't," I say. "This isn't the neighborhood I'd choose, and this place has a lot of bad memories. But I don't want him to have it, either."

"You're angry," he says, "and you have every right to be."

"Of course I do," I say.

"Anger is a strong emotion. It stems from love. Like hate."

"I don't love him," I say. "I don't even feel sad about the divorce. For me, our relationship ended a while ago. Why does that mean I can't be angry?"

"It doesn't. I don't even completely understand anger, and I've been dealing with it for almost four years. You assume it's there, that it'll never go away, until the day you stop to wonder if you still feel it. At some point, it starts to fade. Whether or not you want it to." He shrugs beneath me. "Some people can't accept that, so they convince themselves it still exists."

I hesitate, not sure if I'm offended by the insinuation. "You think that's what I'm doing?"

"No. You're early in the process. I think you're still entitled to be mad. I'm mad for you."

"Don't be," I say. "I'm mad enough for two people."

"First you were telling me what not to talk about. Now you're telling me how to feel?"

"Is that a problem?" I tease.

"Ah, I see how it is," he says. "The boss is back. Trying to tell me what to do," he slips his hand down my stomach, between my thighs, "*again*."

I inhale sharply as he slides a fingertip along me, grazing my clit. I close my legs around him, capturing his hand, then move against it.

He pushes my thighs apart. "Keep them open."

"It feels too good." I struggle against his strength. "Let go."

"No. You're not in charge."

"I should be," I say. "I'm a good boss. Give me a chance to prove it."

"Why should I?"

I inch back just enough to move my ass against his groin, and he rumbles. "I'm used to being the woman on top," I say. "I like to give orders."

Without warning, he pushes a finger inside me. I bite down on my lip. "What kind of orders?"

I have to concentrate harder than I should as he begins to fuck me with his finger. "Get me coffee. Deliver this contract. Make me come."

His cock twitches against my lower back. He drops his mouth to my ear, nipping the shell. "That shouldn't be a problem, boss. Consider me for the position?"

"Which position?"

"Any. But I'd love to learn more about 'woman on top.'"

I turn my head sideways to give him my mouth for a kiss. He adds another finger as I meet his thrusts, grinding against his palm. It's a heady feeling, him hardening against my back when I've barely even touched him. I want to make him feel good too, so I reach back between us.

He catches my forearm. He slows but doesn't stop pleasuring me as he places one of my hands along the edge of the tub, then the other. "You told me to make you come," he whispers in my ear. "That's what I'm doing."

"What about you?"

"It's enough for me to watch you." He pulls his fingers out and circles them over me. I buck my hips and moan louder than I mean to. "Perfect," he murmurs. "Just let me touch you."

I'm not used to this kind of attention, to sitting still. I like to act. To touch and feel and return the favor. But spread open and positioned how he wants me, Andrew has complete control over my orgasm. I curl my hands into fists, frustrated at being both trapped and aroused, but Andrew's too good to fight against. He fucks me with his fingers while gyrating his hips against my backside. I'm all his, and the only thing he asks is that I let myself feel it. It's harder than it looks, but each time I get the urge to take control, Andrew brings me back to the moment with a kiss on my neck, under my ear.

He keeps a steady pace as my orgasm builds slower than before. Reaching along the lip of the tub, he locks his other hand over mine, interlacing our fingers.

"You're doing great," he says. "Relax. Let me make you feel good."

I don't know how he senses my unrest. In an attempt to give him what he wants, what *I* want, I place my head against his chest and shut my eyes. Still, behind my lids, the visual of our intertwined hands remains. I'm warm, inside and out, and Andrew's breath on my skin tickles. He flicks his fingers in just the right spot as he palms me.

"That's it," he says when I gasp, ramping up his assault on my clit. "Come on, babe."

I climb and climb, trying to mount my orgasm. He takes my earlobe between his teeth and with a small nip, I reach the top, bracing myself against the tub as pleasure churns through me. I hold on and make love to his hand for the seconds it takes my climax to work through me, and then I release my muscles, breathlessly falling back against Andrew's chest.

When I open my eyes again, we're still holding hands, my fingers the only tense part of me. I loosen my grip.

"Bubble bath doesn't seem so girly now, does it?" he asks, rubbing his thumb over mine

"I'm glad I thought of it," I say on an exhale.

He laughs, leaning his head into the crook of my neck. Some of his black hair, glossy from the water, falls over his forehead. I push it off, running my hand backward through his hair.

He nearly moans, his long lashes brushing my cheek as he closes his eyes. "It's too long," he murmurs. "Cut it for me?"

I twist my neck to try to look at him. "What?"

"Cut my hair. I took care of you, now take care of me."

I raise one corner of my mouth. I can't tell if he's joking. "I'm not a hairdresser."

"So? It's not hard."

"Are you kidding? You don't just start snipping away. It's an art."

"Who am I trying to impress? No one. I need it cut. You have scissors, don't you?"

"Yes, but they aren't the right kind."

"What the fuck does that mean? Do they have blades?"

"Yes . . ."

"Can they cut things?"

"Yes, but—"

"Then they're the right kind. Come on. You'll save me twenty bucks."

I lurch forward, turn back, and gape at him. "*Twenty* dollars? That's how much you spend to cut your hair?"

"Unless I can get someone to do it free, yeah."

"Oh my God." I slap a hand over my eyes. "Andrew."

"Amelia."

"I run a fashion and beauty PR firm in arguably the chicest city in the world. I cannot be hearing this right now."

He chuckles, but I'm dead serious. I don't lower my hand to look at him. If I do, I know I'll give in to his adorable but misguided idea. "Let me make an appointment for you at my favorite barber tomorrow. If they know you're with me, they'll hook you up. You can even get a shave. It'll look and *feel* amazing."

He takes my wrist and removes my hand from my face. In the dim light of the bathroom, dimples shadow his cheeks as he smiles. "*I* am not a prissy city girl," he states. "Therefore, *I* will not be caught dead at a salon while I'm alive and conscious. Have you ever cut a piece of paper?"

I give him an incredulous look. "Of course."

"Then you're qualified to give me a trim. I cut Bell's hair all the time."

"That poor child. I think I'm going to be sick."

Laughing, he stands, pulling me up with him. "You're all sudsy," he says, plucking a towel off a rack and scrubbing it through my damp hair. He wraps it around me and climbs out to dry himself.

"We could skip the haircut," I say, nodding at his hard-on.

"What, this?" He tucks the towel around his waist. "We'll get to it."

I shake my head. Everyday scissors will give you split ends, but he doesn't seem to care. I suppose he shouldn't if he spends his days getting greasy under the hoods of cars. Still. This feels like a betrayal to my industry.

I find a pair in a desk drawer and return to the bathroom. As I set the scissors on the counter, I catch a glimpse of myself in the mirror. I don't like what I see. My normally straight hair is wavy from the water and frizzy from the steam. Black makeup has smeared under my eyes.

"That's more like it, huh?" Andrew asks, coming up behind me. He meets my eyes in the reflection. "Now you look like you've been thoroughly fucked."

"I look like a mess."

"A mess I created," he says, hugging me. Automatically, I place my hands over his forearms. "We don't look so bad together, do we?" he asks.

I study our reflection. His wet black hair drips water onto his chest. The colorful ink is like a layer of clothes between us, a stark contrast to my white skin. I don't like marks. I take particular, painstaking care of my complexion, and aside from a bruise forming on my chest where Andrew sucked and kissed, I'm smooth. Flawless. "We look like opposites," I say. "You're dark and big."

"You're light and small."

It's true—we look nothing alike. His height dwarfs me, even though I'm somewhat tall. His hair glistens, reflecting the overhead light, while mine is platinum and matte thanks to a talented colorist.

He sets his chin on top of my head. "Our eyes," he says at the same moment I notice.

I nod. "They're the same."

"Almost." He peers at me. "Yours are bluer."

"Yours are the same as your sister's."

"And my daughter's," he says. "'Indigo' is what Sadie's husband calls it. Totally creeps me out when he talks about how beautiful Sadie's eyes are and then tells me in the same sentence how alike we look."

I watch as we laugh together. As he kisses the back of my head. He pulls a bench out from under my vanity to sit on. "All right. Let's do this."

I drape a towel around his shoulders and get my comb from a drawer. "Do you normally make women work on the first date?"

"This isn't a first date."

"I was joking, because you freaked out earlier when I called it one."

"It's more like a second date," he says, ignoring me. "We already had dinner, a walk, and a night cap. *And* you put out—bonus for me."

I comb his hair off his face. I have no idea how I'm going to do this. "So how does date two go then?"

"I don't know." Our eyes meet in the reflection. "It's been a while since I had one."

My heart skips a beat—to my dismay. I ignore it. "Well, I can definitely say playing barber is a second-date first."

"Good. I like to set myself apart."

"You certainly have," I mutter.

"Use your fingers," he says, lacing his hands in his lap.

I set the comb aside and rake his long strands back. "How short do you want it?"

"Hmm?" His eyes are shut, his shoulders slightly hunched.

"Are you sleeping?"

"No." He opens one eye, says, "However you like it" and closes it again.

"You aren't going to watch? What if I mess up?"

"You won't." He scratches his jaw. "Actually, I'll watch if you do it naked."

I don't even respond, just roll my eyes and shake my head to myself. I've seen stylists part hair down the middle. I start with that. "How do you normally style it?"

"It's complicated," he warns.

I furrow my eyebrows, surprised. "Really?"

"Yeah. I normally shampoo it, towel dry it, then go to work."

"Um."

"Sometimes I brush it. And sometimes when it's long and bothering the fuck out of me, I gel it back so I can see what I'm working on."

I sigh, trying to sound annoyed, but I can't help my smile. "All right. If that's how you want to play this, then sit back and enjoy. I'll do my best." I pick up the scissors and run my fingers through one side of his hair. When I have a chunk, I trim off the top.

"That was the first snip," I say, since his eyes are still closed.

I wait to see if he'll stop me, but he just says, "Great."

I continue, doing my best to make sure the trim is even, careful not to cut it too short.

I want something I can get a handful of—even if it's only for tonight.

SEVEN

Standing between Andrew's legs, I make the final snip, and his black hair falls to the floor. Normally, I'd clean up the mess I've made right away, but I'm too busy surveying my work. For as much as my trade requires me to judge other people by their appearances, I feel like I should have a better idea whether or not I've done a decent job. "I'm done."

Andrew blinks his eyes open and looks up at me. "Yeah?"

I nod. "You are officially my first client."

He grins, takes the scissors out of my hands, and sets them on the counter behind me. "You're amazing."

"I'm blocking the mirror," I say. "You haven't even seen your hair."

"It *felt* amazing." He takes me by the waist, and pulls me a few inches forward until he's looking straight up at me. "And you did it how you want it. So I know I'll like it."

I cup his cheek without thinking and look into his eyes. All at once, the moment feels overwhelmingly intimate. I remove my hand. "Are you leaving now?" I ask.

"Leaving? No. Not now." He parts my towel and slips a hand underneath. "Now, I'm going to fuck you again."

I suck my bottom lip between my teeth as my stomach flutters. I came by his hands in the bathtub twenty minutes ago, but already, warmth and need creeps up my chest.

He pulls me forward to straddle his lap. "Wasn't this the position you applied for?" I ask, undulating my hips once.

He groans. "Woman on top."

I slide my hand over his pec. "You made me feel good. I want to return the favor."

"I won't say no." He wedges his hands under my ass and brings me closer. My towel parts, and I'm pressed up against his stone-like cock. I put my arms around his neck, gyrating over him.

"Fuck," he says into my neck, sounding like he's got a mouthful of grit. "I need to be inside you."

"You can be," I say, barely recognizing my own voice, "when I say so."

He runs his hand up to my scalp, grabs a fistful of my hair, and draws back. "You want to play boss for a little bit? Fine. I'll let you."

"You'll *let* me?" I ask, doing my best to look down at him as he holds me in a tight grip.

"Sure. It could be fun to watch."

I grit my teeth and stop moving. I'll show him how fun it can be to do what I say. "There're condoms in my nightstand. Go get one."

In one motion, he stands, lifting me with him. "Yes, boss," he says before setting me on the bathroom counter.

As he walks into the bedroom, his towel loosens and falls off. He leaves it. His ass is tight and tanned, as if he regularly does naked squats outdoors. My mouth waters.

I hop off the counter and follow him into the bedroom, where he's stooped over my nightstand's open drawer. He picks out a condom and holds it up.

"Leave it for now," I say. "You won't need it to eat me out."

He straightens, arching an eyebrow at me. I open my towel and drop it on the floor. He takes a step toward me, but I say, "Stop."

"Why?"

"Just seeing if you can follow orders."

By the way he clenches his jaw and swallows, I can tell he wants to take over. I level my gaze on him, and he stays where he is.

"I have ideas," he says.

I hesitate. Andrew is used to getting his way. So was Reggie. A few times, toward the end of our relationship, he even intimidated me into sex. I let him. He abused his control. I need to know Andrew can stop himself, no matter how badly he wants to be in charge.

"I've eaten a pussy or two in my time," he says. "Have *you?*"

"No," I admit.

"Then consider that a special skill of mine. A good boss knows when to delegate."

I have to admit, he can negotiate. Just the thought of him between my legs is enough to weaken my resolve. I concede. "A good boss also knows how to take suggestions."

"Great." He comes around the bed and sits on the edge before pulling me to him by my wrist. "I *suggest* you sit on my face."

My heart thumps. I want control, but with every sentence from him, my knees quiver harder. "I think . . ."

"Yes?" he prompts, his eyes gleaming. He knows exactly what he's doing to me.

"I think your idea is feasible."

He quirks the corner of his mouth and scoots back to the head of the bed. I go with him, crawling down the mattress until I'm straddling his thighs. For a moment, I'm tempted to skip to the fucking, but then he licks his lips, and my thoughts are reduced to how his mouth will feel on me.

He puts his hands on my hips—a *suggestion*, not an order. I feel the restraint in his grip. I inch forward, grab onto the headboard and lower myself onto his mouth. He hums, vibrating the space around me, but doesn't lick me.

"I wonder how you'll taste," he says, inhaling. "Perhaps like apricot bubble bath?"

My thighs tremble. "Try me."

"I will."

"Now."

He kisses me right between the lips. "Like that?"

"It's a start."

He licks along my slit. "Better?"

"Better," I say. My knuckles are white from gripping the headboard. "But not quite there."

"Mmm." A few tense, anticipatory moments pass. "So am I hired?" he asks.

Through gritted teeth, I say, "Yes, you're fucking hired, now please just eat my pussy."

"Yes, boss." He grabs me by the ass cheeks, pulls me onto him, and sucks my clit into his mouth.

I throw my head back. "Oh . . . my G—"

He spreads me apart with his hands and thrusts his tongue inside me. I squirm, trying to pull back because it feels too good, but he secures me against his mouth. I dig my fingernails into the wood, undulating over him. When he reaches around to play with my clit, I arch backward, overwhelmed by the assault. "Wait," I cry.

He slaps my ass and goes at me harder. My eyes cross. The words I try to form are barely squeaks. I want him inside me when I come, but he's so relentless, I'm already on the verge. I do my best to distract myself to stave off my orgasm.

New York Fashion Week is only five months away. That's twenty—I squeak—*weeks!*

Pantone announced two colors of the year for the first time—Rose Quartz and Serenity.

I hate the word quartz, *and the word* quirky— *apparently, I'm not a fan of "Q".*

But I like quirky things.

Man Repeller's Instagram feed is quirky, and I adore Leandra Medine . . .

Not as much as I adore Andrew's tongue shoved up my—

My thighs shake so hard, if I weren't holding myself up by the headboard, I'd drop down and suffocate him. This isn't working. "Stop, wait," I plead. "Don't make me come."

"*Don't* make you come?" he asks, breathing hotly against my swollen lips.

"Not yet."

Andrew slows, loosening his grip. If he was fucking me with his mouth before, now he makes love to my pussy. When he moans, I feel it everywhere. It's not helping. Gentle or rough, he knows how to work me.

I pull his hands away from my hips and climb off his face toward the nightstand to get the condom.

Andrew wipes his mouth with his shoulder, a smile spreading over his face. I hold out the condom, but he shakes his head. "Your move, boss."

I smirk at him and tear the foil. His cock is practically vertical, waiting for me. I sit back on my calves and watch his face as I stroke him once. He thrusts his hips, a preview of what's to come. I let my eyes wander, appreciating his long, firm, artful body, the abs that flex as he lifts his head to look at me.

"Amelia." We make eye contact. "I'm trying to be patient," he says, "but I've been hard since the bath. I already know how good you feel, and it's killing me."

I'm still throbbing from my core, but teasing him is making me even hotter. I glance down just long enough to place the condom over his tip, and then back to him so I can watch his expression as I roll it on.

His nostrils flare as he takes a deep breath. "Let me fuck you."

"You've been so patient," I say, throwing a knee over him. I lean forward onto my hands, trapping him against the mattress. "That's a quality I value in my *employees*."

He lifts his head to kiss me, but I pull away. His hand is in my hair in a split second, bringing me back down.

I *tsk*. "Are you challenging my authority?"

He removes his hand, but his frustration is clear in the way he grits his jaw. I see the agony in his eyes. Slowly, I bring my mouth to his and touch our lips together. He stays still. "Good," I whisper against him, reaching between us. I position him against my opening. "Now kiss me."

He rakes his hands through my hair, groaning into my mouth with a bruising kiss. I lower myself onto him and slide up and down a couple times, adjusting to his size.

He fists his hands against my scalp. "Can I fuck you yet?"

"No."

"How about now?"

"Let me do it." I sink down until I'm seated. We breathe into each other's mouths, but as he goes to kiss me again, I push off his chest, straighten up, and swivel my hips over him.

"Christ, Amelia," he says, grabbing my waist. I ride him, forward, backward, around in circles. I find my rhythm, drawing up quick and coming down hard.

Andrew pinches his eyebrows together, gasping open-mouthed, as if he's in pain. He thrusts his hips up a little, a small act of insubordination, but it feels too good for me to scold him. I throw my head back when he takes my breasts in both hands, kneading them, tugging on my nipples until I squeal.

"Fuck me," I say.

He slams into me, and all at once, even though I'm still on top, I'm no longer riding him. He's in control again, holding me in place by my middle as he fucks me.

"Jesus," I breathe. "You are so hired. And you've earned a bonus."

He sits up suddenly, flips me onto my back, and cages me with his big body. "Game over. I'm not your employee. There can only be one real boss—"

"But—"

"And that's me." He captures my wrists and raises them over my head, pinning them to the mattress.

"Wait." I struggle to free my hands, but his grip is firm. "I don't like to be tied up."

"I didn't think you would." He doesn't budge. "I like you at my mercy, though."

We stare each other down. He sets his jaw with determination. He hasn't given me any reason not to trust him, but with the sudden racing of my heart, I know I don't.

"I could own you right now, Amelia. But not if you don't submit, at least a little."

I swallow. After the pleasure he's already given me, to be owned by Andrew sounds exquisite, but I won't be able to submit if I can't relax. "Stop." I don't feel good about testing him. I need to know he isn't carried away, though. "Let go."

He releases my wrists. "I wouldn't fuck you like that unless you asked me to."

I shake my head a little. "I won't."

"Okay, but . . . what'll I do with you instead?"

I squirm on the mattress. "Fuck me."

"Yes. But how?" He looks down my body, lingering on my breasts, licking his lips. "Slow? Fast? On your hands and knees? In the ass?"

My mouth drops open. "My *ass*? You've lost it if you think I'll agree to that."

He suppresses a smile, then drops his hips between my legs. "I think right here will be fine," he murmurs, gliding his shaft along my clit.

I lose my breath. I want him back inside me, and I don't care who's in charge.

"What do you think?" he asks.

"Yes, fine." My body flushes, craving him as he teases my slit.

"Yes, fine, what? You want me to take you like this?"

"Andrew," I demand. I grab a fistful of his hair. "Stop teasing me."

"Tell me you need it. I want to hear the desperation in your voice."

I grit my teeth, bite my lip, inhale through my nose. If I don't give in, he'll keep this up. I know he will, because I would if I wanted control more than I wanted to come. I don't. I just want release. "I need it," I say huskily. "Please, Andrew."

He lines his cock up against my opening and buries his face in my neck. "Good girl," he whispers and plunges inside me.

I gasp, overcome by how good he feels, how eager he is. His fingers tangle in my hair.

"God, this is heaven," he breathes onto my neck. "Tight, hot heaven."

I recover from my state of shock and meet his thrusts, taking all of him as deep as I can, moaning as he hits me the right way with each shove of his hips.

"Christ," he bites out near my ear. "I'm going to come. So are you. I feel it." He lifts up, propping himself on his hands. I wrap my legs around his waist right before he rears back and slams into me. I grab onto his unforgiving biceps as he fucks his way to the finish line. All his muscles work together, and the anguish on his face turns me to putty. I dissolve into my orgasm like butter on hot toast, like how I imagine it'd feel to have my soul drift from my body. I barely register Andrew coming along with me, even though he growls loudly enough to wake my neighbors.

Andrew's big, sweaty, spent body pins me to the mattress. I don't move as we each catch our breath. As distant as I'd like to remain, I have the urge to touch his back, guide him down from his climax. I know better, though. This, in the moments when endorphins are flowing and everything feels good, is when bonds are formed, and neither of us can afford to take that chance.

Heavy on top of me, he heaves a sigh. "You kill me," he says. "You literally fucking kill me."

I smile up at the ceiling and give in. I put my hand on the back of his shoulder.

"Mmm," he moans right away. "That feels good."

I massage him a little. "How's this?"

"Perfect. Never stop." He nuzzles my neck. "I'm crushing you."

"No. I mean yes, but I don't mind."

"Good. I don't think I can move. I might fall asleep here."

I don't want him to move. I'm sleepy. Sated. It's been years since I've felt this comfortable. I've never had three orgasms in one day, much less in a matter of hours. Having Andrew on top of me should make me nervous, but it's having the opposite effect—he's safe. If Reggie were to walk in right now, I'd be protected.

Why did I think that?

It occurs to me that living in Reggie's apartment, sleeping in the bed we used to share, has kept him on my mind more than I'd like to admit. There's always a chance, however small, he could show up uninvited. No matter what I think, I'm not safe. Not even from Andrew. Getting too comfortable is a mistake I made with Reggie, and one I don't want to make twice.

My chest tightens. I'm sweating, and not just because of our marathon fucking. I try to breathe, but I can't get a lungful. It was fine, playing around, but now that we've had enough sex to satisfy our libidos, there's nothing left for us but emotionally dangerous territory. I push Andrew's shoulders, but he doesn't budge. "Andrew."

"Hmm?"

"Get off," I say. "Please get off."

"Off?" I hear the drowsiness in his voice, but he rolls over onto his back.

I sit forward and breathe deeply before leaning over to my bedside table. Hands trembling, I manage to get a cigarette lit. With my first drag, I close my eyes and sigh.

"You smoke?" he asks.

"Of course. Not a lot, but this is New York after all."

"Pass it."

I look over my shoulder and give it to him.

"Fuck," he says. "I forgot how good it is right after sex."

"You quit?"

"Mostly, when we had Bell. I still do now and then, but only when she's not around. And never in the house."

I look forward again. "That's why I don't have kids, and I don't want them."

"Because you'd have to quit smoking?"

"Sacrifice. I sacrifice for work, but not for anything or anyone else. Not anymore."

He touches my back, running a calloused, warm palm up my spine, and gives me the cigarette. "Come here."

I almost do. I *almost* come when he calls. It would be so easy to curl up next to him, inhale his soapy skin, fall asleep in his arms. In the midst of a harrowing divorce from someone I thought I loved, it shouldn't be this easy. How can good sex erase my memory so quickly? It can't. I meant what I said—I don't trust myself. "No."

"If you're going to fight me some more, at least cuddle with me while you do it."

I take another drag of the cigarette and put it out. "You should go."

After a few seconds of silence, he asks, "What?"

"You have to go."

"Why? Because I want to hold you?"

"No. Well, yeah, I guess. That's not in our arrangement."

"Arrangement?" I hear the smile in his voice. "We didn't exactly sign a contract."

"Have you changed your mind?" I ask, looking at him over my shoulder. "Do you want this to turn into something more?"

He's mid-yawn, but stops abruptly and shuts his mouth. His expression changes as he realizes I'm serious, and he sits up. "No. I don't see how spending one night in the same bed means *more*."

"It's different for me. I'm a woman. I can't turn it on and off as easily as you."

He looks over at me, his eyebrows drawn. "That's a little sexist."

"It's true, though, isn't it? I want you to stay, and I want to sleep in the nook of your shoulder, and because I want to, I can't. Do you understand?"

He blinks a few times and scrubs his hands over his face. "Spending the night would be too much for you."

"Yes."

"You're scared."

I nod.

He looks down at the bedspread as if he's deciding. "I understand, but . . . I thought we'd have until the morning. I've got a long train ride home, and it's after midnight."

"I'm sorry. I just can't risk it. And I know you don't want me to."

Finally, he nods slowly, staring straight ahead. "Yeah. Okay." He glances at me again. "For the record, I don't want to go. I'd really like to stay with you tonight."

"And that doesn't scare you?"

"I guess." He pulls back the covers. "I can handle it, but if you don't think you can, I'll respect that."

"Thank you." I get up with him and go into my closet for my robe. When I come out, he's in his t-shirt, heading into the kitchen for his pants. Again, I get to watch his perfect ass. Am I an idiot? Should I be thankful for this one night? Would it really hurt to spend a few more hours with him, wake up to his gorgeous face, roll over, and make love while we're still half asleep?

My answer is in my questions.

Andrew and I are adults. We aren't in our twenties anymore, and we know what we don't want better than what we do.

I follow him into the kitchen and watch him button his jeans. After he runs a hand through his hair, it sticks up slightly longer on one side. I frown. "You may need someone to fix your hair."

"I love it."

I raise my eyebrows at him. "You can't even see it."

"I don't need to." He takes a few steps to close the distance between us, bends down to hug my waist, and lifts me so we're face to face. "It's my souvenir."

"Andrew," I warn. "Put me down."

"I know. I'm sorry." He doesn't move. "First, one last kiss."

I peck him once on the lips. "There. Put me down."

"Un-uh." He walks us to the front door. "As far as last kisses go, that ranks pretty low. *Disappointing*, even."

With a sigh and a reluctant smile, I wrap my arms around his neck. "Fine."

"Now the legs," he prompts.

"If by 'one last kiss' you mean sex . . ."

He chuckles, then cups my ass so I can close my legs around his waist. "That's better. Come here."

As if under some kind of spell, I lean in for him. He licks along my bottom lip, and we open our mouths to each other. I can't tell which of us is moaning, or if we both are, and just like that, it's over like he promised. Andrew sets me back on my feet.

"There," he says. "That's a last kiss I won't forget."

"To go with a first kiss *I* won't forget."

"Exactly." He smiles down at me, and the silence stretches between us. It's unfair that the more I want him to stay, the surer I am he can't. I have to bite my tongue to keep from saying *never mind*. "Right," he says. "Bye."

"Don't fall asleep on the train. There're some real weirdoes out there this time of night."

"Thanks," he says with a hoarse laugh. "Your concern seems genuine."

I grin. If anyone can handle himself, it's him. I'm not worried. "Night."

He chucks me under the chin. "Goodnight, Amelia."

EIGHT
ANDREW

I'm one of those assholes who likes Mondays as much as Saturdays. Even though it's never easy to send Bell off to school, I love my work, and there's nowhere I belong more than at the garage. The best part of my day is right now, when my two worlds collide.

I stand on the corner, smoking my last cigarette of the day. I'm normally able to control my nicotine cravings, but after my cigarette with Amelia, I've been finding it harder to resist.

It tastes good. It calms me.

It reminds me of lying in bed next to her.

When a school bus rounds the corner, I put out the cigarette and squint, looking for Bell through the square, tinted windows. The bus stops, and she comes catapulting out, a bundle of energy in a pink and purple backpack. I lift her up.

The driver smiles. "Afternoon, sugar," she says.

I wave and carry Bell down the block. "Aunt Sadie says you pretend that you quit smoking, but you didn't really," Bell informs me. "And she says you have to stop for real."

"I bet she did."

"She says it's disgusting, and you're killing your lungs with black stuff."

I sigh. The last thing I need is Bell harping on me about this. I happily changed my entire lifestyle for her. I learned to cook healthy food. I stopped drinking every weekend. I only get to ride my bike when she's not with me. I don't get close to anyone who might hurt us. This is one small thing I keep for myself, and I never do it around her.

"Aunt Sadie lied," I say.

Bell looks skeptical. "I don't think so. My teacher says smoking is bad for you." She pulls on my t-shirt. "Please, Daddy. I don't want you to put black stuff in your lungs. How will you breathe?"

"We'll see, baby." Guilt gnaws at my heart— which is surely blackened by tar as well. "How was school?"

"Fine. Miss Hughes told me she wants you to come in for a conference."

"For what? Were you bad?"

"No," she nearly yells, completely affronted.

I pull back, sticking a finger in my ear. "Jesus. Calm down."

"I was *good*," she says. "So good, she wants to give me more work."

"Great," I mutter. "More homework for you means more homework for Dad."

She tilts her head, looking pensive. "Why does my teacher always want to meet with you?"

I would laugh if I weren't so annoyed. It's at least the fifth time this school year Miss Hughes has requested a meeting with me, and it always turns out to be stupid shit. I wouldn't mind hearing her gush about what a great student Bell is if it weren't a thinly-veiled attempt to come onto me. "Um . . ."

"Aunt Sadie says—"

"Aunt Sadie needs to learn to keep her big mouth shut."

Bell squeals, wriggling in my arms. "She says Miss Hughes wants to kiss you."

"Christ."

"*Daddy.*"

"Bell-y."

"A lot of the teachers talk to you. And the bus lady. Do they want to kiss you too?"

I shake my head. "You're too young to be talking like this."

"But you always tell me to speak what's on my mind."

"I was wrong. Don't always listen to what Daddy tells you."

She giggles, and like always, it's a knife in my heart, but in the best way. She knows exactly how to melt me. "Don't worry about Miss Hughes, all right? I'll handle it." I put her down and take her hand to walk the last block to the garage. When we get close enough, she takes off sprinting.

The guys who work for me perk up for the first time all day. I'm constantly on their asses about being friendlier to customers, and they constantly ignore me. Bell is the only person who can not only make them smile on a dime, but basically turn them to mush.

Pico wipes his hands on a rag. "Hey, boss," he calls. "You know what next month is?"

"Hmm." I pretend to think. "Shipment of fan belts?"

"It's my *birthday*," Bell says with exasperation.

Pico frowns. "It is? I forgot all about that."

"No you didn't." She puts a hand on her hip. "You've been talking about it for weeks."

"I just can't believe you're going to be ten already."

She stomps her foot. "I'm going to be seven!"

"Really? That's it?" He suppresses a grin. "What do you want for your birthday? Anything but a bicycle."

She drops her mouth open, narrowing her eyes on him. "*All I want* is a bicycle. And it better not have those dumb training wheels."

"Oh. That might be a problem." He shrugs. "Your dad thinks it's too dangerous."

She whirls on me. "What?"

I raise my hands. "You don't even know how to ride a bike."

"I'll learn. My friends already know how, so it can't be that hard. I'll do it right now if you want." We laugh, but she keeps a stern expression. "I'm serious. I can do it."

"We'll see," I say, exchanging a smile with Pico. He and I are custom building one for her and storing it at his place. Bell's never been one to ignore details, and I know what she wants down to the color of the stitching on the seat. Once Bell flits off to bug another one of my guys, I nod at the Chevy Pico's working on. "How's it coming?"

"Fed up setting the timing. Can you try?"

"Yeah." I take his place under the hood and aim the timing gun at the engine.

"Ready for next month?" Pico asks.

"Will I ever be ready for a backyard full of twenty kids under ten?"

He chuckles. "The kids aren't who you should be worried about. You'll have your hands full juggling twenty moms."

I give him a look. "Don't you start in on me too. First it was Sadie. Then Bell just gave me the third degree about why her teachers flirt with me."

"Poor baby."

"Yeah, I am. I just want to be left alone."

"Fuck you," Pico says. "You could have any chick in town, even the married ones, and you have to be a dick about it. You've got Denise Jackson, Prom Queen runner-up, wrapped around your finger, and you don't even care."

"Want some advice?" I say, only half listening as I work. "Don't try so hard. The girls'll come to you."

"Yeah right. It's that easy. My sister says you're disturbingly hot, but I'm just disturbing."

I shake my head. "I have to agree. Rev the engine."

He gets behind the wheel and hits the gas while I check the timing. I motion for him to stop, and he gets out. "Anyway, I wasn't referring to the party," he continues. "I meant are you ready for the other thing."

I glance up at him. The *other* thing is Shana. Since she left a couple weeks before Bell's third birthday, everyone treats me like glass around this time of year. Not that I really blame them. I was a mess afterward. But last year was better. And this year, it's the first I've thought of it.

"Where's the wrench?" I ask.

"Right in front of you." He waits as I loosen a bolt. "Sorry to bring it up, but I had to ask, bro."

"I'll be fine." I am fine. I have to be, for Bell. Shana left without any explanation, and I could've easily turned into my dad—a worthless drunk who drowns his feelings of inadequacy in alcohol and gambling. But Bell needed me.

124

"Boss," Randy calls from the office. "Phone. It's your sister."

I put down the wrench and wipe my hands on my jeans. I'd tell him to take a message, but Sadie rarely calls me at work, especially after I've just seen her. I head into the office, shut the door, and pick up the receiver. "Everything all right?"

"Sorry I wasn't there when you picked up Bell last night," she says. "I had a raspberry sorbet craving so I went to the market."

"Nathan told me. Isn't that his job?"

"I'm trying to walk as much as possible. Keep the weight gain to a minimum."

I shake my head. She's having a baby for fuck's sake. If Sadie and Amelia are any indication, I wonder if there's a single woman in that city who knows how to eat. "Just don't starve my niece or nephew."

"Did you have a nice weekend?" she asks.

"Yep. Already told Nathan all about it."

"Really? I asked, and he said you told him it was good."

"It was."

"So that's not telling him all about it. What'd you do?"

Sadie must be fishing for something. Amelia's the first thing that comes to mind. The only way Sadie'd know anything is if Amelia mentioned Friday night, and she wouldn't. She has more reason not to than me. "I kicked it," I say, which is true. "Shot some pool Saturday night."

"Did you try that pizza place I suggested?"

"Yeah." My mouth waters. I can almost taste the tomato sauce I sucked off Amelia's cheek. "It was pretty good."

"Everyone in the office loves that place."

"Even your boss?"

"My boss? Uh, no, but she doesn't like anything. Especially not carbs."

Feeling something gummy on the sole of my boot, I scrub it on the concrete floor and glance through the office window into the garage. Bell is chattering to Pico about something or other. "What's her deal anyway?" I ask.

"Who, Amelia? I know how she comes off, but she's not that bad. A lot of it is for show, I think."

"What do you mean?"

"She's been through some stuff with an ex and came out a little damaged."

I frown, tightening my grip on the phone. I already know all this from the source herself but hearing it from Sadie just reignites my disgust with Reggie. Before Bell, I had little patience for men who jerked women around. When I'm with a woman, she always knows where I stand. But now that I've got a little girl? Have mercy on gutless fuckers who cross my path.

"Funny you should ask," Sadie goes on, "she's especially schizo today. Her mood was all over the place this morning."

My frown eases into a small smile. She was in a pretty shitty mood when I met her. And a great one when I left her. It was a night I won't forget anytime soon. Her legs entwined with mine in the tub. Her long fingers in my hair. I didn't want to leave her, but I did out of respect. If I'd stayed knowing her feelings could develop into something more, I would've felt like shit in the morning. She's scared. So am I. I'm okay living in fear. It reminds me of the damage one pretty girl can do.

"Did you like *avec*?" Sadie asks.

I blink out of my Amelia-induced haze. Again, Sadie sounds like she's fishing or suspicious. "What do you mean? It's fine, I guess."

"I love the people I work with, especially Mindy. She's great."

"Yeah, uh—" Pico waves me over, pointing at the car I was just working on. There's smoke coming from the engine. "I'm working, Sadie. I have to go."

"I know, I know—just a sec. I have a favor to ask."

"Make it quick."

"*Avec* is nominated for an award by a national PR organization and Thursday night is the gala. Amelia purchased a table for the firm, but Nathan can't come. He has to work."

Bell ambles toward the car, curious about the commotion, and dumbass Pico does nothing. When Pico gestures at me again, I wave my hand for him to get Bell away from it. *Moron.* "All right," I say. "What do you need?"

"Can you please, please come with me? I know it isn't your thing, but I can't show up without a date after Amelia spent that much on Nathan's meal . . ."

An event where Amelia'll be? I didn't think I'd ever see her again—after all, I have no reason to go to Sadie's work, and I steer clear of the city as much as possible. Would Amelia even want me there?

I don't think I care. At the thought of spending another night with her, my insides coil. Friday night was the best sex I've had in four years. It's the most connected I've been to a woman since Shana. I'd be a fool to fall for Amelia, but since I'm not a fool anymore, I don't need to worry about that. The foolish thing would be turning down potential best-sex-ever. "I'll come."

"And I've been so," Sadie's voice cracks, "so emotional lately, I just really don't want to be alone—wait." Her voice returns to normal. "You'll come? Really?"

"Were you seriously going to pull the fucking pregnancy card on me?" I ask. "I have no doubt that works on Nathan, but I've been through this before. I'm not an idiot."

She gasps. "Don't be rude. I *have* been emotional."

"Whatever. I said yes. I have to get off the phone."

"We can meet for a drink before."

"Fine. Text me the details."

"It's black-tie. Wear your good suit—"

I hang up. I only have two suits. She's referring to the one I wore to her wedding since she forced me to get it custom made. Last week, I would've been annoyed as hell to have to go to some pretentious black-tie event in the city. I'm not exactly thrilled about it. But getting to see Amelia is a nice, unexpected surprise and boost to my day. She said sleeping over could be risky for us, but a quick round between the sheets before I have to get back home? Shouldn't be a problem.

I come out of the office and head for the car. "Where's Bell?"

"With Denise."

I glance over to the grassy area by the garage, where Bell and Denise are sitting. Bell sticks out her pinky finger, lifts an imaginary teacup to her lips, and tips it back. Denise waves at me.

"Where'd she come from?" I ask.

Pico grunts. "You know how she likes to pop by."

The car is no longer smoking, and Pico doesn't seem concerned. "You got this?" I ask him.

"Yeah, it's good. Go deal with her."

I stomp over to the grass. Bell is completely clueless as to what Denise is doing, as she should be, but I'm not. Denise isn't. Denise is always getting time in with Bell when she can, trying to get to me through her. "Denise."

She looks up. "Hey, you. Want some tea?" She holds her empty palm open. "A blueberry scone?"

"It's *black*berry," Bell corrects.

"No. No scone for me. Come here, baby." I gesture for Bell to get up, and she stands. "Go in the office and get started on your homework. If you finish before dinner, we can watch something with a princess in it later."

She widens her eyes. "Really? Anything I want?"

"*Frozen* is my favorite," Denise says. "Bell, you're just like Elsa."

Bell whirls around. I try not to laugh. There's nothing I could've said to Denise that'll be worse than what she's about to get. "Elsa is *blonde*," Bell points out. "I have black hair. We're nothing alike."

"I meant that you're brave—"

"That crap isn't even a classic!" Bell says.

"Oh." Denise scratches behind her ear. "I'm sorry. I didn't realize—"

Bell shakes her head, disappointed. "I have to go do my homework."

"Good girl," I say, patting her head before she takes off.

Denise wipes her hands on her jeans and gets off the ground. "You don't have to be a jerk. I'm just trying to help," she says, looking up at me. "It's not good for her to be hanging around all these men all the time. She needs a female influence."

"She has my sister for that."

"Wake up, Andrew. Sadie isn't her mother."

"Then she has me. I do the girly shit. I watch the princess movies. I ask about her feelings. I'm not too proud to buy tampons when the time comes, and she already knows boys are scum so I don't have to worry about the dating thing."

"It's not the same. Being a woman is about more than tampons and Disney princesses."

I level her with a glare. Denise and I have been friends since high school, she knows how protective I am, but she continues to push me. "You think I don't know my own daughter? Mind your own business."

"No. Shana's been gone four years next month. She fucked you over. So what? We've all been fucked over. Get over it. I have."

"She was your friend," I say, reeling back. "*I* lost the mother of my child. But you're wrong. I *am* over it. I just choose not to get back into it." I look her in the eye. "With anyone. You knew that when we started this."

She sighs, crossing her arms. "Have I ever asked you for anything?"

"Not outright."

She looks away. "Why didn't you call me Saturday night when you were at Timber?"

I scratch my jaw. When I go out drinking with the guys, which isn't often, I sometimes end up back at Denise's. Even if it's just for an hour before I have to get home to Bell. Saturday night, though, I wasn't in the mood for just anyone, thanks to a certain sassy blonde with legs for days.

"I slept with someone on Friday," I say.

Denise turns back to me, her eyes big. "What? *Who?*"

"You don't know her. She isn't from around here."

She presses her lips together. "Why do you tell me these things?"

"You have a right to know."

"You don't think I've slept with other guys?" she asks. "I've never thrown it in your face."

"You're my friend, Denise. I don't want you to get hurt."

"That doesn't stir anything in you?" she asks. "Nothing?"

"What?" I ask.

"Hearing that I've slept with other guys."

I shift on my feet and try to conjure an ounce of jealousy. I love Denise—as a friend. As one of the people who stepped in to help with Bell when I needed it most, I'm grateful she's in my life. But that's as much as I'll ever feel for her. As long as she's happy and treated well, I have no comments about her sex life. "If this is getting to be too much, I understand," I say. "We've been hooking up for two years. I wouldn't fault you for developing feelings. But if you are, we have to stop."

She looks at her feet. I know what she'll say. We've had this conversation before. "I'm not."

"Good." I look through the office window. Bell has her head down as she does homework. I put an arm around Denise's shoulder and kiss her head. "You know I care about you. But stay the fuck away from Bell when I'm not around. I mean it."

She sighs, shoves me off, and walks away. "Call me next time you have a few hours free."

NINE

"Shaving cream," I command as if I'm at the head of an army.

"Yes, *sir.*" Bell maneuvers herself onto the bathroom counter and gets the can. She shakes it before squirting some into her hand. Her palm is too small for the amount I need, so I let her slather what she's got on my face before filling in the rest.

She knocks her heels against the cabinet under the sink. "You're going to look so handsome, Daddy."

I glide my razor down my cheek and glance at her in the reflection. "Thanks, baby."

"All the girls will want to kiss you."

With a heavy sigh, I give her a reprimanding look. I don't know if it's normal for girls her age to tease their dads about women. I can't exactly ask around—I don't know any other single dads. I thought I had a while longer before she moved into this phase where she starts to wonder about love and sex.

Sex.

Jesus. Christ.

Could I ever actually work up the nerve to talk about that with Bell, my precious baby? *Fuck*. I hope I'm right that I've got years left to prepare, but I'm worried that might be pushing it.

"Homework's done?" I ask, changing the subject.

"Yup. Are you going to the city?"

"Yes. Uncle Nathan has to work and Aunt Sadie needs me to go with her."

"I love New York City. I want to live there one day."

I slide my gaze over to her. I'm aware of her interest, but this is the first I've heard of wanting to move there. "It's not a nice place."

"But Aunt Sadie lives there, and she has a fun job and cool friends."

"She lives in Brooklyn," I say, "not that that's any better."

"Are you going to a party?"

I rinse out my razor. I don't often leave Bell in the evenings. It can sometimes get ugly. Since she didn't freak out too much about spending a weekend with Sadie, I'm hoping she's grown out of it, but I don't exactly want to test that theory. "Speaking of parties," I say. "Did you decide what kind of cake you want for your birthday?"

"Chocolate with chocolate frosting that has blue and pink swirls," she says. "And mint ice cream."

"Done."

"Will you be home in time to tuck me in?"

Fuck. I tilt my head back, shaving under my jaw. I don't look at Bell, because like an animal, she smells fear. "I don't think so, babe. City's far away. I'll be home late."

She doesn't respond.

I put my razor down and splash water on my face. "I need you to be good for Flora tonight," I say about Pico's mom, Bell's usual sitter. "Even Pico's coming over to play."

Silence. When it comes to Bell, that's never a good sign unless she's doing homework or playing where I can see her.

"You're a big girl, Bell. You'll have fun tonight."

I go into my closet, drop my towel, and pull on underwear. All I hear is the loudening knock of Bell's heels against the cabinets. "Hey," I call out to her. "Pico said he doesn't believe you know all the lyrics to Metallica. Want to practice until he gets here?"

"Which song?"

"'Sandman.'"

Immediately, she launches into the first verse. Her voice echoes through the bathroom as I get into my suit. I button my dress shirt laughing. It's always creepy when she sings it, especially the part that's actually a child's voice, but she loves the song. She's never been a fearful kid. Never believed in monsters

137

or boogey men. She's like me, afraid of things that're actually scary—like being abandoned.

I tuck in the shirt and do up my pants. Sadie probably worries I'll show up looking like a slob since I don't care about these things. But the suit I have from her wedding still fits perfectly, and I have a reason to look good tonight.

I open a drawer with ties. For owning only two suits, I have way too many ties, all less than subtle hints from Sadie to dress up more. I pick up a drab gray one, but a flash of red at the back of the drawer catches my eye. I wore that tie last year when I took Bell into the city for a show around Christmastime.

Sadie mentioned that *avec* was nominated. If I know Amelia, which I don't, not really, she'll be dressed to the nines. That must've been the reason for the expensive cherry-colored dress we picked up from the front desk of her apartment building. I select the red tie. It'll be a message from me to her, a way of both teasing her and showing her I've been thinking of her.

I come out of the bathroom and stand in front of the mirror to get the knot right. "What d'you think, kid? Does Dad look good or what?"

"I don't want you to go," Bell says immediately.

I glance at her. "I know. I don't really want to go either, but—"

"Then don't," she says. "Stay home. We can watch a show about cars."

I chuckle and think, not for the first time, manipulation must be genetic. In that way, she's her mother's daughter. "I can't. Aunt Sadie's expecting me."

Bell crosses her arms, pouting. "Parties are stupid."

"Come on. We don't use that word."

"*Stupid*," she repeats.

"Bell," I warn. "You want to go to your room until I leave?"

"No. I want to stay with you." She sticks her bottom lip out farther. "If I'm good, will you not go?"

"No." I tug on my sleeve and head into the bedroom to get cufflinks from a drawer. Sensing Bell's glare, even through the wall separating the rooms, I ask, "Will you help me? I can't do this alone."

With a huge sigh, she pads over. I lift her up on the edge of the bed and hold the sleeve together for her. "Just put the small part of the cufflink through the holes so it holds the cuff together."

She furrows her eyebrows as she works. "Can I come with you?"

I press my lips together, half pissed that she won't drop it and half devastated. That Bell thinks I'm abandoning her, even for tonight, makes my chest physically hurt. I'm starting to wonder if others have been right about us. If she's too attached. Problem is, she learned it from me. Part of me would rather stay here, dish out ice cream, and play Mario Kart. I'm looking forward to seeing Amelia, but is it worth making my girl feel like this?

Bell's finishing the other cufflink when the doorbell rings. She jumps down and sprints out of the bedroom.

"Stop right there," I call after her. "Don't you *dare* open that door."

"But it's Flora," she cries from the living room.

"I don't care. How many goddamn times have I told you—do not open the door by yourself at night."

"But it's *Flora*."

"You don't know that." I rush into the room after her. "It could be a stranger."

She's hanging on the door handle, her eyes watery, as if she's waited her whole life to answer that door and I've taken it away from her.

"Now that I'm in the room with you, you can open it," I say.

She does. Flora's there, smiling warmly. "Why, hello, Bell," she says, stepping in. "I've been looking forward to this all day."

Bell looks back at me, suddenly shy for all her bravado.

"Say hello," I tell her firmly. "Mrs. Picolli was nice enough to come over and spend her evening with you."

"It's no trouble," Flora says.

"Come in." I hold the door as Bell glowers and then slinks away.

Pico ambles up the sidewalk, his motorcycle parked in the driveway.

"Give ol' mom a ride on the scooter or what?" I ask.

"No, dumbass. She drove herself."

Pico may work for me now, but I've been busting his balls since before we were teenagers. His dad, Flora's late husband, worked for my grandpa.

I slap him on the back. "Do me favor and see if you can distract Bell. She's in one of her moods."

"I'm on it." He pulls a deck of cards from his back pocket. "Learned some new magic tricks recently."

Thank God for his geeky side. It might actually save us tonight.

"Thanks for doing this," I tell Flora as Pico goes to find Bell. "I'm sorry about her. She doesn't want me to go."

Flora takes off her cardigan, and I hang it up for her. "She'll get over it."

"Just when I think she's maturing at light speed, she pulls this crap. I think it's getting worse." I rub my eyebrow. "Maybe I shouldn't go. She's going to cop an attitude with you."

"That's exactly why you should. Believe me, dear, I have five children. I can handle her." Flora eyes my suit. "You look handsome, by the way. Please tell me you have a date to this party."

"I'm just helping Sadie out." My heart thumps once when I think of Amelia. She isn't my date, which

141

means I have to keep my hands off her in public. How can I after last week? I knew the woman an hour before I had her in my arms, kissing her where all of Manhattan could see. It'll be a feat to restrain myself until I can get her alone.

Flora looks as though she's waiting for me to continue, as if I'm really leaving because I have something up my sleeve. "Can I get you something to drink?" I offer.

"I'll take a water."

I lead Flora into the kitchen and get a glass out of a cabinet, even though she's been here a hundred times and knows where everything is. She continues to watch me.

I don't know if it's the maternal vibe she gives off the way my mom used to when we were really young, but her silence has a way of filling the room, pressurizing the air around me until I crack. "Actually, there will be a girl there tonight," I say.

"Really?" Flora sounds surprised. She knew Shana well, knows our history. Then again, there aren't many people who don't. It's not as if Elizabeth is a small town, but sometimes it feels that way. "Who's the lucky lady?" she asks.

"No, it's not like that," I say right away. "Not serious. Just someone who . . . I mean, we're just friends, but . . ."

"I see," Flora says. "A friend like Denise."

My cheeks warm. Pico and his big fucking mouth. Or maybe it was Denise. I wouldn't put it past her to try to get Flora on her side. Flora's one of the few people I respect enough to hear her advice. "Yeah," I say, even though Amelia isn't like any other woman I know, and certainly not Denise. "Like Denise. I'm sorry."

"For what?"

It's uncomfortable talking to Flora about my sex life. Especially since my sex life is extremely . . . *casual.* "I don't mean any disrespect."

"Are you apologizing to me or the women?" She smiles as I fill her water glass. "Everybody needs intimacy. I don't fault you that. I just hate to see you so closed off. I think it hurts the girls, and I think it hurts you too."

"I'm not closed off," I say, passing her the drink. "I'm doing my best."

"Perhaps." She takes a sip. "Listen—don't feel guilty about leaving Bell. It's good for you to live your own life. And I've sat for her enough times to know how to bring out her excitement."

"She's definitely excitable," I agree.

She laughs. "That she is. Go have fun tonight. And if you want to spend the night out, I have no problem sleeping here."

"Oh, that won't be—"

"I'll just plan on spending the night unless I hear otherwise," she says.

"No-o-o," Bell screeches from behind me. I turn just in time to see her burst into tears. Pico mouths "sorry" at me, already looking shell-shocked.

"You can't do this to me!" Bell launches herself forward, gripping my leg with surprising strength. I pick up her flailing body, and she throws her arms around my neck. "No, no, no. Please don't go. I can't fall asleep without you here."

"Bell, calm down," I say firmly, but it comes out softer than I mean. I shoot Flora a look.

She nods encouragingly at me.

Bell sobs into my neck. I rub her back. "You're a big girl, Bell—"

"No I'm not."

"I need you to do this for me. Please. I promise I'll be back before you wake up."

She screams, shredding my eardrums as she fists her hands into my suit jacket. "No, no, no."

Jesus Christ. I'm no stranger to Bell's fits, but normally I'm able to calm her down pretty quickly. I suddenly realize that's because I just give her what she wants.

Flora comes around the counter. "Bell, sweetheart, we're going to have fun tonight, you, me, and Pico. We'll do all the girly things Daddy doesn't do."

"He does them all," she says, kneeing me in the gut.

I double over with an *ooph*, nearly dropping her. Frustrated, I shout "god*damn* it" as pain radiates from my stomach.

"Oh, dear." Flora puts her hand on Bell's back. "I was going to make you an omelet for dinner. I know how you like those. But omelets are for big girls, not babies."

"I'm *not* a baby," Bell says.

"You're acting like one," I tell her. "I thought you said crying was for boys."

She shudders in my arms. It's taking everything in me not to give in. I hate this. I don't even want to go. Sure, I'd love to spend more time with Amelia, but I don't know if I'll get to. Maybe she isn't going. Maybe she has a date. It's not worth traumatizing my daughter.

"Don't you dare," Flora says. "I see defeat in your eyes."

I take a deep breath, hug Bell closer, and try to put her down. She wriggles to keep her arms around my neck, but I pry her off.

"I hate you both," she yells at me. "You went away last weekend and now you're leaving me again. I hate you." She tears off through the kitchen toward her room.

I flinch when she slams the door. She's right. I didn't spend last weekend with her because she was with Sadie. That's three out of seven nights I'll be away from her. At least my dad came home every night, even if he was drunk or pissed off.

I scrub my hands over my face. "I can't do it."

"You should go now," Flora says. "Before she comes back out."

"I can't."

"Yes you can. Andrew, look at me."

I lower my hands, balling them into fists.

Flora's face is earnest. "You're the best dad I know. You're nothing like your father, but you're everything like your grandfather."

I stare at her, my chest tight. Flora's husband and my grandfather used to let Pico and me hang at the garage after school, and without us realizing it, they taught us how to be men.

"You remind me so much of him," she says.

I swallow, feeling not unlike a small child. "He's my role model."

"I know, and it shows." She leans in. "He was a lover, Andrew. He'd hate to know you were throwing your happiness away by not giving someone a chance to love you. Worse, that you're not setting a good example for your daughter."

"How is that setting a bad example? Everything I do is for her."

"Do you want her to live her life for someone else? Even you?" she asks. "Or do you want her to stand on her own, make decisions for herself and be her own woman?"

I look toward Bell's bedroom. I want nothing more than to go comfort her, tell her I'll stay, change out of this stuffy suit. But Flora's right. This isn't healthy. She needs to learn how to be away from me. Not right away. Not for a long time, I hope. But we have to start somewhere.

I nod. "All right. I'll go."

"Good." Flora looks way more relieved than I feel. "Let me know what you decide about staying overnight."

I go into the living room, get my wallet and keys, and reluctantly head out the door before I change my mind.

TEN

Sadie's definition of a bar is different from mine. When I meet my friends for a drink, it normally means beer and a game of pool at Timber Tavern. Tonight, I step into a place with a French name I can't pronounce. The countertops are black-lacquered with white subway tile. The cocktails cost more than most of my meals. For once, I'm glad to be wearing a suit.

Sadie waves at me from the bar. I make my way through the light crowd and stop cold when I spot Nathan next to her. "I thought you had to work," I say from a few feet back. I know when I'm being lured into a trap.

"He was able to get off last minute," Sadie says, waving a hand. "How great is that?"

"Not great," I say slowly, crossing my arms. Nathan keeps his eyes on the ground. "Why'd you make me come all the way here if you don't need me?"

"Because it actually worked out perfectly. My new colleague—Mindy, remember?—her date fell through, and since you were already on your way, I figured you could take his dinner."

I glare at Sadie. I should've guessed this was a set up. Sadie's never invited me to one of her events before. "No."

"Yes."

"You tricked me."

"No," Sadie says. "It just happened to work out."

"Come on, Sadie, I'm not an idiot." Nathan busies himself inspecting the ceiling, the bastard. "Do you guys have any idea what it was like for me to get here tonight? Bell nearly took me down."

"I figured," Sadie says. "She had a meltdown on the subway when we left you Friday night."

I run a hand through my hair. "Seriously? Why didn't you tell me?"

"Because I didn't want to worry you." She shrugs. "I took care of it, Andrew. It's normal for her to have some separation anxiety given the way Shana left, but at some point, you have to stop indulging that behavior."

"You're going to start with me too?" I ask. "I'm her only parent. Everything I do is for her."

"We know," Nathan says, coming over to rest a hand on my shoulder. "Nobody's denying that. But Bell's getting to an age where—"

"Dude," I say, turning to him. "You're supposed to be my bro. A heads up about this would've been nice."

Nate rolls his lips together and removes his hand to scratch the back of his neck. "I am," he says. "Which is why drinks are on me. What can I get you?"

"Whisky, neat. And I want *top-shelf*."

"Of course," Nathan says, smiling a little too hard. He leans in and talks to me through his teeth. "Don't resist. She's just hit month five, and she's getting unpredictable."

Sadie looks up. "What was that?"

"Nothing," we say at the same time.

Nathan and I exchange a glance before he turns away to wave down the bartender.

I nod at Sadie's half-finished drink. "That better be water," I say.

"It's vodka, obviously," she says. "I'm not *that* far along."

"Very funny."

She perks up and waves across the bar. "There's Mindy."

"This isn't a date," I say to Sadie as a pretty brunette makes her way toward us.

"No, of course not," Sadie says. "Just a free meal."

"And drinks," I add. "Plural."

Mindy's smile stretches ear to ear, and her teeth are as white as her tight, long-sleeved dress. "Hi," she chirps, looking between Sadie and me.

She and Sadie hug, and the short dress rides up her thighs. Her tan is incredible, as if she's just returned from a month in the Bahamas. Her brown hair curls around her shoulders, bouncing when she and Sadie separate. I doubt she's even twenty-five, and even though that's not far from Amelia's early thirties, they seem miles apart. I hold out my hand. "Andrew. Nice to meet you."

She looks to Sadie, tentatively taking my hand. "Hi . . ."

"Andrew, you've met," Sadie says in a tone she uses when she's embarrassed. "At my office, remember? She brought you to my desk?"

"Oh. Right." I take my hand back. Her face is vaguely familiar, like someone I've passed on the street more than once. "I'm sorry. I had my daughter, so that day is kind of a blur."

"That's okay," she says.

"Mindy's new to the city. She moved here in winter."

"I'd say welcome, but I don't live here," I say. "I'm in New Jersey."

"Sadie told me. I'm so glad you made the trip tonight."

"Your date fell through?" I ask.

Sadie nods before Mindy even has a chance to answer. "Yep."

152

"I'm talking to Mindy," I say, giving Sadie a look.

"Actually, I canceled it," she says. "I met him online, and he was a little out there."

"Online?"

Nathan hands me my drink and Mindy a red wine.

"That's how people meet these days," Sadie says, nudging me with her elbow. "Online." She turns to Mindy. "I've been trying to get Andrew to sign up for one of those apps—"

"I'm *not* signing up," I say.

"It's not that bad," Mindy says. "I'd say maybe four out of five dates are pretty awful, but—"

I open my mouth. "Four out of *five*? Those are shit odds. It's that important to you?"

"Finding that one great date that could turn into more?" she asks. "Absolutely."

I scoff, shaking my head. "I don't even have time to go on five dates."

"Yes you do," Sadie says. "It's all about prioritizing."

"My priorities are fine, thanks."

She slips her arm around Nathan's waist, looking up at him. "I'd go on a hundred bad dates for Nathan."

"Really?" I ask. "So you'd sit through a hundred bad conversations, a hundred awkward goodbyes, a hundred crushing rejections to end up with 'the one'?"

The three of them stare at me. Maybe they've never been on a truly bad date, but I find that hard to believe. "Yes," Nathan says first. "In a heartbeat."

I shake my head. Nathan, I believe. He'd do it. I'm not so sure about the rest of the world, though. That sounds pretty brutal to me. "Fine," I say. "Should we head over?"

"Not yet," Sadie says. "Let's relax. Finish our drinks. We have time."

The girls take a seat at the bar while Nate and I hang back. Mindy's sweet scent drifts over, and it makes me think of Amelia's strong, distinct perfume, only detectable when I'm close to her—which is maybe the best part. I want at least a whiff of it tonight, which means I'll need to be within kissing range.

I straighten the knot of my tie. "How do you wear one of these every day?" I ask Nathan. "It's fucking strangling me."

"You get used to it." He glances at it. "Red is bold. Definitely not a color I'd guess you'd choose."

I flatten it against my chest. "It's my special-occasion tie."

Nathan sips his drink. "This isn't anything huge. Sadie's more excited about setting you up than the nomination."

"Why?" I ask. "Why can't she just let me be?"

He cocks his head at me. "Dude, she's your sister. She wants you to be happy."

"I'm happy," I insist. "I've got everything I need."

"I guess she thinks you don't." He swirls his drink. "You never think about what it'll be like raising a preteen girl on your own? It's not that far off."

"I think about it every fucking day. She's turning seven next month, and I can literally still feel her as a baby in my arms." I shake my head. Going backward is easier than worrying about what's ahead of us. "You're so lucky, man. I'd give anything to revisit those days. Don't get me wrong. Bell's a human now, and so much more fun, but when she was a baby . . . Jesus. Best feeling."

Nathan watches me closely.

I'm rambling. "Sorry," I say. "I'm just excited for you. Bell and I will be visiting a lot."

"I get it. Sadie had to lay out a budget because I've been overspending on the baby." Nate grins. "You ever think about having another?"

"Baby?" I reminisce about it frequently, but doing it all over again? "I can't imagine it. It's been me and Bell for so long."

"Yeah," he says. "But you could. If you really miss it. You could have all that again."

I thump Nathan on the back. "You're starting to sound like Sadie," I say. "You guys need to get it through your heads—I don't want a baby. I'm not looking for a girlfriend. I'm good on my own."

Nathan frowns at something behind me. I look just as Mindy turns away from us, clearly trying to hide the fact that she overheard me. I shouldn't be sorry—it's the truth, and I make no bones about it. But I feel Sadie's scowl before I see it.

Resigned, I give Nathan a look and take the seat next to Mindy. "How are you liking the city?" I ask.

"It's fun for now," she says. "But I can't see myself staying forever."

I hadn't picked up on her slight drawl earlier. "Why not? Where are you from?"

"Georgia. This place is . . . different. I wouldn't raise a family here."

"Yeah." I lean back in my seat. "I have a daughter, and I couldn't do it. I get anxious just putting her on the bus to school."

She smiles, looking down at her wine. "Bell, right? She's so cute. The resemblance is uncanny. She looks just like you and Sadie."

"Thank God," I mutter. Sometimes I catch glimpses of Shana in Bell, but mercifully, not too often. I worry that as she gets older, the resemblance will strengthen. As if I need the reminder.

Nathan walks up behind Sadie's chair and kisses her on the back of her head. He shoots a glance in my direction and whispers something in her ear. Her face falls. "Oh," she says. "Okay." She leans over to us. "Let's head to the event. We're a little early but they should have a bar to keep you guys occupied."

I stand and help Mindy off the stool. She and Sadie walk ahead of Nate and me.

"Thanks for saving me, man," I say to Nathan.

"I didn't do anything."

"Pretty sure you did, and I appreciate it."

He half-smiles. "I just told her the women's bathroom was out of order."

"Is it?" I ask.

"How the hell should I know?"

We laugh as we step out into the night to make our way to the gala.

ELEVEN
AMELIA

In my bra and underwear, I check my hair and makeup one last time before putting on earrings. They were a gift from Reggie that should make me feel bad but diamonds will always have the opposite effect on a woman, no matter the circumstances.

It should take precisely fifteen minutes to reach the venue, which leaves me five minutes until my car arrives. My red dress is like a work of art, with subtle, intricate details like stitching, gathering and beading only a trained eye would notice. Despite having had a fortunate enough existence that I get to wear things like this from time to time, stepping into a dress like this is never anything less than satisfying.

I pull it up over my hips and zip it halfway. Reaching across one shoulder to close it the rest of the way, I grasp fruitlessly for the zipper. My arm starts to burn from the effort. Just as I'm about to snatch it, there's a knock on my door.

I give up with a huff and go to answer it. The driver's early, and he's not supposed to come upstairs, but at least he can make himself useful by helping me into my dress.

I open the door. "I just need a few—"

I freeze. It isn't the driver on my doorstep, but a man I've worked hard to keep off it. A man who, every time I manage to forget him for a while, seems to sense it and show up.

Once my mind starts to work again, I lean against the doorframe. "Reggie."

"*Bonjour*, muffie," he says.

I cross my arms. The nickname serves to remind me of a better time. For one of our early dates, Reggie surprised me with a weekend in Paris. The first time we slept together, it was in a room that opened up to a view of the Eiffel Tower. The next morning, he fed me muffin and coffee in bed. "Don't call me that," I say. "What are you doing here?"

He massages the inside corners of his eyes with one hand. I notice his dark circles first, then his undone tie, and five o'clock shadow, but it isn't his unkemptness that catches me off guard. I haven't seen Reggie in months, and he's lost enough weight to obliterate his beer gut. His cheeks are no longer pudgy, his posture is straighter, and somehow, he appears to have covered up the bald spot that started forming halfway through our marriage. I almost can't believe what I'm seeing. He looks even better than he did when we started dating.

"Can I come in?" he asks.

"No."

He drops his gaze over my dress. "Wow. You look stunning."

"What are you doing here?"

"I'll explain, but not in the hallway. Come on. This is my home too."

I laugh hollowly. "Not in the slightest. You lost the right to walk through this doorway when you brought *her* here."

He frowns. "Look, muffin—"

"Reggie, I hate that nickname."

"You don't mean that. It's our thing."

"I never told you because I loved you, but I don't anymore, so now I can be honest. It's patronizing and sexist to reduce me to a baked good. And a fatty, top-heavy one at that."

He shakes his head, gaping at me. "I don't believe that."

"Would you nickname a man 'muffin,' or any other pastry for that matter?"

"Not that," he says, waving a hand. "I don't believe you don't love me anymore."

I roll my eyes. "Seriously? *Eleven months*, Reggie. Eleven months of emotional whiplash, me feeling insecure and insane while you were off sleeping with someone else. Why would I still love you after you put me through that?"

"Because love doesn't stop just because I hurt you. Fine, maybe you're still angry, but . . . you love me."

I look him in the eye. "I don't."

"Amelia, listen to me. I understand you want to be done with this—"

"Then let's be done with it."

"We're making a mistake."

I curl my hands into fists until my fingernails bite into my palms. "We're not."

"Just let me come in for a minute."

"I don't have time for this."

As I go to shut the door, he pushes it back open and reaches for me. I don't react in time to stop him from taking my arm. His grip is familiar, like his voice or cologne. "Stop," I say as my heart skips.

"Jesus, relax." He turns me around to zip up my dress. "It's been bothering me."

Even as adrenaline diffuses through me, goose bumps light over my skin when he trails his knuckle up my spine. He knows my tender spots. How to put me on edge. How to get me to yield.

"Why so tense?" he asks, kneading one of my shoulders.

"Let go of me."

"Aw, come on. Don't be like that. I'm massaging you, not trying to break your arm for God's sake."

I search for the words my therapist, Dianne, always says: *Be firm, be confident. You don't owe him anything.* "Reggie, don't touch me. I'm not your wife anymore, and even if I were, that doesn't give you the right."

He removes his hands, showing me his palms as if I'm an animal on the verge of lashing out. "All right, fine. No need to get dramatic. Where are you going?"

I turn back around, brushing my hands down my dress. "Midtown."

"Need a date?"

"No. It's a work thing."

"Ah," he says. "A work thing. No surprise there."

He used to find my dedication to work endearing. He valued it. He brought me dinner on the nights I stayed even later than he did at his job, and we ate picnic-style in my office. When I was really stressed, he surprised me with spa appointments. *Avec* didn't turn a profit for a while, but he never pressured me about the money he'd invested. I was exhausted and crabby most of that time—and he put up with it without complaint. It wasn't until things started going well for me that he strayed.

"What are you here for?" I ask, taking a step back. "Really?"

"I told you. I've given it time like you asked me to, and I still feel the same. I don't want to fight anymore. I want us both to keep the apartment and the business, because I want us to make this work."

"What do you think has changed?"

"Me. I have. Can't you tell?"

I look him over. He knows I can. I'm not blind and the difference is too great not to notice.

"I quit drinking and I'm going to the gym. Hell, I even took a vacation." He studies my face as he adds, "I ended things with Virginia, but you knew that."

Just her name—*Virginia*—makes my stomach flip. "I don't care if you won the Nobel Prize," I say. "You cheated on me."

"I was an idiot. I've done a lot of thinking. With *avec*, you needed me—not just my money, but me. Then, things clicked, and that stopped."

An admission like that from him is a breakthrough of sorts. I'm certain he couldn't have come to it on his own, which means he's likely talking to someone—a step forward for someone who doesn't believe in therapy. I know, because I tried to get him to go when we were together.

"I know what you're doing," I say, unaffected by his progress. After my own therapy and picking apart infidelity with many scorned friends, I could write a book on the behavior of a cheater. "You're trying to turn the blame on me. I wasn't what you needed, therefore you had to look elsewhere."

"You're projecting your insecurities onto me," he says, and now I *know* he's also been working with someone. "I never blamed you. Once you found out about Virginia, I took responsibility. I'm just trying to tell you why I did it so you can see how I'm different now."

I shake my head. "I don't think so."

"I know what I'm getting into this time. *Avec* will always be your top priority, but I'd rather come in second place than not at all."

I'm taken aback to hear him say *avec* will always be number one. Will it? Can it? Every twelve-hour day I work passes quickly as I do my best to keep my head above water. Because of that, I rarely stop to think about the big picture. Is that what I want to be doing the rest of my life? Nearly drowning in details and day-to-day decisions? I don't remember deciding that, but if I continue down this path, *avec* will be all I ever have.

I gave things up in exchange for a successful business. But with Reggie's assumption that there's no room at the top for anything other than work, I can't help wondering if it was ever a mistake to choose *avec* over love. Not over Reggie, because he proved himself unworthy, but he's right that I did put work before him any chance I got.

"I'm glad you ended things with her," I say. "You shouldn't be with someone who had no problem carrying on an affair with a married man for almost a year. But it doesn't change my mind."

His face falls. "I'm not asking you to forgive me on the spot," he says. "But I want to start over. To put the past behind us and try to make this marriage work."

"No. Your attempts to manipulate me won't work anymore."

"Manipulate?" He furrows his eyebrows. "I'm being honest."

I never thought of Reggie as controlling until after I realized he'd been cheating. Somehow, he always managed to make me think his ideas were mine, even the little things, like choosing where to eat. My therapist grilled me one session just to get what she wanted—a simple, meaningless conversation over choosing where to have dinner.

"Where should we go?" Reggie had asked. "Anywhere you want. It's your night."

"How about the Italian place on the corner?"

"Sounds great. Their Bolognese is crap, but the rest of the menu is good."

"Bolognese? That's your favorite."

"It's fine. I'll get something else."

"I guess we could try the new place that opened on Seventh? The one you mentioned last week?"

"If that's what you want," he'd said, kissing my forehead. "Like I said, it's your night."

I wouldn't have remembered that conversation on my own, but Dianne had known exactly what she was looking for. Once I'd relayed it to her, memories of other, similar conversations flooded me. Some as simple as that. Some more complicated, deep emotional betrayals I don't think too hard about.

166

"I guess I don't blame you for trying to manipulate me since I fell for it for years," I tell him.

"That's crazy, Amelia. Maybe I made a lot of mistakes, but I always loved you. I always tried to make you happy, even when I was with her."

"Don't come here again."

"Or what? You have nothing over me. I own your apartment. Your business." He looks me over. "I mean, if you think about it, I even own your body . . ."

I clench my teeth, even though I know he's only trying to get under my skin. "Go to hell."

"You own mine too. I have the paperwork. What good is a marriage certificate if it doesn't prove we belong to each other?"

I'm seething, just like he wants. Reggie would often remind me his money afforded us a certain kind of lifestyle, but this is the first time he's called me his property. In a way, I'm glad he's saying it aloud. He's been treating me like a possession since before he stared his affair. "I want out of this marriage."

He smiles sweetly, as if I'm an indulgent child. "That will pass."

"Let me buy *avec* from you and let's be done with it."

"We've been over this," he says with a sigh. "I'm not giving up *avec*, because I'm not giving up you. You have no way out, muffie." He retreats for the door. "Accept that so we can begin to mend."

167

I open my mouth to argue, but it's no use. We've been round and round on the subject. He may not be able to touch me anymore, but as long as he owns fifty-one percent of my business, he has one greedy hand in my most intimate place. That's how he maintains control.

Reggie leaves, and I lock the door. In my bedroom, I pick up my clutch. I have a missed call from the car service. *Perfect*. If I miss the opportunity to network before the presentation because of my asshole ex-husband, I won't be happy.

I return the call. "Miss Van Ecken," a man answers. "Do you still need a ride?"

"Of course I need a ride," I say. "What, am I supposed to walk?"

"If you like."

My jaw tingles. I've had just about enough of the male species. "Very funny. I wonder if your supervisor will think so too. I'll be down in five minutes—you'd better be there."

I hang up the phone, slip it into my clutch, and sink onto my bed. Belatedly, my hands begin to shake. It's been months since Reggie and I were alone together. Isn't that enough time for me to have moved on? Why do the wounds Reggie left still feel fresh, even if I don't love him anymore? I worry they always will be, but I don't want him back. If I miss him, I don't know I do. Whenever I catch myself thinking about him, I throw myself into work. The night my lawyer advised we start discussing what assets to let go of to move the divorce along, I stayed up until dawn creating a progress report for our newest client. I didn't sleep until I wrote my lawyer back and told him to press on. Reggie shouldn't be allowed to get away with making me feel all the things I did over the course of our marriage—worthless, crazy, objectified, unattractive, dense. He won't get away with it. Not while I'm able to keep fighting.

With a deep breath, I stand and smooth out my dress. The show must go on—it's my mantra, always has been. Without the show, what else would I have?

TWELVE

Before I exit the car, I check my makeup one last time, close my compact, and straighten my shoulders. My muscles have been tense since I slid into the backseat. Getting nominated for an award doesn't excite me like it should. These events have more to do with who's attending than who's being honored. When I step out, the world is my stage.

When I get home, I should relax with a bath.

The thought comes out of nowhere, and for the first time since this morning, I smile. Until Andrew, it'd been months since I'd used the tub. I'd forgotten how comforting a bath could be—until Andrew. *Andrew.* He was exactly what I'd needed when I'd needed it. I barely knew him, but I knew he was different from Reggie. I still don't trust my judgment entirely, but it never felt like a game with Andrew.

I'm still not sure I should've kicked him out.

Right now, I'd love a few more hours with him. But the moment I stopped seeing him as a one-night stand and saw him for what he really was—a considerate, sexy man any girl would be lucky to have—I knew it had to end. I've learned enough in my thirty-two years to know when that shift occurs.

"What's happening at the hotel?" the driver asks.

I glance at him in the rearview mirror. I'm not really in the mood to chat, but he looks at me expectantly. "There's an awards dinner."

"Oh yeah? Are you nominated?"

"My firm is."

"Congrats. What for?"

"Ironically, a campaign we did for a kids' clothing store last year."

"Why's that ironic?"

I return my gaze out the window. "Children and I don't get along. It's not my account. I didn't think it'd be the reason for my first nomination."

He nods. "Children are a pain in the ass. A good pain, though, like the way you feel the day after a good workout. Know what I mean? Or runner's high. I don't run, but I've heard some people get addicted to it. That's kind of what kids are like."

I do know what he means. Bikram yoga can get so intense, I'd cry during each session if I had any fluid left in my body. Yet I attend weekly without fail. "I don't know," I say, "but I have a feeling parenthood is a lot more nuanced than that."

"Sure, sure. I'm just trying to say having your

own kids would be different."

I glance at my lap. Every holiday, I send my sister's kids gifts chosen and wrapped by an assistant, but it's been a while since I visited them. The last time I did, I could barely stand it. The house was a mess. There were toys, food, baby accoutrements everywhere. Walking through the living room was like traversing a minefield, complete with the sounds of battle—constant crying, obnoxious cartoons, and hair-raising screams, from both children and adults.

The driver turns the car onto the street of the venue. "There's a bit of a line," he says. "Shouldn't be too long, though."

"Thank you," I say.

We creep forward a few feet. "Unless you prefer to walk," he adds with a smirk.

I narrow my eyes. And then, for some reason, I laugh. As far as drivers go, and I've been in the company of many, he's pretty inappropriate. He also doesn't cower like the others. "I think I will, actually," I say.

He stops the car so I can get out. "It's a nice evening," he says. "Spring'll be over before you know it. I'd hate for you to miss it."

"Next you're going to tell me to stop and smell the roses," I say.

"You should," he says. "Plenty of bodegas got those little bouquets out front."

"Maybe you have a point." I'm getting soft. His attitude reminds me a bit of Andrew's, and my stomach instinctively drops when I remember how Andrew convinced me to submit to him. I open the door and climb out of the car. "Thanks again."

My heels aren't exactly made for walking, but I'm only a block from the venue. The driver was right—it is a nice night, with a mild May breeze. I stroll around the spotlight in the middle of the sidewalk, past the side alley crammed with smokers, and by the press crowded around the step and repeat.

In the hotel ballroom, I spot a few familiar faces. I air-kiss a marketing manager at Estée Lauder and greet an old assistant of mine who's now a buyer for Barney's Ready-to-Wear department.

It's crowded, so it takes me a moment to scan the room and locate the table I purchased for tonight. As I take a step toward it, a hand on my elbow stops me. "Excuse me, Miss. Can I offer you a glass of our finest single malt whisky?"

I turn to upbraid the waiter for touching me, but find myself face to face with a bottle of sixteen-year-old Glenlivet and a stark red tie where a waiter's uniform should be. I look up into blue eyes that feel more familiar, more comforting, than they should.

"What are you doing here?" I ask Andrew more brusquely than I mean.

Sadie appears out of nowhere, shaking her head at me. "Amelia," she scolds. "Play nice."

I look between the two of them. If Sadie knows anything, she doesn't let on. I'd like to keep it that way, so I shut my mouth and swallow my astonishment. "I'm sorry . . . I just don't understand why the plumber is here."

Andrew raises a dark, heavy eyebrow at me, a punishment of a glance that nearly takes my breath away. I have a feeling he's biting back a cutting response.

Sadie scowls. "He's *not* a plumber. I told you. He's my brother."

"I apologize." I press my lips together to hold in a smile; messing with Andrew comes almost too easy. "I just didn't expect to see him here."

Sadie furrows her brows. "Why would you? He's Mindy's date."

It's the last thing I expected to hear, and it takes me a moment to register what she said—Andrew is here, but not to see me. To be someone else's date. I brush an imaginary lock of hair from my forehead. "I thought Mindy was going out with that awful man from the Internet?"

"He's done," Sadie says.

Andrew, the man who'd made it sound as if he'd chew off his own arm to escape a sleepover with a clingy woman, is here with Mindy, who is definitely on the husband hunt, despite all the warnings I've bestowed on her.

"Oh. Well, nice to see you again," I say, feigning interest in something across the room. "I'm going to grab a drink and mingle. I'll see you two at the table."

"No need," Andrew says, calling my attention back. He produces a tumbler from the crook of his arm and holds it out to fill with whisky. "I've got you covered."

"Where'd you get that?" I ask.

"Andrew is being a total princess tonight," Sadie answers. "He insisted we stop and get Glenlivet on the way. Apparently an open bar isn't good enough for him."

"I was worried they wouldn't have any good whisky," he says. "And Glenlivet's my favorite. What about you, Amelia? What's your preference?"

"Glenlivet," I say warily. He already knows that. I take the tumbler when he offers it. "Isn't this yours?"

"That's nice of you to share," Sadie says. "You're in a weird mood—"

"I think Nathan's looking for you, Sadie," Andrew says, though he continues to stare at me.

"Really?" Sadie asks. "But I was just with him."

Andrew nods. "You know how he gets. Clingy as fuck."

She pushes his shoulder. "What's with you? You're seriously feisty tonight. Let's go find him."

"I'm fine right here," he says.

"Oh. Okay." She hesitates a moment. "You sure?"

I don't wait for them to figure it out. "I'll go get a second glass for you."

I'm not at the bar ten seconds before I feel Andrew's presence at my back. "You look good enough to eat," he says, nearly growling in my ear.

I turn around. His large body blocks us from the

crowd, creating a private little corner. I give him a onceover. In a well-fitted suit, clean-shaven with his hair styled away from his face, he looks like a different man. A man who could bring me to my knees. Oddly, I find I don't prefer him one way or another. Apparently, I've grown an attachment to the plumber look.

And he's grown an attachment to how I taste. "I won't stop you," I respond.

He quirks the corner of his mouth. "It's nice to see you again."

"Why are you here?"

"I was tricked."

"Into being Mindy's date?"

"Sadie's always trying to set me up with women, no matter how adamant I am that I'm not interested."

I arch an eyebrow, tempted to believe him, but unsure if I can. "And what do you think of Mindy?"

He takes my drink from me and sips it slowly. Once he's swallowed, he says, "She doesn't look good enough to eat."

"But she's young," I point out. "And beautiful."

"As are you. Young, beautiful, *and* edible."

I cock my head. "You've got quite an appetite tonight, don't you?"

"You have no idea. I've known since Monday I'd see you tonight. I kept picturing how that red dress would look."

"And?" I prompt. "How does it look?"

"Like I'm going to have you for dessert."

My face warms, and I have to look over his shoulder to keep my composure. "I'm glad it didn't disappoint." I feel his eyes burning into me. "Should we take our seats? Someone might catch on."

"I want to see you tonight."

The way my heart skips, my answer is obvious. I want to see him too, and not just in a dark corner over a glass of good liquor. But his eagerness, his obvious hunger, is clouding my thoughts. I need to keep a straight head. "You're seeing me now."

"You know what I mean. I want a replay of last weekend."

"You're not fooling me." I smirk. "You just want to take advantage of my bathtub again."

He leans in to my ear. "I want to take advantage of *you*."

My breath comes faster. "So that's the reason for the Glenlivet?"

"Maybe." He hands my drink back. "Or maybe it's because I like the taste of whisky even more now that I've sucked it off your skin."

My body hums with his whispered words. I don't let him see how he affects me, though. I hold his gaze and take a slow sip. "Mmm."

"Oh, shit . . ." I hear from behind Andrew. He takes a giant step back and turns. Sadie's husband looks between us. "What's going on here?"

"Nothing," Andrew says. "We're sharing a drink."

Nathan runs a hand through his hair. "You're

178

supposed to be sharing a drink with Mindy."

"Who?" Andrew asks.

"Your *date*," Nathan says.

Nathan looks ready to run and tell Sadie, so I chime in. "It's my fault. I was asking about toilet stuff."

Nathan draws his eyebrows as Andrew turns slowly to me. He looks as if he's about to put me over his knee for that comment, but whether he is or isn't, he isn't doing anything to get rid of Nathan. Once again, I'll have to take charge.

"Go ahead," I tell Andrew. "I'm sorry I kept you from your date, Mr.—" I stop, realizing I don't have a clue what his last name is. "Sadie's brother."

Andrew answers me through gritted teeth. "Beckwith. My last name is Beckwith."

"Right. Mr. Beckwith. Thanks for the advice about . . . toilets."

"You need a plumber?" Nathan asks me. "I can recommend someone."

Jesus Christ. "I was asking for a friend." I lift my chin. "Nathan, will you show me to the table?"

"Of course." He gestures for me to follow, and we make our way through the crowd.

"I can't wait until later," Andrew says behind me, his voice low and gravelly. "Let's leave."

"Are you insane?" I shoot back over my shoulder.

"Probably."

"I just got here," I whisper-hiss.

"Then meet me in the bathroom."

I attempt a scoff at his inappropriateness, but it comes off weak. With him this close, this insistent, it's hard not to be reminded of what it's like to submit to his demands. When I wished for a few hours more with Andrew, I should've specified I'd like to have him to myself.

"At least give me something to hold me over until later," he says. "What are you wearing under this dress?"

"Another pair of underwear for you to steal."

"*What?*"

A few days after Andrew left, I realized I was missing the lingerie I'd been wearing when we were together. The black lace pieces he'd commented on. I'd been alarmed but figured some guys were into that. I throw a glance over my shoulder. "I know you took my bra and panties when you left."

He laughs gruffly over my shoulder. "I definitely did *not.*"

Nathan looks back at us, his eyebrows furrowed. We're talking softly enough that he won't hear what we're saying—but clearly he can hear us speaking.

"I admit, at first I was a little pissed," I say. I have a tendency to splurge on beautiful lingerie. I know when it goes missing.

"I didn't take your dirty underwear, Amelia," he says huskily. "Now, if you want to give it to me, I won't turn it down."

I want to look back to see if he's serious about

not taking it—it doesn't seem like him to lie—but we're suddenly at the table. My eyes go straight to Mindy.

She doesn't notice me watching her, because she's tracking Andrew with big, bright eyes. Did he give her some reason to look hopeful? And if so, why would I care? I got what I wanted from him, and it seems as though I can have it again if I choose.

Andrew pulls out a stage-facing seat for me, and I give him a look. Already, Nathan's suspicious. "Just being polite," he says.

"You wouldn't guess it, but my brother's a complete gentleman," Sadie tells Mindy.

"Aw, sis," Andrew says. "Why wouldn't she guess it?"

As I sit, I respond under my breath so only he can hear, "Perhaps it's stealing a lady's unmentionables. Or the suggestion of screwing her in the bathroom."

Andrew leans down as he helps me scoot my chair under the table. "You're the one who can't stop talking about toilets."

"No, you're right," I say over my shoulder. "You *are* a complete gentleman. Tattoos and all."

"What's wrong with my tattoos?" he asks.

"Tattoos?" Nathan asks from the seat to my right. Apparently we weren't talking as privately as I thought. "How do you know about his tattoos?" Before I can answer, Nathan hisses. "Oh, Jesus. Did you two—"

"Dude," Andrew says. "Shut up."

Sadie turns away from Mindy and puts a hand on Nathan's forearm. "What's wrong, honey?"

Nathan looks to her and back at us.

Imperceptibly, I shake my head, imploring him not to give us away.

"Nothing," he says. "I thought I saw, uh, Karl Lagerfeld."

"Karl Lagerfeld? Here?" Sadie gives him a funny look. "Do you even know what Karl Lagerfeld looks like?"

"Of course," he says, looking flat-out guilty. The man is a shit liar, but fortunately, he's lost Sadie's attention. Her eyes are lasered to Andrew. When I look up, I realize why—he's pulling out the chair next to mine.

"*Andrew*," she says. "We already have a spot for you. Next to Mindy."

"Ah." He glances down at me. I widen my eyes at him, jerking my head to get him to go away. He's turning out to be the least subtle person I know, and Sadie is about two seconds from picking up on our connection. Andrew clears his throat. "I thought it might be nice to sit across from Mindy so we could actually see each other."

Sadie glares at him so hard that he slides the chair back in and rounds the table to sit between Howie, my digital strategy coordinator, and Mindy. Across from me. "But, of course you're right, sis," Andrew says, skating his eyes over me. "This is much better."

To hide my smile, I take a bite of the salad in front of me, shaking my head. Andrew scoots closer to the table, then smooths his tie against his chest. I'd noticed it before, the red bright against his dark features, but now I look a little closer. It's the exact color of my dress. Earlier, Andrew mentioned that he'd been looking forward to seeing me in *red*. Did he choose that tie on purpose?

I look down at my dress and then to Andrew. Mindy's leaning toward him as she speaks, but he's watching me. He nods once as he touches the knot of his tie as if to say—*Yes, I wore it for you*. He thought of me. It shouldn't feel good to know that, but my body warms. I try to stop it. I don't want anything from him, not thoughtfulness, not consideration. They complicate things. I don't want complicated, and neither does he.

A man calls our attention to the stage, and I give him my undivided focus. The alternative is watching Andrew and Mindy get to know each other. Halfway into the second honoree's slideshow, Andrew excuses himself from the table. I look over at Nathan, feeling his eyes on me, as if he expects me to get up as well. I don't move an inch.

I'm listening to the woman's acceptance speech when someone touches my shoulder. I start, looking back at Andrew.

"You dropped this," he says quietly.

Automatically, I open my hand, and he presses

something into it. When he returns to his seat, I check. He's given me a small, rigid envelope with the hotel's logo on it. Inside is a keycard with a room number scribbled next to it.

Gaping, I look up at him, but he's already turned to face the stage. The man is incorrigible.

And, apparently, ready for his dessert.

THIRTEEN

My empty salad plate is replaced with grilled chicken. As the gala's next presenter takes the stage, I can't help but notice how Mindy glances over at Andrew only slightly less than Sadie looks from Mindy to Andrew. Nathan, on the other hand, makes no secret of watching Andrew and me. Andrew's the only one who seems riveted by the presentation, though I get the feeling it's because he's avoiding all the eyes on him.

My palm sweats around the hotel room key Andrew passed me. I should put it in my purse, but just holding it gives me a thrill. What does he have planned? This is a nice hotel—surely there's a bathtub. And a bed. Maybe even a kitchenette with a counter. Or maybe he wants to take me on top of or against or inside something new.

Halfway through my meal, as they're presenting the literary PR categories, Andrew wipes his mouth with his napkin, gives me a pointed look, and scoots his chair away from the table.

Sadie leans over Mindy to get to Andrew. "Where are you going now?"

"Bathroom again." He grins. "Must've been something I ate."

"You're disgusting." Sadie turns back to the stage, quieted.

Andrew keeps his eyes on mine until he's passed me. His intention is clear—I'm supposed to follow, but this is ridiculous. Adults don't really sneak off during a formal event for a quickie. Is he that primal? Then again, he knew me less than an hour before proposing sex. He's not ashamed of what he wants.

And what do I want? I'd be a fool to say anything but him. A fool and a liar. I check my program. *Avec*'s category is toward the end, giving us at least half an hour. I dab the corners of my mouth with my napkin and slide back in my chair. Only Nathan notices me slip away, but in order to stop me, he'd have to speak loud enough to interrupt the presenter. I navigate briskly through the tables, casting a few smiles at familiar faces.

But the closer I get to the door, the less concerned I become with the people in the room. They're replaced by the thought of Andrew's strong, enveloping arms. His hungry mouth on mine. Andrew is a lover and a rebel, voracious and greedy yet attentive and sweet. He's an anomaly I don't need or even want to figure out. I just want to bask in his carnal attention, in the unknown of what he'll do with me next.

He's not in the lobby. I head for the elevator. His red tie, his provocative words earlier, his whisky breath. My heart beats hard at the base of my throat and other places too—my ears, my stomach, between my legs. I'm not nervous. I'm too turned on for that.

I ride the elevator to the eighteenth floor and head down the hall to the room. I only manage to knock once before he whips the door open. His fly is undone, and he's got a condom wrapper dangling from his mouth.

"Not very romantic, I know." He tears the foil with his teeth and pulls me in by my wrist. "I figured I'd get a head start since we don't have much time."

"You got a hotel room?" I ask, tucking my clutch under my arm as the door slams behind me. "Are you insane?"

"You asked me that already, and the answer is still probably." He hands me the condom, wraps his arms around my waist, and pulls my body flush with his. "You have that effect on me."

"There's no time for that," I say, trying to wriggle free.

"For what?"

"Wooing. I'm already here, and the clock is ticking."

"There's always time for wooing," he says, holding me to him. "God, you look so fucking good in this dress. I haven't been able to keep my eyes off you."

"Oh. Are those your eyes I've been feeling?"

"Mine and every other man's in the room."

"You're one to talk," I say. "As if you don't know how well you clean up."

"I *don't* know," he teases. "Tell me."

"You look . . . presentable. It's a nice change."

He barks out a laugh and smacks my ass. "You can't resist messing with me, can you?"

I shake my head. "Nope."

"Good. Neither can I." He captures my mouth with a sudden kiss, and though it alarms me how quickly I melt against him, I don't try to stop it. He works fast, gathering up the long length of my dress until it's bunched at my hips. Spurred into action and trying to keep up with his frantic kiss, I reach down the front of his pants. With just one touch, I moan into his mouth. "You're so hard."

"You have that effect on me," he repeats. "Put the condom on me, then hold up your dress."

I push his underwear down just enough to release him and do as he says. I've barely grabbed the fabric of my dress when he spins me around. He wraps his arms around my front, pressing his pelvis to me, undeniably solid against my lower back. Walking us forward a few steps into the room, he asks, "What exactly should I do with you?"

"Anything," I answer breathlessly, "just do it fast."

The room is predictably lavish with a California King, plush club chairs, and ornate curtains. He stops and bends me over the side of a wooden desk.

"Spread for me, babe," he says. "Pull your dress up higher."

I drop my clutch next to me and bare my ass to him. With a throaty noise of approval, he runs both hands up the backs of my thighs. When he reaches the apex, he pulls my thong around my thighs and tests me with his fingers. My thoughts scatter.

"Wet," is all he says, apparently as engrossed as I am.

He's reduced me to a puddle within minutes, and I'm barely concerned that I've lost any control I might've had. "Please."

He parts my lips with his fingers and presses the head of his cock against me. "I'm going to do this fast," he warns and plows in all at once, jolting me forward on the desk. I groan as he seats himself there with a few small, firm thrusts, his belt buckle digging into the back of my thigh. He pulls me upright by my biceps, and it's as if I'll split in two from having him so deep.

With my back against his front, he says into my ear, "Fast but hard. I'll fuck you until you can't feel your legs, Amelia."

I whimper, a sound I've never heard myself make. "Do it."

"Then, later tonight, I'll bring you back here," he releases my arms to cup both my breasts in his large, calloused hands, "and take you so slowly, you'll beg for fast and hard again." He moves one hand over my eyes, covering my mouth with the other. Instinctively, I arch my back, pushing myself harder onto him. "I'll blindfold you with my red tie so you can only guess where I'll touch you next," he says. "I'll love every inch of you. How's that sound?"

I plead with him against his palm, unintelligible appeals to stop talking and *fuck . . . me.*

He draws back, then slams into me. When I cry out, he asks, "Like that?"

I hear the smile in his voice and nod.

He uncovers my eyes and mouth to gently hold my throat. Skating his other hand down my stomach, he slips his fingers over my clit and moves them in small, wet circles.

"Tell me what you want," he says, his breath hot against my cheek.

My desperation for release reaches a new level. "You."

"Tell me what you need."

"To come."

He begins to move inside me as fast as the angle will allow. What he lacks in speed, he makes up for in depth, in his hands loving my clit. I have the urge to spread my legs, but my underwear traps my thighs. My knees tremble, sending a quiver up my entire body. His hand on my throat should scare me; it gives him complete control. Instead, it possesses me, makes me feel owned and secure—as close to loved as I think I'm capable of feeling.

"I can't hold back anymore." He releases me completely and pushes me down by my upper back, mashing my breasts against the cool wood. For a few desk-rattling minutes, he holds my hips and fucks me like I've offended him.

"I could come already," he grates out. "What do you need?"

"Anything," I say, close but not quite there. "Pull my hair. Slap my ass. Anything."

He closes his front over my back, covers my mouth again, and growls in my ear, "You want to go to the edge?"

I open my mouth to beg for it, but he shoves his finger in my mouth. "Suck." I close my lips around him, and when he says *more*, *harder*, I comply. He removes his finger and saliva dribbles down my chin. Just as I've registered his hand between the crack of my ass, he's rimming my tight bud with a slippery fingertip.

"Andrew—"

He pushes inside, and I gasp. The intrusion shocks and pinches. I break out in goose bumps, shuddering as he hammers my pussy and gently probes my asshole.

Chimes peal through the room, breaking my concentration. I do my best to block out the ring of my cell phone so I don't lose my mounting orgasm.

As soon as the ringing stops, it starts again, and this time Andrew's cell goes off too.

"Answer it," he says.

"I can't," I breathe.

He slides my purse toward us. One-handedly, he extracts my phone and holds it out, slowing his thrusts considerably without stopping. "Say hello."

I grasp at the cell phone and clumsily answer the call from Sadie. "Hello."

"It's Nathan."

"Nathan?" I can barely form a thought other than *I'm full. Of Andrew. So full.*

"Amelia?"

"This is Amelia."

He pauses. "Where the hell are you guys? They're about to do your category."

Andrew wiggles his finger inside me, and I nearly bite off my bottom lip to keep quiet. Being on the phone while Andrew controls my orgasm has the opposite effect I thought it would. Instead of a distraction, it acts as a catalyst, and my climax throbs and pulses close to the surface.

"We're coming," I say quickly. "Ten minutes."

"You don't have ten minutes. Sadie wants to know where you are. I grabbed her phone before she could call."

"Five minutes," I promise and toss the phone aside.

Andrew reaches out, ends the call, and wraps my hair in a tight ponytail. He fucks me hard, pulling me onto him with each thrust until I crescendo like a song and collapse. He surrenders seconds later, digging a hand into my shoulder and cursing as he comes.

My heart beats so hard, the desk pulsates. I don't know how I could possibly move again tonight, much less in the next five minutes, but Andrew has other ideas. He massages my shoulders for a couple seconds and starts urging me up. "Come on. We have to go."

"I can't."

"You have to. You can't miss the announcement."

"Your finger is in my ass."

He chuckles. "I should've warned you—I'm an ass man."

"I never would've guessed," I respond wryly.

"You came, didn't you?"

"Yes."

"And it was good?"

I shrug. "As far as orgasms go—"

He stops me with a short slap on the ass. "Don't start."

I smile. "It was earth shattering. But you can remove it now."

He slides his finger and cock out at the same time, and I can only hope the void he leaves won't last more than a few minutes. Before I can right myself, Andrew tugs my thong to my feet. "I'm taking this."

"I knew it—"

"No," he says, lifting each of my legs by the ankle to strip the underwear off. "You accused me of a crime I didn't commit, so I might as well commit the crime." He stands, shoving a ball of nude lace in his pocket. "Now hurry up, or we'll be late."

I gape at him. "You're going to make me sit in a room full of my colleagues—naked?"

He pulls off the condom and heads for the bathroom. "They won't mind."

Shaking my head, I grab my purse and follow him to quickly fix my makeup. I thumb away eyeliner smears, but my lipstick needs to be reapplied, and I haven't got time. I grab a hand towel and wipe it off completely, staining the terrycloth red.

Andrew looks from it to me as he washes his hands. "Housekeeping'll think I hurt you." He pauses. "Did I?"

"No. It was a shock, and it felt weird, but it didn't hurt."

"Didn't Reggie ever get the ass?" He quirks the corner of his mouth to reveal a dimple. I get the feeling that quirk and dimple frequently get him out of trouble.

"He tried," I say. "Very hard. But he only got as far as you did before I got squeamish. It's . . . unsanitary."

"Mmm." Andrew dries his hands, coming closer to me. He runs his hand over the curve of my ass. "It *is* unsanitary, isn't it? Downright dirty."

Maybe it's because it's Andrew. Maybe it's that I'm not in my twenties anymore, and sexually speaking, I'm less uptight. This time, that small invasion turned me on more than it made me want to stop altogether. "I guess I didn't mind it," I say.

He squeezes one cheek. "I can get a lot dirtier."

My throat dries. We exchange a glance in the reflection, and any teasing in his expression falls away. The heat in his eyes mirrors the warmth creeping up my chest. "How?"

"However you want. Not much bothers me. You're on your period? Great. Let's fuck in the shower. You want me to dress up as a sailor? Ahoy. Let's fuck on a waterbed."

I bite my bottom lip. "A sailor, hmm? That's not very dirty."

"A garbage man then."

I laugh. My phone vibrates in my purse. Reluctantly, I get it out and read the text message from Sadie.

Reading nominations NOW.

I sigh and run my tongue over my front teeth, a habit from wearing lipstick so much. "We should go."

Andrew looks into my open purse and picks out my business card. He flips it over, checks my information, and puts it in his pocket—with my underwear.

"What was that?" I ask.

195

"Me, asking for your phone number."

I don't know where to start with that. He didn't ask, and if he had, I would've said no. "Don't use it."

"Wouldn't dream of it." He fixes a strand of my hair, smoothing it into place. "Come on."

As we exit into the hall, he says, "We barely made it past the doorway."

I shake my head. "Waste of money."

"I have to vehemently disagree. Besides, we're not nearly done with the room. We'll come back later."

My stomach tightens. I don't fight the fact that I want to. I've already had a bite of cake—I might as well have a whole slice.

"I noticed you didn't finish your dinner," he says.

"Oh, God," I moan, my euphoria dispelling. "Don't start with this again."

"I'm not. I'm just saying, maybe you should. You'll need the energy tonight."

I arch one eyebrow, reading him perfectly. If there's any reason to eat carbs, that might be the best one. "You make a convincing argument."

Inside the elevator, he corners me like he did the first night we were together, but this time, it doesn't feel predatory. He lifts my face by my chin and pecks me as if it's the most natural thing. "I'm looking forward to later."

"Me too," I say, glancing at the digital numbers over his head. *Seventeen, sixteen, fifteen* . . . "But I haven't changed my mind about—"

"Spending the night," he finishes.

"I'm sorry. You shouldn't have gotten the room."

"It's okay. We'll make the most of it." He brushes his thumb over the corner of my mouth. "Congratulations on tonight."

I tilt my head, surprised by the change in topic. "It's not a big deal," I say.

"Why not?" he asks earnestly.

Why not? It just isn't, I want to say. It's not, because I've been telling myself it isn't since I received the nomination. "The women I'm up against are older, more connected, and have donated enough money to the benefitting charity to make a statement. I deserve to win, but I won't, because it's all politics. I couldn't not show up, though. It would've been rude, and these things are really about the networking."

Andrew shakes his head. "Being nominated is an accomplishment, Amelia. Don't downplay it."

"But I'll lose."

"So what? How many people ever get recognized for what they do?"

"What do I do?" I ask. "I'm a cog in an industry that makes women feel badly about themselves so I can sell them products to make them feel better. It's a bullshit award in a bullshit business."

Andrew furrows his eyebrows, and I think I must be mirroring his expression. Lately, I've had brief moments where I stopped to ask myself if I'm proud of what I do. But I've never spoken that way before.

It makes me wonder if it has to do with what Reggie said earlier about work being my priority for the rest of my life.

"I thought you loved your job?"

"I do." The elevator dings. "God, I need a smoke. Let's go get this over with."

"Right behind you," he says. "But I'll give you some space to walk in alone."

I nod and now that my sex-induced haze has cleared, a sudden sense of urgency hits me. I trot to the ballroom. As I near the double doors, the echo of the microphone gets louder. The voice is familiar, like an old friend. I open a door and duck inside, hoping nobody will notice me.

When my eyes adjust to the dark, I see Sadie on stage. " . . . grateful for this recognition," she says, squinting out at the crowd.

I pinch my eyebrows together, confused. Why is *she* up there? She wasn't nominated.

"Amelia had to step out—"

My name is projected onto the wall under *Exceptional Women in PR—Fashion*. I gasp silently, covering my mouth. I won the award—and I missed the announcement. I should be up there, but instead, I'm here, disheveled from Andrew's mouth and hands, frozen to the spot.

"—I know she'd like to thank, um . . ." Sadie clears her throat, darting her eyes around the crowd. "She'd like to thank us, her team, and everyone in this room who's ever . . . supported or believed in *avec*. Which is many of you, I'm sure."

I take a step forward and then another and soon, I'm hurrying toward the stage as Sadie holds up the award.

"Th-thank you. Again." She pauses. "And again, I apologize for Amelia's absence. I know she'll be thrilled."

The room applauds. I don't make it to the stage, so instead I stop at our table and steady myself against my chair. Any attempt to get on the stage now would look desperate. Maybe it is a bullshit award, but now it's *my* bullshit award, and my first one at that. The only recognition I've received, in fact—proof that I'm actually decent at what I do. As much as I played it down, I admit to myself that I wanted to win—I just assumed I wouldn't. Everyone at my table looks back, their eyes turning to me in synchronization. "Congratulations," says Howie. "Did you get to see any of it?"

"I—"

"You won," Mindy says cheerfully.

I feel a hand at the small of my back. "You won?" Andrew asks.

I move away from him. I don't want him touching me when all eyes are on me.

"Amelia," he says. "I'm sorry."

I turn away and spot Sadie coming back to the table. "It's fine."

Sadie holds out the small, crystal award and grins. "Where were you?" she asks, nearly bouncing with excitement. She rarely gets giddy, and seeing her happy for me, guilt tugs at my heart. "Can you believe it? You won."

She gives me the award. It's heavier than I expect, and I almost need two hands to hold it. I study it. *Exceptional Women in PR—Fashion.* Other women have babies—I have *avec.* Even if I've doubted it lately, it's never let me down. I've built my world around it. This should've been a big moment for me, but I let a man distract me. It's a classic example of something that would've happened when I was with Reggie.

"Amelia?" Sadie asks. "Do you feel all right?"

I blink a few times. I'm being selfish. This isn't my award—it's all of ours. My team is looking to me, and I've already let them down once tonight. I'm not sure if it's because I missed the announcement, or if I'm in shock, but the pride I would've expected to feel isn't there.

I force a smile. "*We* won," I correct her. "I'd still be working out of a shoebox apartment if it weren't for my team."

"That's not true," Sadie says seriously, and she's probably right.

"Really?" Howie asks, shrugging. "I'm pretty sure it is."

We laugh, and Sadie seems to notice Andrew then. She looks over my head. "Feeling better?"

"Not really," he responds.

"Where were you guys?" Sadie cocks her head at me. "Nathan tried calling."

"We weren't together," I say. I don't want to lie to her, but it doesn't feel like the right moment to announce her brother had me bent over a desk upstairs.

"I know." Sadie squints at me. "I didn't mean you were."

I touch my stomach. "I think I have food poisoning."

"Geez," Sadie says. "You *and* Andrew?"

Nathan snorts, and I glance at him quickly. "Must've been the chicken," he says wryly.

"Or the Glenlivet," Sadie jokes. "Do you feel well enough to stay?"

Food poisoning or not, my stomach aches. I should've been here. I should not have let my love life, if I can call it that, get in the way of what's important. I shake my head. "I don't think so."

"No reason to stay if you don't feel well," Sadie says, and her kindness only makes me feel worse.

"I'll walk you out," Andrew volunteers. "I should take off too."

"No," Sadie says, any sympathy in her voice gone. She nods discreetly at the other side of the table. "What about Mindy?"

"Shit," Andrew says. "I forgot."

"You've barely spoken to her all night," Sadie says.

"Well . . ." Andrew lays a hand on her shoulder. "That's because my mind is on someone else, sis."

I open my mouth to interject before he can out us, but Sadie beats me to it. "For the last time, Bell . . . doesn't . . . count."

"Oh. Got it." Andrew winks, his dimples deepening with a grin that's just for me, and my heart skips. Fuck—I'm in trouble. I don't want a skipping heart. Missing tonight is a wake-up call. I've let myself get too wrapped up in a man I barely know—but it doesn't even matter how well I know him. I can't get wrapped up in anyone—period. "No need to walk me out," I say, tucking my clutch under my arm. "I'm a big girl."

"I know you are," Andrew says slowly, "but I'm leaving anyway."

"I'll get Mindy," Sadie says. "You can share a cab."

"Won't that look bad?" he asks. "If everyone from the firm gets up and leaves right after you win the award?"

"Yes, it will," I say. "You guys stay. Otherwise, I will."

"No, no. Go, Amelia," Sadie says. She bites her thumbnail and looks at Andrew. "If you really don't feel well—"

"I don't." He kisses her on the cheek and looks to me. "Wait there. Let me say goodnight to Mandy."

"*Mindy*," Sadie and I say in unison.

"Right." Andrew shakes Nathan's hand, then leans over to Mindy to tell her something. They look good together. His olive skin matches her golden tan better than my nearly translucent white skin. Our differences are stark, but as much as I want to deny it, we look good together too. So good that I want to smile, and that's a bad sign.

I don't wait for Andrew. I pick up the award and slip out when his back is turned. As I cross the lobby toward the exit, I hear the quick, solid footsteps behind me. I'm at a disadvantage in my sky-high heels.

"Amelia, wait," Andrew says.

I turn around. "I wasn't lying before—"

He holds two plates of cheesecake. "Swiped these from the dessert cart."

I eye the cheesecake topped with raspberry sauce. "I really *don't* feel well," I say. "I'm sorry about the room. I'll pay my half."

He reads me like a book. "Bullshit," he says. "Twenty minutes ago, I was fucking your brains out. You feel fine."

I flush, touching my hair. The back of my neck is clammy. "I'm still leaving."

"What's this about?" he asks. "Mindy? I told you, I was tricked into bringing her. I'm not interested."

"It doesn't matter if you are," I say, drawing back. The edges of the award cut into my palm. "Even if I were jealous, I wouldn't have any right to be."

His eyebrows shoot up, and his concerned expression eases into a slow smile. He takes a step closer to me. I want to step back. I need to. But I don't. "Are you?" he asks, his voice low, "jealous?"

I square my shoulders. "No."

"You're sure? Because I wouldn't mind if you were. If you'd shown up with a date tonight, I would've been."

He only says it to get me to go upstairs with him, yet it still makes me want to smile. "If that's true, then I really *do* need to go home."

"Nah. We've been intimate. It's only natural we'd feel that way. It doesn't mean it's anything more."

His masculine scent is strong—musky with a hint of sweat. Being near him, I can't forget for very long how *intimate* we just were. I can see in his eyes, he believes what he's saying. He wants me to be jealous. "It's not about Mindy," I say with a sigh. "I should've been here for the announcement. I don't want to get distracted."

"I understand." He holds out the dessert like it's some kind of party favor. I accept it, even though I know I won't eat it. "Believe me, it wasn't easy for me to come here tonight. It was a battle for me to get out of the house, a battle I would've been fine losing."

I tilt my head. More often than not, I forget he has a young daughter at home. The word *battle* alone makes my head hurt. "You wanted to stay home?" I ask. "Isn't it a treat to get a night away?"

"Not really." He half-smiles. "Believe it or not, I like hanging out with my kid."

"Oh. I didn't mean—"

"Yes you did. It's okay. To be honest, it's kind of a relief that you're not interested in Bell. A lot of the women I meet see her as a way to get to me."

I shake my head. "I'm sure she's . . . a nice child . . . but I assure you . . ." I don't want to insult him by admitting I want nothing to do with his kid, so I change the subject. "If it was a battle you wanted to lose, why'd you come?"

"Sadie guilted me into it. And if I'm honest, I wanted to see you."

He's impossible to resist, but that isn't the biggest problem. It's that I don't want to walk away. "I'm sorry. It's just not the right time for me."

"When will it be the right time?" he asks. "So I can put it on my calendar. See, I've got it in my head that we're going to have one more night together."

I lose the fight against my smile. "It's not that I don't want to, but I need to focus on my career."

"You said all this was bullshit."

"It is, but that doesn't mean I didn't sort of . . . want to win."

He takes the award from me. "Then I feel awful you missed it," he says, deepening his voice. "Let me make it up to you. I made you some promises earlier I'd like to follow through with."

I inhale deeply, dropping my eyes to his red tie. I haven't forgotten. He wants me slow. Blinded.

Anticipating his next move. "I've been blindfolded before," I say. "I was too tense to enjoy it."

"Amelia."

I look back up at him.

"You'll enjoy it."

Without even a touch, the hair on the back of my neck stands up. The more I try to fight off the fantasy of what he'll do to me for the next few hours, the harder my heart beats. His red tie turning my world black. His skilled hands making slow love to my body. "I can't decide if you're confident or cocky."

"Let me prove myself."

"You already have."

"I'll do it as many times as it takes." He trails his eyes down my dress. I get the feeling he wants to touch me, but he doesn't. "Come upstairs with me. I'll make sure you're comfortable enough to loosen up, and if I can't get you to, I'll relinquish my sex god license."

Just when I think he can't get any sexier, he makes me smile. "Doesn't anyone ever say no to you?"

"And get away with it? Just Bell." He surveys the lobby briefly. "Now, I left my garbage man uniform at home, but—"

I laugh and against my better judgment, walk past him to the elevator bank. "I love it when you talk dirty," I call over my shoulder.

FOURTEEN
ANDREW

Amelia watches me unknot my tie as if I'm about to strangle her with it. If she doesn't like to be tied up, she won't want to be blinded, either. It's a small step toward stripping her control, though. I can't give her much, but she *can* lose herself with me. I'll make her forget for a few hours. When Shana left, I was tempted every day to open a bottle of whatever was nearest, to lash out at anyone who tried to help, to take a long ride on my bike and end up anywhere but where I was. I couldn't because of Bell. If I can make things a little easier on Amelia while she's dealing with her ex, I want to—especially since she'd never ask for help.

I slip the tie off and give it to her. "It's not that scary."

She runs it through her fingers. Next to her dress and matching nails, it's a shade darker, like the inner and outer petals of a rose. "Just the blindfold," she says. "No tying me up on a whim."

I smile, pleased that she trusts me enough to try, and take the tie back.

She turns and looks over her shoulder. "Will you get my zipper?"

"Eventually." I lift the tie up over her head. "You know this isn't just about taking your eyesight away."

"I prefer to pretend it is."

"Defiant until the last second," I say as I cover her eyes. I tie it only tight enough to keep it in place. I don't want to scare her. She starts to turn back to me, but I stop her with a hand on each of her shoulders. "Just stay."

She nods but pulls her hands into fists. I step back, watching her profile. After a few seconds of silence, she lifts her chin. She wants to speak, but she knows I'll stop her. I've never seen her this still. Even in the bathtub, she'd shift whenever she started to relax. I move to stand in front of her, and she turns her head a few inches. Her chest rises and falls a little faster. Without touching her, I bend my head and press my lips to hers. It takes her a moment to respond, and I wait until she parts her lips before I slip my tongue over hers. Her breath stutters. I can't tell if she's shuddering or trembling, so I put my hands over her biceps to calm her.

"I can't," she says. "Take it off."

"You can." I keep a firm grip on her shoulders but run my thumbs over her skin. "I've got you. There's no reason to be upset."

"I'm not upset. I just don't like it."

"I won't hurt you. That's not why I'm holding you. I care about you, and I want you to be strong. You can be in control like this, but not if you're afraid."

After a few seconds, she nods slightly, and the white skin of her long throat ripples as she swallows.

I tilt my head. She *is* afraid. I figured she'd be resistant, given her need for control, but it's unsettling to see how quickly a composed woman like her loosens at the seams. "What scares you about this?" I ask.

She shakes her head. I can't tell if she doesn't know or if she doesn't want to say. She takes a few breaths, and I wait. "It's not just giving up control. It's giving it to someone else."

"I understand. How does it feel to give it to me?"

"Not good," she admits. "But not as terrifying as I would've thought."

I run my hands down her arms, shoulders to knuckles and back up. "Just imagine this. I blindfold you. I tie your wrists and ankles to the bed. I explore every curve and tip and edge and crease of your body with my mouth and hands. How does that make you feel?"

"It sounds like heaven," she says, "and hell. Just the thought of being bound makes my heart race." She jerks a little, even though I keep my hands loose on her.

"Give me your wrists."

She frowns and starts to object. I don't stop her—I won't push her further than she can go. She has to want this too. After a moment, she seems to change her mind as she holds her wrists up between us. I take them both in one hand and check her expression. She bites her bottom lip, but as much as I'd like to steal that lip from her with my own teeth, I don't think it's an invitation.

"Breathe through your nose," I instruct. Her shoulders drop a little, but with my thumb pressed to her inner wrist, I can feel her pulse under the thin skin. "Are you okay?"

She nods slowly. "Just keep talking. Tell me something about you."

"I don't really like talking about myself," I say. "That's something about me."

Even blindfolded, I can sense her rolling her eyes. "Fine."

Despite the fact that she's uncomfortable, I can't help the arousal stirring in me. The red tie is stark against her platinum blonde hair, mussing it where it's pulled around her head. Her lips are parted, her cleavage rising and falling. Then I remember that she's bare underneath her dress—her panties securely in my pocket. I'm tempted to lift her arms over her head and keep them there while I strip her. Instead, I force myself back to the task at hand. Amelia is letting herself be vulnerable with me. I'm not sure if I owe her the same, but the intimacy of the moment seems to call for it.

"All right," I say. "There is something I've never told anyone and until now, never planned to."

She tilts her head up a little bit. "What?"

I clear my throat, hesitating, but Amelia might actually be the right person to tell. Given her own views on children, she won't judge me for it, and she won't always be around to remind me I said it. "Every parent sometimes wonders what it would be like if they hadn't had their kid," I say. "That's no secret."

She nods.

"I never really felt that way. I mean, my life is pretty good. There's this one thing that happens sometimes, though, and it drives me crazy. I'm pretty lucky Bell is clearly a Beckwith—she looks just like Sadie when she was Bell's age. But occasionally she'll make a face or say something a certain way or her body language . . . it'll be exactly like Shana. And I get this gut reaction. Hate. Anger. For that moment, it's directed at Bell, even though she's innocent in all this."

"That sounds normal," she says. "I don't think you're alone in that."

"Probably not. I don't let Bell or anyone else see that reaction, but that doesn't mean it doesn't happen. I feel so guilty after it passes."

Amelia's body has loosened considerably, and I don't even think she notices. "Andrew, nobody would judge you for feeling that way. Imagine how many children look like ex-husbands or deceased wives, and how common—"

With my free hand, I slip the tie off her face. She blinks a few times as her pupils constrict. Her vision adjusts, and her eyes are unguarded, light.

"Still okay?" I ask.

She looks down at my hand around her wrists, how it binds them tightly together. "I think so," she says.

"You're okay." I smile a little. "I shouldn't have blindfolded you."

"No," she says quickly, glancing up. "It was fine, actually. It was . . . good."

"I meant because I like to see your eyes," I say and leave it at that so I don't get sappy enough to send her running.

"Oh." She takes a deep breath and smiles, albeit shyly. "So, were we going to . . . or is that it?"

"Believe me, we're *going to*." I release her hands. "But at least for tonight, I'll let you see."

She tucks some of her hair behind her ear. "Well, next time—"

She stops, but my imagination picks up immediately where she left off. What would next time be like? Amelia blindfolded on the bed? Or her hands bound behind her back, inviting my mouth to her tits? Maybe eventually, over time, she'd let me live out the entire fantasy—vision, touch, control, taste. All mine.

"Anyway," she says, glancing to the side.

I pinch her chin and pull her face to mine, pecking her once on the lips. "Next time would be nice. I have your card." Before she can object, because I know she will, I continue. "Let's just worry about tonight. I still have loads more plans for you. But first," I take my cell phone out of my breast pocket, "I need to be a daddy for a second."

She blinks at me. "A daddy? Is that another . . . fantasy of yours?"

"God, no." I grimace and as an afterthought, hold up my palms. "Not that there's anything wrong with that if you're into it—"

"No, I wasn't saying—"

"It's just that since I *am* a dad, it weirds me out—"

"Oh." Her expression lightens, and she laughs a little. "You have to call Bell."

"Just to say goodnight. It'll only take a moment."

"Of course," she says, crossing and then uncrossing her arms. "I'm sure it means a lot to her."

"And me. Putting her to bed—don't get me wrong, it can be a struggle—but it's one of my favorite parts of the day. She doesn't go down easy, so I have to read to her or have her read to me—" I pause. Amelia's eyes have glossed over. If it were any other person, dismissing Bell would piss me off, but with Amelia, it's better that she isn't interested in my daughter. "I need to learn when to shut up. I go overboard when it comes to her."

Amelia looks down a second, which seems to be the only response I'll get from her.

"I'll, uh, just step out." I take my phone into the hallway. It's a non-smoking floor, but I light one anyway and dial the house.

"Beckwith residence," Flora answers.

"Hey. It's me. Bell still awake?"

"What do you think?" she asks.

I chuckle. "Bottom shelf of the bookcase in the living room. Look for *The Frog Prince*. She loves Grimms' Fairy Tales, but she doesn't yet know that one's her least favorite. It usually puts her to sleep. I only use it in emergencies so she doesn't catch on."

"I'll give it a shot," she says. "But she's been . . . more restless than usual. Maybe you could tell her a quick story? To calm her down?"

"Pass the phone," I say with a sigh. Flora can normally handle herself, so it must be bad.

"Princess Bell," Flora says away from the receiver. "Your prince is on the phone."

"Daddy," Bell screeches. I take a drag while she gets to the phone. "Are you coming home now?" she asks.

"Not yet, Bluebell. Are you being good for Mrs. Picolli?"

"You promised you'd be home before I went to bed."

I exhale smoke up at the ceiling, shaking my head. This is exactly what I was just describing to Amelia. Bell gets the same tone Shana used to get when she's testing how far she can push me. "I didn't say that."

"Yes you did—"

"What have I told you about lying? *We don't lie.* And you never, ever lie to your father. Do you hear me?"

She sniffles. "I'm sorry. I just m-miss you. Please come home."

My throat gets thick in an instant, the way it does when I know she's trying to keep tears in. It's sometimes worse than when she actually cries. I shouldn't have snapped at her, not when she's already upset, but any form of lying is unacceptable in our house.

Suddenly, I can't stomach the thought of smoking, but there's nowhere to put out the cigarette. I keep it between my fingers and scratch my eyebrow. "I'm sorry, kid. I'm not angry. Go get in bed. Flora'll read you a story, and you'll fall asleep in minutes. By the time you wake up, I'll be home."

She hiccups. "No."

Fuck. I know what's coming. I try to stop it, even though I know it's in vain. "Bell, please don't—"

"*I miss you,*" she sobs into the phone. Unlike before, when she was throwing a tantrum, her cries are weighty, hopeless, as if I just confessed to killing her puppy or that I made plans to ship her off to boarding school. They're the familiar, late-night sobs of a confused toddler asking where Mommy went months ago. "I won't go to sleep. Not until you come home. Please, Daddy. I'm scared."

I press the meat of my palm to my forehead. All the nasty things Shana ever said to me, all the names my dad called me growing up, nothing hurts an ounce as much as this. Listening to my daughter beg me to be with her when I'm not is sheer torture.

"Bell, honey," Flora says in the background. "The sooner you let Daddy get back to his party, the sooner he'll be home."

"Leave me alone," she says, but there's no fight in her voice, just wobbling defeat. "He's my dad. You don't know him or me."

"Come on, Bell," I say. "That's not fair to Flora."

"No. I won't go to sleep. I'll stay up all night and wait for you. I swear, I won't even get in bed—"

"Bell—"

"No! No, no, no, no, n—"

"*Okay*," I say, anything to make it stop. "Okay. All right. I'll . . . I'll come home."

She sniffs. "You will? Now?"

"It'll take me a while to get there. Please go lie down and let Flora read to you until I'm there."

"You promise?" she asks, hiccupping again. "Swear?"

I look at the ground. I know in my gut she'll be asleep when I get home. But if I lie to her, and she wakes up to find me not where I said I'd be, I can't bear to think how it would hurt her. "I swear."

"Okay. I'll go to bed, but I promise I won't sleep. Not until you come say goodnight."

"All right." I sigh, not sure what to feel about the fact that the heaviness in her voice has vanished. It's one thing to be played for a fool by a six-year-old, but it's another to let it happen repeatedly. "Put Flora on the phone."

"I can't remember the lyrics to Deep Purple. Will you sing it for me?"

"Deep Purple?" I ask, leaning back against the hallway wall. "I haven't played that for you yet. You been going through my music?" I don't wait for her answer, since I know what it'll be. She loves to steal my phone at the shop and play with it. Instead of downloading games like regular kids, she explores my music. Quickly, I rattle off a verse of "Hush" and a string of nah-nahs. "That's enough," I say. "I'll sing the rest when I get home."

"Okay. Here's Flora."

Flora's barely on the line when I say, "I'm so sorry."

"Don't worry." She lowers her voice. "But she needs boundaries, Andrew. You can't come running every time she cries."

"I know." I take one last smoke, even though I feel a little sick. "I should come back anyway. I'll be home in about an hour."

She sighs. "If you think that's best."

"See you soon." I end the call, turn around, and freeze when I see Amelia in the doorway.

"I smelled the smoke," she says.

"Yeah." I hold it up. "I'm done with it."

She takes it from me. "You have a nice singing voice."

"You heard. Of course you did. You probably also heard Bell's tantrum all the way from Jersey." I scratch under my jaw. "She has me by the fucking balls, that kid."

Amelia takes a drag. "You're leaving?"

I remove the cigarette from her hand, drop it, and step on it before stepping into her. She looks even more delicious with a smear of raspberry sauce on her cheek. "Anyone ever tell you you're a sloppy eater?"

"Well, it *has* worked in my favor in the past . . ."

"You did it on purpose," I say, impressed. "You want a kiss."

"I want to be tasted."

She doesn't have to ask twice. I lean down to suck the sweetness off her face, then shift an inch to her lips. She feels good. Warm. I don't want to go. I don't need to spend the night here, but I do think I've earned a few hours of not being Dad of the Year. Haven't I? After what everyone's been trying to tell me about my relationship with Bell, I'm beginning to question the kind of parent I've been.

Amelia pulls back first, looking me in the eye. "You're not here with me."

"I am."

"You aren't. I can tell." She gnaws on her bottom lip. "But I'd like you to be. Can't you stay a little longer? I promise to get you back before the sun comes up."

I frown. It isn't like Amelia to ask for more. If I could articulate the past seven years in a few sentences to get to her understand, I would. "I'm sorry. I wish I could."

With a simple tick of her eyebrow, I can tell she doesn't like my answer. She steps back. Her red dress is scorching, tight in the all the right places, but still covered enough to make my imagination work. It would take an idiot to walk away from her. But that's what Bell has turned me in to—an idiot. And hard as I try, as good as Amelia looks, I can't get Bell's choking sobs out my ears. "Bell . . . she has a hard time," I explain. "When her mom left—"

"It's not really my business." Amelia turns, walks back into the room, and doesn't bother holding the door for me.

I catch it right before it slams. "Are you mad?" I ask.

"If you remember, I didn't want to come back up here," she says, removing an earring and setting it on the nightstand. "I didn't want to be blindfolded. I didn't even want a second night. But you were persistent. You promised it'd be worth it. Now you're leaving?"

My instinct is to defend myself with my normal response—Bell's my daughter and she comes first. But Amelia's right: it isn't her business. Amelia and I aren't about anything outside this room. "I didn't anticipate this," I say. "I'll make it up to you."

"How?"

I can't think too hard about the naughty ways I'd like to get back on her good side, or I won't be able to walk out the door. "I just need to figure out what to do with Bell. Then I'll come back to the city, any night you want."

She shakes her head. "Not good enough."

Jesus. If Bell's got me by the balls, Amelia likes to bust them. "What do you mean?"

She sits on the edge of the bed. "Look, I'm not saying anything we don't already know. This has been fun, but—"

"How are you breaking up with me if we aren't even together?"

"I put myself out there for you tonight. In more ways than one. I put you before my *work*, Andrew—I don't do that for anyone."

"What do you suggest I do?" I ask, nearly gaping. "Make my child cry herself to sleep?"

"What good is it going to do for you to go home now? You won't get there until after midnight. I don't know much about kids—"

"No, you don't."

"But the first time you and I met, you told me you weren't raising a spoiled brat. Sounds like you've changed your mind about that. She has to learn, and maybe you do too."

"Learn what?" I ask, reeling back.

"In the words of the Stones—you can't always get what you want."

Amelia has no idea she's speaking a language Bell would understand—kid loves The Rolling Stones—and it puts me somewhere between pissed off and impressed. I have no doubt I would've walked out of the room already if I hadn't been hearing the exact same thing from all the women in my life. "Look," I say, "I already told her I'd come home, and if I don't, it'll just make everything worse. I'll call you tomorrow to reschedule. We can—"

"Don't call me," she says. "In fact, lose my number."

My jaw tingles. She's not kidding. "No."

"Yes. It's my fault. I shouldn't have come up here, and I knew that, but I did anyway."

"We had fun earlier," I point out.

"Then let's leave it at that. Fun. That's what we agreed on, isn't it?"

"Yeah, but . . ." I shouldn't be arguing. This is what I do—sleep with women who are easy to walk away from. With each taste of Amelia, though, I want another bite. Even if it's against the rules. "It's not that I *want* to leave, Amelia. Let me make it up to you another time."

She crosses her arms.

That one gesture is enough to ignite an ember of guilt in me. I nearly forced her to open up and trust me earlier, and now I'm leaving her out in the cold. I can feel her closing again, and to my surprise, it bothers me. In her eyes, I'm currently sitting in the same camp as her ex. I want to help rebuild Amelia's faith in men, not reinforce her disappointment in us. Either way, I'm abandoning one of them, messing with their trust issues. But my loyalty can only be to one of them in the end.

I get my things and go home.

FIFTEEN

Flora greets me at my front door. "Bell's asleep," she says before I even empty my pockets. "I'm sorry, Andrew."

"It's okay. I thought she would be." I run a hand through my hair. My fingers stink like cigarette smoke. "Where's Pico?"

"Took off earlier. He couldn't hack it."

I try to muster a smile, but it's forced. I thought once I left the hotel and got on the train, I'd feel better about coming home. I don't. Amelia would've looked edible splayed on the hotel's king-size bed for my hands and mouth. During the ride home, I couldn't decide if coming back was the right choice, but being a good dad is never the wrong one.

I pay Flora. She refuses to accept the way she normally does, and I insist like I normally do until we finally come to our regular agreement—she'll accept if she can have Bell and me over for dinner one night next week.

Once I've locked up the house, I peek into Bell's bedroom. She's on her back, her legs and arms open like a starfish. The kid can sleep in any position.

I slip into the room and look down at her. Her eyes are pink and puffy, her breathing even. I might resent Shana, but I can never completely hate her. She gave me Bell, and Bell gives me a reason to wake up in a good mood every morning. So what if I spoil her? So what if I'd sacrifice anything for her happiness? I'm a father before I'm a man.

Her eyes fly open. She blinks a couple times, taking in her surroundings. "I wasn't sleeping."

I smile. Stubborn every waking—or sleeping— moment. "I know." I sit on the edge of her bed. "What'd you do with Flora tonight?"

"She showed me some cursive."

"Yeah? You don't learn that until next year."

She shrugs. "I wanted to try. Flora says they might not teach it anymore and that's a tragedy."

"A travesty," I correct with a smile. "So you had fun?"

"No."

I frown. "Why not?"

"Did *you* have fun?" she asks.

I pull back a little at the unexpected question. She's getting older and more perceptive, but how much does she understand? If I say no, I'd be lying. "Yes," I say. "Aunt Sadie and Uncle Nathan say hi."

She sighs, rubbing her eyes. "You said Uncle Nathan couldn't go."

"Sadie was wrong." *In more ways than one.* I brush some loose strands off her cheek. "You can have fun without me, Bell. It doesn't make me feel bad. I want you to."

She waits a few seconds to respond, as if mulling this over. "We played a board game. *Pretty Pretty Princess.*"

"Your favorite," I say.

She giggles. "Pico put on jewelry. And the crown."

The image warms my heart, not because it makes Bell giggle, but because Pico embarrasses easily and I know I'll get to fuck with him tomorrow. I'm all too familiar with pink plastic necklaces and jewel-shaped clip-on earrings, but Pico doesn't know that. "I bet he looked very pretty, and I'll be sure to mention that in front of all the guys tomorrow. What about Flora? Did she look pretty?"

"No." She closes her eyes as sleep visibly overtakes her. "She's like a grandma."

I pick up her hand and kiss the back of it. "Just so you know, no matter how old you are, you'll always be my princess. Even when you're a grandma."

She sighs. "You'll be dead by then."

I laugh. *Brat.*

By the time I've kissed the top of her head, she's asleep. I turn out the hallway lights and head to my room. So Bell thinks it'll hurt my feelings to have fun without me. Sadie would say Bell got that idea from me—that I don't know how to be without her. Maybe Sadie isn't entirely wrong.

I strip down to my boxer briefs. Gone are the days I get to sleep in the nude, which is what I'd be doing right now if I'd stayed at the hotel. With Amelia. After a bout of fucking. We'd be skin on skin right now, curled up together. Or would we? Would she have kicked me out already?

I dig out her business card and my phone from my pants before I get into bed. She told me to lose her number, and maybe I should. Now that I'm home, though, where I know Bell is safe and happy, I'm left with the unsettling realization that I truly *did* want to spend tonight with Amelia. I've never been tempted to leave Bell overnight for someone. There's more to Amelia I don't know and her veneer should make me want to stay away, but instead I have the urge to get beneath it. Not just for me, but for her.

I type her a text.

Hello ma'am. This is your service provider performing a routine check to make sure you're satisfied with our services. To be clear, this is not the man you gave your number to earlier and then told him to lose it.

I hit send. She has no reason to respond, but when she does, I release a breath I didn't realize I was holding. I open the message.

I'm satisfied, no thanks to you. Sorry you missed it.

A second later, my phone buzzes with a photo—of her, in the bathtub from the chest down, completely hidden by bubbles. The only skin visible is a bent knee and her red toes curled against the opposite lip of the tub. *Fuck me.* She stayed in the room. She took a bath, without me. Did she . . . satisfy *herself?* Is that why her toes are curled? Is she *touching* herself?

I groan. I could be there now, behind her, learning her body with my hands. I write back immediately.

Move the bubbles a little to the left so I can see how satisfied.

As soon as I send it, three dots appear as she types her response. My heart rate picks up. Phone sex. Text sex. Dirty pictures. Amelia. Naked. My phone vibrates with her answer and I'm worse than Pavlov's dog, my cock stirring in anticipation. I'm a dog all right, and I'm not ashamed to admit I'm nearly panting for a nudie. I open the message.

You have an imagination. Use it.

Fuck. She can't do that. I'll reciprocate if that's what she wants. I lift the comforter, pull down my boxer briefs, take my dick in my hand and stop. Playful, tastefully photographed woman in a bathtub? Sexy. Unsolicited dick pic from a guy you've known a week? Creepy. Reluctantly, I tuck myself back in. I study her picture for any unintentional breaks in the bubbles—accidental nip slip, suggestive flash of skin, anything. There's nothing. I'm going to need more.

When can I see you again?

Mercifully, she doesn't make me wait for a response.

Whenever you want. That's what the picture's for. Goodbye, Andrew.

Amelia is done with me, that much is obvious.
But I don't think I'm done with Amelia just yet.

SIXTEEN

"Butts out," Pico calls through the garage.

I look up from the engine I'm working on, stand, and knock my head on the hood. "*Damn it.*"

"You'd think after twenty years working on cars, you'd know better by now," Pico points out before one last, long suck from his cigarette.

"Fuck off." I rub the top of my head. "Butts out already? Why?"

"It's ten to three, boss. Shouldn't you be on your way to the bus stop?"

"Ah, *shit.*" I toss my ratchet onto a bench and wipe my oily hands on my pants. "Seriously?"

Pico points at the clock, drops the butt, and mashes it with his shoe. "Same as every day."

I head out of the garage and down the block. Bell spots me from the corner and jumps up and down, waving. She and Sammy, a kid from the grade above hers, are already headed my way. Of course the bus is early the one day I'm late. She grips the straps of her backpack and walks faster. When they reach the intersection, Sammy steps off the curb, but Bell grabs his sleeve and pulls him back. Even from fifty feet away, I hear her yelling at him about the importance of looking both ways.

"You're late," she says as we meet in the middle.

"Sorry, kid. Lost track of time."

"You can make it up to me with a piggy back ride."

"Gee, thanks." I exchange a glance with Sammy, who rolls his eyes as if to say *classic Bell*. I squat, and she hops on my back.

"Mr. Beckwith?" Sammy asks.

I never tell Bell's friends to call me by my first name like the other parents. Mr. Beckwith is grown-up and important, at least to people their size. "What's up?"

He holds up a red envelope. "A stranger tried to give this to Bell, but I took it."

My heart stops along with my feet, and Bell tightens her arms around my neck to keep from lurching forward. I take what looks like a greeting card from him. "A stranger? Who?"

"A teacher," Bell says.

"I didn't recognize her," Sammy says with exasperation, as if this is an argument they've had before.

"Oh. A teacher." I wipe sweat from my brow and flip the envelope over. My fingers leave black marks on the red paper. "Is it for me?"

"No, she said it was for me," Bell says. "*Sammy* wouldn't let me open it."

Right. It may be addressed to Bell, but I doubt it's actually for her. It looks like a valentine, even though it's May. Most likely another attempt to get to me through her. I nod at Sammy as I stick it in my back pocket. "Thanks for telling me. You want to hang here for a while?"

"Sure."

"There're popsicles in the freezer," I say. "I'll let your mom know you're here."

I put Bell down, and they run for the sweets. As I scroll through my messages to contact Sammy's mom, I pause at Amelia's last text—the infuriatingly mocking photo—and admire it for the second time today.

"What's that?" Pico asks, suddenly at my side.

I close out of the picture. "Nothing."

"Must be the reason you've been distracted all week," he says. "Could it be *the city girl?*"

"Fuck you," I say. "Is there anything you and your mom don't share?"

Randy holds a wrench in front of his crotch and gyrates his hips. "There's nothing Pico's mom and I don't share."

"Eat shit," Pico says. "You never even met my mom."

231

"Yeah, I did. At last year's Fourth of July barbeque."

Pico glares at him. "Fuck off. She's twice your age."

"So? Pussy is pussy."

"Shut the fuck up," I say. "My daughter's right over there."

"Chill," Randy says. "She can't hear."

"Yes, I can," Bell yells at us. "I heard you say the 'p'-word and Daddy said the 'f'-word."

"Holy shit," Pico mutters. "Kid's got bionic ears."

Randy grimaces. "Sorry, Bell. I didn't mean it."

"It's okay," she says. "Just don't say that again. Mrs. Picolli is like a grandma to me."

I sigh, rubbing the bridge of my nose. "You guys have to tone it down. She's getting old enough to understand."

"*Fuck*'s worse than *pussy*," Randy whispers loudly.

"Is not." As I text Sammy's mom that he's here, Amelia's name pops out at me once again, the way it has the entire week. I hate how we left things. The way she'd trusted me in the hotel room right before I'd walked out. How she'd missed accepting an award she'd earned. A week away should've cooled me off, but it's made me even hungrier, and not for just anyone. I could have my pick of women in this town, but somehow, the city girl's the one on my mind.

I stick my phone back in my pocket and remember the envelope. Pulling it out, I slide my finger under the flap and slip the card out. *Happy Mother's Day* is embossed across the front in pink glitter. "What the actual fuck?" I grumble, opening it. It's blank inside.

My chest burns like I just took a hit of bammer weed. *Mother's Day?* What the fuck kind of demented woman gives Bell, who has no mother, a card like this? As if that holiday isn't weird enough for us. Steam nearly flows from my ears. Even though I don't reciprocate, the moms love to flirt with me. Even the married ones. They can be persistent, but this is a whole new level. I don't know what to make of this. Does a teacher or mother honestly think this is the best way to get my attention?

I tear up the card and toss it in the nearest trash.

"So who's the chick?" Pico asks, his voice lowered. Curse words are one thing, but he knows I'll skin him alive if Bell catches us talking about my sex life.

"Nobody you know," I bite out, dumping leftover coffee on top of the shredded card. "She's too far out of your league."

"Yeah?" he retorts. "Well then she must be out of yours too."

"She is."

"You wouldn't believe the ass I got last night," Randy says. "Two NYU chicks wandered into the wrong bar and ended up getting toasted on Kamikaze shots."

"Bullshit," Pico says. "Maybe in your wet dream."

"Swear to God." He raises his arms. "I invited them both back with me, but only one wanted to go, so the other one sat in my living room and watched TV."

"And you didn't invite me over?" Pico asks, horrified.

"Hold up, I'm not finished. I come out of my room naked and ask the other girl if she's sure she doesn't want to join." Randy's smile turns sinister. "She ends up jumping my dick. I had one riding me while the other ate my asshole."

"Dude," I say. "That's fucking disgusting."

"Two chicks at once?" He scoffs. "Are you nuts? It was insane."

"Not that part. I don't want to believe there's a woman on this planet who'd put her face . . . *there*. You clog the toilet on a weekly basis."

"Well, she did. You ever been sucked off by a twenty-year-old, boss? They're still hungry."

As grossed out as I am, sex is on my mind, and it doesn't take me long to wish I were in the position to call someone up and get some head. Denise would be happy to oblige, and she's a two-minute drive from here, but all I can think about are Amelia's red lips, and at the moment, not much else would compare.

"You're such a goddamn liar," Pico says. "I don't believe a word."

"It's true," Randy says. "Except for that last part about the second girl."

"I knew it," Pico said.

"She was actually a dude."

"Oh my God," Pico says, rubbing his eyes as if he's trying to scrub away a mental image. "Are you serious?"

"Christ," I mutter. Randy has no filter, and his sexual preference is anything that'll fit a dick. After two years working together, Pico still hasn't gotten used to hearing about anything involving another man. Watching Pico squirm is normally too funny for me to do anything but laugh, but I'm not in the mood today. I can't deal with these assholes.

"Where you headed, boss?" Pico asks as I turn for my office. "Rub one out to twenty-year-old pussy?"

"To research homeschooling. I've just decided to lock Bell in the house until she's thirty."

I seriously consider following through. Men are pieces of shit. I don't want anything with a dick coming around once Bell's old enough. Maybe she'll be a lesbian. I knew a lesbian couple once when I was twenty-three and managing a fast food restaurant. One of the girls worked for me and invited me over after we closed. You think that kind of stuff only happens in movies, and it probably does—to other people. I smile to myself as I remember the way they devoured each other and then me. My smile fades and my mind is officially changed. Bell's not allowed to be a lesbian, either.

I pace my office and catch myself glancing at the clock, but I'm not sure why. I have nowhere to be. I take out my phone. Amelia is different from other women I know, and one of the reasons is her blunt honesty. I've reciprocated that. If I want something, I should be able to say so, because that's what our relationship is. And I want something. I want it bad. I start to write to her, but our last interaction sits loudly on the screen. *Goodbye, Andrew.* She thinks she doesn't want to see me, and she's more stubborn than I am. Texting won't be enough to convince her otherwise. I need to see her face to face and convince her to let me spend a night making it up to her.

When I come out of my office, Sammy's mom is talking to Pico. I wave at her, and she smiles but quickly returns to Pico. Then, I notice her full face of makeup, skirt, and heels. *No shit.* She's into Pico. "He lives with his mom," I shout across the garage, just to keep it real.

Pico reddens. "I don't *live* with her," he tells Myra, scratching his head with his middle finger. "She likes the company, and I'm saving to start my own thing."

Seeing Myra, a big, fat, hell-of-an-idea hits me. I've babysat Sammy here at the shop plenty of times. And Bell likes Sammy as much as any of her friends. She might be cool to spend an evening with them, so long as I spin it right, and by spin it, I mean buy them loads of pizza.

I turn in Myra's direction. "Hey."

"Thanks for letting Sammy hang out," she says.

"No problem. Actually . . ." It's harder to get the words out than I thought it'd be with Pico watching. He'll want to know where I'm going. If I want another shot with Amelia, though, I have to man up. I wipe my forehead with my sleeve. "Any chance you could take Bell for a few hours? Maybe even overnight?"

"Sorry," she says. "We're headed to Pittsburgh for the weekend to visit my sister."

"Sure. It's last minute." I glance at Pico. "You?"

He sniffs. "Can't, bro. I'm busy."

I look at him skeptically. "Doing what?"

"Stuff. I have my own life, you know."

"Then I'll ask your mom."

"She can't either."

"Look," I say, "if you're getting me back for the mom comment—"

"I'm taking my mom to Bingo, all right?" He darts his eyes to Myra and back to me. "We do it every month."

I'd ask him to take a night off, but I'm laughing too hard. Myra doesn't seem to think it's funny— she's swooning. Once I've wiped tears from my eyes, I shake my head. "Never mind."

"Why?" Pico looks suspicious as hell. "Where're *you* going on a Friday night?"

I back away. With all Flora's done for me, it wouldn't be right to interrupt her plans. "Forget it."

I find Bell and Sammy in the garage's waiting room watching *Doctor Who*. I've run out of all options but one. Ambushing Sadie—and Amelia—at the office and hoping for a miracle of some sort. "Hey, Bell." I put a finger in each ear, readying myself for her squeals. "Let's go into the city."

Her eyes are glued to the screen. "Huh?"

"Did you hear me? I said *New York City*."

"Um." She shifts deeper into the couch. "I'm okay here."

"Really? I thought maybe you'd want to surprise Aunt Sadie."

"Aunt Sadie?" she repeats, staring straight ahead. She hasn't heard anything I've said. Reluctantly, I mumble, "We can ride the subway."

She blinks a few times and then jumps off the couch, startling Sammy from his own trance. "The subway?"

Bringing Bell along is a last resort, but the truth is, that's where I am. I'll have to convince Sadie to take Bell for a night without raising any suspicion and then convince Amelia to give me a second chance. It'll take some maneuvering, but after a week of trying and failing to get Amelia out of my head, I need to do something, even if it's impulsive. Even if it might be a mistake.

Right now, Amelia's a mistake I'd be happy to make.

SEVENTEEN

It's almost five when we arrive at Sadie's office. Since it's Friday, I worry everyone will have left for the day, but when we exit the elevator, floor seven is buzzing. The male receptionist who greeted us last time looks up.

"Well, hello, Bell." His eyes wander up my body. "I see you brought me an afternoon snack."

"Snacks?" Bell asks. "I have gummy bears in my backpack."

"That's okay." He winks at me. "I prefer a different kind of bear."

"Keep dreaming," I tell him. "Sadie here?"

"She's in her office."

"Office?" I ask. "You mean her desk?"

"Oh, *Sadie*." He smirks. "I thought you said Amelia."

I narrow my eyes at him as I take Bell's hand. We walk through the agency, right by Amelia's office, toward Sadie's desk. Amelia's door is closed, but she has a window that looks into the office and the blinds are open. I glance inside just as I hear, "Surprise!"

I look back in time to see Sadie jump a mile high in her seat. She whirls her desk chair around. "*Bell?* What—"

"We came to ride the subway," Bell says.

"Jesus." Sadie looks wide-eyed from Bell to me, her hand over her heart. "You can't go around surprising pregnant women, Andrew."

I roll my eyes. I've never heard of anyone pulling the pregnancy card as much as Sadie does. "Bell was feeling antsy at the garage," I explain. "She wanted to surprise you."

Sadie glances around the office. "I wish you would've called first. Amelia really doesn't like children in here, and she's in a particularly bad mood today."

"She is?" I cinch my eyebrows. "How come?"

Sadie combs her fingers through Bell's tangled hair. "Jesus, Andrew. Ever heard of a brush?"

"Why's your boss in a bad mood?" I ask.

"What? Something to do with men, I'm sure."

I cross my arms and glance toward Amelia's office again, but I can't see her. Am I the reason for her mood?

Sadie rakes Bell's hair into a ponytail. "Thanks for surprising me, honey. Aunt Sadie has a lot of work to do, though."

While Sadie's distracted, I take a couple steps back, angling my head until Amelia comes into view. She's seated at her desk on the phone, her blonde hair pulled back from her face. She isn't in a flirty, colorful blouse and skirt like when we met but a suit jacket and white button down. As she talks into the receiver, she adjusts black-rimmed glasses I've never seen her wear before. All covered up. It's the bubble-bath-photo bullshit all over again.

"It was Daddy's idea to come," Bell says.

I slowly turn back to Bell to pin her with a look, but she's not even paying attention to me. *Little traitor.*

"But your dad hates the city." Sadie glances up. "Why are you here?"

I shake my head, nod at Bell, and mouth, "Liar."

Sadie cocks her head, then after a moment, her eyes widen. "Oh my . . . *shit.*"

"What?" I ask.

"Um." She smooths her expression. "I-I think the baby just kicked."

"And your first reaction was 'oh, shit'?"

"No. You're right. It was probably indigestion." She looks toward Amelia's office and back at me. "You, uh, couldn't have changed clothes?"

I'm in the white t-shirt and jeans I've been wearing all day. "What's wrong with this? Not good enough for the New York City fashionistas?"

"You've got grease on your face."

"And?" I lick my thumb and scrub my cheek. "I work with grease for a living."

She sighs. "Did you say hi to Mindy?"

"Who?"

She shakes her head and throws up her arms. "Forget it. Jesus. Just forget the whole thing. What're you guys doing now?"

Bell grins. "Dad promised me more ice cream."

"*More* ice cream?" Sadie asks. "How much have you had today?"

Bell giggles. She may not know the word *bribery*, but she's smart enough to understand she's getting away with something. "A popsicle after school."

Sadie's computer pings. "Well," she says, checking an e-mail, "since you're here, let's go get dinner. You guys decide what to eat while I try to sweet talk my boss into letting me leave early."

"Five's early?" I ask, but she ignores me, which is good because I've got a narrow window of time to figure out my next step. This—a few furtive and unreturned glances at Amelia—won't be enough to satisfy me. In fact, seeing her and not being able to talk to or touch her is making things worse. Admittedly, the buttoned-up librarian look is growing on me. "We can bring food here if you can't get away," I say. "Or, I thought, since you had such a great girls' sleepover a couple weeks ago—"

"It'll be fine. I can come in early Monday." She lifts Bell off her lap and stands. "Give me a minute."

New plan. Go to dinner with Sadie, get her to invite Bell over, and then come back for Amelia. I plop into Sadie's vacated chair and watch through the window. Amelia puts her call on hold. As she listens to Sadie, she shifts her eyes to me. I wink.

"What's wrong with your eye, Daddy?" Bell asks.

"Huh?" I look back at her. "Oh. Nothing."

Sadie comes out of the office and heads back toward us. "Good news. Boss says it's fine."

Amelia and I stare at each other. She arches an eyebrow at me, stands, and walks to the doorway. The bottom half of her suit isn't the pants I expected, but a skirt. It stops just above her knees, showing off the long, slim legs that were wrapped around my waist just last week.

"I invited her," Sadie says.

My fantasy skids to a halt, and I whip my head back to my sister. "You what?"

She shrugs casually, but her eyes are trained on my face. "I invited Amelia."

After everything I went through to get here, I should be elated. I hadn't thought this through. The woman I'm sleeping with and my daughter at the same table? The thought makes my stomach hurt. "What about Bell?"

"We can go somewhere kid friendly. Move." She waves me away. "I have to shut down my computer."

I get out of Sadie's chair. This isn't what I had in mind. I do want time alone with Amelia—somewhere my daughter isn't. "Why would you invite her?"

"She needs cheering up." Sadie packs up her desk, glancing at me from under her lashes. "Her ex ambushed her last week, and she's been in a weird mood ever since."

"Her ex?" My body flushes with heat. The ex. Reggie, the cheater, the almost ex-husband—what the fuck is he doing coming around? Here, I'd hoped she'd been thinking of me this week when she'd actually been dealing with him. "When was this?"

Sadie lugs her purse from the ground to the desk. "The night of the awards show."

"Are you kidding? The one I was at?"

"Yes. Why do you care?"

"I don't," I say automatically, but my tone, my clenched fists, my racing thoughts prove otherwise. We were together that night, and she never mentioned him. Unless it happened afterward, which would've meant he was at the hotel. He was with her in what should've been my room. My bathtub. I look back at Amelia, but she isn't in her office. I search the space around us. She's gone. "I need to piss."

"You know where the bathroom is."

"I need to piss too," Bell says.

"*Bell*," Sadie scolds. "Don't talk like that."

"I'll take you at the restaurant," I say to her, walking away. "Stay there."

I head through the office. The receptionist doesn't even look up from his cell as he coughs and points toward a door by the elevator.

I check over my shoulder to make sure Bell didn't follow me, then push through into the stairwell.

Amelia's pacing the small space, a cigarette between her fingers. She looks up quickly. "What are you doing here?"

I ignore her question. "What happened last week? After the awards show?"

"Last week?" Her forehead wrinkles. "Do you really need me to tell you?"

"I mean with Reggie."

She stops to stare at me. "Oh. Sadie told you?"

"Yeah. I don't understand. He came to the hotel? Did you . . .?"

"God, *no*," she says. "It was before I saw you. He showed up at my apartment when I was leaving for the event."

I cross my arms, then change my mind and hold my hand out for the cigarette. She gives it to me. Her deep red lipstick has left a mark on the butt. "Why didn't you tell me?" I ask.

She shrugs. "It's not your problem."

"It feels like my problem," I say without thinking, but it's the truth. "I'm sorry if that bothers you."

She studies my face a few seconds, her eyebrows drawn. "What do you mean?"

I take a drag, thinking about my answer and deciding I don't have one that's as cut and dry as I wish it'd be. "I don't like the idea of him coming around after the way he hurt you, regardless of whether you and I are together." I sound like a chick, and I should stop myself, but I can't. Amelia doesn't deserve to be dicked around, especially not by him. "What did he want?"

Her expression eases a little. She takes the cigarette back from me and flicks off ash. "Just the same old shit. He's sorry. He wants me back. He made a mistake."

I frown. "Like, definitely?" I ask. "He wants you back?"

"I told him to get lost," she says. "I might've been an idiot to fall for him once, but never again."

Despite what she's telling me, I've seen women all throughout my life choose men who weren't good for them, my mother included. I'm not sure if my dad has ever cheated on her, but I wouldn't put it past him. My mom wouldn't even leave if he did. "You deserve better."

She shrugs. "I know."

As we look at each other, the air between us shifts. My irritation over Reggie dissipates as a more pressing need, and the reason I'm here, resurfaces.

I nod at the eyeglasses pushed up on her head. "You wear those often?" I ask.

"These?" She pulls them down onto her face. "Sometimes. For reading."

"I like them."

"How much do you like them?"

I glance over my shoulder, as if someone might hear us. "Come here."

246

"No. I told you—we're through."

"Come . . . *here*."

With a soft sigh, she inches toward me. When we're close enough, she holds the cigarette to my mouth, and I take a drag.

"You were right," I say. "After how you trusted me, I should've held my ground with Bell."

She twists her lips, thinking. "You haven't told me why you're here."

"I made those promises the other night thinking I'd get to keep them. Now it feels unfinished between us." I slide her glasses off her face. "Truth is, I wanted to see you again. I'm here for you."

I dig my fingers into her perfect bun, and she fights to keep her eyes open. "We had a deal," she murmurs. "One night."

"And then we had a second night. Now we'll have a third."

"I don't know, Andrew . . ."

I remove bobby pins and an elastic band from her hair. It falls around her shoulders in waves, a nice change from her normally pin-straight style. I touch the corner of her red mouth, smearing the tiniest bit of lipstick onto my thumb. "I like you put together," I say gruffly. "So I can undo you."

She bites into her bottom lip, drawing my eyes to her mouth. "Undo me?" she asks. "Or just do me?"

I nearly growl. "Right here in the stairwell?" I crook my finger into the waistband of her skirt and pull her even closer. "Because I should warn you. I'm a man on edge. I have been ever since the hotel."

I watch her delicate throat as she swallows, as redness creeps up from under her collar. "Then you shouldn't have left me there all alone."

"No. I shouldn't have." I mean it even more now that I know what she'd been through earlier that night. "I don't want him near you."

"Who?" she asks breathlessly.

"Reggie."

Her lips part as she pulls back a little. "Reggie?"

"How'd he take it when you said no to getting back together?"

She frowns and looks away. "I don't want to talk about this. It's personal."

"Too bad. I want personal right now. What was his reaction?"

Her shoulders slouch a little, and I slip my hand under her hair, to her neck, to comfort her. "He didn't like it," she says. "He isn't good with rejection. He promises this time will be different."

Different? I open my mouth to tell her it won't be, but she cuts me off.

"It won't be. I know that. He just won't hear me."

"Maybe it'd clear out his ears if I kicked his ass."

She laughs softly. "Where'd you come from? A mob movie?"

I grin. "That's how we handle things in my part of Jersey."

She looks hard at me a few seconds, absentmindedly rubbing her collarbone, turning her skin pink. "Maybe I should skip dinner."

"It's five on a Friday," I say. "What could you possibly have to do that's so important?"

"It's . . . not about work."

I know right away what she means, since it's the first place my mind went when Sadie mentioned inviting Amelia. "Bell," I say. I sigh up at the ceiling. "I admit, it's weird. But you and I aren't dating. So it wouldn't be like I'm introducing you to her as a . . . it's not like you're—"

"Don't worry," she says. "I'm not trying to be anyone's mommy."

I look down my nose at her, my interest piqued hearing that once-familiar word. I haven't referred to anyone as mommy since Shana left. "Don't underestimate mommies and daddies," I say. "That stuff about the birds and the bees has to come from somewhere."

She touches the hem of my t-shirt. I nearly shudder when her knuckles graze my stomach. "Speaking of roleplaying, I thought you were kidding about dressing up as a garbage man."

I check my clothing again. "This is what I work in."

"Oh." She looks me up and down, her eyes twinkling. She's giving me shit and enjoying it. "Good thing I find it sexy."

"Yeah?" I ask. "That was risky, sending me that photo in the bath. I almost came back to the hotel room for you."

She purses her lips. "I wouldn't have let you in."

"No?"

She presses her body to mine, rises onto the balls of her feet, and kisses me on the mouth. The way her soft lips mush into mine makes my dick come alive. I've wanted this sweet taste, these red lips, since I stepped into this building. And before that. Since I left her and her sexy dress in that hotel room. I go to wrap my arms around her waist, but she pulls away. She gives me the cigarette before glancing at my crotch. "Better do something about that, handyman," she says and walks around me to return to the office. "We have a whole meal to get through."

EIGHTEEN
AMELIA

Andrew's daughter holds his hand as we walk to the restaurant, but she won't stop turning around and looking at me. It's as if she suspects something. But how could she at her age? She wears a miniature pink backpack, which is funny because miniature backpacks are all the rage right now.

To my left, Sadie fills me in on the latest feature she secured some client on some website. Bell is a beautiful little girl, a spitting image of her dark, mysterious father. She seems well behaved, but in my experience, most kids are until they aren't.

"Turn left at the corner," Sadie tells Andrew. "It's the place with the red-and-white checkered tables out front. They have a kid's menu." She turns back to me. "Anyway, what do you think? Is it time to make a play?"

"For who?" I ask.

"Jo Keller—of *What Jo Wore*? The breakout fashion blogger I've been watching for months?"

Hot, new, promising up-and-comers are my thing. It's partly how I made a name for myself in the industry—carefully researching clients in order to create my dream roster and then ruthlessly going after them, no matter if they were looking for representation or not. But my gut reaction isn't excitement. Taking on a new client means presentations, lunches, dinners and drinks, numbers, negotiation. It costs money. And time—which is another way of saying money. Considering my business is currently up in the air, I don't know that I can afford to bring on anyone new. At least when I was starting out, I had enough energy to make up for lack of money. Since I missed winning the award last week and confessed my hesitations about *avec* to Andrew, my focus has been waning. And the more it wanes, the harder I have to work to keep up.

"Let's hold off," I say.

"Why?" Sadie asks. "She's got staying power, Amelia. Someone'll scoop her up if they aren't wooing her already."

I scratch my eyebrow, glancing at the back of Andrew's head. Strangely, he knows more about my situation with Reggie than anyone in my office. "I trust your instinct," I tell Sadie. "But just keep doing what you're doing. We'll revisit in a few weeks."

"Okay . . ."

Andrew opens the door to the restaurant. Bell and Sadie walk through, and as I follow, he taps my ass. I haven't forgotten that it only took one kiss earlier to make him twitch against me. Or that he came all this way to see me. I might've been able to say no if I'd forgotten about him this week like I'd planned. When he suddenly left the hotel after I'd worked up the nerve to spend a second night with him, I remembered why we had an arrangement in the first place. But seeing him unexpectedly in the office just now made me realize how gray my week had been until that moment. And I didn't want to forget. Time with Andrew—our baths, conversations, sex—has been the most at peace I've felt in months. Maybe even since Reggie left.

The hostess greets us. It's early for dinner, so the restaurant is nearly empty. She leads us to a four-top table with two chairs on each side.

"Do you want to sit by me or Aunt Sadie?" Andrew's deep voice carries over all our heads, like something I could reach up and touch.

"Aunt Sadie," Bell says. She and Sadie claim one side of the table, which leaves Andrew and me standing. I look back at him for direction. I'm not used to being around children, and I've never dated a man with one. Does he need to be across from her? Will he need to cut her food or distract her when she gets bored and starts acting up?

He grins, almost as if he finds my discomfort

amusing, then gestures to the chair facing Bell. He sits next to me.

Almost immediately, a waiter drops off a basket of bread and a paper menu with crayons for Bell. "Evening, folks. Something to drink?"

I open my mouth to order a white wine, but Sadie interrupts me. "Just water for us."

I shut my mouth and frown. Does one child at the table seriously mean all three adults need to remain sober? Directly across from me, Bell tilts her head, studying me as if she's reading my thoughts. For a split second, I'm worried she can. "You work with Aunt Sadie?"

I glance over at Sadie, who answers for me. "Yes."

"Actually, that's not true," I say, lacing my hands in front of me and leaning in. "I'm your aunt's boss. I get to tell her what to do."

Bell smiles. "Like my dad. He's the boss of Randy and Pico and all the guys at the shop. Except Burt."

"Who's Burt?" Sadie asks.

Andrew clears his throat. "Burt is Bell's imaginary friend."

"No he isn't," Bell says, nearly giggling. "He's the man who fixes Daddy's motorcycle when Daddy doesn't know how."

He rolls his eyes. "Daddy doesn't need help. Maybe in your *imaginary* world."

Sadie and I narrow our eyes on Andrew at the

same moment, but he focuses on his menu. "Even experts need help sometimes," he mutters, then coughs into his fist. I swear he says "traitor."

"So do you get to wear a lot of makeup and expensive clothes too?" Bell asks me.

I turn back to her. "All the time."

Her eyes light up. "Cool. I can't wait until I get to wear makeup."

"Which will be never," Andrew says, turning a page of the menu.

"Aunt Sadie already let me."

He jerks his head up. "Excuse me?"

"*B-e-e-ll*," Sadie says. "Are you physically incapable of keeping secrets?"

Bell nods, smiling at me. "Families don't keep secrets. That's what my dad says."

Andrew sighs. "Christ."

I look from Bell to Andrew and Sadie, who seemed to be locked in some kind of stare down. "Did you hear that?" Sadie asks. "Family doesn't keep secrets."

"I heard. And you promised you'd keep that shit away from her."

"Come on—she's a *girl*," Sadie says. "She's curious about these things. We played dress up around the apartment."

"She's not even seven," he argues.

Sadie butters a piece of bread, shrugging. "You keep it from her, and she'll just want it more."

Sensing Andrew's irritation, I address Bell. "Your

aunt and I try to get women to want makeup and clothing from our clients," I say, "but you want to hear a secret?"

Bell leans her forearms onto the table, mirroring my posture. "Yes. I'm very good with secrets."

"It's mostly bullsh—" I stop and look at Andrew. "Not everyone needs makeup. In fact, most women look best with only very little."

Bell looks at her dad. She picks up a crayon, taps it on the table, and squints, skeptical. "Really?"

I nod. "The secret to being beautiful is confidence." As an afterthought, I add my mom's advice to me. "Confidence—and great skin."

She sits up straighter and smiles. "I'm confident. All my teachers say so."

"Oh, so when someone else says it, you believe it?" Andrew asks. "I tell you you're beautiful all the time."

"I know, but you're my *dad*." She rolls her eyes to the back of her head and says to me, "He has to say that."

"Well, he's right." I lean in a little and add quickly, "But just in case, make sure to hydrate, moisturize regularly, and always wear sunscreen."

Sadie laughs, but Bell just pinches her eyebrows together and looks to her dad, apparently done with the conversation. "I'm hungry."

"What do you want?" Andrew asks as he picks out a piece of bread and butters it for her. "Macaroni and cheese?"

She nods. "And Coke."

"No soda this late, you know that." He offers me the bread basket. "Roll?"

"Are you going to butter mine too?" I ask with a hint of a smirk.

"Amelia doesn't eat bread," Sadie says.

Andrew mocks me with a gasp. "*Really?*"

"Not even sandwiches?" Bell asks.

"No," I say. "Not macaroni either."

"Why not?"

"Because carbohydrates make you f—" I pause. Bell's eyes are big with curiosity. The people I pay to listen to me aren't even this attentive. Her young brain is soaking up my words like a sponge. My own mother comes to mind, a well-to-do, naturally thin Texan who couldn't understand why her daughter was overweight when I had constant access to any type of food I wanted, any time of day. Even though I lost the weight as a teenager, whenever I talk to her, she asks about what I'm eating, a subtle way to find out if I've reverted to my eleven-year-old self.

I feel Andrew staring at me. Considering how concerned he is with my diet, and how protective he is of Bell, I don't think he'll ever forgive me if I finish my sentence. "Carbs, like bread and pasta, make some people . . . *tired*," I say instead. "And in my line of work, it's not good to be tired."

"Oh." She takes a bite of her roll. "Not me. I love sandwiches. I can eat them all day and not get tired."

I sip my water. "What's your favorite kind?"

"Pastrami with mustard."

"That's a lot of sandwich for a little girl," I point out.

"I can finish it," she says. "Most of the time. If not, Dad eats the leftovers. He's a human garbage disposable."

"*Disposal*," I correct, but she doesn't hear me over Andrew and Sadie's laughter.

"Now you answer," Bell says. "What's your favorite food?"

"Hmm."

"Glenlivet doesn't count," Andrew says.

I giggle, but stop when I notice Sadie's stare. "Inside joke from the award ceremony," I tell her, clearing my throat. "Remember?"

Sadie nods slowly. "I remember . . ."

"Anyway," I say, returning to Bell, "I love Brussels sprouts."

Everyone groans. Bell makes a face. "Ew."

"You can't be serious," Andrew says.

"I'm not." I laugh. "Cupcakes are my weakness. Especially those huge ones from Crumbs with all the frosting and toppings."

Andrew and Sadie turn to me. "*What?*" they ask in unison.

"I don't eat them often," I say, reeling back from their glares, "but that doesn't mean they can't be my favorite."

"I like cupcakes," Bell says. "What's your favorite

movie that's not for grownups?"

Andrew coughs again and turns his head to me. "Not *Frozen*," he says through his teeth.

"What's *Frozen*?"

"Are you kidding?" Sadie asks.

I look around the table at three open-mouthed stares and get the sudden sensation of being the old person at a table of teenagers who's never heard of Snapchat. "Oh, right," I say, forcing a smile. "*Frozen*. The one about penguins."

Bell squeals and dissolves into peals of laughter. Her face reddens as she tries to catch her breath. "No," she gasps. "Not even close."

Andrew puts his hand on my knee, creeping it up the inside of my thigh. Instinctively, butterflies flurry inside me. My body only knows his touch as a precursor to sex, and I get instantly warm, my stomach tightening. But then he slips his hand into mine, squeezes it, and doesn't let go.

"I-I don't really know any of the new stuff," I stammer, partly because of Andrew's unexpected affection and partly, I realize, because I was enjoying Bell's idolization of me, and now she probably thinks I'm just another clueless adult. "I prefer the older Disney movies from when I was growing up."

Bell gasps and yells, "Me too."

"Hush," Andrew says, glancing at the other patrons. "We're in public, Bell."

She clasps her hands together, ignoring him. "What's your favorite? Mine's *Beauty and the Beast*."

"That's a good one," I say. "Is that who you're named after? Belle?"

"No. She has an 'e' on the end of her name, but I don't. I just like how the beast was mean to her, but she was always nice to him anyway and then they're in love. And she reads."

"You like to read?" I ask.

"Yes. My dad reads to me every night."

I look over at Andrew. He keeps his eyes on Bell but curls his lips just a hint, one dimple deepening in his cheek. A tattoo creeps out from under his sleeve, the dark shadow visible through the thin white fabric. He's a man's man, macho as I've ever known, but every single night, he puts his princess-loving daughter to bed with a fairytale. And that's a problem for me—because I didn't think I could find him any more irresistible than I already do.

Out front of the restaurant, I sling my purse over my shoulder and offer Andrew my hand, even though we made a fairly embarrassing scene arguing over the bill. "Thank you for dinner."

He eyes me coolly, keeping his hands in his pockets. "No problem. You only had a side salad, after all."

"Thanks for noticing," I say dryly, lowering my hand back to my side. Apparently his fixation with my diet hasn't subsided. "I should get back to work."

Sadie gasps. "I just had the best idea." She opens

her mouth, pauses, and shakes her head. "No. Never mind. Your dad'll never go for it."

Andrew groans, but Bell bounces on the balls of her feet. "What, what, what?"

"Well . . ." Sadie hesitates. "Uncle Nathan and I have started decorating the nursery. I thought maybe Bell would like to come over and help—"

Bell whirls to Andrew. "Can I, Daddy? *Please*?"

He widens his eyes at her. "You *want* to?"

"Yes," she says. "I have ideas. I want to so bad. Please?"

Andrew and I both look at Sadie, and she arches an eyebrow at him. "She wants to. Because you won't let her. See how that works?"

He doesn't look amused. "You're giving me a lesson in parenting?"

"You can pick her up tomorrow," Sadie says, casting me a glance. "Or Sunday, depending on how complicated things get. With the nursery, I mean. Come around lunch, and we'll do a picnic in Prospect Park."

Sadie and Andrew are close, unlike my sister and me. It never really bothered me, but I feel a hint of envy over their relationship. Bell is surrounded by family, and it's about to grow by one more. *My* Sunday afternoon plans? Brunch with a college friend I only keep in touch with because she works in my industry, not because I like her, followed by spending a few hours in the office.

"All right," Andrew says. "But just tonight, not

261

Sunday. Bell has gymnastics tomorrow afternoon."

"Thank you," Bell says, her voice an octave too high, then takes Sadie's hand and pulls. "Come on."

"Whoa," Andrew says. "No goodbye kiss? Since when?"

Bell runs into Andrew's open arms and hugs his neck. "I'll take a picture of the nursery on Aunt Sadie's phone and send it to you."

"Don't forget," he warns.

She kisses his cheek and turns to stare at me. Neither of us speaks. I'm the adult, but it's not like I can just shake her hand with a 'nice to meet you' or 'let's do lunch sometime' so I just look back at her.

"Say goodbye to Amelia," Andrew says to her.

"Bye, 'Mila."

"Ameel-ee-a," Andrew corrects.

"That's what I said. 'Mila."

She continues to stare at me like she did on our way to the restaurant. I can't quite read her expression, and my discomfort is at an all-time high. To my extreme embarrassment, I put out my hand. "Nice to meet you."

"Are you going to kiss my dad?"

I cover my mouth, stunned by the absolute last question I expected. "Excuse me?"

"Jesus, Bell," Andrew says, his words uncharacteristically clipped. "How many times have I told you not to—"

His chastisement is drowned out by Sadie's fit of laughter. "Andrew and Amelia," she sings.

"Kissing in a tree," Bell picks up, her eyes lighting with excitement. "K-i-s-s—"

"For Christ's sake, Sadie," Andrew says. "Don't encourage her."

"Fine, fine. Hey—*avec* is on the way to your train, Andrew," she says. "Maybe you could walk Amelia back."

"That's not necessary," I say.

"But it's on the way," Sadie points out. "What are you going to do, walk a few feet behind him?"

Aha. Sadie knows. Andrew and I no longer need to keep this secret from her. But Bell's presence, while surprisingly welcome, makes me more conscious of Andrew's real life. It makes me awkward. She's a real person now, something I can't ignore.

Sadie smiles, takes Bell's hand, and pulls her away. "We'll get a cab to our station. See you tomorrow, Andrew."

Once we're alone, I look at Andrew. "Did you tell her?"

"No." Andrew crosses his arms. "It was Nathan."

"He knows?"

"He thinks he does, and he definitely said something to her. That's why she invited you."

I twist my lips. "But then why would she leave us alone?"

"Isn't it obvious? To give us time together."

"I doubt it. She wouldn't be that cool about her

263

boss and her brother. Correction—her *man-hating* boss, and her *heartbroken* brother."

He quirks his lips into what's becoming his signature smile. "I'm not heartbroken."

"You aren't?" I ask, turning to face him. "I thought we had a pact."

"Are you heartbroken?"

I am a lot of things where Reggie is concerned—angry, embarrassed, regretful. Do I miss him, though? No. Maybe, sometimes, the idea of him. The husband I thought I would have. "No."

"Are you . . ." He shuffles a step toward me. "Man-hating?"

I let my gaze drift from his galaxy-blue eyes down his slightly stubbly throat to the collar of his t-shirt. "All men, as a unit, yes. Individually, though, exceptions can be made."

"Hate me or love me, fate has put us together again with nowhere to be. What should we do?"

"Maybe *you* have nowhere to be. *I* have to go back to the office." I turn on my heel, but he catches my elbow.

"You're not going to back to the office."

I try unsuccessfully to wriggle out of his grip. With his warm hand on me, and halfway under his spell, I can't remember why I'm not supposed to spend another night with him. I just know it's better that I don't. "Yes. I am."

He pulls me to him so his face hovers over mine. "No . . . you're not."

"I have work to do."

"And I have you to do."

I smirk. "Very cute. But—"

He cuts me off with a kiss so quick, it's over before I realize it's happening. He smiles. "I know what I said about—"

"Don't," I say, taking my arm back. If he tries to renege on our no-strings deal, I definitely won't be able to take him home tonight, and there's a side of me that's fighting for it.

"Don't what?" After a moment, he glances off to the side and then back. "I was going to say . . . I know I made a big thing about the Tahitian vanilla, but I might've changed my mind." He smiles a little. "I haven't been able to stop thinking about it."

If he's trying to tell me something else, I won't hear it. "I was serious about not seeing you again."

"I know you were. That's why I'm here—to change your mind."

I watch his lips as he talks to avoid his mesmerizing eyes, but they're just as hard to resist. Those lips can kiss. They can suck. They can tip me over the edge. I don't want to get even close to the edge, though. It hurts when you fall. "You shouldn't have come."

"I'm aware of that."

He knows this is against the rules. So do I. Yet I'm here, considering another night.

"I kept picturing that gorgeous body of yours," he says. "You know it's beautiful, right? Even if you'd had a piece of bread at dinner, you'd still have a smoking-hot body."

"Why are you bringing that up?" I ask.

"I'm not." He looks me over. "Was dinner okay, though?"

"That restaurant wouldn't be my first choice, but—"

"Not that. Bell."

"Oh." Seeing Andrew in his element, any doubts I might've had about his character, due to his gender, were squashed. It also means I can't ignore the fact that there are other people involved. I look away as I admit, "It was fine. Better than fine. I had a good time."

"I don't know where she's getting that kissing stuff, but it's freaking me out."

I furrow my brows and turn quickly back to him. "Maybe she's confused. About you being a single dad. It's confusing even for me."

He tilts his head. "Is it? Why?"

"You're kind of a rare breed. I can't exactly put my finger on it."

Tentatively, he slips an arm around my waist and tugs me against his body. I let him. "Try," he says.

"You might not like it."

"I don't care."

I've known Andrew as a man, a one-night stand. Now I know him as something else, someone who normally wouldn't appeal to me. "Kids are foreign to me. I'm not really into them. I never thought you being a dad could make you somehow . . ."

Suddenly, I realize I've been tracing the outline of his flower-cluster tattoo through his t-shirt. I stop.

"What does it make me?" he asks.

"Sexier." I sigh and look into his eyes. What's left of my resolve melts. "It makes you sexier."

"Seeing you with Bell was sexy as hell, Amelia."

I widen my eyes, shocked. "But I tried to shake her hand. I'm not *that* kind of woman—I . . . I made a complete *ass* out of myself."

He chuckles. "You did better than you realize. I don't think you can do wrong now that she knows how you feel about *Frozen*."

"Picking a favorite Disney movie is a lot of pressure."

"She loves *Beauty and the Beast*. So how about we go back to your place and I'll play the beast, you be the beauty, some inanimate objects sing, and then we fuck. That's how the fairytale goes, right?"

I smirk, but something pulls deep in my stomach at his bluntness. And from the look on his face, he knows exactly what he's doing to me. "You're not going to let this go, are you?"

"In all seriousness," he says, "I came here tonight determined to see you again. I've been sexually frustrated since I left you. But watching you with Bell . . . that was new for me. And it feels weird."

"Bad weird?"

"No."

I swallow. I don't need to hear any more. It could cut the night short if he says too much, if he asks for more than a hook-up, and now I want tonight to happen. And I don't want it to be short. "Fine," I say. "You win this round."

"I'll make sure we're both winners by the end of the night." He winks. "So, are you taking me to your office to put me to work, or are you taking me home?"

"I'm taking you home," I say, "to put you to work."

NINETEEN

When Andrew and I arrive at my apartment, I drop my keys on the side table and start to take off my blazer.

"Don't," Andrew says behind me. I freeze. "Let me." He takes the lapels and peels the jacket over my shoulders so slowly and deliberately, it makes me think of making love and how different it might be with him. Different from fucking. Different from Reggie. "I like this outfit."

I look over my shoulder. "So do I. Careful with that."

"Yeah?" he asks, tossing it on the ground. He presses his front to my back and undoes the button between my breasts without looking. "It's just clothing."

"No it's not. It's Theory," I say, but my argument dissolves as he works his way down my blouse.

He rids me of that too and drops it on top of the blazer. "If it makes you feel better," he says, "you can rip my shirt off."

"Your ten-dollar Hanes t-shirt?" I ask, smiling a little.

"It's ten dollars for a pack of three."

I laugh, but my humor is replaced with urgency as he gathers up my skirt. "I especially like this," he murmurs in my ear as he pulls it up my hips and cups a hand between my legs. "Easy access."

He rubs me, and I drop my head back against his shoulder. "You don't waste any time, do you?" I ask, already breathless.

"I've been waiting to touch you since you sent that photo," he says. "Next time, lose the bubbles."

"But what fun is that?" I pant as a throbbing ache forms under his fingers.

"You're right." He takes his hand away. "It's more fun to tease."

"All right, all right," I concede. "Next time, no bubbles, swear."

"Good girl." He resumes touching me, leisurely but with purpose. With his other hand, he pops open the hook of my bra. "You're way too easy to undo."

"It's you, not me. You're good at undoing."

He takes my breast in his hand, massaging it at the same pace as my clit. "You've been thinking of me too," he says. "I can tell by the way your body's responding."

"Maybe," I admit.

He stops touching me completely. "Maybe?"

"Yes. Yes, okay? I've been thinking of you."

He hugs me from behind and walks us farther into the apartment. "How about we try to make it to the bed this time?"

"Or the bath."

He nips my earlobe with his teeth. "I'm going to make up for leaving you at that hotel, believe me. I hope you're ready to take a week of pent-up sexual frustration."

Even if he hadn't told me so, I'd have known by the hardness suddenly pressing into my lower back. He's eager. I'm melting. The more under his spell I get, the more I want to give him control, let him have his way with me.

"What do you want tonight, Amelia?" he asks.

"I have some ideas." I extract myself from his grip, turn, and walk backward into my bedroom. He follows, licking his lips. I close my bedroom curtains and pull him to me by the waistband of his jeans. I open the button, unzip his pants, and push them down around his ankles along with his underwear.

He takes himself in his hand, his hard, impressive length leaving no doubt that he's been thinking of this all day.

"You're easy to undo," I say.

"You're good at undoing me."

I cover his hand with mine. Together, we stroke him a few times before he pulls away and it's just my fist around him—warm, solid. "I'm good at a lot of things."

"Like what?" he asks, pulling his shirt over his head, dropping it at our feet.

"My job," I say. "And giving orders. And yoga."

"Yoga," he repeats. "I might need a demonstration."

"First things first." I drop to my knees.

He puts a finger under my chin, raising my eyes. "Look at me when you taste me for the first time."

I test him with my tongue, gliding it under the ridge of his head, watching his strained expression. "Mmm."

"Kiss it."

I do as he says, brushing my lips along his shaft and over the soft, round head until his next command.

"Ruin your lipstick," he says. "I want my dick red with it."

My insides tighten with his unexpected, roughly-spoken demand. I take him in my mouth, but it's not enough. I pull back and smear my lipstick all over his dick, down to his balls.

"Good," he says through gritted teeth before raking a firm hand through my hair. "Now clean it all off."

I salivate, suddenly quivering with this firm, insistent side of him. I obey, flattening my tongue and pulling him deep. I bob my head a few times, then release him with a wet pop. I suck the marks off his shaft until they're completely gone, which is no small feat considering I wear the kind of lipstick meant to last all day. He lifts his cock to his stomach, pumping it in his fist a few times and thrusting his balls against my lips. Hungry for him, I suckle them until his knees practically give out and he has to sit on the bed.

"Touch yourself," he says. I go to put my free hand between my legs, but he says, "Both hands."

I wet two of my fingers with my saliva and push them inside myself. With my other hand, I massage my clit.

"Suck," he says, grit in his voice.

I open instinctively. He guides himself back into my mouth. With my hands occupied, I'm forced to get him off just by bobbing back and forth. I do this with as much gusto as possible, working myself at the same time, until he pulls on my elbow. I raise my arm and suddenly, my fingers are in his hot mouth.

He groans, tonguing my juices off. "Your mouth, your pussy—how do you always taste so fucking good?"

The sensation of sucking and getting sucked makes my thighs shake. I just want to come, and he must be able to sense it, because he pulls my head back by my hair and says, "Your turn."

Gasping for air, I only have a second to gape up at him before he squats, takes me by my waist, and lifts me up like I weigh nothing. I involuntarily yelp as he throws me over his shoulder. "Andrew—"

He slaps my ass, stunning me into silence, then yanks my thong down and my skirt up. As I dangle over his back, he holds my legs in place with one arm and thrusts his fingers inside me.

"Oh, *God*," I moan as he fucks me hard.

He bites my ass cheek, and I squeal. I have nothing to hang on to, so I wrap my arms around him, wanting to return the favor, but he's too tall and I can't reach.

Maybe it's the angle or the shock or the blood rushing to my head, but in no time at all, I'm coming. Upside down. In his complete and utter control.

"Fuck," he says. "You are *ripe* for the picking tonight." He walks us around the bed to the nightstand. "No more foreplay. I'll fuck you now, and we can resume later." His fingers disappear from between my legs as I hear the drawer open.

Since we walked through the door, he's had me at his mercy. And to my surprise, I love it. It's getting me off. I didn't think I'd ever like to be dominated so completely, and it makes me wonder about the other barriers Andrew might be able to break down. "Andrew?" I ask.

"Hmm?" he asks, rifling through the nightstand.

"You asked what I want tonight." I have to get the words out quickly, before I lose my nerve. My heart pounds in every part of my body, and not just because I'm upside down.

"Yeah? You finally going to let me tie you up?"

A mix of fear and excitement thrill up my spine. "No," I say. "Better."

"What then?"

"Look in the back of the drawer."

After more rustling, he pauses. "Fuck. Seriously?"

He lowers me onto the mattress. He's almost intimidating in his height and broadness, with his cock hard and reaching. He looks down at me on my back, holding the bottle of lube from my nightstand and a small, silver plug shaped like the smooth bud of a rose.

"Where'd you get this?" he asks.

"Reggie brought it home after a night out drinking."

"All right then," he says, sounding disappointed. "My fault for asking."

"We never used it," I say. "I mean, obviously he tried, more than once. I wouldn't."

He lets his gaze travel down my body. "But you'd let me?"

I admire him too, the tattoos I'm coming to know better, the fine dark hair on his thighs and calves. His strength is evident. He could hurt me, but he won't. I'm willing to have him in this intimate place. Maybe it's a fuck-you to my ex, but I want Andrew to have something nobody else ever has. And above all, most importantly, I've been curious about anal since Andrew fingered me in the hotel room—and I *enjoyed* it.

Our eyes meet at the same time. "I would love to," he says. "But not if you have to think that hard about it."

If I had any doubts, his concern is enough to cut through them. "I want to. I didn't, with him, but you—you're different."

"Smart," he says simply. "You knew, on some level, you couldn't trust him."

"But why do I trust you? I barely know you. We aren't even—" I look away. It occurs to me he might see this as a step in the wrong direction, an intimacy that goes beyond what we agreed to. "It doesn't mean I—"

"What if it does mean something, Amelia?" I turn back to him. "You do know me. We've been honest with each other from day one. That's why you're comfortable doing this. You know where I stand. I know where you stand. There's no secrets between us."

Andrew would hurt me now to save me later. Maybe that's why I trust him. I'd do the same for him. I get up onto my elbows and crook my ankles around the backs of his thighs to pull him to the edge of the bed. "Get rid of the condom."

He arches an eyebrow at me. "You sure?"

"I want to feel you. Are you clean?"

He nods. "I haven't gone without a condom since Shana, and I was tested after she left. Just to be sure."

"Same with me and Reggie."

With a grin, he tosses the wrapper over his shoulder and pulls my skirt down my hips, discarding it on the ground. I retreat on the mattress as he crawls toward me. "I told you I was an ass man."

"I'm not sure if I'm an ass girl."

"You will be when I'm done with you." When he's above me, he lowers his mouth, ghosting it over mine. "Then we'll be a match made in heaven."

"I don't know about that," I tease, then raise my lips to his.

He cups the back of my head and eases his weight on me. Leisurely, I slide my tongue over his, deepening the kiss. He curls his fingers into my hair and groans, grinding his hips against me. "I'm going to make you feel so good. Flip over, babe."

He lifts up to give me room, his bicep muscles bulging. When I'm on my stomach, he sits on the backs of my thighs, straddling me.

I hear the cap of the lube pop open. My insides clench before he even touches me. Since I can't see, I'm forced to fill in the blanks as I listen to him squirt lube into his palms, the gooey sounds as he rubs his hands together.

"Your ass was one of the first things I noticed about you," he says, spreading my cheeks apart with sticky fingers.

"It's the first place I—" I suck in a breath as he slides his fingers up my crack, "—first place I gain weight."

"Thank God," he says through a chuckle. He grabs both my cheeks, kneading them. "Otherwise I might've missed you."

I'm more turned on than self-conscious, so I push back against his hands. "Patience," he says. I hear the grin in his voice. "I can't exactly dive in."

I search for a witty comeback but lose my train of thought as he starts to explore. He teases my clit with his thumb as he presses one finger into my anus. "If at any point I'm going too fast—"

"I'll tell you," I promise.

He works it in to the knuckle. Since we've done this before, and he's nice and slick, it doesn't take long before he's adding a second finger. I breathe evenly against the bedspread. My hairline prickles, my body warming with each stroke.

"Good?" he asks.

I answer by gyrating up into his hand.

He stills me. "Not yet. Give me control of your orgasm. I promise it'll be worth it."

I try to swallow, but my throat is suddenly dry. I relax back into the mattress. It takes all my concentration not to hump the bed. Without warning, he slides his thumb in my pussy and before I know it, he's thrusting three slippery fingers in and out of my asshole.

"Jesus," he mutters. "You should see yourself. You're making me hard as a rock."

Flooded with sensations as his fingers work me from both ends, I plead, "Then fuck me. I'm ready."

He stops massaging, stops searching, and a second later, cool metal slides along the back of my thigh. Will it hurt? Would I mind if it did? He pulls one cheek aside, draws his fingers out, and replaces them with the tip of the plug. He doesn't linger, but starts working it in, slowly, but without hesitation. He spreads and stretches me. It's an uncomfortable feeling, but not enough to ask him to stop. "Is it in?" I ask.

"You'll know."

He's right. After a few more pushes, an acute pinch takes my breath away, and then there's a pull within my body as it accepts the plug. I gasp as my muscles contract around it.

"There," he murmurs. "Still good?"

I inhale deeply, adjusting to the feeling and the knowledge of getting plumbed by an alien object. He doesn't give me a chance to think too hard about it. Rising, he guides me up with him until I'm on all fours. I'm about to ask what he's doing when there's a familiar pressure between my legs.

"Relax," he says—I've tensed up. "I'll do all the work. I'm going to make you feel so good, baby. You'll come apart at the seams."

"And you?" I ask, taunting him.

"Don't worry. I'll get mine too." He tugs me back onto him by my hips, filling me gradually, absolutely. I'm fuller than I've ever been, unnervingly so, but as he withdraws and slides back in, pleasure overtakes everything else. "*Fuck*," he says.

"What?" I ask, alarmed by the intensity in his voice.

"I can feel the goddamn plug," he says. "It's bulging right against my shaft. I'm trying not to come like a fucking teenager."

I'm distracted by the roundness inside me and the sharp awareness that Andrew's controlling both of my holes right now. I drop my head between my arms, but he pulls it back up by my hair and his control begins to slip. Skin on skin, the both of us covered in lube, he gets faster, slicker, relentless, until he's slamming into me, and my entire body is shaking with the need for release.

"Normally, I'd make you wait for your climax," he says, panting. "But the more relaxed you are when I fuck your ass, the better."

He takes me right to the edge with his unyielding thrusts and then shoves me over so I'm climaxing mercilessly. At one point, I can't even hold myself up anymore, and I fall onto the mattress, spent.

"Good girl," he murmurs, slowing down. "I didn't even have to put you into position." Still hard as a rock, he slides out of me while working the plug free. I writhe underneath him with the strangeness of being deflated, emptied after I was so full. He squeezes more lube between my cheeks. "Feels so goddamn amazing to be back inside you," he says. "I'm barely keeping it together. Don't worry, I won't last long."

Because I'm so turned on, my instinct is to tell him it's okay if he lasts until the sun rises and sets again, as long as I can come a third, fourth, fifth time—but what if I'm not able to handle it more than a few seconds? What if I can't reach another climax because it hurts? For a split second, unable to see his face, I'm terrified he'll be so far gone, he won't be able stop.

"You must be nervous," he says. "I've never heard you this quiet."

As soon as I hear his voice, my panic subsides. This is Andrew. He hasn't given me any reason not to trust him. If he had, I wouldn't be here at his mercy. "I'm ready," I say.

"I've got you," he says, somehow knowing what I need to hear. "Remember, if it's too much . . ."

"I'll stop you."

He massages my anus, inserting a couple fingers again, loosening me up even more. Even though I want to stay where I am, spent and wobbly, he positions me back onto all fours. By the time he's pressed up against me and pushing inside, my face burns hot. This feels wrong—forbidden but also physically wrong. A cock like his is too big for such a small hole. It sends a thrill down my spine that I'm doing something new with *him*, something so wicked, so outside my comfort zone. Andrew pulls me apart, probing me—huge, foreign, determined. He enters me so slowly, it must take every ounce of his restraint as he slides out a little and back in, slightly deeper than before, breaking through my barriers.

He skates his hand up my back and grips my shoulder, firm but comforting. "Inhale."

I do what he says, as if I'd forgotten something so basic. Maybe I had.

"Now exhale," he instructs.

I blow out a long breath, and it moves through my entire body.

"And repeat. Just like that," he says. "Like when you do yoga."

"Yoga?" I can't help snickering, and after a second, he laughs with me, deep and reassuring. I relax around him, and he slips deeper, causing me to gasp.

"Tell me when you want it," he says with a few short, shallow thrusts.

If his plan is to go so slow that I get more impatient than afraid, it's working. "I want it."

"No," he says, massaging the base of my neck. "Tell me when you really fucking want it. When you need it."

I nod, and remind myself to unclench. His words alone loosen anything I've been holding on to. With a control I can feel in his every movement, he works me open. Soon, I'm taking him all the way, morphing from anticipating each intrusion to craving it. My body accepts more and more of him. After two orgasms already, I should be sated, but they seem to have made me more feverish. I hunger for another one like I've been on the verge of it for months. I want to know how good it can be to let him loose.

"Now," I beg. "I can't wait anymore. Make me come."

He doesn't question me, just pulls out almost all the way and adds more lube. He grabs my hips in both hands and eases in, slow but firm, all the way to the hilt. The pinch of pain from taking him all at once provokes a guttural noise from the back of my throat.

In response, he reaches around to play with my clit. "Help me make you feel good, babe," he says. "Stay steady."

I move down onto my forearms to brace myself, keeping my lower half propped up for him. He moves faster. If he was taking my ass before, now he claims it, fingering my pussy at the same time, spreading my wetness around my clit, dividing my attention. My body shudders, overwhelmed, sucking his fingers deeper while both fighting against and accepting his cock.

I pinpoint the exact moment he lets go—he begins to slip and slide out of me, sloppy, no longer self-possessed as he digs his fingers bruisingly into one hip. His hand between my legs gets frantic, searching, vibrating, plunging. Just sensing his control fall away makes me crazy. I push back, and his answering groan is strong and primal, not only filling my ears but rattling my body.

"That's it," Andrew grunts, fucking me through the first wave of my orgasm. "Come on, Amelia."

I dissolve into it, breaking piece by piece, with no choice but to submit to the intensity of my climax. As I finish, Andrew closes his front over my back, pushing even deeper into me as he breathes hotly into my hair. He doesn't last long in that position and within seconds, he rips at the comforter with two desperate fists and explodes inside me.

He's out of breath, muttering inaudibly into my ear over and over. My back, damp with sweat, sticks to his chest. He drops his forehead to my shoulder and with a few wet kisses on my sensitive skin, I shudder.

"You loved every second of that," he says.

"It wasn't what I expected," I admit.

"But it was good?" he asks.

I sense a hint of doubt in his voice. I want to reassure him with a look, but we're in no position to see each other's faces. "Incredible," I say. It feels weird to be grateful to him, but I am. He doesn't know, couldn't know, how far I've come in the last two weeks thanks to him. I thought sex had to come with strings. The last few times I did it before Andrew, it was a weapon, not pleasure. "Thank you."

"For what?" he asks. "I should be thanking you."

"Thanks for, you know, being present. And conscious of what you were doing." It hurts me to say. I never thought I'd be the kind of woman who allowed a man to break her, but I was on the verge of that a year ago. "Thank you for thinking of me first."

"You're always first," he says as if it's fact. "That's how it should be when you let someone into your bed."

I'm suddenly painfully aware that he's about a thousand pounds of pure muscle on top of me—and that he's still inside me. "We should clean up," I say, shifting to get free, "and if you think about it, there's really only one sensible way to do that."

"You don't mean . . .?"

"I think I have just enough Tahitian crème left to make it a good one."

"Mmm," he responds. "Well, if taking a bubble bath is the only sensible thing to do, then I guess it would be foolish not to."

TWENTY

Andrew rests as I head into my bathroom, working the aches out my arms and legs. Once I've cleaned myself up and started the tub faucet, I catch a glimpse of my reflection. I'm red in the face, as if I've just done sprints, and my hair is tangled and damp around my neck. I look owned, as I wanted to be, and I know Andrew likes that, so I resist the urge to fix myself up.

I pass through the bedroom, where Andrew lies on the bed with his eyes shut, to the kitchen. I pour two drinks before dropping them off in the bathroom.

Andrew's clearly passed out, but he knows the rule about sleepovers, so I don't feel bad waking him. "Your bath is ready, sir."

His answering sigh turns into a soft laugh, but his eyes remain shut. "I wasn't sleeping."

"Sure you weren't." I smile, return to the bathroom, and shut off the faucet.

"Or maybe I was," he says as he comes in, scratching his hair, mussing it in every direction. "Was it a dream?" he asks. "Or was it really that fucking good?"

Something about seeing all of him in the dim lighting, his tall, broad-shouldered frame and colorful torso, makes me warm and fuzzy inside. I put my arms around his middle. "The second one."

He takes a second to hug me back, an almost imperceptible hesitation. "I hoped I'd end up here tonight," he says, rubbing my back. "I'm glad I did."

I smile up at him. "So am I."

He isn't smiling. "How glad?"

I loosen my arms enough to pull back. It's likely my sudden affection has caught him off guard. Me too, a little. It's hard not to feel closer to him after what we just did—and after spending an evening with his family. That doesn't have to mean more than it does. It isn't an invitation to stay the night or anything. I drop my eyes to his chest. "I'm not sure."

"Amelia." He waits until I look up again. "It's okay. I want you to be honest."

Honesty. It's what we do. It's the main reason we've made it this far. "Tonight was different," I admit. "We might've broken through a few walls without meaning to."

He nods. "I think so."

"It'll make things harder when we part," I continue. "Maybe I'm okay with that, though."

He raises both eyebrows. "You are?"

The alternative is that tonight didn't happen, and I wouldn't take it back, so the only option is to be okay with it. "Yes. I mean, it wouldn't be a good idea to keep going down this path, but—"

"Why not?"

I tilt my head at him. "Because I won't always be okay with it the next day. We're already having a nice time tonight, so we might as well just . . . keep doing that. We can't really go backward, can we?"

He studies me, expressionless. I have no idea if I've completely scared him off or if he understands what I'm saying.

I keep talking. "We've crossed into different territory. Anything after this would be a conscious choice. I mean there's family to think about, and work . . ." I'm drowning, and he's not making any move to jump overboard with me. With a sigh, I say, "I'll understand if you want to leave now."

To his credit, he doesn't look longingly at the bathtub. I know how badly he wants to get in. Enough to get him to stay? "Do you want me to?" he asks. "Leave?"

I run the back of my hand over my hairline. Our intense sex plus the steam from the bath is making me a bit too warm. "No. Not yet."

The lines between his eyebrows ease as he nods. "Good. I'm not ready to go. You look hot."

My cheeks heat, a feat considering I'm already sweating. "Thanks."

"No, I mean you look *hot*." He goes to the bathroom counter and opens the top drawer. "As in, warm. Do you have a hairband or something?"

"Um . . ."

He finds a clip, stands in front of me, and rakes his hands through my hair. He gathers it behind my head, then twists it up to secure it. "Better?" he asks. "And you do look hot, as in sexy, as well."

I try unsuccessfully to hold in my smile. How can a man of his stature and beauty ever be described as cute? But that's what he is right now.

Like before, he gets in the tub and pulls me down between his legs, but this time he washes me, dipping my loofah in the water and running it over my back.

"If we were dating," he says, "I get the feeling we'd be a very clean couple."

I smile and hug my knees. "It's nice, though. A bath kind of forces you to slow down. It's not like either of us gets a lot of free time."

"I'm not complaining." He soaps my arms and the back of my neck. "I've been thinking about what you said the other night. About work."

"What did I say?" I ask, only partly focused as I enjoy the scrape of the sponge and the goose bumps it inspires.

"That it's a bullshit industry."

"Did I?" I close my eyes and sigh. "I was upset. I don't really feel that way."

"What about those things you said to Bell earlier?"

"They're true. Confidence is the main ingredient for beauty. But I make a living convincing people there's more to beauty than that, and so do thousands of other people in this city alone."

"Right. Have you ever considered doing anything else?"

"No. Why would I? It's demanding, but that's what I want."

"What if you cut back?"

"For what?"

That shuts both of us up. I don't blame him for falling quiet. I never used to think hard work and success could paint such a sad, lonely picture. My life is exactly how I designed it. I get to do what I dreamed of as a girl—what many girls would consider a dream job. Fashion, celebrities, parties in New York City. Yet lately, something about the work is missing. It feels less like a dream and more like a job.

"What was it like?" Andrew asks. "When he cheated?"

I look over my shoulder at him. The question, though out of nowhere, doesn't feel abrupt. In fact, considering the conversation that led him there, it hits a little close to a nerve. Would Reggie have cheated if I'd been a different kind of wife? Like the daily-luncheon, charity-heading arm candy of his colleagues? "Do you have to ask? Surely you've been cheated on."

"Why do you assume that?"

"Almost everyone I know has. Most, if not all of my friends."

"Not me. Shana was the only person who's been close enough to hurt me. She didn't cheat, though."

I turn, if only to hide the surprise in my expression. I can't remember if he'd told me that before because the truth is, I wouldn't have believed him. I'm not even sure I do now. Maybe Shana did cheat, and he just doesn't know it.

I lean forward and take our drinks from the counter, passing his back. I've talked about Reggie a lot with my girlfriends. We bond over bashing our exes. This is different, though. I'm naked with a man I've let get a little closer than I meant to. My past is not an easy place for me to go even when I'm dressed and sitting in my therapist's mild, eggshell-colored office.

After a courage-bolstering sip of whisky, I say, "It's kind of like slaving over a lobster dinner for someone you love, and when they get home, they tell you they don't eat crustaceans. While you watch, they dump everything in a blender and hit *shred*. Only, that crustacean is your heart."

"I see," he says.

"And then they don't even drink it. They pour it down the drain. And turn on the garbage disposal, just in case there's anything they missed."

He chuckles softly, which, despite my macabre disposition, makes me smile. "I think I get the idea, though your cooking analogies could use some work. Who was the woman?"

"The wife of one of the stockbroker's in his office. I remember when I found them, my throat just closed. It was like choking. I really thought I'd die on the spot."

"You *found* them?" he asks.

I put my cheek on my knee and look into the bedroom. "I didn't mention that?"

"Definitely not." He must follow my gaze, because he then says, "*There*? In your bed?"

"I had an appointment near here, and I decided to come home for lunch. It was that stupid." The worst part is not anticipating something like that, being caught completely off guard. At least if I'd seen a trail of clothing on the way to the bedroom or even heard them, but no. I'd just walked right in to get a sweater from my closet and nearly tripped right onto the bed with them. "He was never very creative."

Andrew puts his hands on my shoulders and squeezes once. The simple gesture is more soothing than he probably knows. "Isn't it hard to sleep there?"

I shrug. "It's just a bed. I'm not going to go through the trouble of replacing it. I got rid of the sheets, of course."

He snorts. "Then you're stronger than I am."

"Am I?"

"Emotionally, yes. But physically?" He leans forward as he pulls me back toward him to speak in my ear. "I'd love the opportunity to kick . . . his . . . ass."

His warm breath tickles in just the right way. "So would I."

"I'm not kidding."

I turn back as much as I can. "Is that so?"

He tucks some loose strands behind my ear. "I'm not a boy who goes to some fancy office during the day and thinks it's okay to dick my woman around. I'm a man, Amelia. I treat women like treasure. I treat my girlfriend like the love of my fucking life. And I treat an asshole like an asshole."

The intensity in his voice raises every hair on my body. I can't resist picturing it. Andrew and Reggie face to face would be terrifying in real life, but maybe, in my fantasy, it can be a little thrilling too. "How does an asshole get treated?"

"If he ever comes around while I'm here, he'll leave knowing it's his last visit."

It feels like the only thing I've ever wanted to hear, but my self-doubt is never far, and I know once Andrew leaves, *he* won't come back. He won't be around the next time Reggie shows up. "You're sweet."

"I just threatened to kick some ass, and I'm sweet?" I hear the smile in his voice. "Are you *trying* to shred my ego?"

I don't believe Andrew is all talk—I think he really believes he'd do it. He seems to have temporarily forgotten about Bell, though. Devoted dads don't go around taking risks like that. "What about Shana?" I ask. "Am I now expected to say I'll make her pay too?"

He grunts good-naturedly. "Nah."

He doesn't offer anything else. It occurs to me I don't know much about Shana, at least not the specifics. Is it that I haven't asked? Or that he hasn't offered? "How long has it been since she left?"

"Almost four years. Right around Bell's third birthday."

"That must've been awful."

"Well. You know."

I shift, and the tub squeaks. Andrew has no problem pressing me for information on Reggie, but he doesn't seem as keen to share himself. I've given him a lot tonight, though. "What was it like? When she left? What about Bell?"

"Come here." I lean back against his chest, and he puts his arms around me. "It was pretty much how you'd imagine. I was clueless. Sadie helped as best she could from an hour away."

"What about your parents?"

"They're closer, about fifteen minutes from here. But they're not that involved."

"By choice?"

"It's mutual. I mean, not so much for my mom. She wants to see Bell more. I just hated growing up there, and I don't really want Bell to get too close to them."

"Why not?"

He shrugs under me. "They'll just disappoint her."

"Isn't that what parents do?" I ask. When he doesn't answer, I realize my mistake. "Not all parents, obviously. Not you."

"It'll be a while before we know, won't it?"

I furrow my brows. "No," I say. "There's no question. Bell is so fortunate to have you as a dad."

"I do my best." He clears his throat. "How'd your parents disappoint you?"

I run my hand over his arm, admiring the fine dark hair. "It's the other way around. I didn't go to business school. I'll be divorced at thirty-two. I barely talk to them or my niece and nephew because I'm so swamped with work. It's not exactly the conservative Texan way my sister went."

"You're from the South?"

"Yep. I think they hoped I'd move home at some point and marry a nice, upstanding lawyer, doctor or banker . . . like Reggie, actually."

"Don't tell me they were fans of his."

"My mom loved him before she'd even met him. I should've known then it was doomed. When I told her I was leaving him, she nearly had a heart attack."

"Because he cheated on you?"

"Lord, no," I say. "That's not an excuse to leave. It's an 'opportunity.' She thinks I should identify how I've neglected my husband and step up as a wife."

"Fuck that," he says.

"Yeah. Exactly. Fuck that." I follow it up with a sip of Glenlivet. The words taste just as good as the whisky. "She would hate you."

He laughs. "Blue collar mechanic from New Jersey with an illegitimate child, a motorcycle, and tattoos? Can't imagine why."

"That's not what I see."

"No?" he asks, nuzzling my cheek. "What do you see?"

I pause. "A loving father who takes control of his life. An artist."

"I'm an artist?"

"I think you are." He is, at least, a work of art, his inky black hair, his skin a parade of vivid imagery, his muscles as sculpted and perfected as a masterpiece. I may have called him a mechanic our first night together, but his garage is clearly important to him, and if he treats cars like anything else he loves, I'd bet he brings a certain artistry to his craft.

"What about your dad?" he asks.

"My dad doesn't care for Reggie. Thinks he's slimy."

Andrew sighs deeply. "Dad knows best, young lady. You should *always* listen to your father."

I smile. "He didn't tell me until after Reggie and I were done. I guess my mom made him bite his tongue. He's not without his disappointment, though. Education is his thing. I was supposed to go into business."

"You *are* in business."

I put on my best dad voice. "'Fashion is frivolous' is what he always says. At least I went to college, so I haven't totally let him down."

"NYU?"

"Parsons, majoring in fashion marketing. I took a PR internship knowing I wanted to start my own firm as soon as I had the experience under my belt."

"I always knew I wanted to do my own thing too. I'm not cut out for the corporate world."

"How'd you end up with a garage?"

"My grandpa was huge into cars. My dad is a bum, but not his dad. He worked for a guy who owned a garage, and they taught me everything they knew."

"Does your grandpa help out with Bell?"

"Never met her, sadly. He died young from a heart attack, but I kept going to the garage. I skipped college to work and save money. When Gramp's friend was ready to sell the garage, I had enough to make a serious offer."

I knew Andrew was smart, but I didn't realize how ambitious he was. I never stopped to ask how he ended up with his own business. I can picture him picking up extra hours while his friends wasted time at college. "I have to admit," I say, "I find that pretty sexy."

"A high school-educated mechanic does it for you?"

"You're doing better than a lot of people."

"I can't disagree there. Love my job, and I get to spend every day with Bell. It's a good life."

I glance at our tangled legs through the melting bubbles. Dark versus light. I wonder, since Andrew has worked so hard to make the life he wants on his own, if it were even possible for someone to come in and make it any better. That isn't any way for me to think. I bend my knees and extract myself from his grip.

"Where are you going?"

"Nowhere. I have a surprise. Close your eyes."

"What could you possibly give me to make this night any better?" he asks, but when I look back at him, his eyes are shut.

I stand to reach a drawer with a box of cigars my dad left behind during his last visit. I cut one with a guillotine, light it, and put an ashtray on the edge.

"What the hell are you doing?" he asks. "Was that a lighter? Should I be worried?"

When I get back in the water, I sit opposite him and nudge his calf with my foot. "Here."

He opens his eyes and takes the Cuban I'm holding between us. "Seriously?" he asks, rolling it between his fingers. "You're the fucking best." I smile proudly as he smells and then puffs on it several times. "Sure you want to waste this on me?" he asks, blowing a cloud of white, silky smoke between us.

"Can you think of a better situation for one?"

"Better than a post-fuck bubble bath? I don't know if one exists." He grins. "Why're you all the way over there?"

"I don't need you accidentally lighting my hair on fire."

With his free hand, he lifts my ankle to his mouth and kisses the inside. "It's nice to be taken care of for once."

"Don't get used to it," I tease. "I suck at putting others first."

"Are you crazy?" he asks, pulling a face. "I haven't felt this relaxed in a long time. Why would you think that?"

"I don't cook. I hire someone else to clean. The fridge is never stocked with your—" I pause before 'favorite foods' comes out. I'm airing Reggie's grievances, things my therapist and I have supposedly worked through.

"That's your ex talking."

I shake my head. "It's all true, though." I look him in the eye to drive home the point that we're better off apart. "I don't do those things. I'm not a homemaker or a housewife. After I found out about the affair, Reggie and I had a few huge fights. It was one of the things he always brought up. I didn't take care of him the way he needed."

"Forcing yourself into your husband's box is not how you take care of him." He leans forward, resting his elbows on both sides of the tub. "You want to know how to take care of a man?"

I bite my bottom lip at the intensity in his eyes. Whatever he needs, he's going to tell it to me straight. "Okay."

"What you just gave me in there," he points to the bedroom then gestures over the bath, bumping a little ash into the bubbles, "and now this? I feel like a king."

I look over at the bed, and for a moment, I'm embarrassed. I'm not sure what I expected him to say, maybe something more profound or romantic. "Sex," I say. "That's all it takes with you men, isn't it?"

"No," he says. "I'm talking about something deeper. You didn't withhold."

I don't really register whatever excuse he just spit out. Sex isn't enough to sustain a couple. Eventually, it becomes a chore. Not every time, but enough. Of course that's what Andrew needs from me. Not that I should be surprised—what else have I given him?

"Hey," he says, calling me back to the moment. "Where are you?"

"I'm here," I say, drawing my knees to my chest. "We should dry off. The water's getting cold."

"Oh, no you don't," he says, nabbing my ankle again. "What's wrong?"

"Nothing."

"Not nothing. Something. I can tell."

I sigh. "Really, Andrew. I'm not your girlfriend. You don't have to do all this with me."

"Tell me what upset you."

"For Christ's sake, I'm not upset. But when you tell me sex is all a man needs to be happy, it doesn't sit well. I'm still trying to work through my issues with Reggie, so I don't really think it's healthy to—"

"Whoa," he says. "Back up. I didn't say that's what I need to be happy. I'm talking about how you trusted me in the bedroom. The other night, in the hotel, when you let me blindfold you? You took care of me by letting me take care of you."

I shake my head and wave my palms. "Fine. I don't know. You're right—let's drop it."

"God damn, he did a number on you, didn't he? What are these issues you mentioned?"

"None, nothing, not a one." I try to pull my leg back, but he won't release it.

"If it has to do with sex, I need to know," he says, and I don't think I've ever heard him so determined. He's bordering on angry. "You let yourself be vulnerable with me—that's a lot of responsibility on my shoulders."

"Okay, it won't happen again. Promise. Now, can we please—"

"Amelia." He levels me with a look. "What is it? He made you feel bad about your body? Is that why you have issues with your diet?"

"It's more . . . complicated than that. And you and I? We don't do complicated, Andrew."

"I'm willing to try. I wish you would too."

I sigh, looking from side to side, trying to figure a way—physically and conversationally—out of this. In the end, though, he's right. Andrew is in dangerous territory, and he doesn't know it and that's not fair to him. "When you and Shana were together," I start, "and one of you didn't want to have sex—say, maybe, she was tired from being up all night with Bell—how did you handle it?"

He looks over my face. "I don't understand the question."

"How did you handle it if you wanted sex and Shana didn't?"

He's quiet for a few seconds, probably trying to put himself in that position again. Great. I'm trudging up painful memories for both of us. "I still don't understand," he says. "If she didn't want it, I guess I turned over and fell asleep. Or went to watch TV. Or I went and jerked it in the shower. What are the other options?" His face falls. "I already told you, I never cheated on her. Are you saying Reggie would leave and find it somewhere else?"

"No." I shift against the back of the tub. Even though the water is cooling down, it seems to be getting warmer. "I mean, eventually he did with Virginia. But a few months before the affair started, we were growing apart. We both worked a lot. I think Reggie felt me slipping away and got more controlling."

"How?"

"When he wanted sex, he didn't handle it like . . . a normal person. He would push and push. He'd try to coax or guilt me into it, saying if he'd wanted someone to tell him no, he wouldn't have bothered getting himself a wife. Basically insinuating that I owed him."

"You *owed* him?" Andrew asks, shaking his head in disbelief. "That's utterly ridiculous."

"That was when he was sober. When he'd been drinking, he'd call me names, he . . ." These are only things I've told my therapist, and hard as it was, hell if it wasn't a lot easier than laying it out for my new, naked lover who, so far, is too shiny and perfect to hear this kind of thing.

"Keep going," Andrew says, "otherwise I'll be forced to fill in the blanks and that won't be good."

Part of me wants to include Andrew. As great as Dianne has been at coaching me to get past Reggie's sexual harassment and emotional abuse, I've felt alone a lot of the time, and Andrew—he asks questions. He *wants* to know. I take a deep breath. "He'd accuse me of getting it somewhere else and call me a whore. Or on the flip side, I was 'too lazy to even lie there and spread my legs.' He'd follow me around the apartment, insisting, calling me names. A few times he blacked out and cornered me," I swallow, glancing around the bathroom, "once in here."

Andrew's eyebrows are in the middle of his forehead. All his angles, his jaw, his nose, his shoulders, seem sharper, more alert. "What would he do?" he asks.

"It wasn't often. He made me touch him until he got hard. A couple times he pinned me to the bed until I gave in. I'd just do it to make him stop."

"Jesus," he says. "That's force."

"No," I say. "I mean, yes, my therapist has said the same, but we were married—"

"So? No wonder you don't like to be restrained."

I ball my fingers into a fist. Having a hand around my wrist is the simplest way to make me feel helpless. "Actually, I've never liked it. This obviously didn't help, but I've refused it with partners I had before him too."

"And Reggie knew that?"

"Yes."

He shakes his head. "Have you confronted him about this?"

"No. I'm still working on it with Dianne, and I'm not ready to go there with him. Not sure if I'll ever be."

Andrew lets go of my ankle so fast, it's almost like I've burned him. "Jesus Christ, Amelia. Why didn't you tell me all this before? I wouldn't have been so overbearing, so dominant. At the hotel. Just now, in your bed."

"No. You've helped me without even realizing it," I say, shaking my head. "You have no idea how great you've been."

He stubs out the cigar harder than necessary. "I'll kill him. I'll really kill him."

"I didn't tell you this to make you angry," I say. Without thinking, I reach out and take his hand, trying to call him back to me. "I want you to understand. Why I sometimes freak out. Why I'm so grateful to you for respecting me."

"You shouldn't have to be grateful for—for—" He swallows, puts his other hand around mine and brings it to his mouth, kissing my knuckles. He looks up at me but doesn't speak, just stares, his expression hard. After a few seconds, he presses his forehead to our hands, as if in prayer. "I'm so mad."

Seeing his struggle makes my throat thick. "I shouldn't have told you."

"No. I mean yes, of course you should have. I'm not mad at you; I'm mad at the situation. At him." He says *him* like the word itself has wronged him.

"I'm not a victim," I tell him. "I got out. I'm stronger than him, believe me."

"How did this . . . why did you marry him?"

"He didn't act that way most of our relationship. When *avec* started doing well and I could stand on my own, it drove a wedge between us. That's when the name-calling started. After he met Virginia, he wanted sex with me less, but when he did and I didn't, he took it as an insult."

"You never thought about leaving him?"

"I still loved him. I couldn't see the big picture. He'd been manipulating me in my business dealings and personal choices for a while without me realizing it, so it almost happened like a shift." I take my hand back. "When I started therapy after the split, my doctor listened to it all, and she's been helping me understand how wrong his behavior was."

"But you're so strong," he says. "So independent. It doesn't make sense."

"I'm still human. I fell in love." I pause as we stare at each other. "Stupid, I know."

He looks me in the eye. "Not stupid."

"No? Maybe not the first time. But I know better now."

"So do I."

I smile timidly at him. "That's why we're such a good pair."

"Yes, that's why," he says. "Not because of amazing sex. Or our unintentionally intimate conversations. Not the fact that I care about you."

He's gone and done the exact opposite of what he promised, and yet, when he says it, I know I feel the same. I care. He lets the comment hang. Either he's wishing he hadn't said it, or he's letting me adjust to it. I shudder with a mix of excitement and fear.

He misreads my reaction for cold and stands to swipe a towel off the rack. "Come on," he says, holding a hand out for me.

I take it, letting him help me up. He wraps the towel around my shoulders and rubs them, warming me up. "I mean it," he says. "I care about you. Since we started this, I've wanted you to be happy, but now—now, I want you to be safe, and that comes from a different place."

I may be able to open up, but telling him how I feel doesn't come quite as easily. I wipe the leftover bubbles off his chest like steam from a mirror to reveal the tattoos underneath. They're such an important part of him, like a hidden appendage, but until now, to me they've just been ink on skin.

"What do they mean?" I ask.

He looks down at me, as if debating what to share and what to keep private. He takes my wrist and pulls my hand away from his chest.

My heart drops. After everything we've just gone through, it feels unfair to be shut out.

But he replaces my hand on his left shoulder, over the first tattoo I noticed, a cluster of rich, purple-blue flowers. They droop lazily onto his upper pec. "Bluebells," he says. "For Bell. I got them when she was a baby. Shana's favorite flower."

They resemble upside down bells, sagging but vibrant, small individually and striking as a bunch. "They're pretty," I say, "and also a bit sad."

He nods. "That was Shana." He moves my hand down his pec to a skull and crossbones, only the bones are a wrench and a hammer crossed in an "X". "I drew this in memory of my grandpa, a fix-it guy with a special love for cars. He lived clean for most of his life. He's my role model, unlike my dad. My dad," he slides my hand under his arm, over his ribcage, to a script of words I can't see well enough to read, "is a drunk and a gambler. This says '*the things I cannot change*'."

"That's from the Serenity Prayer," I say, glancing at his half-finished whisky. "Are you an . . . alcoholic?"

"No, but I could've been. My grandpa was. He cleaned himself up when my grandma got pregnant. My dad didn't, though. When I was a teen, my dad drank and picked fights with me. I'd leave the house and meet up with friends to get wasted. But Sadie was always in the back of my mind. I knew, no matter how obliterated I wanted to get, I had to come home for my little sister. I didn't want to leave her there alone, and she worried about me."

"She kept you from going over the edge." I glance at the flowers again. "Like Bell."

He nods. "When Shana left, I just wanted to numb myself. Not going to lie, it wasn't easy—raising a child, a girl no less, by myself while my heart was broken. Some nights, it got to be too much. I wanted to say fuck it, drop her off with a sitter, and go on a bender."

"That's understandable," I say. "What matters is that you didn't."

"I got '*the things I cannot change*,'" he says, "because life doesn't always go as planned, and that can be a good thing. There are things I *can't* change, and it does me no good to try. I also got it to remind myself of what I avoided and how easy it is to go down that path." He winks. "Plus, it hurt like a bitch. I made a deal with myself—if I ever get blackout drunk, I have to add a line the next day. Fortunately I don't plan on it."

"Aha. Pain therapy." I smile and glance at the tattoo I'm most curious about—and most hesitant to learn about.

He squeezes my hand and lets go. "I got the rest before Bell. Stupid shit. Things I thought mattered."

"Even this one?" I go to touch the illustration of an anatomically correct steel heart made of machine parts, like it's the guts of a clock or car engine. Except that it's a *heart*. He stops my hand. I look up at him. "What?"

He shakes his head a little. "I got that when Shana left."

"So it's not before Bell."

"No."

"What is it?"

"A hard heart. Steel. Can't be broken." He releases my hand, kisses my forehead, and gets out of the tub.

As he dries himself off and wraps the towel around his waist, I'm left standing there with most of my questions answered—yet somehow less informed. Steel casing seems appropriate right about now, considering I can't seem to get through to him where Shana is concerned. I should leave it. We've been through a lot already. And yet, I've admitted to myself I care about him when I promised myself I wouldn't. He made it clear he's not emotionally available, and for the first time I wonder if it's because he never wants to fall in love again, like he said, or if it's because he's still in it. "Andrew?"

He glances over his shoulder but doesn't look at me. "Hmm?"

"Do you still love her?"

He pauses, but only for a second before he picks up his drink, downs the rest in one gulp, and then does the same with mine. "I don't know. I did, but it's been almost four years since I've seen her, so . . ."

Unfairly, my heart drops a little. I've been warned. I have no right to be upset if he still pines over his ex. I don't understand it—I've never been tempted to give Reggie a second chance—but I don't have to.

I realize I'm alone in the bathroom, standing knee-deep in cold water. I pull the stopper from the drain and change into a black cotton nightdress before I find him in the kitchen rinsing out the tumblers.

"What was she like?" I ask.

"Who?"

"*Shana.*"

"Oh." He pauses. "Volatile."

"And?"

He places a glass on the drying rack. "How specific do you want me to get? She's a woman. Women have a lot of different person—" He stops, smartly so.

"What?" I ask tersely. "What were you going to say?"

"Nothing. They're just complicated is all."

"I wouldn't know anything about that," I say. "Men are a fucking breeze."

He wipes his hand on a dishtowel and turns to lean back against the counter. "Look, it's really not worth getting into. I'm in a good place now. I don't want to drudge up old shit."

"Do you think it was easy for me to talk about Reggie?"

"No, but I'm glad you did. It'll help the healing process. It's better to be open about these things. I just can't."

I balk. "That's unfair."

"Maybe."

That's it. *Maybe.* "Why'd she leave?"

He crosses his arms. "How should I know? There was no note."

I take a step back. "She didn't even tell you she was going? She just left in the night? How is that possible?"

"I don't know." He runs a hand through his damp hair, slicking it back. "I understand how she could leave me, but not Bell, even if she didn't want her."

He says it so bluntly, a statement both cryptic and telling, so sure and sad, I don't even know where to start with it.

"Don't look at me like that," he says. "I don't want anyone's pity."

I school my frown. "I'm sorry, I just—it's shocking, is all."

He looks down at the ground between us, and I take the reprieve to study him with new eyes. His tattoos are less intimidating now that I know their meanings. Oddly, though men with ink are typically considered tough, Andrew's artful body makes him softer. Sweeter. I wonder if he's always been this way, or if Bell is the reason. Shana hardened his heart and simultaneously gave it a weak spot.

"You going to make me leave now?" he asks.

My thoughts clear, and I meet his eyes. His beautiful, blue, piercing, searching eyes. Eyes that belong to a man who has the potential to hurt me. Look how far we've come in only one night. "You don't want to?" I ask.

He shakes his head slowly before pushing off the counter. He stalks toward me. I place my hands on his chest as he wraps his arms around me. "I didn't set that rule. You were the one who wanted that."

I didn't *want* that, though. I needed it. Sleepovers are scary. They're fitting yourself to a new body, they're that split-second confusion when you wake up with unfamiliar arms around you. Staying the night means morning breath, awkward exchanges over a whirring Keurig, closing the bathroom door in your own apartment for the first time in years. He's right. I set the rule. I haven't *wanted* him to leave since the first night we spent together, though. And now, I know about him. He knows about me. We're damaged, our edges ragged, but is that why they seem to fit together?

"What do you want?" I ask him.

"I already told you. I want to spend the night with you."

"And if I say no?"

"I'll argue my case." He adds, "Respectfully. If you don't want me here, I won't stay, but if you do but you're still afraid, I won't let that be the reason we spend another night apart."

He says *another night* as if there've been endless nights apart. There haven't. Not by a long shot. He really does want this. My forearms, rigid until now, give against his chest.

"I'm spent, Amelia. Let me sleep," he says. "I'll spoon you like you're my favorite ice cream. Promise."

I curl my hands into loose fists right over his heart—his real one, not his hardened one. "What does this mean, though?"

He kisses the top of my head and leads me into the bedroom. "It means good things."

Good things.

Reggie meant good things once. It doesn't feel the same with Andrew, though. With Reggie, everything is measured and calculated. I was never quite sure if he got that from his work, or if he exceled at his job because he was innately that way.

Andrew, on the other hand, is upfront. Honest. It's what attracted me to him that first night I met him.

I can trust him.

But after all the mistakes I made with Reggie, all the times he was out with *her* behind my back, the fact that I let him take from me without fighting back or even speaking up—it makes me wonder . . .

Can I trust *myself?*

TWENTY-ONE
ANDREW

When Amelia wakes, I'm standing at the foot of her bed in my underwear, sipping coffee and watching her. Like a fucking creep. *Great.* As if the first morning with a girl isn't awkward enough.

"Morning," I say, breaking the silence. "How'd you sleep?"

"Good. Really well." She sits up, rubbing one eye like Bell does after a deep sleep. Her blonde hair is tangled and full of static, messier than I've ever seen it. Finally, I managed to ruffle her. Hair mussed, makeup gone, skin pink where I've left little marks with my mouth and hands.

"God," I groan, "you look—" I stop. I hadn't meant to say anything out loud.

She grimaces. "I know. The bubble bath sounds nice in the moment, but it makes me all sweaty, and my makeup runs, and the humidity destroys my hair—"

"Beautiful. I was going to say you look beautiful."

She shakes her head. "You don't have to say that. You already got me in bed."

I pass her my coffee. "You have a lot to learn about me."

"Oh yeah?" She curls her hands around the mug and takes a sip, humming pleasurably. "Teach me."

"I don't pass out compliments. Never have, never will. I have no reason to. When I say something, it's 'cause I mean it."

Two red patches form on her cheeks. "All right."

"Something else about me you should know going forward," I say.

"Forward—"

"I don't find beauty in the glossy stuff."

She blinks up at me, and I think she's attempting to suppress a smile. "Where do you find it?"

"When you get done up with your hair and makeup and dress—I like it if it's for me. I like when you're messy, like now, if it's because of me. I don't find my daughter beautiful because she has nice hair or unusual, blue eyes. She glows like a beacon from the inside. When you let me see you without hair and makeup, it makes me feel like you're beginning to trust me, and that . . ." I pause, taking in her alarmed expression. Steam from the coffee coils around her face. "It's really beautiful," I finish.

She swallows. "Andrew . . . please don't tell me—"

"I'm not telling you what you want to hear."

"That's not what I was going to say. I believe you. I just . . . don't tell me what you tell other girls. That's all I ask."

She wants to be special. Or, at least, different. Is it because she's jealous? I let a slow smile spread over my face and don't respond for a few seconds, enjoying the way uncertainty sets on her face. "Is that all you ask?" I repeat. "Or are you asking me not to tell other girls anything at all?"

She glances into the drink. "I mean, that wasn't really our deal . . . we haven't discussed anything other than—but last night . . ."

I wait. I could rescue her, but I want to hear what she has to say. Honesty has been a two-way street for us, and if it's going to work, it has to stay that way. I'm not going to guess what she's thinking just so she doesn't have to own it.

She looks up again, a new determination in her eyes. "I don't know what I want," she says. "And that's the truth. The idea of other girls makes my stomach hurt. But I can't ask more of you, because I don't know if *I* can give more."

I feel a slight pinch of disappointment, but then it's gone. This isn't Amelia's fault. It's that motherfucker ex-husband of hers. After what she told me last night, I can't expect her to trust me just because I ask it of her. I'll have to prove to her I'm worth it, and for the first time since Shana left, I'm up for the challenge. Amelia is broken. I can help her through it, because I was broken too.

Was? My thoughts grind to a halt. I *was* broken? I've known for some time that my resentment toward Shana was weakening. When I thought of her, anger was no longer instant; it took me more time to work up to it. But am I finally past it? It's been almost four years to the day. Everyone who knew Shana and me said 'give it time.' I'd thought it was bullshit. Maybe I've been here awhile and didn't realize it until Amelia came along.

She's gnawing on her bottom lip. I've left her out in the cold with no response. "There are none," I say.

She tilts her head. "None what?"

"Other girls. There are girls that I—" I believe in honesty, but I don't think it's necessary to go into more detail about Denise or anyone else than I already have. Other girls lost their appeal the night I met Amelia. But they left the picture completely last night at the dinner table when I watched Amelia with Bell. She wasn't perfect, and I realized I didn't need her to be. "I've had a lot of casual sex in my life. What we did last night wasn't that. I like this better."

Her lips twitch before she gives in to a hesitant smile. "Well, you know where I stand—in terms of sexual partners. You had to clear the cobwebs away that first night."

"Good thing I find cobwebs sexy."

She laughs quick and loud, caught off guard, and then her shoulders relax against the headboard. "So, why were you standing there staring at me when I woke up? Contemplating the most efficient way to arrange my body parts in the freezer?"

"I'm sorry. I wasn't trying to be weird. I was actually thinking," I glance around the room, "how much it bothers me, you living here."

"Because she was here?"

"Her, him. You've felt unsafe here. You've had your heart broken *here*." I point at the ground I'm standing on. "We need to get you the hell out of this apartment."

She pulls back a little, raising her shoulders around her neck. "What?"

"I know you've been fighting for it, but why? Why would you want to live here, where they've been? Where he made you feel like nothing?"

She looks away, her brows furrowed. "Honestly, I don't. I thought maybe I'd sell it once I won it— that would really piss him off. But I can't just let him walk away from this unscathed."

"Believe me, he's scathed. He lost you."

She looks back at me, her expression softer. "It's not enough. Don't you understand—it's about principle. I want to put him through the wringer."

"But you're putting yourself through the wringer. Don't *you* understand? The best way to hurt him is to move on with your life. You'll never be able to do that while you're here."

She raises her eyebrows at me. "What makes you so sure? Reggie hurts from his wallet, not his heart."

I shake my head. All the money in the world can't buy back a man's pride. Seeing Amelia with me, knowing she's strong enough to leave him behind—that'll do more damage than an apartment. And it's what's best for Amelia. "I'm a man. I tend to know how they think."

She sighs. "My therapist doesn't think it's healthy either, but I can't just up and leave. This is my home."

"Amelia, you're one of the strongest women I know. You can up and do anything." I check her bedside clock. "I have a few hours before I need to go get Bell for her gymnastics class. Let's get breakfast and go look at some places. Just to get you moving in the right direction."

"But—" She stammers. "I can't just *move*. We're in the middle of planning a huge fashion show at work while simultaneously building out an influencer marketing division. Do you have any idea how grueling it is to try to keep up with the teen market? I'm creating a whole team just for that. Not to mention the fact that before I can even think of moving, I have to worry about selling this place—"

"You told me he owns it."

"He does."

"So fuck it. Leave it behind. You don't owe him anything."

She sits forward to set the mug on her nightstand, clutching the sheet to her chest. "You can't be serious."

I can't be, but I am. Amelia was right that first night—sleepovers are dangerous. It was just great sex until she opened up to me, let me in, showed me her fear. And then slept in my arms. Now it's real. And I'm more than a little uncomfortable with her living in her ex's apartment, especially now that I know the extent of his scumbag ways. As long as she's here, she's still under his thumb. "Does he have a key?"

"Yes, but the doormen know—"

"Amelia, listen to me. The more I think about it, the more my skin crawls. You shouldn't be accessible to him at all."

"I'm not, really," she says. "We're only supposed to communicate through our lawyers."

"But he showed up here recently. How'd he get past the doorman?"

She opens her mouth to respond but pauses. "I'm not sure, actually. I didn't think about it, but Frank's not really a fan of mine. He'd probably hand Reggie the keys."

"*Great.* So your disgruntled doorman is in cahoots with your crooked ex." I half-roll my eyes. "Look, I get it. You want to repay him for the pain he's caused. I'm telling you—the quickest way to do that is to sever all ties, give him what he wants, and find happiness somewhere else. If he feels an ounce of love for you still, it'll kill him. If he doesn't, you're better off getting out before he does even more damage."

"It's not that simple."

"Call your lawyer," I say. "Tell him you'll give up the apartment and anything else Reggie wants in exchange for regaining complete control of *avec.*"

"*Everything?*"

I kick the foot of the bed like I'm testing the air in a tire. "They're just things, and they're weighing you down."

"What about alimony?"

"Do you really want his money?" I ask. "You've come this far. You run a successful business."

"I want the money because he does."

"Is it about that or about hurting him?" I ask. "If it's the money, that's fine, but you need to figure that out before you go any further in the process."

She readjusts the sheet under her arms and then shakes her head. "No, it's not about the money."

I blow out an exhale. I can offer Amelia stability, but I'll never hit Park-Avenue-apartment status, nor do I want to. "So," I continue, "imagine his face when his lawyer tells him you're willing to give up everything—including his money—just to get away from him once and for all."

"Oh, God." She curls her fingers into the edge of the sheet. "He'd have a coronary right there. In his world, there isn't a person who can't be bought. It's just about finding the right number."

I nod slowly. I shouldn't be surprised she gets it—she's a smart woman. But I've seen other smart women blinded by whatever it is she feels—or felt—toward Reggie. "*You* can't be bought, Amelia. Teach him a lesson."

She straightens a little, as if she needed to hear that, but why? I shouldn't have to remind someone of her caliber of that. It lights a fire in me that after everything I've been trying to teach Bell, one misogynistic, entitled asshole could potentially destroy her with enough time and skill.

"I—where would I even start?" she asks.

"It's New York City. You could have a new apartment squared away by the end of the weekend if you wanted. Pick out some new furniture. I'll get the guys to move it in. Done."

"I can't," she says as she shakes her head in disbelief. "You're making it sound too easy. There's more to it than just picking up and moving."

I hold up my hand and count off the steps on my fingers. "One—choose a neighborhood. Two—see some places in the neighborhood. Three—pay first and last month's rent, security, whatever. Four—I move you in."

She opens and closes her mouth. "What would I tell Reggie?"

My jaw tenses just hearing his name. It isn't like me to react this strongly to someone unless it involves Bell, but as we go, I'm disliking Reggie more and more. Whether or not Amelia and I move forward,

I'm ready for her to be done with him. "Why do you have to tell him anything?"

"I guess I . . . don't?" she says. "I guess I can just . . . tell my lawyer?"

"Good." I look her over. I'm surprised it took me this long to react to the red tint of her cheeks, her hair tangled from my hands, the thin white sheet hugging her breasts. Sex. I can't not think of it seeing her this way. I adjust myself in my underwear. "So, uh, let's get going," I suggest. "Because I have to pick up—"

She smiles coyly at me, beckoning me with one finger. "Come here."

I raise an eyebrow. Even though I know I could be hard and between her legs in moments, I tease her. "Real estate talk does it for you?" I ask. "Good to know."

"*You*. You do it for me."

"If I get on this bed," I say, "we'll never get out of here." I hold out my hand, and she sticks out her bottom lip. I'm more than eager to snatch that bottom lip between my teeth. We fell asleep quickly last night. I feel a little like I should've made love to her after our bath, showed her I can be more than hard and demanding in bed, but we were exhausted. "Come on. I promise to do you good next chance we get."

"Fine." She gets up and stretches. Immediately, I regret my decision, her long, white arms reaching for the sky, her tits high and full. I shake it all out of my head. I want it. But with someone like her, it's a long-term game. It always was, I just didn't know I wanted to play. Helping her detangle from Reggie is the way to prove to Amelia I meant what I said last night. That despite all my efforts not to—I care about her.

TWENTY-TWO

"It had a *fireplace*," Amelia says, waving the open-house flyer at me. "A real, working, wood-burning fireplace."

"I heard you the first ten times," I say and put my arm around her shoulders so she knows I'm teasing.

"Why are you not more excited about a fireplace? DeBlasio banned them in new construction, so they're a dying breed."

I shrug a little, glancing sidelong at her. "I guess because I have one at my house."

"You do?"

"Well, *I* don't live in a—" I lean in to read the spec sheet of the apartment we just looked at, "*six-hundred* square foot box. Jesus Christ, that's small."

"I don't mind the size. It's just me. Do you actually use the fireplace?"

I nod. "During winter."

"Where do you get the firewood?"

"I chop it myself."

She gapes at me. "Seriously?"

"No." I chuckle. "I get it from the supermarket."

She shakes her head in disbelief. "I haven't lived in a real house since I left home at eighteen. Reggie and I gave up a place with a fireplace for a bigger bathroom. What's your house like?"

I squint ahead of us. The sun is high today but with the mild temperature and slight spring breeze, it feels just right. "I bought it a couple years ago. The one-bedroom place Shana and I rented was getting too small for me and Bell. My place is three beds, two baths. Huge master bath," I add, "but unfortunately, no tub."

"Hence the extreme fascination with mine."

"I wouldn't call it *extreme*—"

"What else?" she asks.

"Hmm. Most important parts: a high-end kitchen and a decent-sized backyard."

"A backyard," she muses. "Wait, why's the kitchen important? Do you cook?"

"Babe, like you wouldn't believe."

"Liar."

"How do you think Bell gets fed—Flora, Fauna, and Merryweather?"

"*Sleeping Beauty*?" she guesses.

"You weren't lying about liking Disney classics." I wink. "Anyway, Sadie taught me to cook and I

330

ended up being all right at it. Now, to put it modestly, my culinary skills put all the women in my life to shame, Sadie included."

Amelia grins. "You're like a real grownup."

"Yep." I look down at her. She's different today. Looser. Not as careful. I love how worked up she gets, how blunt she can be. But this side of her? I earned this. It makes me appreciate it all the more. "You should come see it—the house," I say and pause to assess how I feel about the invitation. I can't just have a woman over the way most guys can. Thing is, I haven't ever wanted to, not since we moved in. It's new territory for me, but my gut says having Amelia over would be the right thing. "Bell—it's . . ." I pull Amelia into my chest to push through a group of tourists. "It's her birthday next weekend," I say when we're past the crowd.

"Oh." She keeps her eyes forward.

"You should come." It's a big step. I know it is. I don't even know exactly how Amelia feels about bringing Bell into her life, and I realize it's something I should ask her because I plan on seeing more of her going forward. I kiss the top of her head. "If you want," I say. "If not, I'll bring you by another time."

She glances up at me shyly, I think because she's going to accept my invitation. Instead she asks, "Where do you go when you want a bath?"

"Uh . . . nowhere. It wasn't on my list of requirements when I was house hunting."

"It's okay." She crumples up the spec sheet. "You can just use mine."

"What are you doing?" I ask.

"That place doesn't have a tub."

"But it has a fireplace."

"I've decided I'd rather have a tub." She holds up the brochure to the first place we saw. "This place has one."

It's a small gesture, but it says everything. Maybe Amelia isn't quite ready for Bell's birthday party, but she isn't looking for a place just for herself. She sees me in her future. She'd give up the fireplace to make me happy. I lean down and assault her cheek with a series of short kisses, and she breaks into an uncharacteristic fit of giggles.

"Oh my God," she says breathlessly. "Stop. It tickles."

"That only makes it more tempting." I nibble on her earlobe. "I made the biggest mistake of my life this morning."

"Oh yeah?" she asks, unconcerned. "What was that?"

"Passing up an opportunity to ravage you. Just spending time with you is like foreplay."

She wiggles her shoulders in my grip. "I agree. That was a mistake. Ravage me here."

"In the middle of the street, for everyone to see?" I mock-gasp against her cheek. "Nah. I want you all to myself. When I fuck you, I want only my eyes on your body."

"What about your hands?"

"You know what I mean," I say, pinching her side so she squeals. "Now that I know how ticklish you are, you're in a world of trouble."

Just ahead is a blocked-off street lined with umbrellas, tents and carts separated by tables of tchotchkes or rolling racks of clothing or furniture. "Well, if that isn't serendipitous," I say, nodding toward the Hell's Kitchen flea market. "First, we manage to find three apartment open houses, and we're already onto furniture."

She squeezes her arm around my middle. "I've always wanted a big, vintage wooden armoire," she says. "Reggie said they were too old and heavy, though."

I steer her across the street toward the crowded stalls. "Well, good thing I'm stronger."

Her gloriously-naked-for-once lips spread into a wide smile. "You've never even met him."

"I don't need to. I already know."

We slow together and make our way down the first row of mismatched, homeless items. She ducks out from under me to look at some jewelry and picks up a silver locket. "My dad gave me one of these as a girl. I wore it every day until I started high school and thought it wasn't cool anymore. I think I still have it somewhere." She frowns. "You should get something like that for Bell for her birthday."

I look at the necklace. It wouldn't have occurred to me. Bell loves dress up as much as the next girl.

Since I have nothing of worth to offer her—Shana took her jewelry with her, and my mom gambled away her things long ago—Bell's toy chest is littered with plastic costume jewelry. "She's too young," I say. Jewelry, makeup, hair, and all the other shit women do, all the things Amelia and her firm shill—I want them nowhere near my daughter.

Amelia glances over her shoulder and studies me a moment, as if she senses the shift in my mood. "Maybe," she says, replacing it gently on the velvet pad.

She walks a few feet ahead, and I stop at a booth where some other men have gathered. I push a few old license plates aside to inspect a pile of car parts.

The woman manning the table nods at me. "I know you."

"Yeah?"

"Beckwith Motors in Elizabeth, right?" she asks. "My husband and I have been there for work on our '66 Mustang."

"Right. I remember. Orange with stripes?"

She nods. "That's it."

"We did a coupe-to-fastback conversion for you."

"Good memory. You guys are the best in the tri-state area for classic restoration. That Camaro I always see there—it yours?"

I nod. "Been working on it for years. Every time I get started, we get swamped."

"'68?" she asks. "I think I got something for that." She pulls out a bin from under the table, drops it in front of me with a thud, and picks out a thin, chrome triangle about the size of my forearm.

"Vent window frame?" I ask.

She nods. "Right side."

I glance over at Amelia, who's testing the drawers of a *massive* armoire. *Fuck.* I didn't know she'd take me seriously about that. If she picks something out today, I'm not actually sure how I'd get it to her apartment. And then we'd have to move it again when she finds a new place. I shake my head at myself. *Good call, dipshit.*

I turn back to the woman. The other men have dispersed, and we're alone. "How much?"

She shrugs. "I'll give it to you for ten."

It's worth more, but I think she knows that. The piece I have now is a replica, which means I'm eager to swap it for an original. I slide my wallet out of my back pocket and pass her a ten.

"How's that little girl of yours?" she asks, bagging it up.

"Perfect," I say, my standard response, and I feel a pang in my chest. I miss her, and though I'm having fun with Amelia, I look forward to picking Bell up soon. I look over my shoulder again as I stuff my wallet back in my pants, but Amelia's no longer at the armoire. "She's turning seven soon."

"Wow. Guess it's been a while since we were there."

I scan the market, furrowing my brows when I don't see her. Even in jeans and a blouse, Amelia wouldn't blend in. Not to me, anyway. When I spot the back of her head through the crowd, muscles I hadn't realized I'd been clenching loosen. Until I notice she isn't alone. At first, I think she's haggling with the man in a baby blue polo in front of her, but then he puts a hand on her upper arm. She shrugs him off immediately, and I'm speed walking in her direction.

As I get closer, I become more aware of her body language. Her head is ducked, as if she's whispering. Her arms are crossed. The man looks over her head, darting his eyes toward the car parts booth as if he's looking for someone. Me? Clean-shaven with studied posture and ironed clothing, he isn't a flea market salesman.

I strain to hear their conversation, but I can't until I'm a few feet away.

"What are you even doing in this part of the city? At a *flea market*?" she asks. "You live across town, and you hate this kind of thing."

"Amelia?" I ask.

The man looks over her head. His eyes lock on me like laser beams are about to shoot out and slice me down the middle.

Amelia turns around, facing me. Tension cords her neck and collarbone. She touches my arm. "Let's go."

"Who is this?"

"Reggie," she says. "Or, as you know him, my asshole ex."

My back stiffens. Her nervous energy makes sense now, but it only reminds me of the reasons she's upset. He's here, in the flesh, the "man" who not only cheated on Amelia for a *year* but who manipulated her for longer and used sex as a weapon. A punishment. Something I'm now working to undo.

Even if I have reason to be angry, I understand almost immediately it's not the way to get under this man's skin. He's just as skeevy as I pictured with the smooth-skinned face and hands of a little boy rather than a man. I put an arm around Amelia's neck, bringing her into my side. To my surprise, she relaxes against my body, and it only makes me feel more protective.

"What's this about?" I ask him.

"It's between me and my wife," Reggie says, eyeing my over-the-top display of affection. "If you'll excuse us."

Amelia opens her mouth, but I don't give her the chance. "Your soon-to-be *ex*-wife," I correct. "My *current* girlfriend. You can say what you have to say in front of me."

"Tell your boy toy to go wait across the street with the other greasers," he says with an upward tilt of his chin toward Amelia. "It's got nothing to do with him."

His attempt at insults has the opposite effect he means it to, and my anger simmers into a less-threatening irritation. Name-calling is a sure sign of a loser who only fights dirty.

"He's my boyfriend, Reggie," Amelia says.

"After three weeks? Bullshit. You've never even mentioned him."

"Why would I?" she asks. "You had a girlfriend while we were married. I figure it's okay that I have one now that we're divorced."

"We're not divorced," he says.

"Logistics."

"All I want is an hour. Come sit with me. You owe me that."

"I don't owe you anything."

"Fine—then you owe it to us. It's like you've blocked out the first couple years entirely," he glances at me, "when it was good. It was so good, muffin."

I nearly gag at the pet name. Alerts are firing off inside me. I don't like that he thinks she owes him anything, even time. I force myself to let Amelia handle it, though.

"I haven't forgotten," she says, and I check her expression to see if she's serious. "It's just that . . . the bad outweighs the good by so much, nothing you do from this day forward could ever even it out."

He shakes his head. "You don't know that. We can get back there."

"Hey, man," I say. "Back off. I just told you she's my girlfriend."

"Marriage is a commitment, a journey," he continues, avoiding my glare, "and you're treating it as if it can be tossed out like garbage."

"I tried," she says, but her heart isn't it.

"No you didn't," Reggie says quickly, as I keep my mouth shut, watching him do his thing with my own two eyes. He heard the quaver in her voice just like I did. "You ran out when you found out about the affair and never gave me—*us*—a chance to put it right. How is that trying?"

Amelia glances away. I've had enough. "It's over, man. You need to go home and sort shit out with your lawyer."

"It's not over," he says slowly, "until *I* say."

Amelia scoffs. I'm sure she can feel the tense and release of my bicep against her neck. He can call me what he wants, but as far as I'm concerned, he's done jerking her around.

"What fantasy world do you live in that you think I need your permission to leave you?" she asks.

"The one in which I own fifty-one percent of you—your business, your apartment, your bank account." He tilts his head. "I paid for the bed you fucked him in. I might as well own your left tit."

I lunge for him before I even make a conscious choice, but he leaps out of my grasp, anticipating my attack. Amelia clasps onto my elbow, pulling me back with all her weight. "That's what he wants," she says. "A reaction. Don't give it to him."

Slight as she is, she's able to subdue me long enough for the initial shock of his words wear off. "You piece of shit—"

He looks at her. "It's the truth, and she knows it. You can play boss all you want in the bedroom, but you know who's in charge. *Me.* Your only choice is whether you decide to fight against me, or alongside me."

"Go to hell," she says, stepping around me. I gently take her bicep, keeping her closer to me than him. "You're a sad, lonely man with nothing better to do than swindle people out of their money and make me miserable."

He laughs loudly. A small crowd has gathered, and a couple teenagers have their cells aimed at us. I wave to get the boys' attention. They stuff their phones in their pockets before I even say, "Put it away."

"Sad? Lonely?" Reggie asks. "You don't know anything about my life. Women smell money, Amelia, and I've got lots of it. They're all over me. But you know something? I haven't touched a single one. Because I have a good woman at home, one who doesn't make me want to go find someone else. Virginia is—"

"*Virginia?*" Amelia asks, her body stiffening against me. "You told me it was over with her."

"I lied. She's left Robert. As soon as you and I divorce, I'm proposing to her. *She* makes me happy, something you never did. *She's* there when I leave for work and when I come home. She doesn't treat me like I'm second place to a *job*."

"Is that why you came to my place the other week, begging me to take you back?" she asks.

"You're right—I must've gone temporarily insane," he says. "You nag, you question every decision I make, you act like I didn't give you everything. Virginia is grateful and never makes me feel like I'm not enough. She fulfills all my needs—s*he* doesn't even have to try to be beautiful and sexy, unlike some women."

"Watch it," I say, stepping between them. "I'm restraining myself for her sake, but you're on my last fucking nerve."

"If you have all that, then why won't you let me go?" she pleads.

His eyes go blank, as if she's just asked him the square root of the Brooklyn Bridge.

"I think you should leave," I tell him.

He doesn't even look at me. "You first."

I step closer to him. "I'm sorry. I didn't mean that. What I meant was, get the fuck out of here before I kick your ass all the way to Hoboken."

Finally, he looks up at me, and for all my rage, the fire in his eyes is a little alarming. Whatever this thing with Amelia is, it runs deep for him.

Before I can figure it out, he sets his jaw and retreats. The haze over his eyes clears, and now, he's focused on me. "Fine." He holds up his palms. "I guess she's allowed a revenge fuck considering the circumstances. But I know what we have," he says, "and it doesn't go away just because I made a mistake."

He stalks off, roughly pushing his way through the crowd. Once I'm comfortable with his distance, I turn around. "'A *mistake*,'" I mock. "He has a seriously fucked-up perception of reality."

Amelia's hunched over with her back to me, pinching the bridge of her nose. I put an arm around her. "Hey," I say. "He's gone."

She ducks away from me too suddenly for me to stop her, especially since it's the last thing I expect. "I just need a second."

"That's fine." With my arms empty, I cross them over my chest. "What's going on?"

She shakes her head, looking at the ground. "I can't believe him. I thought it was over."

I want to pull her back to me, but I can practically see the emotions working through her. Whatever just caused tears to form at the corners of her eyes is being replaced with anger. As much as I want to do something, I don't know what will help, so I wait.

"How could he want that *home wrecker*? I've read about adultery, and a lot of the time, infidelity isn't about romance. Cheaters are selfish, self-indulgent—"

As she talks, I glance at the same spot on the ground she's staring at. *This* is why she's so upset? Because he's with someone else? I take a deep breath and try not to read into it. As my anger settles, regret replaces it. Regret that I didn't knock him out cold. Regret that I almost lost my temper. Back in the day, hotheaded reactions were par for the course. But I have too much at stake to fly off the handle now. "Amelia."

She looks up as if she'd forgotten I was there. "I'm sorry." She absentmindedly dabs at her eyeliner. "Whenever something is going right for me, he ruins it. It's like he has a sixth sense."

"He's just trying to get under your skin any way he can. He might not even be with her, he's just using it to get you to react."

She closes her eyes and nods. "No, I know. You're right. Still—"

"You should be more upset about the way he spoke to you."

She puts her hands in the back pockets of her jeans and finally looks up again. "Yeah. He gets like that when he's hurt or embarrassed. He's proud."

"Proud or not, that's inexcusable."

"I know. I'm making excuses again."

"Again?"

She shakes her head. "When I started therapy, I would make excuses for him to Dianne. I thought we'd worked past it, though."

"Maybe it's always a work in progress," I offer, trying to be helpful. I've never been much for excuses—making or accepting them. Try as I might, though, I'm not sure I'll ever understand the power he has over her. How he managed to get her into this state within minutes, or how she can't see through his words. What I do understand, though, is Reggie. Now that Amelia has opened up to me, and now that I've met him, I have him pegged. Power. He wielded it over her, and he feels it slipping away. He's an insecure man who works in one of the most powerful industries in the world in one of the most powerful cities in the world—and it's a dangerous combination. Power, control, influence. He gets them through sex, money, and love, and he gets those through manipulation, coercion, intimidation. The pieces go together to complete a puzzle. If I can figure him out so quickly, why can't Amelia?

I run through the conversation as best I can. Maybe if I show her the idiotic tools of his manipulation, she'll understand and calm down. Money—check. He said he had lots of it, and implied any sane woman would want a piece of it. Love— check. Virginia has his love, and it's better than Amelia's ever was. Sex—check. He diminished my relationship with her. I'm torn between two different instincts—one to protect Amelia from Reggie, the other to protect Bell by staying levelheaded.

"I hope he and I don't cross paths again anytime soon," I say, "not for his sake but for mine. I can't afford to lose my temper."

"I understand." She nods slowly, dazed. "I'm sorry you even had to meet him."

"What was he doing here? What does he want?"

"One minute he wants me, but then he brags about being happy with her." She's no longer looking at me, but off to the side, as if addressing someone who isn't there. "I think you're right—I doubt they're back together, but in the moment, when he's saying those things, I'm there again. I'm back in *my* bedroom watching them go at it for a full ten seconds before I start screaming."

I watch her closely, my teeth clenched. I'm not sure I wouldn't have killed another man in my bed. "He knows how to get to you."

She nods. "Whatever will hurt the most, that's what he says. And it does. It's not like I want him back, but when he rubs it in like that . . ."

"I get it. You loved him." I remember all the nights I'd lie in bed, cursing Shana. I never wanted to see her face again—and I missed the way she fit in my arms. The little snort she made when she laughed too hard. "That love doesn't just go away overnight, unfortunately."

She swallows, and we exchange more than a simple look. I study her, and she does the same to me. Here we are on the precipice of something new, and neither of us knows what'll happen. I'm not even sure we know enough about our own feelings yet, much less each other's. Does she still love him on some level? Do I still love Shana? Is there a chance in hell she'd go back to Reggie? The thought should wrack me with fear, send me running in the other direction. She could leave, just like Shana, and I'd be the blind fool who believed her when she said she was over her ex.

But when that realization is finished working its way through me, I'm still standing in the same spot. Somewhere along the way, she became worth it to me. The threat of pain that comes with keeping her in my life—it's not enough to scare me away. In fact, it's the threat of competition that stokes a fire in me. It makes me want to put up a fight.

And then, as if I'd spoken my thoughts aloud and she didn't care for what she heard, she sniffs and turns away. "You should go. You'll be late picking up Bell."

I check my watch. "I still have a few minutes."

She tucks some of her hair behind her ear and seems fascinated by something in the street. "Yes, but I should run too. It just hit me how much work I have to get done this weekend," she says. "I should've done it last night, but—"

"But instead you came three times," I say, hearing the roughness of my own voice.

She bites her lip harder than I think she means because she releases it right away. I've brought her back to what's important. Us. For a moment, I think she'll come to me. She doesn't. "It was great," she says stiffly. "I had a *great* time. I just need to . . . go."

"Great?" I ask. "That's all you've got?"

"Maybe," she says. "So what if it is? I said it was great, I didn't say *okay* or *complete shit*."

I raise both eyebrows at her, noting the sudden flush of her face. "Okay, you're mad, I get it," I say. "I don't get *why*, but—"

"I appreciate that you stuck up for me, but you're *not* actually my boyfriend, Andrew. This part is ugly and hard and I'm telling you, as nicely as I can, although you're pushing me, that I want to be alone."

"Hold up. You just completely flipped on me." She won't look at me as she inches backward like a caged animal. "Why? Are you having second thoughts about getting back together with him?"

She widens her eyes, stopping in her tracks. "I would never, ever—he disgusts me." Her face crumples. "Didn't you hear anything I said last night?"

"Of course I heard. I heard every goddamn word," I say, reeling. I'm raising my voice but I've been holding back too long, and I can't seem to control it. "*I'm* disgusted. I'm outraged. But I don't understand why you're suddenly acting like I'm the bad guy. I just want to protect you from whatever black hole you're standing at the edge of right now."

"You're being dramatic," she says.

The accusation is so ridiculous, I laugh. "Babe, I don't do drama. Neither do you, which is one of the many things I like about you. I see your mind spinning, though. You're going down a path that's not good for you. I'm just trying to bring you back."

She presses the heels of her hands against her eyes. "I know. I *know*. I wasn't expecting him to say all of that. I feel like I'm right back in the middle of it, so . . . so fucking *stupid* and blind and—"

"Hey." I pull her hands from her face and hold them. "You're not stupid. You're not blind. You trusted him, and he manipulated and betrayed you *on purpose*. He knows what he's doing."

She looks me in the eyes. "This isn't what you signed up for. We were supposed to spend one night together, and now you have to deal with this mess—"

"I don't have to. I could walk away right now if I wanted. I'm not here out of obligation."

She goes quiet, frowning. "You're a good man."

"Then don't push me away. I told you I care, and I do, and I said I was your boyfriend, and you know what? It felt fucking good to say it. Because I think that moment on the sidewalk you told me you'd never be mine, in a way, you already were. I didn't know it, but you won me over right there."

Her hands loosen in my grip. She looks close to tears, and just like with Bell, it grabs onto something at the core of me and holds on. "You're right," she says. "I'm being crazy. I'm—I'm . . ."

"It's okay," I say. "You can be crazy. Just don't walk away . . . even though we sort of had a pact that we *would* walk away."

That gets me a smile, albeit a slight one. "What a mess."

"A mess we created, so it can't be bad."

She glances at our intertwined hands and shifts her eyes to my watch. "You really should go, Andrew."

I let go of her with a nod and a wave of relief. There's still something off, but I think I've gotten through to her and that's all I can do now. I need to go get Bell, and there's a small part of me that wants to be a few minutes late or ask Sadie to take her to gymnastics instead, which is how I know Amelia's right—I need to go get my girl.

"Let me walk with you," I say. "At least to the train. You're upset."

She shakes her head. "I'm going to the office."

"Then I'll walk you there—"

"I'm fine. Really. I'll get a cab."

I put my hands in my pockets. "Are we good? Can I call you tonight?"

She hesitates and then nods, smiling. "Yes. Of course. Once I've gotten some work done, I'll feel better. I'm always anxious when boxes on my to-do list go unchecked for more than a day."

I don't tell her I understand because I'm not sure I do. There are times, when my mood is dark, that burying myself under a hood feels like the only thing I can do. It got me through a lot with Shana and that's possibly the reason the garage is doing so well today. I guess that's how Amelia feels, so I can't really begrudge her that, even though I think she works too hard.

She turns away.

"Hey, whoa," I say. "Can a boyfriend get a kiss?"

She stops and turns back slowly. Her expression is passive. I can't tell how she feels about my new title, and it makes me a little uneasy. She takes a few steps toward me, rises onto the balls of her feet, and kisses my cheek. Before I can grasp her, keep her there, show her how to really kiss her boyfriend goodbye, she's hurrying off, slinking between the barricades that block off the street. Clutching her purse to her side, she steps into the street. Within seconds of raising an arm, she's hailed a cab that scoops her away.

TWENTY-THREE

At times, occasionally, I've been accused of exaggerating when it comes to Bell.

But evidence doesn't lie.

As soon as Bell walks into gymnastics, her friends perk up and yell for her to join them. Her coaches wave. Parents smile. She brightens up any room she's in, including one as large and well-lit as this gymnasium. She takes off for the group of girls gathered in the center, and I start to call her back but stop myself. I'm not into this new thing where she forgets I'm around as soon as she sees someone else, but that's what I'm supposed to want for her. She should be excited about what's ahead of her rather than too anxious to leave my side. Still, my gut sinks watching her skip off.

But then, she skids to a halt and turns around. She sprints back to me, and I *ooph* as she jumps into my arms. "Promise me you'll stay and watch," she says.

"When have I ever not?" I kiss her forehead before removing her shoes and putting her down. "I'll be right over there in the bleachers."

I sling Bell's hot pink, rainbow-glittered duffel bag over my shoulder and find a seat. I didn't use to *ooph* when I caught her. Either I'm getting older, or she's getting bigger. I prefer to pretend it's neither of the two.

Kiki Brown spots me and shuffles her daughter in my direction. "Andrew," she says, fixing the collar of her white blouse. "How are you?"

"Fine." I nod at her daughter. "Hi, Brynn."

"Where's Bell?" she asks.

"Don't be rude," Kiki says with a nervous laugh. "Say hello first."

"Hello. Where's Bell?"

"*Brynn.* Try again."

Jesus Christ, I want to say. *Let the girl go see her fucking friends.* Brynn scowls but says, "Hello, Mr. Beckwith." Then, she goes quiet since she can't ask the only thing she wants to know. "Um. How are you?"

I point to the group. "She's with the girls, warming up."

Brynn drops her things and hurries away.

"Sorry about that," Kiki says, her bracelets jingling as she picks up Brynn's bag. "We're working on her manners."

"Fuck—manners? Was I supposed to be working on those?"

She hesitates as if she's not sure I'm joking and then gives in to a smile. "It's never too early. How was your Friday night? Have some fun?"

She asks me something along these lines every time I see her, as if my life is one big bundle of fun and oh yeah—I have a daughter too. This Friday, it happens to be true, but that's not what she wants to hear. She's just keeping tabs on my love life.

"It was fine. Yours?"

She rolls her eyes. "Ron had some bullshit in the city that apparently prevented him from making it home." She glances toward the girls and stretches her hands toward the ceiling, arching her back, showing off a sliver of her flat stomach. "We were up late arguing. I could use a coffee."

"Yeah," is all I can think to say. I was up late too. There could've been some arguing, I was with Amelia after all, but I couldn't tell you who won. I smile to myself.

"My treat?" she suggests.

"Nah. I stay for the practices."

She widens her eyes. "Always? Don't you get bored?"

"Not really. I don't have anything better to do."

"Nothing at all?" she asks, half-smiling. "We should work on that. Find you something better to do."

I look past her at Bell, who's directing the girls into a circle for their stretches as the coach stands back and lets her. Give the kid an inch, I swear. Her coach should know that by now. "What I mean is, I really can't think of anything I'd rather be doing."

"Oh, I don't believe that." She plays with the strap of Brynn's bag, sliding her hand up and down the polyester. "There must be at least *one* thing you'd rather be doing than sitting here."

I'd rather she just came out and said what she wanted. This suggestive flirting annoys me, especially when Bell is a few feet away.

It's not just the fact that she's married that gets to me. It's that she and her friends think I'd have no problem taking an hour to give her what she isn't getting from her husband because I've got tattoos, a bike, and a bastard child by my wild ex-girlfriend. As if I have no principles or standards.

"Not a thing, Kiki," I say quietly in case anyone is within hearing distance. "I suggest you look elsewhere. Like at home. You might find something to do there. Do you mind?"

"Mind?" she asks, touching her collar.

I nod at her. "You're blocking my view."

"Oh." She adjusts Brynn's bag on her shoulder and mutters, "Well, I'll just . . . coffee—"

She walks away, her heels clomping on the gym floor. I could almost feel bad about embarrassing her if I had time to wonder what drives her to come onto someone who doesn't want her. But I can't muster enough interest. Between Bell and Amelia, I don't have much more attention to spare.

As if on cue, because God knows the woman has a sixth sense for bad timing, I see her. She steps out of the shadows, and the air around me evaporates. She's worse than a sucker punch.

Nobody ever took my breath away like Shana.

Shana is the same as I remember her: jeans painted on from hip to ankle, a low-cut halter in any shade of dark, and jet-black hair that's either slick-straight or, like today, wild and curly. She walks toward me with her hands in her back pockets, her elbows out, her hips sashaying from side to side. She has a small waist, and T&A that make men stupid. It takes her long enough to reach me that I can see the edges of new ink from the waistband of her low-rise jeans.

Neither of us speaks. As if I have a clue what to say. I used to fantasize about this moment and how I'd react. Sometimes I'd hug her as she broke down in regretful sobs. Sometimes I'd shake her good and hard, demanding to know why. Now, all I can do is stare and wait for her to evaporate in front of my eyes.

She doesn't.

"Hey," she says, removing one hand to wipe her palm on her jeans.

She looks the same. As if she was just out at the salon for a few hours.

"How are you?" she asks.

"That's it? *Hey, how are you?*" I keep my voice low. I can see Bell, and it's enough to remind me that I don't want to call her attention over here. "What the fuck are you doing here?"

"I . . ." When she looks up, her eyes are big and watery. "I don't know. I mean, I do, but, like, it's complicated. So, yeah. How are you?"

"I haven't heard from you in nearly *four years*."

"I know." She rubs her nose. "I know I don't have any right, but . . . it's good to see you. I've missed you."

Bell giggles. My steel-encased hard heart becomes a fist. "You can't be here."

"I—"

"What do you want? Tell me quick and go."

"I don't want anything—"

"You wouldn't be here if you didn't want something. What is it? Money? Christ, Shana."

She balks. "Money? If I wanted money, I wouldn't come to you. You never had any."

I mash my molars together. Two minutes, and we're already having the same argument. That's got to be some kind of record. "You're right," I say. "I'm broke, so there's nothing here for you. Move along."

It's a lie. Those first few years we had Bell, I invested any extra money I had into the garage, leaving only enough in our bank account to cover Bell's basics. I'd worked like a dog once I had Bell to take care of, but it meant Shana and I'd had to go without. That hard work has paid off now that the garage is doing enough business to keep us busy around the clock, but Shana wouldn't know that. Unless, of course, she can sense it, which wouldn't surprise me.

"I've been doing a lot of thinking," she says. "I told myself to stay away. I had no right to come back into your life, but I just can't help myself. I'm not the girl I used to be."

"You can stay away," I say, keeping an eye on Bell, who is, so far, oblivious to what's happening over here. "You just don't want to, and you always do what you want. You are the girl you used to be."

"My parents *died*, Andrew."

I whip my head back to her. "What?"

"First, my mom. Breast cancer." Her voice cracks. "Six months later, my dad started to lose his mind. It happened so fast. One day, he just didn't know me anymore. I had to put him in a home."

"He's alive, though."

"Yes, but he might as well be dead. He doesn't remember anything beyond the immediate short term."

Shana's parents had her late, but they're too young to have both gone like that. Ashamedly, for a split second, I wonder if she's lying, but not even she would stoop that low. They're strangers to me now, but once they were Bell's grandparents. "I'm sorry," I say.

"I called a few times, but—" She swallows. "I didn't know what to say." She takes a step toward me and I automatically put my hands up. Her mouth falls open. "My parents are gone—I'm not *contagious*."

"No," I say suddenly. "You don't get to come here and play the sympathy card. You don't have the first clue what we've been through." My voice is rising, and a couple of the moms look over at us.

"You keep looking at her," Shana says fondly. She glances over her shoulder at the girls. "I don't even think you realize you're doing it. She's really beautiful, Andrew. I can't even believe how big—"

"Don't—don't look at her," I say, panic knotting in my chest. I stand up, towering over her even more than usual since I'm on the third step of the bleachers. "Don't even *look* at her."

She turns back to me. "There's no need to overreact. I promise, I'm not here to cause trouble." She snorts. "And you say I'm dramatic."

I swing an arm between us. "You don't think this is dramatic? Ambushing me out of the blue in the middle of Bell's gym class?"

"You didn't know I was in town?" she asks.

"How the fuck would I?"

"The card I sent home with Bell. I thought you'd see that and understand—"

I take a step down to the first bleacher, and she shrinks. "You *talked* to Bell when I wasn't around?"

"I didn't tell her who I was. I was gently sending you a message that—"

"How fucking dare you."

"I'm her *mother*."

"No you're not. You're nothing to her. She doesn't even know about you. She never asks. Never."

She gapes at me. "Oh my God, Andrew. That's so mean. And it's a lie."

"No it isn't," I say, and almost unbelievably, it's true. Bell has yet to come to me and ask why all her friends have moms and she doesn't. "I'm enough for her. Because I've taught her to be smart. Independent. That way she'll never get fucked over again."

"*Andrew—*"

Bell looks over at us, tilting her head, and I snap in the most contained way I can manage so I don't alarm her. I shove my hands in my pockets and school my expression and my tone. "Get out of my face," I say slowly. "Right now, or I swear to God, if you ever come near her again, I'll file a restraining order. If you ever come near her again while I'm not around? I'll make your life a living hell."

Her nostrils flare. "Jesus. When did you get to be such an asshole? You were always trying to control me, but you were never mean. Not like this."

She turns and stomps out, making no secret of her discontent. The few moms in the crowd look either at me or her, because fuck this small town, of course they know who she is. They know my situation.

I plaster on a smile and Bell waves emphatically at me. "Watch me," she yells. She starts her floor routine, then stops abruptly and says "No, wait, watch," and starts over, even though I have no clue what she did wrong. I grin as my heart pounds right up against my chest. When I've lost her attention to tumbling, I scrub my hands over my face.

Fuck shit fuck. For a long time, I wished Shana would come back, just so I could tell her to fuck off. Now, though, I don't want to do that. I don't want her here at all. Bell and I have figured it out without her. We have balance. We're happy. I don't need revenge. I don't need to prove anything. I just want Shana to leave us alone.

My head throbs with an avalanche of thoughts. Will she come back? What does she really want? I won't give her anything. Not money. Not access.

She has some nerve accusing me of being controlling. Anything I ever did, anything anyone does, is a reaction to her. She cares about no one but herself and the rest of us have to cope. I can't get ahold of my thoughts. I only have half an hour before Bell's finished and I have to get it together.

I take out my cell phone and dial Sadie's number. She picks up on the first ring. "Forget something?" she asks since we were just at her place.

"No." I train my eyes on Bell. Her complete obliviousness is the only thing keeping me sane right now. "Shana just showed up at gymnastics."

"*What?*" Sadie asks. "*The* Shana?"

"Yes of course *the* Shana. Do you know another one?"

"Oh, she has some massive balls," Sadie says. "I knew it. We should've seen this coming."

"Yeah?" I agree and then pause. "No. Why?"

"Because she'll never do better than you and Bell. I just hoped she'd never realize it. What does she want?"

"I don't know. Money, I hope."

"Money? Really?"

"It's better than the alternative."

Sadie grows quiet as that sinks in. If Shana isn't here for money, she's here for Bell. "She can't," she says. "She can't just show up here, and expect . . . *anything*." Sadie launches into a rant, and it's a relief to hear outrage as passionate as my own.

And then I get tired, having slept very little the night before, and my shoulders feel a thousand pounds, as if I've been carrying a heavy load and only just realized it. "I gotta go," I say. "Bell's almost done."

"What are you going to tell her?"

"Obviously nothing."

"I don't know, Andrew. You can't protect her forever. She needs to know about Shana. Maybe it's time—"

"It's not time," I say through a thick throat. *I* am Bell's parent. Her only parent. There's no room left for Shana. "Now is definitely not time."

"Call me later," Sadie says with a sigh.

Ten minutes until practice ends, and I'm both weary and amped. I have the sudden urge to talk to Amelia, who will understand how this feels. Not in the fuming-mad way Sadie does, but in the knockout-punch to the gut that Amelia's experienced. She's dealing with her own boxing match and maybe, just maybe, hearing each other's voices will help.

I pull up her number, lean my elbows onto my knees, and let it ring. And ring and ring. I get her voicemail. "Hey," I say after the beep. "It's me. Call when you get this. Any time. Even if it's late."

I hang up and watch the wind-down of the class until Bell cartwheel-skips back to me.

"Did you see me?" she asks.

"Yes, baby," I say as she climbs over the seats to me like a monkey. "You were great."

"You say that every time."

"Well, you're great every time."

She gets on my lap and puts her arms around my neck. "The coach thinks I'm ready to try a backflip next class."

Moms filter into the gym to pick up their daughters, some waving in our direction. There are no men in here. "Backflip?" I ask, focusing on what she's saying. "Backflip—really? It's not too advanced?" I cringe as I say it. I might as well have just dared her to try.

"No," she says. "It's not that hard. I could probably do it right now—"

"Not so fast," I say. "I've told you. No gymnastics off the floor." I don't even like her doing them at home or in the backyard without a coach's supervision. I pat her knee. "Get your stuff. Let's go home."

"Why were you talking to that lady?" Bell asks. "She's the teacher who gave me the card."

I shake my head because my throat is suddenly thick. "No reason."

"Was it about me?"

"No. Never mind, Bell. Get your stuff."

She juts her bottom lip and climbs off my lap. She twirls around between the seats, teetering, hopping, almost flying off the bleachers. She gasps. "Ohhh. I know why you were talking to her."

I grab the strap of her gym bag, haul it up to the seat below me, and unzip it. "Shoes."

"Don't you want to know what I know?"

I get her cardigan out along with her flats. "Nope."

"She wants to *kiss* you," Bell screams loudly enough to make everyone in the gym look over. She makes a kissy face, sticks her butt out, and wiggles. "She lo-o-o-ves you," she sings. "She wants to ki-i-i-ss you."

"Stop it," I say. "I'm warning you."

She jumps up on the bench and spins in a circle.

"Get down."

"All the teachers and mommies want to kiss my daddy," she croons. "He's the most handsome, most nicest daddy——" She stumbles over her own two feet and falls onto her knees, nearly toppling over the side before I grab her.

"Goddamn it, Bell," I shout, pulling her to her feet. "I told you to get down."

She looks up at me silently, her eyes wide.

I'm instantly chastened by my own reprimand. I rarely yell at her, but the combination of intentionally defying me and risking her safety in the process makes me snap.

Her face crumbles, and she hiccups with her first wave of tears. "I-I'm s-sorry."

"Ah, shit." I run both hands through my hair, sit on the bench, and pull her onto the seat next to me. "I'm sorry. I didn't mean to yell at you."

When I put an arm around her, she turns into my chest and sobs. I have to restrain from crushing her. "I'm sorry, Bluebell. I'm not mad. I'm just——" I shake my head. "You don't understand what you're saying, and I've told you——it's inappropriate."

She warbles something unintelligible.

"Why do you keep talking about kissing?" I ask, pushing through my discomfort. "Are you curious about it?"

She pulls on my t-shirt a few seconds and lets go to look up into my face. "I don't know. When I go to Sarah's house, her mom kisses her dad. Is it bad?"

My stupid, hard heart cracks down the middle. I take her hand and close both of mine around it. "No, it's not bad."

She looks around a little bit, her brows furrowed. "But you get mad."

I'm a bad parent. I don't know what the fuck I'm doing. My heart hammers. Whether or not I'm ready, we're having this conversation. "What do you want to know?"

"Why don't you have a girlfriend to kiss? Like other dads? Don't you want one?"

I close my eyes. What . . . the . . . fuck. She's just a little girl. How can she possibly be thinking about this, much less worrying about it? "I'm not like other dads, Bell."

"I know," she says, as if it's a fact. "Does that mean you won't ever have someone like Sarah's mom? Her parents are happy when they kiss."

"Do you think I'm not—" I swallow through the lump in my throat. "Not happy?"

"I don't know."

"You make me so happy, Bell. Daddy is very, very happy."

"If you do find someone to kiss, then what? Will you go somewhere else?"

I cinch my eyebrows together. "Where would I go?"

"I don't know. You kissed my mom. She left."

"I . . ." I look down at our hands. "I didn't know you remembered that."

"Not really. I don't remember anything. Don't be sad."

She's lying to protect me, something she most likely learned from me. "I'm not sad. I'm glad you remember, I just didn't know you were thinking about all this." I have to breathe through my mouth for a few seconds to quell the pain in my chest. "You have questions about your mom?"

"I think so, but I know she makes you sad, and I don't want that."

I have tried, with every fiber of my being, to shield Bell from all this. I keep it inside as much as possible, and I never talk about Shana in front of her. It's beyond me how she's figured this out, though it shouldn't be, because she continues to surprise me daily. "You're getting so goddamn smart and big. How? When?"

"I'm not big. I'm still half your size."

I chuckle. "Yeah. What do you want for dinner?"

"Pizza," she says so quickly, I wonder if she really does or if it's an automatic response.

"All right, tell you what," I say, picking up her bag and standing. "We'll get some pizza and go home, and you can ask me all the questions you have."

I hope, that in the time it takes to order a pizza and drive home, I'll be able to figure out the answers to questions I've avoided thinking about for four years.

TWENTY-FOUR
AMELIA

When Sadie knocks on my office door, it takes me a few seconds to invite her in. I've been avoiding her for days as best I can in a small office where we have daily meetings. We haven't yet been alone in the same room, but I've caught her staring at me a few times.

Ever since I bolted from Andrew at the flea market, I've wanted to reach out, explain why, and make it right. I can't get myself to complete the call, though. I once found Reggie charming, clever, and kind—all things I consider Andrew to be. Now that I've seen the other side of Reggie, I'm afraid it was there all along. I just turned a blind eye to it. How do I know I'm not doing the same with Andrew?

"Come in," I say.

Sadie closes the door behind her, brings her laptop to my desk, and turns the screen to me. "How's this look for the IncrediBlast event next month?"

I glance over the invitation, but I find it hard to care. I used to take self-abusive joy in micromanaging, in having my stamp on every single thing that passed through this office. The truth is, it's a goddamn invitation that people won't decline just because the kerning's a little tight. I look up and sigh. "The kerning's a little tight."

"I thought so too."

I look at her over my glasses. "You could've e-mailed it to me."

"I needed to take a walk," she says. Her desk is thirty feet away. "How are things?"

"Things are fine."

"I meant with Andrew. I'm not blind, Amelia. I know you're sleeping with my brother."

I pause, then slide my specs off completely and set them on the desk. "And? Are you upset?"

"Why would I be?"

"You know how I am about men. And he's your family. I didn't think you'd like it very much."

"Admittedly, at first, I was a little shocked," she says. "You two don't really make a lot of sense. But then I decided I was too impressed to feel anything else about it."

"Impressed?"

"I've been trying to get him interested in someone for years. That's why I tried to force Mindy on him."

"Right. Mindy." I sit back in my chair. "You should've tried harder. She really would've been a good fit for him."

She tilts her head at me. "You think?"

"She's young, energetic, beautiful. She wants kids. Well, I'm not sure how she'd fare in Jersey, honestly, but—" I stop at the perplexed look on Sadie's face. "Oh. I'm ending things with him."

"I didn't realize. Andrew's not very forthcoming about these things."

He wouldn't be, if not because he's fairly private, then because I asked him not to be. We've only known each other a short time, but it's as if the harder I resisted him, the closer we became. Which might be fine for a normal couple, but we're far from normal. We can only be dysfunctional together, since we don't function all that well apart.

I'd forgotten that for twenty-four hours, but seeing Reggie at the flea market over the weekend brought it all barreling back to me. Andrew and I might be able to make this work, and if I were younger, it would be fun to try. But now I know better than to walk willingly into the lion's den.

"I'm sorry," Sadie says. She makes a move like she's going to leave, and I'm surprised by my disappointment. I have no one to talk to about this, and it's been bothering me for days.

"It's just too complicated," I say. "There's *avec* and Bell and New Jersey and the city, and, well, maybe he thinks those are things we can work through, but how could we? He's never going to move here, and he shouldn't have to when he's got Bell to think of."

Sadie slides to the edge of her seat. "Are you telling me you and my brother have talked about these things?"

"Well, not at length—"

"And he thinks it could work?"

"I suppose. He came with me to look for a new apartment, and we talked about the future some. But that was before things were . . . over."

Sadie's mouth falls open. "I don't believe it. Andrew never talks about anyone in the future tense. Not since . . . never mind."

My cheeks redden. My urge is to downplay what I said—maybe I exaggerated. I didn't, though. We really had an amazing weekend up until I spoiled it. "Since Shana?" I ask.

Sadie widens her eyes. "You know about Shana?"

"Yes," I say. "A fair amount, actually."

She blinks a few times, looking around my office as she seems to collect her thoughts. I can't seem to read her shock. Is she upset? Happy? "So why's it over?" she asks.

"I don't have to tell you how screwed up I am after Reggie. You already know. Andrew and I ran into him while we were together, and it reminded me of everything I'd been through this year. Andrew got the brunt of it. Just for being there."

"But he didn't leave," she states.

"No, but is that the kind of woman you want with your brother? One who's too emotionally scarred to operate with any normalcy?"

Understandably, she stays quiet.

I sigh. "I care about him, but maybe I was too rash thinking I could get involved with someone so different from me. He has tattoos and a motorcycle and his garage. And I—I'm probably too stuffy for him. We just don't click, you know?"

"But do you *click*?" she asks, arching an eyebrow. "Like when you're together?"

My face heats. There's only one possible answer to that question. "Yes."

"That's not enough, though," she says.

I can't tell if it's a question or a statement. I hesitate. "Bell." Just her name says it all. "Out of everything, she's the most important thing to consider. I mean, what if we try this, and down the line, it's time to move in together, but I won't go to Jersey and he won't come here. Then what? We've put her through all that for nothing. Just to have another parental figure ripped out of her life."

Sadie laces her hands in her lap, unusually quiet.

"You understand, don't you?" I ask. "Would you have gone out with Nathan if he'd been your complete opposite in every way?"

"Probably not."

"Thank you," I say. "If you could just explain that to your brother. I'm not sure how he'll take it. He seems to think we have a shot."

"Okay," she says. "I will."

I realize then I was bracing myself for resistance, though I'm not sure why. All along I've suspected she wouldn't want us together. But she hasn't actually spent time around us while we weren't hiding our relationship. She doesn't realize how good we are even though we aren't supposed to be. "You'll convince him for me?" I ask.

"I see your points." She taps a finger on the arm of her chair. "You're all wrong for each other. What are you going to do—go to *Jersey*?"

"Exactly," I say, but for whatever reason, her agreeing with me has weakened my resolve, and the word comes out wavering. "I mean, some people commute, I know. But back and forth, that's an extra two hours I don't have."

"I totally get it. That was one of my concerns moving to Brooklyn. I've gotten used to a slightly longer commute. It can be nice to have some extra time to relax to and from work. But that's not the point."

"No," I agree, "that isn't the point."

"You are so not the mom type," she continues. "You'd have to take Bell to gymnastics, probably even her competitions as she gets older. And help her with homework or girl problems that Andrew won't understand, like her first crush or how to use a tampon. Stuff I thought I would do." She nods, as if she's adding more to the list in her head. "You might have to do, like, bake sales for her school. Then again, Andrew is a really good baker, so maybe not."

In just a few seconds, I've been forced out of my office and into some alternate reality. The shift in topic is so quick, I'm suddenly in a kitchen in New Jersey, Bell's schoolbooks spread out on the kitchen table as Andrew makes cookies. The kitchen is warm—why? From the oven? Or the people?

It's *so* not my life. It doesn't sound like a bad life . . . it just isn't mine. Couldn't be mine. Could it? Can I see myself at that table, helping Bell with homework, sneaking glances at big, strong, tattooed Andrew as he bakes?

"Right," I say, but it comes out as a whisper.

"Andrew needs someone who can make him happy." She watches me closely, as if waiting for me to say something. "Someone that makes him smile and laugh. Other than Bell."

"I agree," I say. "I mean, he does when we're together, smile, and laugh, but I can tell it's not how he is all the time."

She thins her lips, nodding. "He's got a tough exterior—it's hard to break through. That was why I was surprised he told you about Shana."

I shift in my seat. "Yes, well. We didn't mean for the conversation to go that way, but it did."

"So, what're your plans tonight?" she asks.

My fantasy fizzes and fades. The warmth recedes with it. There's work to be done. There's *always* work to be done, no matter if we're busy or not. Normally, I don't think too hard about that, but now, the thought depresses me. "Nothing," I say. "I'll probably stay here."

"Nathan wants to try this new restaurant in Meatpacking." She shrugs. "I'm not really into Indian right now, but he's been bending over backward to make sure I'm comfortable."

"That's, um, sweet," I say.

She nods. "I know you don't really like him, but he's been amazing."

"It's possible that I . . ." It's hard for me to admit when I'm wrong. I start again. "It's possible I don't know the full story. According to Andrew."

She smiles a little. "You don't. But you don't really have to like Nate," she says. "It's not like you ever spend time together. You're just my boss."

It's a bit harsh for Sadie, who's generally pretty even-keeled, not one to make a scene or go out of her way to make her opinion known. Maybe that's why it stings a little. I had almost been part of their unit, the three of them, but that's gone now. Sadie knows it too, yet by the smug look on her face, it's as if she's rubbing it in.

In fact, this whole conversation, she's been putting ideas in my head, like Andrew as a sexy baker, and then tearing them down.

Of course. Sadie knows me well. She understands that pushing Andrew on me would've scared me off. I narrow my eyes. "Sadie?"

She stands quickly. "I should get back to work."

I gasp. "You're using reverse psychology on me."

"Do you honestly think I'm that calculating?"

"*Yes.*"

She covers her mouth and laughs. "All right, fine. Yes, I tricked you, but my intentions are good, Amelia. Andrew's held everyone at arm's length so long. If he smiles and laughs with you, if he opens up to you—that's rare. Don't take that away from him, and by him, I mean me, because I want my brother to have what Nathan and I do."

I may be surprised by her approval, but she looks completely at ease about it. "What about everything else?" I ask. "All the reasons not to?"

"I can tell that you like him. And that he likes you. It makes no sense and it's a miracle. Don't throw that away." She absentmindedly touches her growing belly. "I love Bell with all my heart, but you have my approval. Even if it doesn't work out, I think it's really important for her to see her dad happy right now."

Me, make Andrew happy? But I do, don't I? It's been a while since I've done that for anyone. Reggie had to find someone else for it. Andrew isn't Reggie, though. I know that deep down. Andrew's more important to me than I've allowed myself to believe. Maybe Bell too.

Is that enough reason to put us all at risk of getting hurt? Since day one, I've tried to protect us from the long-term. We could be together for a night. For three nights. Hell, if I had a month left to live, I'd enjoy him every day of it and as much as possible. Does that really mean anything, though?

As soon as the question forms in my mind, I know the answer. It actually does mean something.

Maybe it means a lot.

TWENTY-FIVE
ANDREW

There's still an hour until butts out, and even though I rarely partake like the chimneys I work with, today, I come up from a tricky engine feeling particularly agitated. I've been at it all morning. I've tried everything I can think of to get it to work. All the guys have taken a look. The only option left is to call in Burt. Burt knows everything there is to know about automobiles, and that's why his hourly rates are astronomical. I end up eating the cost since it's not the customers' problem I can't do my job.

I wipe my hands on a rag and throw it at the car. "Fucking piece-of-shit lemon," I say. "Someone get me a cigarette."

"Only got one left," Pico answers, closest to me.

"So? I gave you a job when you were homeless and had never seen the inside of a car."

"I lived with my mom," he says defensively. "And I'd worked at Bob's Motors for months before you finally hired me."

"Whatever. If someone doesn't put a cigarette in my hand in five seconds, it'll be butts out permanently. Don't fucking test me right now."

Pico mutters, making a show of digging into his back pocket. He passes me one from the pack he has left, which is half full. He stares dumbly at me.

"Do I look like a *fucking* boy scout?" I ask.

"Huh?"

"What am I supposed to do, go out front, knock a couple rocks together, and produce fire?"

He flips me off before tossing me his lighter.

Randy chuckles a few feet away from us. It's the kind of sinister laugh that gets under my skin and bubbles at the surface. "Everything all right, boss?"

I take a soothing drag. "Fine."

"You seem a little on edge," he says. "When's the last time you got laid?"

"Ask your mom." Acting like an immature teen makes me feel oddly better.

Randy *tsks*. "Might be time for a trip to Timber. You've been nasty ever since the city girl blew you off."

"She didn't *blow me off*." I sound sulky even to myself.

"Well, something happened. You gotta get yourself some pussy, who cares what kind."

"I said I'm fine."

"I got a blowie last night," he volunteers. "Not bad, but not worth the fifty bucks. I'd stay away from Timber's back alley if I were you."

"You're such a piece of shit," I say.

"Maybe, but at least I'm having a great day."

"Believe it or not, blowjobs aren't the answer to everything," I say and stick the cigarette between my lips to pull up Burt's number.

"No? Name one situation that doesn't improve with a blowjob. I bet you can't even think of one."

I hate the fact that I'd give my left nut to get laid right now. When I get this way, agitated, overwhelmed, I need release. If not emotional, then physical. Sex. Fucking. It's been almost a week since I've heard from Amelia. She's glaringly absent, and her timing is shit with Shana trying to get her claws in.

I haven't seen Shana since the gymnasium, but she called the house last night. Bell was in the bathtub, and I was halfway through dishes. I'd had to wedge the receiver between my ear and shoulder thanks to wet rubber gloves.

"Andrew, babe," she'd said, and her tone, her words, were so familiar, for a moment it felt as though she were calling from the market to ask if we needed milk. "Just meet me for a drink. One drink."

Cornered and on the verge of feeling like one half of a couple again, I was terse. "I'm a single parent," I'd told her. "I barely have time to wipe my ass let alone sit and chat."

If she responded, I didn't hear it. I was already back to the dishes, but as I'd scrubbed and rinsed, dried and tidied, Shana had grown bigger in my mind. The first time I saw her, she was walking away from me. She wore jeans one size too small, her ass round and firm like an apple. It always seemed to be swaying. Looking back, her strut never faltered. Not when she left bed in panties and a tank to feed Bell. Not when she came home drunk off her head. I never stopped to wonder if it was just the way she walked or if she'd trained herself not to break character.

Sex with Shana, in the beginning, was an addiction; I was worse than a kid in a candy store. After Bell, it died off, and we had nothing to say to each other that didn't involve accusations or insults. Her resentment over Bell needled me to an unhealthy level.

Amelia feeds a different kind of hunger in me. She isn't candy, without nutrition or value, but a well-balanced, well-flavored meal. Her wit, her ambition, draws me in as much as her figure. She's surprisingly funny. Adventurous. And somehow, despite our boundaries, the sex is more connected than casual, more intuitive than cautious.

A week without it has made my entire body raw as an exposed nerve. Whenever I look at the photo of her in the bathtub, all I see is what I can't see. She mocks me, and it darkens my already black mood.

Randy's still running his mouth about all the ways blowjobs can improve your mood when a Mercedes with blacked-out windows pulls into the driveway and stops. The car idles, but nobody gets out. I give it a onceover, but nothing looks wrong, and it sounds in good shape. Generally, yuppies stick to their dealerships for auto work. "Go see what he wants."

Pico has his hand down his pants as he scratches his crotch. "'K."

"On second thought," I say, "I'll go."

The car's back door opens, and a man on his cell phone gets out. It takes me a moment to place the slicked-back hair, the expensive-looking pinstripe suit that creases and gaps in the wrong places, as if it's a size too big. If possible, Reggie looks even slimier in a suit than a baby blue polo.

Reggie checks the sign above my shop. When his eyes land on me, he says something into the phone before he hangs up.

"What the fuck?" I mutter for probably the hundredth time this week.

Randy's back goes straight. "What's wrong?"

Reggie and I walk toward each other, meeting in the middle. "What can I do for you?" I ask.

Reggie glances past me, into the garage. "Nice place. Sorry I couldn't get here sooner. I never really make it to this part of . . . Jersey."

I crack my knuckles as loudly as possible. The tip of his nose is red and peeling, as if he just got back

381

from somewhere sunny. I wonder what the hell Amelia ever saw in this guy. "What can I do for you?" I repeat.

He looks back at me. "Just one thing, really," he says with a labored sigh. "Amelia. She's not really your type, is she? I don't think you're hers, either."

I shrug. "How is this your business?"

"It is." He puts his hands in his pockets. "She's got a lot going for her—class, looks, value. She belongs with a man who can give her what she deserves. That's not a mechanic."

"She's a big girl," I say. "Maybe we should let her decide."

He sniffs, possibly, I think, because he's not getting the reaction he wants. "She's a little mixed up right now. Hurt. When that goes away, she'll regret this fling you guys are having. But, thing is, I'm not very patient, and I don't really like the idea of my wife screwing around with some fuck-up from New Jersey, so I'm ready for it to be over."

I laugh, a sound that's menacing and hollow even to my own ears. My irritation is rising up my chest. I don't care what he thinks of me, but that he's still calling her his wife needles me, even if Amelia seems to be through with me. "You'll have to talk to her about that."

"I've tried, believe me. I assumed it was nothing at first, but when you get family involved, it starts to worry me." He straightens his suit with a derisive glance at my coveralls. "I don't think Amelia is dumb enough to fall for a guy like you, but I can't take the chance."

My face warms. I have to work to keep my breathing even. I don't know what family he's referring to. The only family Amelia and I have brought into this is Sadie, Nathan and Bell, and I can't have this fuckwad even looking in their direction. "Get the fuck off my property."

"Or what? You'll kick my ass all the way to Hoboken? You're a thug."

I take a menacing step toward him. "*I'm* a thug? I'm not the one trying and failing to intimidate everyone in his path."

"Whatever Amelia told you, it's a lie."

His comment comes out of nowhere. I was referring to myself, not Amelia, although it applies. "What was a lie?"

"All of it. She's spun quite a tale with you and her therapist. She and I were happy. I never hurt her."

I lift my chin. If he really believed I was just a fling, there'd be no reason for him to assume Amelia would tell me any of what she did. "She didn't say you did," I lie.

He shakes his head like he's chastising a child. "I have an offer."

An offer can only mean one thing—some way to convince me to stay away from Amelia. I don't believe for a second that he'd go head to head with me like a real man. "You better think carefully about how you proceed," I say slowly, since he seems to have issues with comprehension. "I'm no thug, but I have no problem trying the title on with you."

He arches an eyebrow. "Is that a threat?"

"You're goddamn right it is. Caught me on a bad day. Keep talking, and you'll save me a trip to the punching bag tonight."

He raises his palms. "Message received. You're bigger than me, and I'm not an idiot. Muscle over brains, and all that. I'm not here to get violent." He reaches into his jacket pocket and pulls out a checkbook. "Let me talk in a language you understand. This'll be the easiest money you've ever made."

I'm barely able to unclench my teeth enough to get the words out. "You're going to pay me to stay away from her."

"Break up with her, and stay away. Simple. Everyone gets what they want."

Break up with her. He doesn't realize it might already be over. "And what do I want?" I ask.

He glances up at the sign of my shop. "Money, I guess. I'm sure you have no trouble finding women in your part of town. Money's not as easy to come by, though."

"And what does Amelia want?"

"She doesn't know. She may think you're meaningless sex, but she's a woman. They always get attached." He leans in as if we're old pals. "Trust me. I almost had to change jobs because of the crazy bitch I cheated with."

My hands shoot out to grab him, compelled by some force outside my control. This time he doesn't anticipate it, and he sucks in a breath when I catch his lapels. He darts his widened eyes over my shoulders. I sense Pico and Randy at my back. "You gutless asshole," I grate out. "Get in your foreign car and drive yourself back to the city. Go up to your pretentious apartment, clean the shit out of your pants, and stay the fuck away from us."

"Ten grand." His voice breaks, and he has to clear his throat. "Ten grand, clear and simple. I write the check, you stay on your side of town, and it's done. Free money."

My hands shake, and the loose skin under his chin jiggles. "Fuck you."

"T-twenty," he says. "Name your price."

As always, when I feel threatened, Bell pops into my mind. Amelia is there too, morning-after disheveled, unguarded on her bed. Women are objects to this man. Something to show off. Something to control. I'm so angry, my mouth won't open so I can respond. I need to let go. For Bell. For Amelia. I'm no good to them if I get arrested for pummeling him.

"You can shove your checkbook," Randy says from behind me when I don't answer. "Better yet, I'll do it for you. You look like you got a tight asshole. That's my favorite kind."

Reggie's face goes white as a sheet. "Are you fucking insane? It's twenty grand. You don't even have to do anything."

Then I hear it. "Daddy?"

My heart stops, and my burning rage runs suddenly cold. I release Reggie and take a step back, inhaling through my nose. Bell and Sammy stand ten feet away.

"What's wrong?" she asks, looking at all of us.

Reggie's mouth curls into a smile. "You must be Bell. Your daddy and I were just playing around."

She scowls. "My dad doesn't play like that."

"Don't look at my daughter," I say evenly, under my breath, and Reggie turns back to me. "Pico," I say over my shoulder, "take the kids for ice cream."

"But—" Bell protests.

"No buts," I say without taking my eyes off Reggie.

Randy shuffles them off. Reggie straightens his suit and takes a pen out of the same pocket. His hand jerks as he writes out a check. "Beckwith, correct? So, how much will it take? Keep it within reason."

"You think, just because you dress up and get your lazy ass driven around and you hire people to clean the piss and shit off your toilet, that you're better than me?" I laugh, and this time it's genuine. "You have no idea how wrong you are. You're a bad man. And I'll tell you, now more than ever, I'll do whatever it takes to keep Amelia away from you."

He shakes his head, removes a card from his pocket, and hands it to me. "Call me when you've changed your mind. A guy like you wouldn't turn down this kind of money for a woman."

"A guy like me?" I ask. "You think you know what kind of guy I am?"

He looks me up and down. "Without a doubt." He gestures behind him, in the direction of the city. "The kind who grew up within sight of everything but had nothing. Still has nothing, even after years of labor. The kind who gets desperate. It's sad, really."

I cock a smile. "Maybe. I'm also the kind of guy who can make a woman feel so good, she'll offer just about anything I can dream up." I lean in as he had, lowering my voice, getting chummy. "The kind of guy who loves to go where no other man has been before. Not even her husband."

When he understands what I mean, he frowns. "She wouldn't."

"She would. And she fucking loved it."

His nostrils flare, his skin reddening from his neck up. "Bullshit," he sputters. I wipe spittle off my face. "If she did, I'd know about it."

I chuckle. "Sure you would."

He replaces his checkbook in his jacket as the redness in his face fades. "No, you're right . . . I'd have no idea what she does behind closed doors. How would I?"

At the front of my mind is only one thing: Bell and Sammy are right around the corner. "Get off my property."

He walks back to his car, and the door opens before he even gets there. He slides in and slams it shut.

"Yo, what the fuck was that?" Randy asks from behind me.

"A man with a small dick who has the need and resources to try and make up for it."

"Damn," he says. "I assumed because of your mood things were over with her."

"They might be." How did I end up here? I never thought I'd be pining over a prissy city girl who seems to have more interest in her wardrobe than my daughter. Only, I'm not sure I believe that's true, even if she wants me to think it is.

"You could've taken the money then," he points out.

I turn my head over my shoulder. "Would you have?"

"Obviously," he says with a sniff. "But nah. Not really. Too fun to watch that clenched asshole squirm."

My shoulders ease when I remember that Randy spoke when I couldn't, and he knew exactly what to say. "Thanks."

"We should've kicked his ass."

"If only he'd come at us ten years ago."

Randy blows out his cheeks with a sigh. "We're getting so old, man. What happened to the days when we could just fly off the handle?"

Down the block, Pico leans out of the ice cream shop, checking that it's all clear. I wave him over. Reggie put me in that position in front of my daughter. I have every right to be pissed, and there's nothing I can do about it. "Those days are over."

TWENTY-SIX

My Camaro isn't made for city streets. Confined by Lexington Avenue traffic, even though it's Saturday, the car rumbles and protests each time we start and stop. Bell bounces in her car seat and accidentally kicks the dash.

"Watch it," I say.

"Why?" she asks.

"You'll mark up the leather. Just stay still."

"Why?"

"Because I said so."

"Why?"

I hit the brakes a little too hard. "Because I hate driving in this fucking city, and you're distracting me."

"There's valet."

"Valet," I mutter. "Do you think I'm made of money?"

"There," she screeches, pointing at a pair of reversing taillights. A Honda maneuvers away from the curb, and I drop my foot on the gas. The car in front of us brakes and starts to back in, but I'm already partway there. The guy lays on his horn.

"Close your eyes," I tell Bell.

"Why?"

"Because I said so."

She sighs but obeys. I stick my middle finger out the window and keep it there. He can have this spot over my dead body. After a few seconds of our standoff, a pedestrian yells at him for blaring the horn. His tires squeal as he hits the gas, and he flips the bird right back at me. I pull into the parking spot.

"You're the one who didn't want to take the train," Bell points out.

I get out of the car and walk around to her side. She's been talking about Aunt Sadie's surprise baby shower for days, but she still knows to wait until I open her door. I let her out of the car seat and take her hand to lead her into Gramercy Park Hotel, then up to the terrace on the eighteenth floor that Nathan reserved for the afternoon.

I spot Nate right away. It isn't hard in the explosion of floral arrangements and miniature pastries. A table at the entrance has the start of a gift pile, and I tell Bell to add ours.

Nathan's brows are gathered as a woman in a suit taps her clipboard, showing him something. He scratches his forehead and glances up at us.

"Andrew," he says, desperately motioning me over. "You've got to help me, man. They ran out of raspberry macaroons. Sadie craves raspberry *everything* right now."

"Dude, she's not going to give a rat's ass." I check the sheet of paper filled with pictures of desserts and their names. I point to a frosted cupcake that's topped with chocolate shavings. "You got these?" I ask the woman.

"Yes, sir."

Nathan looks too, nodding. "Everyone likes chocolate. Those'll be fine." He mops his brow as she walks away. "This is way harder than it looks."

"When does Sadie get here?"

He checks his watch. "Ten minutes? Jill told her they were going for lunch at the restaurant downstairs."

"Then what?" I ask.

"That was the hotel's event planner, and she has some games and stuff set up. Jill takes over when they get here. Then we've got to go. This is like, chicks only."

"No shit," I say. "Husbands don't typically plan baby showers."

"I know." He half-smiles, somehow proud of this, and looks at me sidelong. "Looking forward to seeing Amelia?"

I look out at the buildings surrounding the patio. "She coming?"

"Yeah. She didn't tell you?"

It's been a week since Amelia left me in the middle of the flea market. Since Shana dropped into my life like a bomb, and Amelia wasn't around to help pick up the pieces. "Nope."

"Ah. How about we go next door and grab a beer when they get here?" Nathan asks. "You can tell me all about it."

Sometimes, Nathan's all-knowingness is helpful, and other times *not*. I sigh and take a good look around the room at tiny teacups, satin bows, and diaper tower centerpieces. "Uh, yeah. I think I'll actually head over now." The prospect of spilling my complicated feelings about Amelia to Nathan appeals to me slightly more than running into her. "I'll meet you there."

"Are you sure? Don't you want to say hi to Sadie?"

"I'll catch her later." I check on Bell. She's already chatting up the only other child in the room, who looks a couple years older than her, but who politely listens to Bell ramble on about God knows what. "Poor girl," I mutter.

"Don't say that," Nate says. "I'm sure she's put up with worse than you."

I arch an eyebrow and turn back to him, but he isn't looking at Bell. I follow his line of sight. Amelia breezes onto the terrace, reading her watch. She scans the outdoor space and asks the woman nearest her, "Has she arrived?"

"Not yet," the woman answers.

"Good." She visibly relaxes, but only until her eyes land on me. Tightening her hand around her purse strap, she draws a long breath, her chest expanding. Like the schmuck I am, I look right at her tits. Her neckline plunges enough for me to get an eyeful, and her white dress ties off to one side. She touches a simple silver pendant around her neck, pulling my attention to her collarbone. Every strand of her hair is predictably smoothed into place. I don't understand how this woman could be the exact opposite of what I want and yet the center of all my fantasies.

She takes a few steps toward me, and because I don't need Nathan hanging on our every word, I meet her halfway.

"I thought this was a girls' thing," she says.

"I got a girl," I say, nodding at Bell.

"Oh." She absentmindedly runs both hands over her dress. "Of course. I didn't even think—"

"I tried to get ahold of you."

With a sideways glance, she nods once. "I know."

"And?"

"And nothing," she says. "I don't have a good excuse."

I appreciate her honesty, but then again, me appreciating her honesty is partly what got us into this mess in the first place.

"I'm glad you're here, though." Her eyes soften. "I've been working up the courage to call. Is it all right if we talk after this?"

"We can talk now." I look over her head instead of into her eyes. I don't need that mesmerizing blue playing tricks on me. "I went through some shit last week. That's why I called. I could've used someone to talk to."

"Someone?" she asks. "Me?"

"Yeah." I cross my arms. "I ask you to be my girlfriend, and you respond by ignoring my texts and pawning me off on your receptionist."

"What happened?"

I shake my head. For the last week, I've been brooding, worried about what Shana's presence means, fielding Bell's equally valid and unnerving questions about her mom. The simplest ones are the most impossible to answer: *Where is my mom? Why did she leave? Is she ever coming back?* 'I don't know,' is what I wanted to tell her, and basically what I'd said in a lot more words. I'm frustrated Amelia stayed just outside my reach when I could've used her comfort.

That's a whole week to begin putting my walls back up. "Suddenly I don't feel like confiding in you."

She frowns. "I was going to call. I just needed to get my head on straight."

"Is that how you do relationships?" I ask. "Because that doesn't work for me. I need communication, especially after what I've been through."

She looks at her hands. "I understand. At first, I didn't respond because I thought maybe you and I were fooling ourselves to try this. There are so many reasons not to."

I don't need her to list them; I've been doing that the past few days. "Then?"

"Then I decided maybe falling for each other isn't convenient, but maybe it could be pretty great."

I'm taken aback at the unexpected response. I'd assumed she'd spent the last week convincing herself we wouldn't work. "I thought so," I say. "I fell for you."

She lifts her eyes to mine. "You did?"

"I started to. I wouldn't spend the night with just anyone. I wouldn't help just anyone search for a new apartment to get her away from her ex. I wouldn't hate just anyone's ex as vehemently as I do yours."

She's quiet as she chews on her bottom lip. Somehow, her lipstick remains unperturbed. "I wasn't expecting to see him like that, with you," she says slowly. "I wasn't mentally prepared for him, but suddenly . . . he was there, two worlds merging into one. And it reminded me of the truth."

"What's the truth?"

"Things fall apart. People lie. Cheat. Hurt each other, accidentally or on purpose. I don't want to rely on anyone but myself. How do I know you won't hurt me like Reggie did?"

"You can't know that. But don't you get it?" I ask. "You did the same thing to me that Shana did. She disappeared. You disappeared too."

She shakes her head quickly. "I didn't *disappear*. I was taking a breather. Figuring things out. I thought you'd understand, given our situation."

"I didn't. I don't." I stick my hands in my pockets and look up at the commotion by the door. Sadie has arrived, her hands over her mouth, her eyes wide. She launches herself into Nathan's arms. When I see them together, I know love exists. I'd just thought it wasn't for me. For the first time in years, I wanted to be wrong about that.

"What happened?" she asked. "Why did you want to talk to me?"

"If you'd called me back, you'd know." I take a step back. It isn't easy. I still feel strongly for her, but I have more than myself to consider.

"Is it about Bell? Is she . . . is she okay?"

I get a surge of regret with her question. Her concern for Bell touches me, but it's too little too late. Amelia isn't Shana, but if she's spooked this easily, she could be. "Bell's fine. We'll get through it."

"I'm sorry, Andrew." She glances nervously at the group of chattering women. At Bell. "I . . . I like her. I didn't even know children like Bell existed. She's so mature but free. Wise, but still naïve and innocent. I'm not sure I'm ready to jump right in with her, but—"

"Don't." I pull at my collar as my throat feels like it's closing. I only see Bell crying all those late nights, confused about where her mom was. "I can't go there."

Sadie waves me over, and Bell notices, perking up when she picks me out of the crowd. She'll be over here in a flash, I can tell.

"Let me make it up to you," she says. "We can go for real food after this lunch. Pizza, beer, and then my place to talk. I'll make myself sick with carbs if that's what it takes." She smiles a little, but I just stare at her.

"I have Bell."

"She can stay with Sadie tonight. You're already here in the city. Don't make the same mistake I did."

"Which mistake?" I ask.

"I let my fear come between us. I know that's what you're doing right now by not giving us a chance to work through this."

I scrub my hands over my face. "Don't turn this on me—"

"Please, Andrew. Just—don't shut me out. I can make it right. Forget the pizza. I'll open a bottle for us. I'll draw you a bath with all the Tahitian vanilla I can find. We'll be you and me. We'll drink, soak, and talk. About everything. We'll figure this out."

I look at the ground, as if that will stop the tempting picture she's painting, a picture of us in our little bubble. Who were we kidding? We can't live in there. We can't hide from our problems in a bathroom.

Bell's Mary Janes *click-click-click* as she runs up and attaches herself to my leg. "She was surprised! Did you see?"

"Yeah, baby." I smooth my hand over her hair. Amelia looks between us expectantly, as if she's waiting for me to say something. "I'm going to take off," I tell Bell. "I'll come back to pick you up in a bit."

"You have to go?" Bell asks.

I pray against the odds that she won't melt into a tantrum. The last thing I need is a roomful of women judging my parenting. "Yes, this party is girls only. I'm not a girl."

"But . . ." Her hands curl into my jeans.

"I'll be right next door with Uncle Nathan."

"Hello, Bell," Amelia says, touching the pendant around her neck. "Nice to see you again."

"Amelia," I warn. "Don't."

Bell looks up as if she hadn't noticed anyone at all. "'Mila?" She releases my leg to face her. "What's that?"

Amelia releases the locket suddenly, as if she hadn't realized she was playing with it. Her fingers are stiff. "It's . . . a necklace."

"I *know*," Bell says irritably, "but what kind? It looks old."

"It is." Amelia curls her hand against her chest. "I just found it in storage. I haven't had a chance to clean it yet—with silver, you should really take care of it, have it polished . . ." The thin skin of her throat ripples when she swallows.

Bell's eyebrows are wrinkled. Because she doesn't give two shits about how to care for silver. Amelia has no idea how to talk to children, which should bother me, but I'm more captivated by their awkwardness.

"I hear it's your birthday tomorrow," Amelia says. "My dad gave me this locket on *my* tenth birthday."

"What's a locket?" Bell asks. "Can I see?"

Amelia hesitates before she reaches behind her to remove it. She squats, her back straight as a rod. I doubt she's ever bent down to anyone else's level before. "You put a picture inside."

"Inside? How? Can I open it?"

"The clasp is a little tricky—" Amelia starts to undo it and thinks better of it. She hands Bell the necklace. "Go ahead. You try."

Bell fumbles with the small, oval pendant while Amelia obviously restrains herself from interfering. Finally, Bell pops it open and gasps. "Wow. Is that you?"

"As a baby," Amelia says.

"I love it," Bell decides. "I want one with my picture."

"Well, you'll have to wait a few more years. Until you're old enough." Amelia glances up at me. "If your dad says it's okay."

I have to look away. I want to be angry, like I am when Denise tries to get to me through Bell. It doesn't feel like that's what Amelia's doing, though. She doesn't know how to connect with Bell, and I'm not sure she even wants to—but she's trying. For me.

Bell gives back the necklace and takes Amelia's hand. "Come on. I'll take you over to say hi to Aunt Sadie."

Amelia closes her eyes for a brief second and then stands. "Please," she says to me under her breath. "I didn't know I wanted this. I'm sorry that I do, but I'm also not."

"Come on, 'Mila," Bell whines, pulling Amelia's hand. "You can go, Dad. We'll be okay."

Amelia keeps her eyes on me. "Tonight, my door is open for you," she says. "I hope you'll walk through it."

TWENTY-SEVEN

Nathan sips his club soda and sets it on the bar with a sigh. "Thank God that's done. I don't know what I was thinking planning a baby shower in the first place, and then I had to go and make it a surprise."

"You were thinking it would make her happy." The loving look on Sadie's face when she stepped onto the terrace said it all. "And you were right."

"I've been feeling helpless," he admits. "She's going through everything that comes with pregnancy—swelling, heartburn, mood swings—and I'm just over here fumbling through."

"I know that's not true. Sadie told me she'd have lost it a long time ago if it weren't for everything you do for her."

He smiles a little, looking over at me. "Yeah?"

"Definitely." Sadie hadn't exactly said that, but her eyes twinkle when she tells me about how Nathan brings home whatever she's craving without her even asking. And how he spends hours researching cribs online. I take a drink of my Coke. "Look at us. At a bar drinking sodas. We're pathetic."

"I promised Sadie from now on I'd cut out alcohol. Show of support. She misses her wine."

"And I have to drive back to Jersey tonight, which wouldn't have stopped me from having a beer or two in the past."

"And then Bell happened," he infers. "We're whipped by our women."

I lean back on the barstool. "I'd say so."

"We must be crazy to bring another one into the mix."

I glance over at him, tilting my head. Nathan is more observant than I give him credit for, but for once, he's wrong. Despite the fact that Amelia and I weren't very discreet just now, he seems to have missed the fact it's over between us. "Actually, Amelia and I aren't . . . we're done." I nod behind us. "That's what all that was about at the hotel."

Nathan raises his eyebrows, no doubt sensing the lack of conviction in my tone. I don't mention Amelia's invitation. Do I want to go to her, let her put a Band-Aid on this with a bath, whisky and sex? Yes. I still want her. But it doesn't change the fact that when she freaked out, she turned away from me when she should've done the opposite.

Finally, Nate says, "*Oh*. You mean Amelia."

"Yeah. Why? What other woman are we bringing into the mix?"

"Your niece."

"Niece?" I ask. "But I don't have—unless Sadie . . . but she doesn't know the sex. Does she?" I widen my eyes and leap off the stool. "Dude. Are you telling me you're having a girl?"

Nathan laughs loudly enough to turn a few heads. "Did you not notice the entire party was pink?"

I think back to the set up, which was disgustingly girly—because it was for a bunch of women, I thought. Now, details set in—the fact that the lace tablecloths and satin bows were the color of bubble gum. "I figured that's just how baby showers were."

"The cake said 'It's a girl.'"

"Oh." My chest tightens at the thought of a baby girl, and it's not so disgusting anymore. It's *fan-fucking-tastic*. It's nearly tear inducing. I'm flooded with memories of Bell crawling for the first time, of how we dressed her up in a red velvet dress and black patent leather shoes for Christmas dinner, of falling asleep on the couch with her on my chest, the rest of me buried under dolls. I grin and slap Nathan on the back. He jolts forward. "No shit. A girl. Congratulations. They're the most amazing . . ." A lump forms in my throat. "I can't even put it into words."

He nods. "I know, man. I know. I was there," he says, referring to the last seven years with Bell. "Sit down before you hurt yourself. Or me."

"I can't even . . ." I get back on the seat, shaking my head. "I'm speechless. Sadie must be over the moon."

"I took a risk announcing it like this," he says, "but Sadie said she was ready to tell people last week, so I assumed it would be okay."

I grimace. "You didn't clear it with her?"

"How could I? It was a surprise."

"A little advice," I say, "I don't care if she's Mother Teresa—when dealing with a pregnant woman, assume *nothing*."

"She didn't seem mad about it," he points out. "Not at all."

"That could be. But still. Don't think you're off the hook yet. She could strike at any time."

"You make her sound like a rattlesnake hiding in the bushes."

"Two words." I hold up my fingers and count down. "Shana and hormones."

"Ah. I see why you'd be traumatized," he says. "So . . . she's back, huh?"

"No. I don't know. I'm hoping if I ignore her long enough, she'll go away."

He shakes his head. "Sorry, man. Wish I could say it's a surprise, but you never know with her. Is that why you're putting the brakes on with Amelia?"

I glance up at the Yankees game in time to see Masahiro Tanaka strike out his batter. Nathan and I raise our glasses toward the TV and cheers. Since Jersey doesn't have a major league baseball team, I root for the Yanks, my only concession where New York is concerned. "Not exactly," I answer Nathan. "It's more complicated than that."

Nathan sighs. "Is it? After four years, are you seriously not ready to open up at all? To bring Amelia into Bell's life?"

I nod out of habit more than agreement. I'm used to hearing it from Sadie, but Nathan is generally understanding of my stance on love. Am I not ready? Can I not open up? That isn't the case. I already opened up to Amelia. Seeing Shana again should've sharpened that fear of falling for someone new, but instead, I turned to Amelia for support. I stop nodding and shake my head. "No, actually. I mean, yeah, Shana fucked me up. But I think I'm finally . . . over it."

"Because of Amelia?" Nathan sounds surprised.

"Not completely. I just needed time and distance from Shana, and I have that now. But also, seeing Shana again, I felt nothing at all—except protective of Bell. No anger, no hurt." I spin my glass on the bar. Would I have felt the same if Amelia weren't in the picture, though? She's not the reason I'm ready to move on from Shana, but she was the reason I suddenly wanted to. "And yes," I add, "because of Amelia."

"You really like her."

"I do."

"Then why . . .?"

I look at Nate. He's a romantic, always has been. He'd love for everything to work out for everyone. It's not that simple, though. "She's scared. I was willing to take that risk with her, but she freaked out and left me hanging when I needed her, and I can't risk that happening again. Not with Bell in the picture."

"Well." He hesitates. "Didn't she just get divorced?"

"Not even. They're still battling it out."

"And you've been doing this for four years. Remember what it was like in the early days? Wouldn't you have freaked out too?"

"Yeah. I understand it, but I just don't think she's ready."

"If you feel that way, why'd you get involved with her in the first place?"

"We agreed to keep it casual. No feelings."

"And you're upset that she held up her end of the agreement."

I look at him sidelong, not sure if I'm impressed or annoyed with his emotional ninja skills. "There's more to it than that."

"Is it? Jesus. I've never seen Amelia giddy, but that's what she is around you. Normally she's all business, all the time, to the point I wonder if she even knows how to smile. Not with you, though."

I wave him off. "It's the sex."

He laughs. "Probably. But I think it's more for her."

He's right. I know it. She knows it. It started out as sex, but I think we knew that first night it would never be just that, even if we never saw each other again. Fuck. Knowing others can see what we have makes this even harder to swallow. "I don't know. Maybe I'm wrong," I admit. "But she's going through what I went through years ago with Shana. I sure as fuck wasn't ready back then to get involved with anyone."

"So who better to guide her through that than you?" he asks, leaning his elbows on the bar. "I just haven't seen you excited about anyone since Shana. And Amelia, I've never seen her like this. I'd hate to see you both walk away because of pride or fear or whatever you're hung up on. Everything else aside, how do you feel about her?"

"I told you. I like her. All the things you just said—excited. Giddy. Protective."

"Then don't give up on her," he says, and I don't have to question why he's so adamant. He's been through his own shit with Sadie. He fought for her then, and he'd fight for her again. That kind of love is a gift, and maybe I've been given the opportunity to fight for it as well. "Amelia has her rough edges," he says, "so do you. If you two somehow fit together, that's a little bit of a miracle, isn't it?"

It's true—I can't imagine anyone out there worse for me than Amelia. She should be with someone like Reggie, someone wealthy, influential, ambitious. I should be with someone who could spend a day talking shit and smoking cigarettes at the garage with me and the guys.

"Plus, Bell seems to like her," Nathan adds. "I saw how she grabbed her hand before we left."

My chest tightens. Bell is noticing Amelia, and because she's just a kid, she'll trust her. If that's supposed to make me happy, it doesn't. What happens if Bell turns ten, and Amelia isn't there to give her a locket? I didn't worry about these things before Shana, and since her, I've never cared enough to worry.

I nod at Nathan as if I'm agreeing, so we can end the conversation. Because I won't be able to put into words the fear of Bell and Amelia getting close, and even if I could, he wouldn't understand.

He will, in about three months, but until he has a little girl of his own, he won't realize the lengths he'll go through to protect her.

Or the ways a father would unflinchingly sacrifice his own happiness for his daughter's.

TWENTY-EIGHT

My mood has been foul since I picked Bell up from the baby shower. Maybe sensing this, Pico invites us all to his mom's place for dinner. I don't want company, but the alternative is sitting at home, wondering if I'm making a mistake by not going to Amelia's. Twice, I've gotten out my phone to tell her I'm not coming, to put a definitive end to our relationship, and twice I've chickened out.

Bell sits at the kitchen table with crayons and a coloring book. Between her, three guys, and all the place settings, there's barely room for Flora at her own table.

"Got to get a bigger set up, ma," Pico says.

"Why are there two extra settings?" I ask.

"Antonio has invited a lady friend," she says.

"A what?" I ask.

Randy perks up as well. "A lady friend?"

Pico shrugs. "Didn't I mention? I'm sure I did. Yeah."

"No," we say in unison. Pico hasn't been on a date in over a year, and he hasn't gotten laid in that long either. We would know.

"She's lovely," Flora says. "Her son too. Sammy, is it?"

Bell's head pops up. "Sammy's coming?"

I gawk at Pico. "You're dating Sammy's *mom*?"

"Yeah. Why? Were you interested?" he mocks. "Too bad. She chose me."

"I'm not interested." I nod discreetly at Bell. "But you'll have that to deal with if things go south."

The doorbell rings, and Pico leaves the room. He's changed out of his clothes from the shop and fixed his hair. Maybe I haven't been paying as close attention as I thought. He returns with Myra, who has her hands on Sammy's shoulders as she leads him into the kitchen.

"Hey, Bell," he mutters, his gaze bouncing from her to me to Pico to his mom and back to Pico. Sammy's a year older than Bell, and he seems to already grasp what's going on. Fuck dating as a single parent.

Bell passes Sammy a yellow crayon and shows him what she's working on—a monkey at a zoo. "You can color the bananas, but stay inside the lines. My dad will probably put this on the fridge."

I smile sheepishly as Pico and Randy groan. I think Flora might even snort. "I can't remember a time I saw a wall without a coloring book page taped to it," Randy says, referring to my office at the garage, which is covered with them.

"Myra understands," I say, turning to her. "Don't you hang Sammy's things?"

"Not if I can help it," she says. "He didn't exactly get the creative gene."

Bell pauses, her concentration lines easing, as if she's deciding whether or not to proceed with this duet she's just orchestrated. She checks Sammy's work and, seemingly pleased, returns to coloring.

"Thank you for having us," Myra says.

"You know you're all welcome any time," she says. "Even if it is extremely last minute."

"Sorry about that, Mrs. Picolli," Randy says. Despite tormenting Pico with mom jokes, he's been nothing but polite tonight.

"It's no trouble. What's the occasion anyway?"

"Beckwith needs the stick removed from his ass," Pico says. "We figured your spaghetti bolognese'd do the trick."

Bell swaps her brown crayon for pink, inspects the bananas, and says, "Let's turn the page. The next one is under water."

Sammy shrugs.

"What's the matter, Andrew?" Flora asks. "Lady problems got you down?"

Amelia wasn't at the baby shower when I returned to get Bell. It was better that way. I didn't say I'd show tonight, and she shouldn't expect me to.

I don't really have much to say to these guys about that. Amelia's an alien in our world of coveralls, carbs, and car parts. There is, however, one name that will make them all understand the reason for my permanent scowl.

I glance once more at Bell. The tip of her tongue is stuck out the side of her mouth as she alternates between green and blue to fill in fish scales. "Bell, ears."

She slumps her shoulders and makes a noise from the back of her throat. "But—"

"Ears."

She slams her crayon on the table, puts both hands over her ears, and begins reciting the alphabet.

I look back at the table. "Shana's back in town."

"*What?*" Pico asks.

Flora brings an oven-mitt-clad hand to her mouth. "No."

I nod at Bell. "Showed up at gymnastics last week."

Pico's nostrils flare. "What a cun—"

"Antonio Leonardo Picolli," Flora says. "Language."

Bell giggles, the way she always does when she hears Pico's full name, and I realize she's stopped talking.

"What comes after G?" I ask.

She sighs. "H, I, J . . ."

"What'd she want?" Randy asks.

I shake my head. "Don't know. Don't care."

Flora *tsks*, shaking her head as she pulls a stack of dishes from a cupboard. "You better find out. That girl won't just go back where she came from. Not until she gets what she wants."

My muscles clench, some animal reflex to feeling threatened. "Good thing I'm too busy to worry much about it," I say, which is only partly a lie. I haven't thought about Shana since seeing Amelia this afternoon, that's for sure. My stomach drops. Dusk is setting in. Amelia must be expecting me soon.

"Is that Bell's mom?" Sammy asks, saving me from my own thoughts. We all look at him. He taps his crayon on the table.

He might be too young for this conversation, but he looks about as concerned as I feel, and it's a small comfort. "Remember the woman who gave Bell the red envelope?" I ask him.

He nods. "That was her?"

"Yeah. But Bell and I haven't talked about that yet."

"I won't say anything," he says, nodding.

"I think I have some garlic," Flora says. "Want to take it with you?"

I furrow my eyebrows. "What for? I have garlic at home."

"Not for cooking," she says, a smile sliding over her face. "For warding off evil."

"What evil?" Bell asks, bouncing excitedly in her seat. "Zombies? Monsters?"

"Something like that," I mutter and point at the drawing. "Look—Sammy's coloring outside the lines."

"What!" She grabs his crayon. "What are you doing? Do you have a stick up your ass?"

"Bell Beckwith," Flora scolds, but the rest of us burst into laughter. She has no idea what she's saying, but she looks pleased with herself to have gotten such a raucous reaction.

"I don't know where she gets this stuff," I say, looking pointedly at Pico and Randy.

Flora dishes out pasta. Except for Myra and Flora, we each eat portions as big as our heads, Bell included.

Later, while Bell's in the bathroom, Flora says, "Why don't you all go get a drink? I can watch the kids."

I shake my head. "I'm not in the mood to fight with Bell tonight."

"She won't even notice. Sammy's here."

She means to comfort me, but her words sting. Is that what I have to look forward to? Bell blowing me off for boys? I make a mental note to revisit the idea of locking her in the house until her hair is gray.

"I can help." Sammy rolls his eyes but blushes. "I'll even watch *Beauty and the Beast*."

I arch an eyebrow at him. "You'd do that?"

He suppresses a smile. "Sure."

He knows Bell's moods, her favorite movie, and he's got her back. Maybe I don't have to be so terrified of what's to come. "You're a good man, Samuel."

"Thanks, Mr. Beckwith."

I grin. "Call me Andrew."

Buck, Timber Tavern's longest standing bartender, hands me a pint. "You got company, Beckwith," he says, nodding behind me.

I close my eyes and sigh. *What now?*

"Hey," I hear.

I look sideways as Denise slides onto the stool next to me. "What's up?" I ask.

She sets her purse on the counter. "I'll have a Stella," she tells Buck, waiting until he serves her to speak again. "It's nice to see you, Andrew. Been a while."

"I've been busy."

She nods. "I'm sorry about before, when I yelled at you. It's just, like, I care about you. You know? And Bell."

"I know." I take a seat too and lean my elbows on the bar. "Truth is, you're probably right."

"Am I?" she teases.

"I guess. Bell and I are codependent. I just don't know how to parent any other way. I don't know if I want to."

"I know I don't have children, but I have three older brothers."

I take a swig and recall all the times I blew Denise off, especially right after sex. "Thanks for the reminder."

"And I've been doing lots of thinking about this," she continues. "You aren't doing her any favors by scaring off women who get too close."

I look over at her. Pico, Myra and Randy are nearby, cracking balls on the pool table while they wait for me to start a game. "By women, you mean you."

She shrugs. "Just someone who might want to be part of your lives. You're not going to be able to fight her battles for her forever."

"You don't know that," I say, folding one corner of a cardboard coaster. "I can't think of anything better to do with my time than follow her around and make sure people treat her right."

She smiles a little. "You're a good dad. I bet you'd be even better if you were happy."

"Christ. What is it with you people? I *am* happy—"

I stop when I catch her wide-eyed expression. "*Shit*," she says as color drains from her cheeks.

"What's wrong?" I turn on my stool to follow her gaze. In the doorway, dressed in head-to-toe, skin-baring black clothing, is Shana. Scanning the bar. She spots us, narrowing her eyes.

"What the fuck," Denise says. "Did you know—
"

"Yeah," I say. "She got back about a week ago."

Shana strolls toward us. "Well, well, well," she says. "I guess the rumors are true. I didn't think you had it in you, Denise."

"What're you doing here?" Denise asks.

"Spoiling your date, it would seem."

"It's not a date." Denise's expression sours. "And what do you care? What right do you have to say anything? You left them."

"Some friend you are." Shana shakes her head slowly. "How long did you wait to move in on my man?"

I groan. If I thought I could flee the bar, I'd try, but Shana would never let me off that easily. "Come on. It's not like that."

Shana keeps her eyes on Denise. "I shouldn't be surprised. I knew you always had a thing for him. You were supposed to be my friend."

Denise flinches, dropping her arms to her sides. "I was a *great* friend to you, Shana. I invited you into our circle of friends because Andrew cared about you. You're the one who up and left without a call. Didn't even say bye. What was I supposed to do?"

"Fuck my boyfriend, I guess."

"Look, we didn't plan it," I say in Denise's defense. "We were friends. It just happened."

Shana glares at Denise. "So it's true then. You back-stabbing bitch."

Denise's mouth falls open. "Are you kidding me? Do you know what everyone in this town said about you when you left? I was the only one who defended you."

I nod after I take another sip. "It's true. Everyone talked shit. Denise said you had your reasons, though. Not sure why she had your back."

"You have a funny way of showing support," Shana says. "Pity you couldn't get a seat at the table, though. Have to settle for his scraps."

Denise's eyes water. "Why do you think that is? You completely fucked with his head."

Shana smirks. "You of all people should've known nobody could replace me. Especially not you. Andrew and I were made for each other. But you knew that, didn't you?" She tilts her head. "Andrew likes a strong woman. Not someone who'll swallow her self-respect just to get in his bed for a night. You're pathetic."

"That's enough," I say, and both women flinch at my raised voice. "Leave Denise out of this. She might be the only friend you have left here."

"Not anymore," Denise says.

"You think I care?" Shana asks. "Why are you still standing here?"

Denise's face reddens as she looks between us. I remember what Flora said earlier—Shana won't go quietly. And the more I ignore her, the harder she'll try to get my attention. "Just give us a few minutes," I tell Denise.

Denise storms off, and I can tell I'll pay for dismissing her. She's a good friend, and I don't want to hurt her, but I can't have any distractions while taking on Shana.

I look down at my sleeve. Shana's playing with the edge of it. "It's true, you know," she says.

I take a long pull from my beer to cool off. "What is?"

"You and me. We're made for each other."

A fiery anger rises up my chest—outrage, injustice, frustration. It flames out before it reaches my lips, though. Why? For so long, I've wanted the opportunity to rail at Shana. There's so much to say, I don't even know where to begin. I'm afraid if I say one thing, it'll all come pouring out, and I don't want to give her the satisfaction. I've never been good at controlling my reaction to her. What if that hasn't changed? If she can still get under my skin, does that mean I still love her?

"Andrew, babe. Look at me." She's close enough that I catch a hint of her scent, the same passion fruit-something-or-other shampoo she always used. Again, it's as if she never left. I glance into her eyes knowing I'll find that familiar twinkle. It was there more often than it wasn't, whenever she'd try to get me to do something. "No one will see," she would say, smiling mischievously and unbuckling my pants as I drove the two of us back from a day at the shore. Or, more soberly, "A one-year-old won't know the difference," when we'd argue over the quality of baby products to buy.

"I got scared," she says to me. "Can't you understand that?"

"You think I wasn't?"

"Nothing scares you."

How wrong she is. My conversations with Amelia and Nathan are still fresh in my mind. Fear of the future is the reason I'm not with Amelia right now. Fear of abandonment has kept me from letting anyone into our lives in years. If Shana only knew how the love I have for Bell sits in my chest like a bowling ball all the time, crushing my organs, my lungs, my heart. I have the fear of a parent, the most potent, pervasive, life-altering kind there is. "What do you want, Shana? Why are you here?"

"I want my family back."

I would throw my bottle against the back of the bar in blind rage if I weren't laughing. The gleeful noise travels up my throat, filling the space between us, and Shana looks appropriately confused. "You don't know what you want," I say. "Because you don't know what you've missed. You have no idea what the last few years have been like."

"It must've been terrible." She grazes her thumb under my sleeve, and my traitorous skin breaks out in goose bumps. "I can't even imagine the hell it's been, raising a child on your own—"

I pull back, curling one corner of my mouth into an easy smile. "Hell? They've been the best years of my life."

Her eyebrow lowers as she opens her mouth. "I find that hard to believe."

"Then don't," I say. "Really, don't believe it. Go back to thinking children are demons."

"I don't think they're *demons*. Just because I wanted something different doesn't make me a villain." She waits for me to agree with her. It might be true, but I'm not ready to concede anything yet. "You and I had some good times," she says. "They got me through a lot of lonely nights."

"Being with Bell is better than all of it. That little girl is everything to me."

She bites her bottom lip, shaking her head in disbelief. "I want to feel that way too," she says. "I do. I didn't want to be a mom then, but as my family gets further away, and I get older . . . I need to feel grounded again."

"A phone call now and then would've been nice," I say. "Just to let us know you were okay."

"My mom—"

"I spoke to her right after you left. She said you were safe. Honestly, after I heard that, I wasn't sure I even wanted to know. It meant there was nothing wrong, no reason for you to leave. Just me and Bell."

"It wasn't what I expected," she says carefully. "Motherhood. I didn't want it, but it was even worse than I thought. My options were to stay and torture all of us or leave. What would you have done?"

"I can't put myself in that position," I say. "I always wanted it. It's the best thing that ever happened to me."

She purses her lips, looking affronted. Of course she would take my devotion to Bell personally. "I was young."

"Too young. Too young for me, too young to know what you wanted."

"I'm older now. I'm not going anywhere."

"What makes you think I'd put my daughter—or myself—through that again?"

"Because I'm her mother," she says. "And you love me. Or, you did. Didn't you?"

I glance down at the bottle. "Yes."

"Do you still?"

I don't want to look at her, but I do. I have to know if she can still transfix me. That sparkle is back in my life, that neat curve of her mouth. At twenty-seven, she looks even better than she did four years ago, having grown into her features and shed some of the roundness of her face. If I look closely, I can see cover-up under her eyes, but she doesn't need it. If she has dark shadows, they don't show.

"Let's get out of here," she says under her breath, tracing her fingers along my hairline, behind my ear. "You and me again. I've spent a lot of nights thinking about you. It doesn't get any better than us, does it? You know it doesn't. Did Denise even come close?"

"No," I admit but I'm not thinking of Denise. Amelia is the one Shana should be worried about. Shana and I had great sex, but Amelia and I connect on another level. I understand, with her, what it is to make love. The realization that I've lost the only real connection I've had in years, maybe ever, aside from Bell, saddens me.

"Come on, then."

I look at Shana. "Where are you staying?"

"A motel a few miles from here."

"A motel?" I ask.

"I was hoping . . . I mean, not now. Not tonight, maybe not tomorrow. But I'd like to come home at some point."

Home. My home. "I don't live at the apartment anymore."

"I figured," she says. "I drove by, but someone else was there. Where are you now?"

Even though she may already know—even though she could ask ten different mutual friends and find out—I can't help keeping *home* close to my chest. It's my safe place. It's Bell's safe place. "A house not far from here," I say, intentionally vague.

"What's it like?"

I shrug. "It's a home."

"Sounds wonderful." She leans in closer to touch my jaw, her fingers confident, as if checking for stubble. When I don't pull away, she kisses the corner of my mouth. "I'd love to see it."

She's hesitant but assured; it's a half-kiss, like she's testing me. It doesn't have the potent effect I'm used to. It makes me think of Amelia and my first tomato-sauce taste of her. I jerk back. "No."

The vehemence with which I say it surprises me, and from the look on her face, it surprises her too. Because the twinkle in her eyes is still there. The mischief in her smile. The ass and tits. She hasn't changed. No matter how mad I've been in the past, those things always worked on me. But right now, I'm not falling for it.

"*No?*" she asks.

"No," I repeat, my confidence building. "This isn't going to happen. Not tonight. Not ever."

She sighs, pouting slightly. "Are you seeing someone? Tell me this isn't because of Denise."

"It's not Denise," I say, and like *home*, I can't bring myself to say Amelia's name. Not to Shana, who could shred a football team with one look. Amelia may or may not be mine, but just her name gives me back some of the strength Shana's trying to suck out of me.

Shana puts her hand in my lap, sliding it up my thigh, dangerously close to my crotch. "Andrew. Babe. It's *me*. Just come with me tonight. I've missed you so much." She leans into my ear. "If you feel the same in the morning, I'll leave town. I promise."

I catch her wrist and move her hand away. "I said no."

The look in her eyes changes almost imperceptibly, from excited and daring to irritated. "I'll let you put it anywhere," she says, her voice extra husky. "Remember how you liked that? Me, on my hands and knees. You used to spend all night—"

I pound my fist on the bar. "I'm not who I used to be, Shana. I'm not that man anymore."

She flinches but still puts her hand on my bicep. "But he's in there, that man—"

"No. He's not. When you left, you took more with you than a bag. I loved you. The fact that you could just walk away without a backward glance taught me a valuable lesson about love—it's destructive. And cruel."

As soon as I say it, I question if I still believe that. The words feel rehearsed. It's a breakthrough for me—and I can't help thinking I have Amelia to thank for it. She's helped me see that I might deserve a second chance at love. That maybe it can fulfill rather than obliterate. That she could be the one for me.

The thought catches me off guard.

All this time, I was worried that I might still be in love with Shana. I hadn't thought to ask myself . . . what if I love Amelia?

I can't think like that. I've already made my decision, and even if I change my mind now, it might be too late.

Shana's expression smooths. "I never meant to hurt you like that, honest. Try to understand that I left so I wouldn't hurt you any more than I already had. But the way I did it was selfish. I got scared and ran when I should've talked to you. I'm not like that anymore."

I stand up, push my bottle across the bar, and leave a few bills for Buck. "Then we understand each other. You're not the same. Neither am I. *We* are not the same."

I walk to the exit, in desperate need of a cigarette. Her boots click against the wood floor as she follows me. "That can be a good thing," she says. "We both had to grow up."

I push out into the mild night and stop. I don't have any cigarettes. When I turn, Shana's there, holding one out for me.

Reluctantly, I take it from her. "You don't even know if you want this," I say. "You're bored, so you're creating drama."

"If I wanted drama, I would've done this tomorrow at Bell's party," she says. "I would've made a scene. That's not what I want. I'm trying to be better."

"This is you not making a scene?" I ask, exhaling smoke, looking down my nose at her. It doesn't shock me one bit that she knows about Bell's party.

"Yes. I still love you."

"I'm sorry to hear that."

"Andrew, *stop* it. Stop being a jerk."

"What do you want me to say, Shana? Give me one fucking word I can say to you."

"Do you really, honestly not love me anymore?"

I understand why she finds that so appalling. *I* didn't even know, until tonight, that I'm no longer in love with her. It wouldn't matter if I were. It'd never be enough for me to let her back into our lives in any meaningful way. "I promised myself I'd never fall in love again after you left."

"And I'm sorry I hurt you that badly, but in a way, I'm not. I don't want anyone else to have you. I guess I'm still a little selfish. I want you for myself."

"You had me. You left."

She fists her hands, and finally, her façade drops. I see it happen, because I can read her just as well now as I could then. "You act like you were a fucking saint, Andrew. You weren't. Do you think I just up and left for no reason?"

I work my jaw side to side. For so long, I've placed all the blame on her shoulders so I wouldn't have to face the truth. "Why'd you go?" I ask, but I know why. I always have.

"There's no one magic answer," she says. "I didn't want to be a mom. I told you that so many fucking times, and you told me I'd change my mind when the baby came. You said if I didn't want to get pregnant, *I* should've been more careful. What about you?" She points a finger at my chest. "You had nothing to do with it?"

My heart thumps. I pushed her into motherhood, then expected her to love it because that was how normal people felt. I didn't realize what I was doing at the time. It took time and distance for me to understand it might've been hard for her day in and day out caring for a baby she didn't want.

"And after I had Bell, you gave me no support. Everything was about her. *Everything*. When I cried or complained, you couldn't believe someone wouldn't want that perfect little angel of a girl. You made me feel like some kind of monster."

I take a drag. She's trembling, her eyes full of tears. That first year or so after she left, I wanted nothing more than to have her in front of me, begging for a second chance, but now, it doesn't give me any satisfaction. Instead, I feel guilty and sad for what we've been through. "I'm sorry," I say. "I wasn't a good boyfriend to you."

"You were in a lot of ways," she says. "Except where Bell was concerned. She could do no wrong, and how was I supposed to compete with that?"

"I just—" I put my hand over my chest. "She's my heart, Shana. She *is* everything."

"She can't be, Andrew. Do you know what it'll do to her to grow up seeing you sacrifice everything for her? Does it send a good example that you're giving up love, happiness, family?"

She says *love, happiness, family* with some timidity because she's referring to herself. I don't associate her with any of those words, though. Amelia's the one I see. She's the one I've given up, not Shana. Amelia has the potential to give me love, happiness, family— and with those, the potential to hurt me. "I'm scared," I admit. Amelia knows I am. She *didn't* disappear like Shana, but by believing she did, I had an excuse to push her away. "I'm scared to love her."

"I don't need you to love me," Shana says, misunderstanding me. "Not right away. I just want my family back."

"What does that even mean?" I ask.

"It means . . ." She takes a tentative step closer. "If you can't love anyone, then can't you not love me? I'll come home and be a good mother to Bell. A good wife to you."

She gauges my reaction, but I can barely think straight, much less form an opinion on what she's suggesting. A pit is growing in my stomach. Amelia's at her apartment, waiting for me. Hoping. Except that it's getting late. Maybe she's given up on me already. I've let her down by not showing up, and knowing Amelia's history, I may not get another chance.

"Think about it," Shana says. "If you really don't love me anymore, then there's no risk. We'll be a family, and we'll make it work, and maybe one day when I've proven myself, you'll let me in again."

Against my will, Shana paints me a vivid picture that differs greatly from what Amelia and I could be. No risk. A safe home, where I love a woman as much as I'm capable of, but not as much as I should. And she's okay with it. She doesn't ask for more. If she leaves again, it won't hurt.

I think about the last month with Amelia. For the first time in a long time, I was excited about something other than Bell. Excited to see Amelia, to learn about her, to get overcome by intimacy I fought against. I don't regret getting close to her.

It hits me—I don't regret my time with Shana, either. It gave me Bell. It gave me hindsight—about the kind of partner I was, and the ways I fucked it up. I'm a better man for having loved her. I'm a father because of her. The pain she caused me is nothing compared to the joy she brought into my life. And there might be more happiness out there if I push past my fear and go get my woman.

Shana, of all people, has opened my eyes. But about one thing, she's wrong—she and I weren't made for each other. And I don't love her anymore.

"I can't," I tell her.

"Because you're afraid?" she asks. "How would you feel if Bell never tried anything because she learned not to from your fear?"

"It would kill me," I admit. I can't pass that onto Bell. I need to man up and face what scares me. "But I'm not saying no because I'm afraid. Maybe things would've turned out differently if you'd stayed, but I don't think so. I think eventually, we would've realized that this," I motion between us, "was real, but it wasn't right."

"How can you say that?" she asks. "It was incredible. Not all the time, but . . ."

"It was good." I nod. "But when it got hard, we failed. That isn't the kind of relationship I want. Running away when things get difficult is not the example I want to set for our daughter."

"So you're just going to be alone forever?" She crosses her arms, frustrated.

"No." Amelia and I were fools to think we knew better than the rest of the world. That we could willfully resist love.

I stamp out my cigarette and head back into the bar to tell Pico I'm borrowing his bike.

I need to get to the city fast—before Amelia loses all faith in me.

TWENTY-NINE
AMELIA

The bath I prepared earlier looks pathetic, the bubbles having fizzed and melted over an hour ago. I feel too pathetic to get in alone. I yank out the plug. The drain gurgles and sucks as I put on my robe and head into the kitchen. I put away the twenty-five-year-old bottle of premium Glenlivet I spent way too much money on during my walk home from the baby shower.

It's past eleven. Four hours since I dressed in a silky, red La Perla negligée. Two hours since I drew a bath, hoping Andrew and I could sink right in, no bullshit, and get things figured out.

Well, I figured it out, but apparently too late. I want him. I know the price, and I'm willing to pay it. Even though it means putting my heart on the line again, that I might end up worse off, I can't stop wondering what it's like at that kitchen table with Bell. How it would be to crawl into Andrew's bed each night. I've glimpsed a different kind of life, and while it was exciting at first, now it feels like a sickness—I won't ever be able to rid my mind of that happy picture that was within my grasp.

I get the Glenlivet back out. Might as well indulge—there's nobody to save it for. Maybe someone exists out there for me. Andrew's shown me I could be capable of love again. But the thought that that someone isn't Andrew makes my throat thick. That someone won't pry me open with bubble baths and good liquor. He won't force me to see that my pettiness over the divorce hurts me more than it helps me. He won't have Bell. I can't believe a month ago, I thought work was the most important thing in the world.

There's a knock at the door, jarring me from my thoughts. My heart, which was firmly planted in my stomach, soars. It can't be him. I'm not that lucky.

But it has to be.

My legs wobble as I leave the kitchen—fear, excitement, and adrenaline rushes through me. I can't even wrap my head around what this means.

Andrew came for me.

Despite all the promises we made each other to keep love out of it, he's here. It's more than a bath and a drink. More than sex. He wants to make this work as much as I do.

This is real.

"It's open," I call. I want his arms around me. After floating in uncertainty for a week, I need to be grounded by him. The door opens, and I stop to untie my robe. My skin flushes as I anticipate his hands on me, the look on his face when he sees me in red.

When Reggie walks through the door, I'm confused. Disoriented. I clutch my robe instinctively, tying the sash. In that same second, he locks the door. "Bonjour, muffie," he says as he walks toward me.

The hope and excitement I'd felt over getting Andrew back dissolves. Reggie's in front of me in an instant, looking me over with bloodshot eyes, grinning so hard he's sneering.

"Why so tense?" he asks when I retreat. "You look like you've seen a ghost."

The disappointment that Andrew isn't coming is as crushing the second time as it was moments ago. It's as heartbreaking as my irritation with Reggie is pervasive. "What are you doing here?"

He chuckles and loosens his tie, undoing the top button of his dress shirt. "What am I doing in my own home?" His cheeks and nose are unnaturally red. "Have a drink with me, muffin."

"For the last time, *stop* calling me that."

"I only do it because it bothers you. It's better than getting no reaction from you. Surely you're smart enough to realize that by now. Aren't you?"

Either I realized it and reacted anyway, or I'm an idiot for not seeing it. I look away. "I don't want you here. You need to go."

He holds out an arm, showing me to the kitchen. "Just one drink. I'm celebrating."

"Celebrating what?" I ask warily.

"I've got a new venture on the horizon." He lumbers toward me, and to keep my distance, I let him steer me into the kitchen. "Those fuckers thought they could fire me, but they forget what I know."

"You were *fired?*" I ask. I'm not surprised he lost his job—he's probably done enough shady shit to land him behind bars—but so few people see through him. He either charms them into turning a blind eye, or they do it on their own.

"Head of the company tried to move me off my biggest client's account. I asked how he felt about me going to the press to expose him for insider trading." Reggie's breath smells of liquor, his words verging on slurred. "The fucking idiot fired me instead. He'll pay Monday morning. I have dirt on everyone, Amelia." He winks at me. "You know I do."

Reggie was always liberal with his secrets when it came to me. He didn't have many friends growing up, and his dad belittled him constantly. I was the confidante he'd never had. Drugs, bribery, "borrowing" client funds—Reggie's colleagues are guilty of it all, and so is Reggie. I never wanted to know the details, and I don't now.

"I thought you quit drinking," I say, changing the subject.

"I did, but slipping up once in a while isn't so bad, is it?" He mock-gasps as he goes for the Glenlivet. "Well, I guess for *some* people, it's grounds to end a marriage."

I snatch the bottle and hold it to my chest. "This isn't for you."

He sets his jaw but squats to search the liquor cabinet. "Who's it for?"

My heart sinks. I pick up my phone from the kitchen counter to check it for the hundredth time tonight. This whisky's for someone who isn't coming. It's for no one. Suddenly, I feel exposed in my thigh-grazing robe and nightie. I can't risk sending Reggie the wrong signal. "I'll be right back," I say, turning for my bedroom.

He grabs my ankle. "Don't go."

I fumble to keep the bottle in my hands and drop my cell instead. "Reggie, *let go* of me. I just need to change."

"I've seen you in less. What's the big deal?" He sticks out his bottom lip but tightens his grip. "I'm not in the mood to fight, babe. Please, don't make me angry."

Even though Reggie has terrorized me in the past, he and I had a few good years before that. My natural instinct is not to fear him, but now I wonder if I should. "Okay," I say to appease him. "I'll stay."

He lets go and picks my phone up before rummaging through the cupboard. He chooses a bottle of his old favorite, Maker's Mark. It's been in there since before he left. "By the way. If you're waiting for your new boyfriend," he says, "don't bother. He isn't coming."

I put the Glenlivet back on the counter, sliding it into the corner farthest from his reach. I don't want to talk about Andrew. "Give me back the phone."

"I paid him a visit," he says, sticking my cell in his pocket.

Blood drains from my face. *No.* Reggie can be ruthless. And, as I saw at the flea market, Andrew can be confrontational when pushed. He puts his hands on Reggie just for the way he spoke to me. How would he have reacted having Reggie in his territory? "You didn't," I say, *hoping* this is another one of his lies.

He screws the top off the bourbon and picks up one of the glasses I'd gotten out for Andrew. "I went by the garage to offer him ten grand to stay away from you. That's how much I love you, Amelia. *Ten grand.*"

My stomach knots. I don't even have to ask if Andrew took it. It's the thought of Reggie going to his workplace, to where Bell might've been, that has me seething. "How dare you," I say.

Reggie looks surprised. "Me? He took the money! The schmuck didn't even realize I would've paid double."

"You have no right to interfere in my life. No right."

"I did it out of love." He sighs. "Did you hear what I said? He took the money. You should be thanking me."

I don't believe Reggie for a second—I don't. But the fact that Andrew didn't show tonight tugs at my conscience. He made it clear I'd hurt him enough for him to walk away. I don't know if I could fault him for taking Reggie's money when we were over anyway.

I shake my head, disappointed I'd even consider the possibility. "Give me back my phone, and get out," I say. "Take the bourbon with you. I haven't been able to stomach it in a long time. Hell, take the Glenlivet if you want. Just go."

"Have you forgotten who owns this apartment?" he asks, sniffing as he scratches his red nose. "I can come and go as I please."

"No, you can't. This is my place. We agreed on that because *you fucked another woman*. Remember?"

"Oh, come on with that shit already." He wipes his hairline with his sleeve and fills the second glass. "I've taken my punishment like a good boy. How long are you going to throw that in my face?"

"I'll make you a deal," I say, crossing my arms. "Stop coming around, and I'll stop bringing it up. Win-win."

"That's not a win for me. I want you back." He passes me the drink. I put it on the counter. "I want you on my arm and in my bed. What'll it take? What do you want to hear?" he asks. "I regret all of it."

I arch an eyebrow at him. "And that should surprise me?"

"No. You told me I'd regret it, and I do, and you said I'd come crawling back, and I have. Just tell me what you need me to do to make things right."

I glance at the glass of bourbon he poured me. I haven't so much as looked at Maker's Mark since he left because it reminds me of him. What do I need? To move forward for good. To close this chapter. To take back my life. I pick up the drink, study it, and take a sip as I look him in the eye. Bourbon's fucking good. Why shouldn't I drink it if I want? "Nothing," I say. "I don't need anything."

"Everyone needs something. I need you. I need my life back in order."

"And what do I need?" I ask.

"Love. Money. Your business, your home. I can give you all of that."

"I'm better off than you think."

"I don't believe that. You needed me once; it's still in there. You might pretend not to love me anymore, but love doesn't vanish just because you walked in on me with another woman."

"Actually," I say, "you might be surprised to hear that's exactly what happened. It's as if I was wearing a blindfold and it fell off in that moment, and . . . I've been seeing clearly ever since."

The muscles of his stubbled jaw tighten. "You're just saying that because you're still angry. To get back at me."

"I'm really not." I peer at him. "You know things were starting to change between us before you met her."

"Because of that fucking sinkhole you call a business."

I take a step back at the rage in his voice. If we were together, I'd be disappointed he's this drunk after his obvious effort to do better. "Why do you care so much?" I ask. "You're with Virginia now."

"I lied about that. We're not together."

Andrew was right. Reggie claimed to be with her to get under my skin, and he succeeded. "You can't expect me to believe anything you say—especially when it comes to her."

"It was over before it began," he says. "I swear. I haven't even seen her in months."

"Really?" I lean a hip against the counter. "So if I called her up right now, she'd back that up?"

"I'm not sure," he says. "She might lie. We didn't exactly end on good terms."

"I see." I can't help my shit-eating grin when I ask, "Did you cheat on her too?"

His cheeks are pallid, as if he might be sick. "No. She assumed when you and I split that I'd be with her, but I never wanted anything—"

"Except sex. You wanted that badly enough to jeopardize your marriage."

"You're deliberately trying to piss me off."

It *is* satisfying to see him squirm. When I think I'm starting to get over the pain, I remember how it felt to see them together, tangled in my sheets, the ones I picked out from Restoration Hardware, paid for, carried home, washed, and made the bed with. I remember learning the affair had been going on almost a year—like I'd been walking down the sidewalk and had had an anvil dropped on my head. It was a one-two punch, getting it from both sides. "You're the one who came into my home," I point out. "I'm just making conversation."

"*Our* home," he says.

"Not anymore." I take a fortifying breath. Though Andrew's no longer around to help me through this, I know I still need to give up the apartment. While I'm here, I'm holding onto Reggie, and that's the last thing I want to do. Reggie won't like losing even more control over me than he already has, but that's partly why I need to go. "I'm getting my own place. You can have the apartment back, and you can keep your money. I don't even want alimony."

He tilts his head. "Excuse me?"

"I give up." As I say it, I straighten my back. It feels nothing like surrender. The opposite even. It's a form of liberation. "You win."

"I don't think so," he says with a dismissive wave.

"The only thing I want is my business. I'll buy you out. You get to keep alimony and recoup your investment. You get it all."

"I don't get *you*."

"That's not up for negotiation."

"I've had a long time to live with my regret," he says. "Every day that goes by, I feel it more. I don't like myself without you. I'm a jerk."

"You were always a jerk," I say. "But neither of us noticed, because we were in love."

"*Are* in love."

I shake my head slowly. I'm not sure how many other ways there are to say it. It was nice to gloat for a few minutes, but he's bordering on pitiful.

"I have something for you." He sets his drink down carefully, as if he suddenly wants to appear sober, and takes an envelope out of his suit jacket pocket. "What if we just start over?"

I frown. "What is that?"

"Tickets to Paris. I'm taking you back to where it all began, only this time, I want to spoil you even more. Champs Elysées. First class seats. My secretary booked us a suite in the same hotel."

I stare at him. "You can't be serious."

He shows me the tickets with a half-smile. "This is how serious I am. I know I've made my intentions clear, but I want to prove that I'm ready to do this for real. Let's make love on that moonlit balcony again. Marvel at the Eiffel Tower, eat pastries, sip *café crème*."

I open my mouth, but nothing comes out. It's a happy memory, that first night we spent together in Paris—he hadn't showed me yet how consumed he was by money and status. But that's all it is. A memory. Reggie has made a living on his persistence, but this is borderline delusional. In the last year, I haven't given him any indication I want to get back together, much less spend a romantic vacation with him.

"You *are* serious, aren't you?" I ask. "After everything you've done to me, and after everything I've said, you *actually* think we have a chance."

"There's always a chance. No door is ever completely closed."

"*No*. Reggie, you're starting to worry me. You need to accept that this isn't going to happen."

"I can't."

"You have to. I'm already making arrangements to move out—"

"You aren't leaving this apartment."

"Yes, I am—"

"You *aren't* leaving this apartment," he booms, snarling as he swipes a glass of bourbon onto the floor.

I jump back as it shatters, clamping my hand over my mouth. He lunges forward to grab my shoulders. "What the hell is your problem?" he asks, shaking me. "I treated you like a queen! I made *one* mistake. Get over it already."

"Okay," I say, keeping my voice even. "Okay. You're right."

"Don't fucking patronize me." He pushes me back while keeping ahold of me, and my heel slams against a wall.

"*Stop*, Reggie—you're hurting me."

His expression crumbles, and he releases me. "I'm sorry, muffin. But you won't *listen*. We need each other. I just want you to stop pretending we don't."

Reggie doesn't like not getting what he wants from people. I've seen him come home and rage over competitors, clients, even the boy who delivers his mail. During the course of our relationship, I started to learn how far I could push him, but it occurs to me—just because we're not together anymore doesn't mean I don't still have to play by his rules. "All right," I say, slowly moving back so he doesn't think I'm running away. I just need him out of my apartment. "I'll listen. You and I can have a long talk. Tomorrow. When you're sober."

"Tonight," he says, inching forward until I've retreated into the hall. "Now. We'll work this out now so we can be together tonight. Do you know how long it's been since I *slept*? Really slept?"

My stomach flips. I will never, ever sleep in the same bed as him. Nor will I let him near my body after the way he abused his power in the past. "I promise we can talk tomorrow," I lie. I turn for the front door, but he grabs my wrist.

"Reggie, please—"

He pulls me the opposite direction. Instinctively, I try to wrench free, twisting until my skin burns. When I realize he's heading toward the bedroom, I panic. "I don't want this," I say. "Let me go. I don't want you."

He turns on me, grabbing my other forearm. "You'll fuck some piece-of-shit mechanic from Jersey and not your own husband? Are you some kind of whore?"

My chest stutters with shortened breaths. "No. I—this isn't about him."

"You're right. It's about you and me."

"There is no you and me," I say, needing to make myself as clear as possible. "Now let me go. You know I don't like to be restrained."

"I'll let you go," he says, but continues clutching me, "once you tell me how sorry you are for putting us through this. Once you prove your love for me. I'll hold you here all night if I have to."

THIRTY

Reggie kicks two club chairs together in the living room, keeping me bound by his hands, and orders me to sit in the one facing him. To an outsider, we'd look like lovers unable to let go of each other even in the comfort of our home.

I'm sweating. My wrists throb from his grasp. Reggie knows I don't like to be restrained. I've told him several times.

"You don't *really* want to be with him," he says. "You're just trying to get back at me. You've succeeded. What'll it take to get you to call off this divorce?"

"I told you, this is not about him. It's about us." I glance around. The apartment is smaller. The walls are definitely closing in. I pull on my hands, but even when he wasn't in shape and I'd been working out regularly, Reggie was stronger than me.

"What's wrong, muffin?" he asks. "You afraid of your own husband?"

"You know I don't like to be held like this."

"Because it reminds you you're weak. Alone. Out of control. You talk a big game, but you're just as weak as any other woman. Virginia was the same— that's why she hopped into bed with me first chance she got. I barely had to smile in her direction."

I close my eyes, tune Reggie out, and grasp for the strength I need. It's Andrew I see, looking down on me in the hotel room after he'd removed my blindfold.

"I won't hurt you. That's not why I'm holding you. I care about you, and I want you to be strong. You can be in control like this, but not if you're afraid."

Strong. I *am* stronger than Reggie, maybe not physically, but mentally. Emotionally. I know his weaknesses better than he does. I will the tension out of my body. At first, it doesn't budge. I breathe in slowly through my nose and exhale, the way Andrew coached me.

"You're still my wife," Reggie says. I sense him closer, his warm, alcohol-tinted breath near my face. "I know you still want me. I see it in your face. You get this look when you're turned on."

Panic flares in me again, but I breathe through it and hold onto the image of Andrew and his poise as he held me. I'm not aroused—I'm scared. That's what Reggie sees, what he wants to see. Terror. The stiffness in my arms begins to ease. I open my eyes.

"I'm not turned on," I say. "I want you to let go of me."

He stands, pulling me up with him. "You don't know what you want," he says softly, sliding his thumb over the pulse of one wrist. "I do, though—I always have."

"I'm telling you what I want. You have to respect that."

He drops his forehead to mine, but as much as I'd like to, I don't jerk away. "Give me a chance to remind you how good we are," he says, looking down the front of my robe. "Come on, babe."

My heart hammers against my chest, but I keep my expression calm. This is what my therapist and I have gone over and over. "I said no, Reggie." I swallow. "If you push me until I have no choice but to give in, that's rape."

He reels back, his eyes popping open. "Rape? What the . . . are you *crazy*?"

"No."

"We're married. We've had sex a thousand times."

"It doesn't matter," I say. "If I don't want it and you bully me into it anyway, that's force, and I won't stay quiet. How will that look for your reputation? Your 'new venture'?" My shoulders are back to where they should be, my breathing evening out, and though my nerves buzz, I find strength in my own words. "I'm not afraid of you."

"I don't *want* you to be afraid—"

451

"Yes, you do. You like me insecure and weak. That way, you can coerce me into anything and make me believe it's what I want."

"You're talking crazy, Amelia. Frankly, I thought we were finally getting somewhere, but what you're saying concerns me."

It's taking everything in me not to fight him off, to try to pull away again, but that's what he wants. He loves the struggle of emotionally wrestling with his prey, of fighting for the win. I keep my arms and hands limp. "You have five seconds to let me go," I say.

"Then what? You'll go to the police? You'd look like a fool charging your own husband with rape."

"Five."

He shakes his head at me. "You've lost it. I don't even know you anymore."

"Four."

"You're not acting like the woman I married. You think I can't get any twenty-year-old I want? And I was willing to take *you* back?"

His words sting, even if I know that's the only reason he says them—to hurt me. Even if I don't love him anymore. I clear my throat. "Three."

We both startle at a knock on the door. "Amelia. It's me."

My breath catches. The deep voice is clear, calm.

"*Andrew*," Reggie growls under his breath. He cuts his gaze to me. "Don't say a word."

My heart hammers. "He knows I'm in here," I say. "We were supposed to meet tonight."

"Amelia?" Andrew calls. "I'm sorry I didn't come sooner. Please open the door."

I hear the emotion in his words. I desperately want to see his face, to tell him I need him. I open my mouth to call out, but Reggie clamps a hand over it and the other around the back of my head.

"Don't even think about it," he says. I could practically get buzzed off his pungent, bourbon-soaked breath. "This isn't his business."

"I'm not leaving, Amelia," Andrew says, trying the handle. "Not until we talk."

"Huh." Reggie digs his fingers into my cheeks. "Trouble in paradise?"

I shake my head hard.

"Sure sounds like there is." His jaw ticks as he stares behind me at the front door. I can practically see the wheels in his head turning. "Answer the door," he says.

I widen my eyes. Andrew'll fly off the handle if he finds Reggie in here, trying to intimidate me. Doesn't Reggie realize how badly Andrew could hurt him?

"Tell him you don't forgive him," Reggie says. "Send him on his way. For good."

I choke back a sob and shake my head again. Andrew won't buy it. He's too stubborn.

"And make it convincing," Reggie says, as if reading my mind. "Because if he suspects I'm in here, he'll come after me like he did at the flea market. I don't think I need to tell you what'll happen if he so much as plucks a hair off my head."

I stare at Reggie as the truth sinks in. He *does* know how badly Andrew can hurt him. Andrew warned me he never wanted to cross paths with Reggie again—because he can't afford to get physical. If he does, Reggie would press charges in a heartbeat. If not out of wounded pride, then to get Andrew out of the picture.

"I already have footage of him grabbing me," Reggie says, calmer now. "That, plus an arrest charge, would be enough to take his daughter away."

Bell. Footage. What? My throat closes. This is my fault. I should've been more aware this past month. Reggie's fallback plan is always blackmail. Intimidation. Extortion. Of course he's been keeping tabs on us, accumulating anything he can use. I suck in a breath as best I can with his hand on my mouth—and nod.

Reggie releases me. "I'll be listening."

I work out the ache in my jaw and stagger down the hall. As much as it kills me, Andrew can't know Reggie's here. He told me himself—he treats an asshole like an asshole, and that's exactly what Reggie is. Andrew's threatened to kick Reggie's ass for less. I've heard it with my own ears. I have no idea how far he'd go in the heat of the moment, especially finding Reggie in my home. Reggie knows it too. I tighten the sash of my robe, inhale deeply, and open the door.

Andrew's leaning both arms on the doorway. He looks me over. "Finally. I was getting worried."

"Hi." My voice is scratchy, so I clear my throat. "Sorry, I was in the shower."

He furrows his eyebrows. "Your hair is dry."

I touch my ends. "I mean, I was about to get in."

"Can I come in?"

"No," I say quickly.

He nods a little. "I don't blame you for being upset. I'm late. Really fucking late. I've had a weird and shitty day, but that's no excuse. I don't deserve a chance to explain since I didn't give you one, but I'm asking anyway." He makes a fist with one hand. "Let me in for a little bit before you kick me out for good."

I have to bite back the urge to cry. He's disheveled, obviously upset, and I can't comfort him. I can't ask for his comfort. I grasp for strength. Everything in me is screaming to tell him the truth: I don't want him to go; I need help; I don't know if I can handle Reggie on my own. But Bell needs her father more than I do, and I can't put them at risk. "I don't forgive you. Please leave." It's as much as I can say without breaking down.

He closes his mouth, tilting his head. "What's wrong? Why is your face so red?"

"Please, Andrew," I say, allowing more emotion into my voice. "Just go. Don't make this harder."

He pleads with me, his deep-blue eyes sad, beaten down like I've never seen. "Just a few minutes."

"No."

"I rode all the way here—"

"You should learn that when a lady says no," Reggie says behind me, "she means no."

My heart leaps into my throat. *What the fuck is he doing?*

Andrew looks past me, pushing off the doorframe. "What is this?"

Oh my God. Andrew might think Reggie's here because I invited him. "I can explain," I say.

"There's only one explanation," Reggie says. He comes up behind me and grabs my ass so hard, I inhale a sharp breath. "She chose me. Didn't you, muffin?"

Andrew looks between the two of us. "Is that true?" he asks me.

My mind is spinning. I don't know the right answer. If I say yes, it'll kill Andrew. But if I tell him Reggie's blackmailing me, Andrew might snap and do something stupid. I can't have that. From the start, Andrew and I had an understanding: hurt me now to save me later. I owe him that. My urge to protect him trumps my fear.

"It's true," I say with as much confidence as I can muster. "I asked him here."

Andrew narrows his eyes. "Why?"

I don't have to reach too deep. I know how to hurt Andrew, and that's what I'll have to do to get him to leave. To stay away until I can deal with Reggie. "I thought about what I said earlier, and I was wrong. I can't be what you need," my voice cracks, and I clear my throat, "what she needs."

"She . . .?" Andrew asks.

My stomach drops. "Bell."

Andrew's jaw ticks. "I see. You can't, or you don't want to?"

"I don't want to."

"You don't want me," he says. "Don't want my little girl."

I have to look away from his scrutinizing gaze. Hot tears scald the backs of my eyes. "No."

"Well. Fuck." He shakes his head. "I've been an idiot, haven't I?"

"Oh, don't be so hard on yourself," Reggie says. "You couldn't have known it would end this way. Well, actually, you could've, if you'd listened to me from the start. But what's done is done. Go on back to your little life. Amelia's had her fun."

Andrew swallows and drops his eyes to me. The sadness is gone, and now they're just sharp with anger, hurt. "All right. I'll go if that's what you want."

It's not. It's not what I want. My heart urges me to speak, but my brain knows better.

"But do one last thing for me, Amelia, will you?" Andrew asks. "Before I go . . ."

I can't even open my mouth or I'll scream. I want to launch myself into Andrew's arms, but I'm afraid. For both of us. "What?" I rasp.

Andrew nods. "Move a foot to your left."

My mind goes blank, confusion coming on fast. I'm sure I've misheard. "What?"

"*Move.*"

I leap aside when Andrew lunges into the apartment, grabbing Reggie by his shirt. He barrels him back into the nearest wall, and Reggie *oophs* like he's had the wind knocked out of him. "How fucking dumb do you think I am?" Andrew asks, nearly rattling the walls with the deep rumble of his voice. "Did you honestly think I'd believe this? That she'd choose a scumbag like you?"

Shock freezes my limbs, keeps my mouth from doing anything but hanging open. My instinct is to pull Andrew off, but the way he's hulking out, a full-grown man wouldn't be able to separate them.

"Get out of my apartment," Reggie says through his teeth, wheezing.

"This isn't your apartment—it's Amelia's. You have a real bad habit of showing up places you aren't wanted, don't you?"

Reggie straightens, despite his obvious disadvantage. I know him. He feels cornered, and Reggie fights with words and threats, not muscles. "You should've taken the money. Amelia might fight and resist me, but eventually she'll come crawling back when she needs something. Money, sex, companionship—I'm the one she'll turn to. You'll be a chump, but you could've been a chump with ten grand in your pocket."

"Amelia's been trying to get away from you for a year, yet you keep slinking back. Who's the chump?"

"Fuck you," Reggie says, spittle flying. "You're delusional. You should be locked up. You can kiss your daughter goodbye. I'll have you thrown in jail so fast for this—"

Somehow, Andrew grows even bigger. Toe to toe, with Reggie cowering, Andrew looks almost twice Reggie's size. The muscles in his back tighten through his t-shirt. "You're going to bring my daughter into this?"

"Somebody has to. You're a fucking Neanderthal. Whoever left you in charge of a small child should be ashamed."

Andrew raises his fist. Reggie looks more amused than afraid. This is what he wants. Once Andrew hits him, Reggie will have what he needs to take him down.

I grasp Andrew's bicep, pulling it with all my strength. "Bell," I cry out.

He pauses.

"Think of Bell. Don't make this mistake."

After a few tense seconds, he drops his fist but keeps ahold of Reggie's shirt. "Here's what's going to happen," Andrew says. "You're going to go home, sign the divorce papers, and hand them over to your lawyer."

Reggie scowls. "Says who?"

"Me. From this moment forward, you'll stay away from Amelia. You won't have a choice, since she'll be getting a restraining order—"

"She wouldn't—"

"She would, she will, and if that isn't enough to keep you away, then I'll have to do the job myself."

Reggie eyes him. "Is that a threat?"

"You think *I'm* a Neanderthal? Just wait. My friends are nearing middle age, and they're just itching to prove they're as tough as they used to be. Don't think they'd have any problem proving it on you."

Reggie turns to me. "Are you hearing this? This is the kind of man you want to get mixed up with?"

I could never explain to Reggie how Andrew is ten times the man he is. Money and status mean nothing to him compared to family, love, security. The confidence Andrew wants to give me is far more valuable.

Reggie wriggles, and Andrew lets him go. "Get out," Andrew says.

"You have balls now, but just wait," Reggie says. "I have what I need to take both of you down. Even you, Amelia."

I feel Andrew's eyes on me, but I keep mine on Reggie. Reggie's been circling this all night, so I face it head on. "What do you have?" I ask quietly.

"It's me or him. This is your last chance. If you aren't my wife, you're my enemy. Decide."

I start to remind him that this isn't about either of them—it's about me. Whether or not I choose Andrew and Andrew chooses me back, I will never return to Reggie.

Reggie holds up a hand. "Before you respond, know this. *Avec* and I come together. Without me, there's no *avec*. That's how I bring you down."

THIRTY-ONE

Andrew and I go completely still, as if a vacuum has sucked the air right out of the room. I've been white-knuckling *avec* like a rope in a tug-of-war for a long time, trying to keep the bigger half on my side. I've built it from the ground up. It defines me. It's a piece of me so large, it's taken over every aspect of my life.

I no longer know if I want it because I love it, or because I'm afraid of who I am without it.

Now, I might be forced to find out.

"We'll fight it," Andrew says.

I blink out of my daze. "How? He has money. Power. Attorneys."

"I don't care. We'll find a way."

"I have more than that," Reggie says. "I have you on tape, screwing another man in my kitchen while you're still legally married to me. I have that same man threatening me in a crowded place and then again in front of his daughter."

My heart drops. "How?" I ask, but I know the answer. I shouldn't have underestimated Reggie. Nothing is too far if it means getting what he wants. He'd hired a private investigator often enough while we were together to track people who'd wronged him. I wouldn't be exempt from that just because I'd loved him once.

Andrew's chest rises and falls as he glares at Reggie. "You're sick."

"Maybe, but at least I'm not stupid. Amelia had a whole year to gather evidence against me for the divorce, and what has she got? Nothing."

"Because I trusted you," I say, covering my stomach as it drops. *Gathering evidence.* Reggie has invaded my home—my *privacy*. And Andrew's. It didn't occur to me he'd take it this far. "I never suspected . . ."

"You do anything with those videos," Andrew says, "and we'll—"

"What?" Reggie asks. "You can't touch me. Not physically. Not financially."

Andrew goes quiet. He *can* touch Reggie, and do a great deal of bodily damage, but not without serious consequences.

"I know things about you," I say. "I may not have evidence, but I know things." His secrets are at least a year old, but he's been fucking people over all his life. Surely there's someone with more power than him that he's pissed off. Reggie opens his mouth, but I cut him off. "Don't worry—I'm not going to do anything. I'm not going to go to your old clients and tell them they're knee-deep in an investment scheme or to the FBI to suggest they look a little closer at your taxes. My integrity is more important than revenge. Andrew and I are above your petty threats."

"You can't prove any of it," Reggie says. "But it doesn't need to come to that anyway, Amelia. You can still fix this. I haven't done anything permanent. Come back to me, and you can erase the evidence yourself."

"Fuck off," Andrew says. "She'd be better off getting wrongfully slandered than entering into another abusive relationship with you."

"Why don't you let her answer for herself," Reggie says, sounding mildly amused. As if he expects me to buckle because of what he's told me tonight.

"Ignore him," Andrew says. "He doesn't have shit."

I frown at Andrew. "I think he does."

"Then we'll fight it, like I said." He watches me closely, his dark eyebrows gathered, his forehead creased with concern. He truly believes he and I have a chance against Reggie, and he cares enough about me to try. Even if it means putting himself in the middle of it. He's wrong to think we can take Reggie on, but knowing he's behind me gives me renewed confidence—in us and in myself.

I turn to Reggie. "You win. Although I guess it really depends how you look at it." My throat is dry as a desert. I wish I knew in my gut if this was the right decision, but I don't. All I know is that no business is worth this disillusioned, washed-up asshole's manipulation. And it's certainly not worth putting Andrew and Bell in the center of it. "You can have *avec.*"

Andrew steps closer to me. "Amelia."

I shake my head, still staring at Reggie. "It's okay. I'll start again. I'll do something bigger and better. Or maybe I won't. But it's my choice. I don't know what you want with a fashion and beauty business—maybe you just need to run it into the ground to feel like a man, or to spite me, and that's very sad. Take the alimony and the apartment too. I'll give you everything; I'll let you keep every cent. You'll need it when you end up alone, having to live with the person you've become."

Both men's eyes are on me, and for the first time in a long time, at least where work and Reggie are concerned, a sense of calm settles over me. I loosen my grip, physically, uncurling my fists, and figuratively. I accept defeat. Though I love my business, there are more important things in the world. Part of me sees, like a pinprick of light on a dark horizon, how letting go of something that leaves me constantly drained could be a good thing.

"You're going to choose a man you've known for weeks over your husband. Your business?" Reggie asks. "Things you've invested years of your life in?"

"I'm choosing myself. You may have every material thing that means anything to me, but I'm richer than you'll ever be." Andrew's presence is strong beside me, and I take his hand. "And yes. I choose him too."

Reggie raises a red, meaty hand. I don't know what he intends to do with it, but I don't find out. Andrew shoves him backward toward the door. "Do what you have to do," he says. "But get the fuck out. Now."

"You're just a bunch of . . . of . . ." Reggie turns and slams his fist into a wall, then curses in pain. "Remember—when you're jobless and living with a bum—you could've had it all, Amelia. If you'd chosen me."

I don't give him the satisfaction of a response. He's half out of his mind anyway. Andrew and I wait, still and silent, until he's out the door. We don't even move until we hear the ding of the elevator.

I exhale a sigh of relief. Andrew comes around to face me. "Are you all right?"

"Yes."

"No, you're not." He gently pinches my chin to lift it, inspecting my jaw. "He put his hands on you?"

"I'm okay," I say and look up at him from under my lashes. As the threat of danger recedes, understanding takes its place. Andrew's *here*. "You came. You came for the bath, for the whisky—"

"I came for you." Just when I think he's going to kiss me, he stops himself. "And I'm not going anywhere from now on."

My heart swells. But there are bigger things on my mind than romance. "How'd you know I was in trouble?"

"I would never believe you'd go back to him unless he was forcing you to. And on my ride into the city just now, I came to some realizations."

"About us?" I ask hopefully.

"No. I'd already decided about us."

I open my mouth to ask what he decided, but he cuts me off.

"I started putting things together—like how he found us at the flea market and then knew where I worked. When he came to the garage, he made a strange comment about what you do behind closed doors, but I didn't catch it because I was worried about Bell. It just kind of clicked that he was probably keeping tabs on us. Makes sense considering his fascination with control."

I shake my head. "You were right. Except it was more than keeping tabs."

"I had no idea it was this bad, but now that I do—I think he's the one who stole your underwear."

My gut pangs. As soon as Andrew says it, I know it's true. Reggie was in my home when I wasn't. He went through my things. He filmed me in my most intimate moments. I cover my mouth. "What are we going to do?"

He takes me in his arms, and once I'm pressed against his chest, I realize I've been waiting for him to do that since he walked in the door. Finally, some of my tension eases. "We'll be getting a restraining order first thing Monday," he says, kissing the top of my head. "I can't have some disgruntled ex-husband taking my girlfriend's most intimate things."

My anger drains as I look up. Andrew's eyes say it all—he believes in us. He came for me. He thinks we can do this. "Girlfriend?"

"You got scared. Then I got scared," he says. "We want to believe we don't need each other."

"But you think we do?"

He closes his mouth, letting my question hang. I wait, anticipating his answer until I realize I'm not going to get one. He's wants me to provide it. Do we need each other? It's a strong word. Family needs family. Husbands need wives. Little girls need their mothers. "You need someone for yourself? Or for Bell?"

"No, I can do it on my own. In fact, it'd be easier." He glances at the ceiling. "If I bring anyone into our lives, she has to be so many things, Amelia. Solid, smart, loving. A good example to Bell. Not a woman who just wants the role of mom and wife because it's available."

"But there are plenty of women who do," I point out.

"Yeah. But none of them are right, they never were. Not even Shana." He rubs my back. "I want to be honest with you. Earlier tonight, I wasn't going to come. I went to a bar instead. I thought it was best for us both if we ended this. Then, Shana showed up."

I freeze, inhaling a short breath at the name. As if I wasn't already struggling hard enough for Andrew. Now, I'll have to go up against the mother of his child? A woman who's clearly cast some kind of spell on him? "She's back?"

"That was why I wanted to talk to you last week. She randomly showed up at Bell's gymnastics practice."

My heart drops. The day Bell had gymnastics was the same day I left Andrew at the flea market. I'd thought he was calling to talk about how abruptly I'd run off, and I'd had no excuse, so I hadn't answered. But it was to tell me about Shana. "I'm sorry."

"I know," he says. "I am too." He checks his watch. "We'll talk more at the house. I really need to get home to Bell."

"The house . . .?"

"I'm not leaving you alone tonight."

"Oh." I pull back a little. "You don't have to do that. Reggie won't be back. I've wounded his pride in more ways than one, and from now on, I have a feeling his lawyers will be the ones trying to corner me."

470

"You're coming to my place," Andrew says, ignoring me. "Tomorrow, I can bring you back here, or . . ." He tucks some of my hair behind my ear and smiles a little—I'm sure he's thinking about messing up my hair to boost his ego. "Or you can stay."

I blink up at him. "What about Bell?"

"Her birthday party's tomorrow, and the house will be crazy, chaos really—there'll be kids and horny moms and toys everywhere, but . . ."

"But?" I ask, not hiding the hopefulness in my tone.

"I'd like you there in the middle of it."

I bite my bottom lip to keep from screaming yes. My life has changed drastically in the last hour, and what Andrew's offering feels . . . safe. Stable. But it isn't my home. "I can't just show up and stay the night," I say. "It'll confuse Bell."

"I have a guest room. She should be in bed by now. If she has questions, we'll answer them." He nods toward my bedroom. "Go get some things. I mean it. I'm not leaving without you."

I open my mouth to protest, but I don't know what to say. The truth is, I want to go. I'd like to watch Bell turn seven, and maybe some wholesome chaos would even be good for me. It'll distract me from the reality that I've just given up the one thing that has consumed my life for the last few years.

The only thing I gave any real value.

Avec might be gone.

For good.

THIRTY–TWO

As if I haven't endured enough shock tonight, when I follow Andrew out of my apartment building, he leads me directly to a motorcycle.

"Um." I make a face. "Andrew?"

He turns back to me. "Yeah, babe?"

"You didn't mention this . . ."

"Oh. This is Pico's. Believe me, mine's a thousand fucking times better than this hunk of scrap metal. But I was in a hurry to get to you. No time for traffic."

"That's sweet," I say. "But it's a motorcycle."

"And?"

I think of my poor, fine hair, which was not made for hats, a shame because I've been coveting one from the Marc Jacobs fall line. If I'm not willing to give up a good hairdo for Marc, I'm certainly not going to do it for this. I show him my duffel. "I've got my overnight bag, so maybe I should get a cab—"

"To Jersey?" He comes over and chucks me under the chin. "Aw. Don't be nervous. I got this. You don't have to do anything."

He thinks I'm afraid. I play along. "What if I fall off?"

"I take that back. You do have to do one thing: hold on."

He climbs on the massive thing, handling it like it isn't hundreds of pounds of metal and leather. Once his helmet's in place, he starts the bike, his biceps stretching his t-shirt as he grips the handles. With each rumble, the sidewalk trembles, vibrating up between my legs.

My stomach drops. He says something about my bag, but I'm not listening. I get a glimpse of the kind of teenager he must've been—reckless, sexy, brooding. I've never been much for bikers, what with their grizzly beards, greasy hands, and head-to-toe leather. But with Andrew's bad boy showing, I'm swooning. I wonder if he's ever had sex on the bike. If it's even possible.

He holds out a helmet. "You coming?"

"Nearly."

He arches a quizzical eyebrow at me. Is it possible he rides a bike because he loves it, and not because he knows how sexy it makes him? I take the helmet, all notions of wrecked hair vanishing, and cross the duffel over one shoulder. I stick it behind us, get on, and scoot as close as I can get. His six-pack middle is hard under my arms.

"Sure you got a good enough grip?" he asks and laughs, his stomach tightening underneath me.

"Oh." I ease up. "Am I hurting you?"

"Just the opposite, babe." He checks for traffic before pulling away from the curb. I squeeze him again, this time out of fear of being flung off the side. He whips down the center divider line, weaving between cars. I've never moved this quickly through the city, even in the absence of traffic. I get a thrill from the way the skyscrapers blur together, from the wind whipping around us, from the edge of danger he rides along.

"You good?" he calls over his shoulder.

"Great," I say into his ear, slipping my hands under his shirt. His stomach is warm. It's hard to tell with the bike vibrating underneath us, but I think he shudders.

We pass through Lincoln Tunnel and shoot back into the night. An ache forms in my ass, but it's nothing compared to enduring twenty minutes of stimulation while curled around a sexy man. But once we're out of the city, and then the outskirts, traffic falls away. Aside from the growl of the bike, we make our way down the freeway in silence. The ride is no less exciting, but somehow peaceful.

Andrew exits the freeway toward Elizabeth, and eventually we enter a quiet, tree-lined neighborhood. He stops at a colonial-style white house with a lawn so well kept, it's richly green, even in the dark. There's a mailbox and a blue front door—nothing out of the ordinary, but surprisingly traditional. And nothing like I'd imagined.

I climb off, stretching the stiffness from my legs. "This is your place?" I ask.

"This is it." He nods me toward him, unclips the helmet strap from under my chin, and eases it off my head.

"Is it a mess?" I ask when he smooths his hand over my hair.

"Yes. Just how I love it." He leans in and surprises me with a kiss. "Is that okay?" he asks.

I nod. "It's good."

"Just good?" he asks. "Is good great? Is it unsure? Can you be more specific?"

I'm not sure I can describe how it feels to kiss Andrew again when I didn't think I'd get another chance. "You know when you've been searching for years for a pair of leather boots in a very specific color, like Merlot red or Chestnut brown, and *finally*, Louboutin comes out with a pair that exceeds your wildest dreams? And you go to the store and ask for your size, and they actually have them, and you slip one on . . ." I sigh.

Andrew rolls his lips together. "You lost me at that L-word."

I scrunch my nose. "What, Louboutin?"

476

We stare at each other. "Okay," I say, trying again. "Let's say the boots are a pair of jeans and the brand is Levi's."

He slow-blinks at me. "You think I've ever gone into a store and asked for a specific pair of hard-to-find jeans and then been elated that they had them . . .?"

I roll my eyes. "*Okay*. Then how about the feeling when you buy a car part and it clicks perfectly."

"Ah." He nods. "Sure. I get it."

He may be indulging me. "That feeling. It's just . . . right, you know?"

"Right," he repeats, slipping his hand under my hair, around my neck. "Well, that's better than good by a mile."

I grin. "Yes, it is."

"How are you doing? Earlier—that was a lot to handle."

"It was, but—"

"But nothing," he interrupts. "It was a lot, Amelia. You must've been scared."

I relax my shoulders a little as he begins to knead my neck. I have to stop my eyes from rolling back into my head, and as my muscles loosen, my resistance follows suit. "It was unnerving. I expected you, so when he walked in the door so nonchalantly—"

"You thought it was *me*? Holy shit. I didn't even think of that."

"At first. It's supposed to be a safe space, a home, but it wasn't in that moment."

"And it won't be ever again," he points out. "Not after this. We'll find a new place next week. You can stay with me until then. You won't have to spend another night there if I have my way."

My instinct is to protest, to say I'm fine. Fear is weakness, and I've always tried to beat it into submission. But it seems Andrew and I have both learned a lot about fear these past few weeks. I nod. "I would like that."

"I've been in your position," he says. "When Shana left, I was scared she'd come back. I was scared she wouldn't. I thought that being afraid meant I was a pussy, but looking back, I'm just human. There's bravery in facing fear when it's easier to bury it."

Andrew is one of the most intelligent, empathetic people I've known, and I never would've guessed just meeting him like I did. "I was terrified," I admit. "He held me in place and wouldn't let go. I panicked."

Andrew's nostrils flare with an inhale. "*Fuck*, Amelia. He restrained you? Thank God I showed up when I did."

"But I remembered when you and I worked through that fear," I tell him, "and the thing is . . . I was able to calm down. I think that confused him. He thought I'd be more afraid."

A spark flashes in his eyes, as if he's trying not to react. He studies me until his breathing evens out. "I'm sorry."

"Don't be. If anything, you saved me before you even showed up."

He pulls me to him by my neck and kisses my cheek. He smells like a blend of light sweat and soap, as if he were mid-shower when he'd suddenly decided to hurry to my apartment. "Let's go inside," he says. "I could stay here and kiss you until the sun comes up, but . . ." He glances toward the house. "If Bell heard the bike, she might come to the window thinking I'm home. And I don't want her to see us like this. Not until I have a chance to talk to her about it."

I step back quickly. "Of course. I should've thought of that."

"It's fine," he says, holding out his hand for mine. "I'm going to talk to her. I want her to understand."

I let him lead me up the sidewalk. "I'd just like to point out that we have her permission," I tease. "She sang us the k-i-s-s-i-n-g song, after all."

He smirks. "She doesn't have a clue what she means. She kept talking about kissing, and it was pissing me off."

"Why?" I ask.

"Because she's too young for that."

I bite my bottom lip. I'm not so old that I can't remember being a young girl, curious about sex. I don't remember thinking about it at her age, but Bell has been through a lot for her seven years. Not having a mother around might be confusing for her, especially if she's picked up on the other moms or teachers trying to get to Andrew through her. "Maybe she's just confused, Andrew. I don't think punishing her would help."

"It doesn't. And you're right, she's confused as hell. It's been a weird week of trying to work through it." He glances back. "Look at you with your maternal instincts."

To my surprise, I blush a little. I don't admit to being insecure about much, but motherhood is intimidating to say the least. The fact that I'm open to even *wanting* it speaks volumes.

"I had to have a talk with her the other night," he says, releasing my hand to unlock the door. "We got into stuff I'd been avoiding. It was beginning to feel—well, unavoidable."

"Like what?" I ask as he leads me inside.

"Her mom."

Instinctively, my heart clenches. I know how hard it is for Andrew to talk about Shana with adults—but Bell? At the same time, I can't fathom what Bell must be thinking. "How did it go?" I ask hesitantly, unsure if he's open to discussing it.

"It wasn't easy. But nothing ever is where Shana's concerned."

"How'd Bell react?"

He pauses in the entryway and glances down at me, as if he's debating how to respond. Or if he should. I realize with a painful pang that he doesn't want to tell me, even after all this. I've tried to pry him open before, but I only get so deep before he closes back up. Either he doesn't trust me, or he's still trying to preserve some part of himself.

Before either of us can speak, an elderly woman comes out of the kitchen. "Andrew, honey," she says, "I was worried when I got Pico's call to bring Bell here. Is everything all right?" Her gaze stops on me.

"I'm sorry," he says. "I had a hell of a night, and I had to run into the city to get Amelia."

"Ohh," she says, nodding. She offers her hand with a knowing smile. "The *city*. Then I guess that would make you the city girl."

"The city girl . . .?" I take her hand as a slow, uncertain smile spreads across my face. I hope she hasn't just embarrassed him by mentioning some girl from his past. I am a city girl, but Andrew hasn't even opened up to Sadie about us. "Um, I'm not—I don't think he's talking about—"

"She is," Andrew says, seemingly amused by my mumbling. "This is her. Amelia, meet Flora. How'd Bell do tonight?"

"Fine, fine." Flora smiles warmly without sparing Andrew a glance and puts her other hand over mine. "It is so, so lovely to meet you. We all adore Andrew and want to see him happy."

Andrew glares at her. "Flora. Maybe you're jumping the gun a bit?"

She releases me and picks up a sweater off the back of the couch. She places it over her shoulders. "I hope not, dear. I really hope not."

"I'm staying in the guest room," I blurt. They both look at me, and my cheeks burn. "It's just—" I start. "I don't want you to think . . . with Bell, I'm not trying to—"

Flora chuckles. "Stay wherever you like," she says. "Personally, I think it's a waste to dirty two sets of sheets." She leans in toward me. "If you only knew what I'd give up to spend a night next to a man like this."

"Oh, God." Andrew runs both hands through his hair and turns his back to us. "This is not happening."

"I'll be back in the morning to start the cake," Flora sings, patting her purse at her side.

"Actually," Andrew says, turning back, a wary look etched on his face, "I thought Amelia could make it."

I gape. "*Me?* I can't—I've never . . . *I* . . . *don't* . . *bake.*"

He chuckles in a most irritating way. Flora joins in, to my dismay. "That's a wonderful idea," she agrees.

"It's not." I give Flora a serious look. "I'm a terrible baker. Absolutely awful. The last time I made muffins, they were gluten-free and vegan. My assistant gagged, spit one out, and eventually went home for the day."

"*Vegan?*" Andrew exclaims. "Never mind. You don't have to bake."

I plead with Flora. "It would be so great if you could just—"

She shakes her head. "You'll do fine, honey. Just make it with love, and it'll turn out great."

Make it with love. That doesn't really help. I'd prefer a more concrete tip, like using buttermilk or cage-free eggs. "Maybe you could come early and help me?" I ask.

She looks at Andrew. They exchange a smile, as if they're in on a private joke. I'm pretty sure *I'm* that joke.

"I think that would be fine," she says. "Everything's already in the fridge. I'll swing by around ten, and we'll do it together."

I sigh with relief. "Thank you."

Andrew leans in and kisses her on the cheek. "Thanks, Flora. For tonight and tomorrow. You're a huge help."

"It's no trouble. Goodnight, you two."

Andrew closes the door after her and locks it. He turns to me and rolls his eyes. "Sorry about that."

"It was sweet. Is she a friend of your mom's?"

"She's Pico's mom."

"Oh, right. Of course." I pause. "What's a Pico?"

"A guy who works for me. A friend." He grins. "We still have quite a bit to learn about each other, don't we?"

I nod. That's one way to kill the mood—a stark reminder that we're about to embark on something huge while we're still strangers in a lot of ways. "I probably shouldn't have come here tonight."

"Really?" He closes the distance between us and lifts my chin with his knuckle. "You sure? I was just thinking the opposite. I'm glad you're here."

"It's not too soon?"

"To sleep in my guest room?" He winks. "Come on."

As he leads me through the house, I finally get a look around. It's a good size, much more spacious than my apartment, which is big by New York standards. Like the exterior, the decor is traditional but with modern updates such as hardwood floors, clean lines, and—to my delight—an exposed-brick fireplace.

He notices my gaze. "It's a little warm tonight," he teases. "Let's give it a few months."

A few months. With Andrew. Glee wells up my chest. "Can I get a tour?" I ask.

"Not much to see," he says. "I'll get us a drink. Make yourself at home."

He may believe there isn't much to see, but to me, it's like opening the second volume of his life. When he leaves, I stand in place and look everywhere I can. There isn't more than necessary in the room—a wood coffee table with a remote positioned next to some car magazines. An overstuffed brown leather couch that faces an obscenely big flat-screen TV. A table in the entryway with a dish for keys and spare change. Sparse but tasteful. If I remember our conversations correctly, Shana never lived here. He bought this after she left, so he must've decorated it himself.

It doesn't look like a child lives here. The biggest indication is a large bookcase with shelving that appears to be divided between the two of them. The lower half holds coloring books, crayons, fairytales by the Brothers Grimm, Disney DVDs, and a small, stuffed unicorn. I browse the books at eyelevel. Manuals on cars and motorcycles. Some crime fiction. I pick out a book with a spine that reads *On Grief and Grieving* and flip through the first few pages. It's been four years since Shana left, but is Andrew really over her? What would I have found here even a year ago?

And there's the small detail that she's back in his life. As much as it concerns me to go head to head with someone who once captivated Andrew at every turn, I know I can't back down. Because he deserves better. Bell deserves better.

"That should be in a Goodwill box," Andrew says from behind me. "It was a gift, honest."

I turn around, holding it to my chest. "Your house is tidy for having a small child."

"It doesn't always look like this, but Bell is pretty good about picking up after herself. I told her that's what adults do, and she listens."

I take a deep breath. My emotions are raw tonight, close to the surface, perhaps not the best time to get into a deep conversation. But if I'm going to sleep under Andrew's roof, I have to speak up. "I need to know about her."

He pauses, looking me over. "Bell?"

"No. I mean yes, her too, but this—" I hold up the book. "This is a book about losing a loved one to *death*. How badly did Shana hurt you?"

He comes further into the room with two glasses of amber liquid and sets them on the coffee table. "I told you, I didn't buy that book or even read it. Sadie gave it to me. There aren't exactly many books on what to do when your girlfriend disappears overnight and leaves you with a small child. Sadie overreacted."

"You're holding back."

"I'm not," he says. "I just don't see the point of living in the past."

"You want me to trust you. I've told you everything there is to know about Reggie and my life, but you're still shutting me out. I understand why, but I can't accept it." I gesture around the cozy family room. "Not if I'm going to become part of this."

He glances at the ground. "Why give her that power over us? It happened four years ago. I'm not getting back together with her, believe me."

"I do, but Sadie gave you this book for a reason. You can't just pretend it never happened because it hurts too much to revisit."

"It doesn't hurt. I don't feel anything about it."

"I think I'm falling in love with you," I say and stiffen. I'm as surprised by my declaration as Andrew looks to hear it. *Shit shit shit.* This was the last thing I wanted. But standing here in his home is not as terrifying as I thought it would be. Maybe it isn't what I envisioned for myself, a home in the suburbs, a young girl, a good, hard-working man, a career up in flames. But somehow, he and Bell and this home— they fit into the puzzle of my life like a piece I didn't know was missing. Andrew wasn't a complete picture until this moment, until I could see him here, as a father who comes home to his daughter every night. As a man who runs a household by himself.

Silence stretches between us.

"Is that what you want?" I ask finally. "Does it scare you? Would you rather keep everything to yourself? If so, take me home now. Because you got it wrong. We both did." I point at the steel machine tattooed on his chest. "Hard hearts break easy. It's the soft ones that survive hit after hit."

He stands there in the stillness that follows, and as he does, the truth of my words sets in—for me, and, I think, for him. He was upfront from the start. Love wasn't on the table. Is an ultimatum really fair? Maybe not. But this is what I need. It would hurt to walk away after all this, or to be left behind, but if he can't move on from his past . . . then we have to say goodbye.

And it has to be now.

THIRTY-THREE

Andrew hasn't blinked in what feels like minutes. I've hit him with an unfair ultimatum—let me all the way in or let me go. It would be easier to take it back and trust we'd get there in time, but I can't. I'm not prepared to endure what I went through with Reggie, who I don't think I ever loved absolutely, with Andrew, who I think I could.

"We've always been able to be honest with each other," I say. "Tell me what you're thinking."

"I don't want you to leave," he says right away.

"I'm not asking for the world, but if you want me to stay, I need more."

With a swallow, he nods. "I know. I didn't even realize I was . . . keeping you out. It wasn't on purpose."

I replace the self-help book on grief on the shelf and go to him, rounding the couch. "I don't blame you—we had a deal. But now we have a new one."

After a few tense seconds, one corner of his mouth lifts. "We do? What would that be?"

"We're allowed to fall in love."

He raises his eyebrows. "And?"

"That's it. We take it day by day. We stay honest with each other." I chew my bottom lip. "Or, we walk away like we originally planned. But I know I'll always wonder what could've been if . . ." I'm out on the ledge alone. I'm tempted to look at my hands, but I hold onto a thread of courage. This is new for both of us, and he deserves my patience.

"If what, Amelia?"

"If I had let myself love you."

His expression sobers. "I would wonder too. Always." He sits on the couch. Taking my hand in his, he tugs me down next to him. "She made us my favorite dinner that night. Back then, I didn't cook. I didn't clean or do much of anything around the house, honestly. I was just trying to get the garage going, and that took up a lot of my time."

"You sound like you regret that," I say.

He nods. "Part of what I struggle with is the fact that I wasn't a good boyfriend. I thought I made up for that by being a good dad, but Shana didn't see it that way."

I bring our laced hands to my lips and kiss his knuckles. "You blame yourself."

"Sometimes." He pulls my legs over his lap, and I settle back against the opposite arm so I can see him. "We all went to bed that night. When I woke up, Bell was crying in her crib. Shana was nowhere to be found, but she didn't have a job or anywhere she had to be at six in the morning. Once I'd calmed Bell down, I went into my closet. Most of her things were gone. I panicked and called the police, but they knew better. When I admitted her things were missing, they told me to wait a couple days."

He leans forward and picks up his drink before passing me mine. "So, she was gone. I called her mom, who said Shana was safe but that was all she could tell me. I would've gone to her parents', but they lived hours away, and I was saddled with Bell and work. Plus—I was fucking bitter. I wasn't about to go banging on her door, begging her to come back. Eventually, when I was ready to face her, her parents said she was no longer there."

"Where was she?"

He shakes his head. "Either they didn't know, or they wouldn't tell me. Her mom wanted to come visit, but I held Bell like ransom. It was a way of punishing Shana, not letting her parents see Bell."

"Didn't they fight you?" I ask. "They're her grandparents."

"Not hard enough." He clears his throat. "All of this happened right before Bell's third birthday. I would've been happy to crawl into a hole and drink myself stupid, but I couldn't. We had friends and family coming over. I spent the party explaining Shana's absence and getting a sickening amount of pity. At one point, I actually went into the bathroom and puked."

"God," I say, covering my heart. "That's awful."

"I was fucked. Because I worked a lot, Shana had handled almost everything when it came to Bell. Sure, I helped out in the evenings, but I had no idea what went on during the day. Sadie and Nate came for a weekend and forced me to man up. I wanted to go straight to the bar and drown myself in liquor."

"That's why you got that tattoo," I say.

He nods. "The stress of suddenly being a single parent, plus the fact that I'd loved Shana, sent me into a black hole. But I couldn't let that show when I was around Bell, which was basically every hour of every day."

"What about the garage?"

"My guys held it down." He looks into the distance and nods. "They're my family. At home, Flora and Denise stepped in. Flora was a friend of my grandfather's, and Denise was Shana's close friend, so they knew Bell. My parents were useless."

I shake my head. Flora was more than a babysitter, Sadie more than a sister, Denise more than a fling. They'd seen Andrew and Bell through a horrible time. "How'd you get through it?"

"Bell. And my grandfather. He was my role model, and I just kept thinking—if he were here, what would he do? I asked myself that every day for years, and every day, I got my answer. He was a real man. He faced responsibility head on. Once he decided to get sober, he never looked back."

"I'd like to have met him."

He smiles a little. "He would've loved you. Grandpa had two weaknesses—women and cars."

"What about your grandma?"

"They split soon after my dad was born, she moved away, and she passed a few years ago." He pauses, swirling his drink as he thinks. "So that's it."

"That's it?" I ask. "Until now? Did she say why she left?"

He squeezes my knee. "It's not easy for me to say. I'm afraid of what you'll think of me."

I shift against the arm of the couch. If there's anything to fear about Andrew and his situation, I want to know now. "Go ahead."

"She never wanted to get pregnant. Bell was an accident, but I pressured Shana . . . I wasn't exactly open to other options." He glances at his hand on my leg. "Motherhood was hard for her. She cried a lot. She didn't connect with Bell. And I made her feel as bad as possible about it, because I didn't understand. How could she not want this perfect baby that was somehow the tiniest and most enormous thing in my life?"

My chest pangs with regret. When I first met Andrew, his status as a father didn't appeal to me. Children were nuisances. He never made me feel bad about that—it's not like either of us had planned on me meeting her—but now that I'm getting to know Bell, I feel protective over her. "Knowing how important Bell is to you, that must've been difficult for both of you."

"I was an asshole. I didn't give any merit to her doubts or concerns. Considering her penchant for drama, I assumed she was just trying to get a rise out of me—which she usually did. I wasn't always this . . . sensitive."

I laugh. Big, hulking, gruff Andrew—*sensitive*? I'm about to protest, but Andrew really is more sympathetic to and understanding of my needs than any other man I've dated. As tough as he comes off, he takes care of what he loves. Shana's mistakes are my gain. "What changed?" I ask.

He blows out his cheeks with an exhale. "A lot. Bell taught me so much about the opposite sex. She started to come into her personality. I can't fathom ever discrediting how she feels or trying to change or control her like I did with Shana. That, and with time, I gained perspective on my relationship with Shana. I saw how I'd let her down. Where I could've done better."

"But it couldn't have been all you," I say. "You said she was dramatic."

"Absolutely," he says. "She wasn't exactly the gold standard of girlfriends. More than once, I'd come home to find Flora watching Bell because Shana had taken off with some girlfriends. She wouldn't check with me because she knew I'd say no.

She'd come home wasted and make enough noise to wake up the baby, then bitch about the fact that Bell was always crying."

I cover Andrew's hand, not to console him, but myself. It's uncomfortable to hear about another woman's family and how she let them down. "I'm sorry."

"She kissed me." The direct statement surprises me enough that I take my hand back. "At the bar, before I came over tonight. She tried to get me to go home with her."

I stare at him. Andrew watches me open and close my mouth. This is my weakness—other women. Unfaithfulness. I trust Andrew. Enough to ask what I want to know. It's a step forward that I'd even be able to trust his answer. I pull my legs from his lap and sit cross-legged. "Did you sleep with her?"

He narrows his eyes at me. "No. I realize you think all men lead with their dicks, but some of us are capable of controlling ourselves."

"But it wouldn't have been cheating," I say, picking at nothing on the couch. "We weren't together."

"I'm aware. No matter how potent Shana can be, it would never be enough to make me forget about what she did to Bell. And, as it turns out, she isn't enough to make me forget about you."

I bite my bottom lip. We've demanded communication from each other from the start. The simple act of sharing Shana's attempts means more than I thought it would. I unfold my legs and crawl to him. He checks over his shoulder, presumably toward Bell's bedroom, before pulling me into his arms. "With Shana, it was just lust," he says. "I'm not in lust with you, Amelia."

I glance up at him. "Is that a good thing?"

He kisses me on the tip of the nose. "Do you think I could've honestly stopped myself from coming to your apartment tonight? That I could've ever accepted that money to stay away? Do you really think I'm not falling in love with you too?"

I get a rush of adrenaline, as if I'm at the edge of a cliff, one toe over. Any fear I might have is hidden by excitement, though. I'm not going to fall. I'm *jumping*. "You are?"

He nods. "I am, but make no mistake—just because I'm not in lust with you doesn't mean I'm not crazy horny too."

I laugh. "You're such a poet."

He smiles. "Just keeping it real." Andrew locks his lips with mine for a hard, steamroll of a kiss that takes my breath away. He explores my mouth with his tongue, sliding his hand up my waist over my breasts.

"What was that for?" I ask breathlessly when he slows down.

"I missed you," he says. "I missed your confidence. Your humor. Your sexy red lips."

I smile a little. "They're not red tonight."

He lets his gaze fall to my mouth. "Yeah, baby, they are."

"Well, when you kiss me like *that* . . ."

"I missed other things too," he says, lowering his voice, leaning into my ear. "Having you spread out on the bed, just for me. For my eyes, my hands." As he speaks, he lifts my top, touches my stomach. "I want you."

"I'm right here."

"It's not enough. I've never even had you in my bedroom. I want to undress you, stretch you out on my bed, fingertips to toes, your hair splayed on my pillow, and I want to take you over and over until you can't handle it another second."

I inhale sharply and turn to wrap my legs around his waist. "We can't."

"We can."

We whisper like two teenagers trying not to get caught. He shoves his hand down the back of my pants, yanking me against him so my clit connects with his hardening cock. "Jesus," we say in unison.

"It's not allowed," I protest. "Somebody has to be the adult here."

He chuckles. "Believe me, what we're about to do is reserved for adults only."

As soon as it's out of his mouth, a click sounds from the hallway. We detangle at lightning speed, jumping apart a second before Bell wanders into the room, rubbing her eyes. "Daddy?"

"Bell," he says gruffly before clearing his throat. "Hey, baby. You have a bad dream?"

"No. I'm thirsty."

Andrew runs a hand through his hair, side-eyeing me. I fix my top, tugging on the hem even though it's in place.

Bell blinks a few times as she registers me. "Who are you?"

"It's Amelia," Andrew says. "Remember? From Aunt Sadie's work?"

"'Mila." She nods and yawns. "I'm thirsty, Dad."

He half rolls his eyes. "All right, all right, I'm going." He picks up our drinks and mouths "sorry" at me.

The man is at her beck and call, and I don't blame him. She looks adorable enough to eat right now, half asleep, her hair a rat's nest of tangles. Maybe I should be annoyed about getting interrupted, but I just want to pull her into my lap and pet her until she falls back asleep. It's not an urge I'm used to having. Bell somehow manages to be both a vulnerable child and mini-adult, which fuels my curiosity.

She stumbles to the couch, flopping next to me like a rag doll. "It's my birthday tomorrow."

"I know." I'm about to tell her that technically, it's been her birthday for over an hour, but I can all too easily imagine how her excitement could lead to an all-nighter. As much as I like her, I also like my sleep. "Do you mind if I come to your party?"

She looks up at me again, blankly at first, and then recognition seems to dawn on her. "Are you my dad's girlfriend?"

I open my mouth, half with surprise, half to respond. Nothing comes out but an awkward guffaw. "I'm his friend," I say. "And I'm a girl."

"I'm not a baby," she says. "I'm going to be seven. You can tell me."

And with that, I realize what it is I like so much about her. She doesn't need to be coddled or treated like a little girl the way I assumed all children would. I proceed cautiously, but I don't baby her. "What do you think a girlfriend is?"

She looks at me from the side of her eye. "Um. Like, you make him happy when he's sad. You go out to fancy restaurants." She brightens. "You can have a picnic. Or you come over for dinner."

I nod a little. "There is a *lot* of eating involved when you're a girlfriend."

"Not crabs, though," she says.

"Crabs . . .?" I laugh loudly when I realize what she means. "*Carbs*. No, this girlfriend doesn't eat carbs." I can practically hear Andrew's exasperation in my head, so I amend. "Well, maybe a few carbs won't be so bad. We'll see."

"You can come over Thursday," she suggests. "On Thursdays, we have breakfast for dinner. My dad is a really good cook. He makes the best omelets in the world."

I smile at the picture she paints. Being a girlfriend is slightly more involved than guzzling food all hours of the day, but it's simple in her eyes. Make him happy. Eat a lot. Kiss . . . "Would it be okay with you if I were his girlfriend?" I ask.

She sighs, her tiny body deflating into the cushions. "I don't know. He says my mom's not his girlfriend anymore and never will be. She left when I was three. I don't think she's coming back."

I press my lips together, suddenly, inexplicably, overcome with a wave of tears. Because of what's behind her, but more because of what she has ahead of her. When she's older, it won't be so cut and dry. She was abandoned—there's no way around it. I have the urge to protect her from that, even though I know I can't. What I could do for her one day, though, is be there. That could ease the sting. "You have your dad, though. He's not going anywhere. And your Aunt Sadie and Flora and that man with the strange name."

She giggles, seemingly unaffected by the intense conversation. "Pico." She coughs a little and says out of nowhere, "I want you to come to my party."

I was going to anyway, but my relief is immense enough that I smile. "I'd like that."

"Back to bed, Bell," Andrew says from behind us, and I realize he's been gone much longer than it takes to get a glass of water. "It's late."

She gets up and plods back to her room. Andrew follows. He reappears a few seconds later, quietly shutting her door behind him.

"Either she's exhausted or she's showing off," he says, gesturing for me to come closer. "Normally, getting her to sleep shaves a few days off my life."

I smile. "She's sweet."

"She's bossy." He massages my shoulder. "Ready for bed, *girlfriend?*"

I blush. "You heard all that."

"Yeah. And it was pretty fucking cute." He kisses me on the lips. "I like it, her calling you my girlfriend. I think I'll call you that too." He nods behind him. "My bedroom is that way. I'll get your bag."

In the hallway, a few pictures hang—Bell's school photos and some of Andrew and Bell with Sadie and Nathan. I stop in the doorway of his bedroom. It's as simple as the living room. Only the necessities. The comforter on his solid, wood-framed bed is white like the walls. Nightstands flank the bed, one with a lamp and alarm clock, the other one with a book. Nothing more.

Andrew comes up behind me, drops my duffel at our feet, and wraps his arms around my middle. "Hey."

"Hi."

"I haven't brought anyone here before," he says. "You're the first."

Warmth fills me. I look around the room. It's his safe space, and he's inviting me in. But Bell's presence sticks to me like an extra limb. I feel her a couple rooms away. I turn in his arms. "Thank you. I'm going to stay in the guest room, though."

He furrows his eyebrows. "What? Why?"

"This is about more than us."

His face softens. "I know, but you heard her. She's okay with it."

"She doesn't understand it," I say. "Let her get to know me before she wakes up and finds me in her dad's bed."

He cups my face, running his thumb along my cheekbone. "I appreciate that, but I'm a grown man. I can make love in my own home."

My breath catches. Andrew and I have made a few different kinds of love, but something tells me it'll be different in his bed—his domain. My insides tingle with anticipation, but I swallow them down. "I'm new at this," I say. "The kid thing. I don't want to screw it up."

"You will screw it up. So many times. So many ways. Seven years later, and I'm still figuring out how to be okay with the fact that every day, I fuck something up."

I wrap my hand around his wrist and kiss his palm. "You're a good dad. A good man. A good boyfriend."

"Easy for you to say," he says, grinning. "I've only officially been your boyfriend for five minutes."

With a last kiss, he shows me to the guest room, where he leaves me alone with my bag. I perch on the edge of the bed. I've slept by myself almost every night the past year, yet suddenly I feel Andrew's absence acutely.

I have to give him credit for what he's done. He's the personification of "actions speak louder than words." I can trust him. I knew it early on, but I wasn't sure I could trust myself. After a few minutes have passed, and I haven't moved, I stand up from the bed and tiptoe into the hallway, back to Andrew's room. I knock lightly.

Andrew opens the door in only his boxer-briefs, filling it with his six-foot-plus frame. Without a word, he pulls me in and locks the door behind us. He engulfs me in a hug, consumes my mouth with his. Separating only to discard clothing, we stumble to the bed, leaving a trail of underwear. He ushers me under the covers, climbs over me, and hides us under the comforter. "Back-up plan," he teases, "in case she breaks down the door." I smile into his mouth. He nabs my bottom lip with his teeth. "Have I ever mentioned how it feels when I'm the reason for your smile? Like a million bucks."

My grin fades. I touch his face. He's so good to me. And if he keeps this up, I won't have a chance. I'll fall over-the-edge in love with him.

"What's wrong?" he asks, but I think he knows I'm perfectly fine, because he kisses the tip of my nose.

"I'm happy."

"I'm glad." He nuzzles my neck and cups me between the legs. "I want to make you even happier." He slips a finger into me, and I suck in a breath. "You're ready," he says.

I nod. After the night we've had, the high-highs and low-lows, the loss of what I thought was my identity, the possible gain of a family, I want to feel connected to Andrew more than anything right now.

He removes his hand to position himself against my entrance. He cups my head, keeping my eyes locked on his. Our mouths reach for each other as he pushes into me. I groan as he fills me—fully, completely, relentlessly, until he's rooted as deep as he can get. And then, as promised, he makes love to me, his thrusts slow but firm, his mouth hot and greedy on mine. My body melts into the mattress for him, my eyes glued shut from pleasure. He overwhelms me, engaging all my senses—giving me his taste, his moans, his cock, his briny scent and, finally, he says, "Let me see you."

I open my eyes and come first under his half-lidded gaze. He rolls me over on top of him. After an intense orgasm, I'm nothing more than a bag of bones, so I prop myself on his chest with my hands, but my arms nearly give. "I can't stop shaking," I tell him.

"Don't worry. I've got you." He holds me up by my waist as he takes me. When his breathing shallows and his grunts intensify, he slides a hand up to grip my breast. He bucks up into me and erupts.

He fills me for the first time.

After what we've been through, it binds us in an irrevocable way.

THIRTY-FOUR

When I emerge from the guest bedroom in the morning, I'm embarrassed by how late it is. I normally leave for work around seven, but thanks to the large, cloud-like bed, the complete stillness of the suburbs, and the workout Andrew gave me last night, I overslept. I barely remember waking up at dawn to sneak back to the guest room. After a shower and dressing in my party outfit, it's ten in the morning.

I follow the only noise in the house, which comes from the kitchen. Bell and Flora are surrounded by baking ingredients, from a heavy bag of flour to a carton of eggs to a colorful array of mixing bowls.

"Morning," I say.

Bell whirls around, and her eyes double in size. "Mila!"

My heart drops. What was I thinking, wandering in here like this without considering how it might look to Bell? I should've waited for Andrew to come get me. I look hurriedly at Flora for direction, but she just shrugs, so instead I address Bell. "I hope you don't mind that I stayed in your guest room—"

"You . . . look . . . *beautiful.*" She covers her mouth with both hands. "You're wearing that to *my* party?"

"Oh." I look down at my dress, a colorful DVF wrap from the spring collection with enormous, budding flowers in pink, orange and red. "Yes. Do you like it?"

"I love it." She tiptoes toward me, holding out her hands.

"Bell, honey," Flora says. "That's an expensive dress. Wash your hands first."

Bell has her father's purple-blue eyes, and they're saucer-sized with wonder. Her giddiness reminds me of standing in my mother's impressive, Texas-sized closet, surrounded by glamorous pieces that always smelled of Chanel No. 5. As much as I shelled out for this dress, I'd rather spoil it than this moment—a young girl's budding love affair with fashion. "It's okay," I say. "You can touch it." I hold out the fabric. "This is Diane von Furstenberg. The fabric is silk. Flora's right—it is delicate and beautiful, so you want to treat it with respect."

Bell wipes her hands quickly on her pajamas and then gently takes it in her small hands, stroking one of the flowers.

I glance up at Flora, who's smiling at us. "Where's Andrew?" I ask.

"He and Antonio ran out to pick up some last-minute things."

"Antonio?" I ask.

"My son. Pico."

"Oh." I nod. "Right. Should we start the cake?"

Flora hesitates and nods at Bell. "It could get messy, especially with this one."

Bell goes rod straight, as if possessed by some great idea. "Daddy has an apron. I'll get it."

"You look very . . . put together," Flora says while Bell rummages in a closet.

"You mean overdressed."

"Just a touch. The heels alone—you'll sink in the backyard."

There are jeans, a t-shirt, and sneakers in my duffel bag, but I purposely chose this dress. It may be a party for a seven-year-old, but it's a party nonetheless. I wouldn't wear anything more casual if it were in the city, after all. This is who I am, whether New Jersey likes it or not.

Bell finds the apron and brings it to me. "Here you go."

"Do you think I should change, Bell?" I ask, taking it from her.

"*No*," she says. "Please don't!"

"Me neither." I tie the apron around my waist and neck. "I can't think of a better occasion to dress up for."

Flora chuckles to herself, muttering, "It won't last."

Bell squeaks, and I look down at her. Her face is bright red with exertion, and I quickly figure out she's doing her best to hold in a laugh.

"What?" I ask, glancing down. I hold out the apron and crane my neck to see it upside down. There's a silhouette of a man with a spatula next to a grill. I read it aloud. "I Like Pig Butts and I Cannot Lie."

Bell bursts into a fit of giggles, wheezing from her effort to keep it in. Her glee spurs my own. Laughter travels up my chest, and soon, I'm no better than her, an immature pre-teen laughing at a butt joke.

"Now there's a sound I could get used to," I hear from behind me. I turn around. Andrew fills the doorway in a black t-shirt and jeans, his muscles straining as he holds several canvas shopping bags. My already big smile widens. "Hi."

He looks me over, hair to shoes, then fixates on my chest. "Nice apron."

"It was that one or World's Best Dad," Bell says.

"You have a point," he says, winking at her. "That title's reserved."

Another man comes into the kitchen, shouldering Andrew out of the way to slump groceries on the island. "Good God. Your dad went a little crazy at the store."

Andrew shrugs a shoulder. "Don't want to run out of food."

"They're first graders, not wild animals," the man says.

Andrew arches an eyebrow at me as he sets his bags down too. "You'd be surprised."

I return his stare, and suddenly, I forget anyone else is in the room. With just a look, last night's lovemaking rushes over me. He promised me all sorts of naughty things in his bed, yet all he did was treat me like a princess, give me an orgasm, and let me fall asleep on his chest.

I like being here in his kitchen, with his friends and family, but I also want to be alone with him. Can there be romance with a young child in the house?

"Bell, Antonio," Flora says. "Let's get the rest of the groceries."

"There're only a couple more bags," the new person—Antonio—says. "And is anyone going to introduce me to the city girl?"

I put out my hand. "Amelia. Nice to meet you."

He wipes his palm on his jeans and takes it. "Call me Pico."

Andrew glares at him. "Listen to your mother and get lost, a-hole."

"*Oh*," Pico says, nodding with a sly grin. "Got it. Come on, Bell. How about a piggy-back ride?"

"Yes," she screams and hops on before he's even at her level.

The three of them disappear, and not a second too soon. Andrew closes the space between us and gathers me in his arms. "You disappeared on me this morning," he says in my ear.

"I told you I would."

"It'll be the last time."

"But—"

"But nothing," he says. "You sleep under my roof, you're in my bed. Understood? I'll have a conversation with Bell first chance we get."

"Okay," I relent. What's he doing to me? I used to be immovable when I wanted my way, and suddenly my argument is a simple "but" followed by my submission?

"What're you smiling about?" he asks.

I shake my head. I can't explain, so I just say, "You."

"You look sexy as hell, by the way."

"Is it the pig butts that do it for you?" I tease.

"It all does it for me—apron, dress, heels, hair. You're way too beautiful for a kid's party."

"This is me," I say. "City girl. Take it or leave it."

"I'll take it." He kisses me on the lips, then the corner of my mouth, making his way to underneath my ear. Sliding his hands down my backside, he takes two handfuls. "God, I love this ass. It's enough to get me worked up again."

The front door slams, and I push him off by his chest. "You'll have to put it on hold a little longer."

He grumbles, but as soon as Bell enters the kitchen, his glower vanishes. "How's it feel to be seven years old, kiddo?"

She twirls. "Amazing. I feel like a new person." Everyone in the room smiles, and Bell notices, batting her lashes at each one of us. "Daddy, I know what I want for my birthday."

Andrew looks suddenly terrified, as if she just told him she could see dead people and there was one right over his head. "But—your birthday is now," he says, and I hear the stress in his voice. "I already got your gifts."

Unperturbed, she continues, "I want a silk dress, just like Mila's."

Slowly, Andrew turns his head to me, his eyes accusing. "Is . . . that . . . so?"

"I may have introduced your daughter to designer fashion." I grimace. "To be fair, that's a love you're born with. She would've discovered it eventually."

"I see." He looks around the room, taking stock. "Well . . . I'm thinking a dress like that is pretty expensive. I suppose I could take back all your gifts, and exchange them for one—"

"No," she says quickly, jumping up and down. "Next year. I want it next year. It won't fit me now anyway."

Andrew glances at me, his eyes glimmering. "Good point. Next year it is, then. Amelia can help me pick it out."

I return his smile. I can't think of anything I'd rather be doing a year from now.

Bored with the baking, Bell has migrated outside to help her father and his friends set up the birthday party. Andrew and Pico cover a long picnic table Andrew rented for the kids to sit and eat. Standing at the sink, I watch Bell through the kitchen window as she bosses grown men around the yard. She doesn't want the plates and silverware in piles—she wants the table set "like the grown-ups do." She won't stand for "baby" music. She wants Zeppelin, The Rolling Stones, Black Sabbath, and Taylor Swift. Andrew revealed, after some prodding, it took him three hours to build a playlist suitable for a children's party.

"You know Andrew has a dishwasher," Flora says.

I turn my head to her quickly, startled by her voice. "What?"

"You've been washing that bowl for five minutes."

"Oh." I didn't have a dishwasher when I moved to city or for years after. Not until Reggie and I got our apartment. Even then, I continued to hand wash everything. I rinse the bowl and set it on a drying rack.

"What's on your mind?" Flora asks.

I glance back outside. Andrew scans the backyard, squinting against the sun. It looks as though he's doing nothing, but I know he's making sure everything is perfect for Bell. He's devoted to her happiness. I can see why Andrew loves being a dad. It's not always pretty, but it's meaningful. He doesn't fix cars for a living—he raises a human being. I have a reputation for doing my work well, but what does that mean at the end of the day?

A realization hits me hard. Even with everything I'll have on my plate come Monday morning, I haven't thought about *avec* since last night. It's probably the longest I've gone in years without mentally listing all the things I have to do or wondering about website statistics or inventing creative ways to impress my clients. The most surprising part, though, is that I don't feel any guilt about it. But it's not because I'm going to lose it. I know in my heart of hearts, I'll go down with the ship as deep as I need to until all of my clients and employees are taken care of. It's this, what surrounds me, that has kept me from work. Bell's party, Andrew's family, my safety—it all seems more important than sending out an e-mail on time.

Andrew throws his head back and laughs at something Bell says. My heart comes to life. *He* is more important.

"Work," I tell Flora.

"You're thinking about work?" She sounds disappointed.

"No." I glance at her. "I'm thinking about how I'm not thinking about work."

"I see." She tilts her head at me. "How does it feel?"

"Weird. I forget there's a world outside of it."

Flora joins me at the sink, looking out the window. "She's his world. I worry he won't be able to make space for anyone else, even though he needs to."

I'm surprised by her bluntness. Last night, she was more than obvious about pushing me onto him.

"Since Shana, many others have tried," she says. "I've seen it with my own eyes. I can't blame them." She shakes her head and looks up at me. Despite her words, there's no pity, no defeat in her eyes. They're sparkling. "None of them made it here. And it has more to do with you than it does Andrew."

I study her a moment. "What are you saying?"

"Andrew fought against it because he thought his life needed to be about her. He thought he'd had his chance. What he needed was the right woman to make it worth it again. Someone strong and smart and challenging."

Though her words resonate deeply with me, I can't help but point out the obvious. "But it isn't just about him," I say. "This whole life is foreign to me."

"Does that worry you?"

"Of course." I pinch the apron between my fingers, showing it to her. "I'm not a mom. I don't do bake sales or minivans, and frankly, I don't think I ever will. I don't cook—even my vegetables are takeout. How am I supposed to be responsible for the health of a small child?"

"I don't know if you're aware, but Andrew is an excellent chef. For only learning to cook four years ago, he's astounding. When something's important to him, he never half-asses it."

"That's not really the point—"

"Moms—and families—come in different shapes and sizes. You don't have to drive a certain kind of vehicle or dress in khaki Bermuda shorts."

I gasp. "Bermuda shorts—oh, God. You're making it worse."

She laughs. "I'm saying not all moms look alike. There are just a few really important things you have to be or do. I don't think you need me to tell you those."

Bell folds her arms over her chest, surveying the picnic tables, her stance the exact same as her dad's when he inspected their work a minute ago. I think of my own mom, who was, for the most part, good to me. But she did her own damage, all while looking exactly as a mom should, according to the rest of the world.

What would I have to be to Bell? A role model, a support beam, a cheerleader. What would I have to do? Love her unconditionally. But am I capable of that? Loving a child seems like it would be more graceful and simple than surrendering your heart to a lover. Already, I feel protective of her. Proud of the headstrong, independent girl she is. If I let myself love her, though—what happens if Andrew and I don't make it?

"If I do this," I say, "it's for good. I can't just walk away if it gets hard."

Flora nods her head. "It's true that Bell isn't as tough as she acts. But Andrew is teaching her strength, and if one day you leave, she'll survive."

"That's very . . . practical."

"I'd hate to see you walk away, or worse, not give them a hundred percent of yourself because you're worried about hurting them down the line. They're survivors."

Andrew squats to Bell's level, his brows furrowed. He listens to whatever she says with complete focus, as if she's giving him directions to a fortune.

My heart surges with adoration. "I'm not going to walk away," I say. "It's more that I'm not sure how not to be a businesswoman."

"That's what I'm trying to tell you. You can be both. So you cut back on evenings and weekends. So you work from home more. Don't you own your own business?"

I swallow. Letting go of *avec* won't be easy. Already, I feel a void. Work will always be important to me, and I know I'll figure out something else.

Ultimately, I have to believe in the decision I made because the reasons were right. "Yes," I say.

"Maybe you get some clients out here. Or open another branch." She shrugs. "You're the boss—that's what bosses do. Adapt."

Wise old woman. "It'll take some rearranging."

"That can be a good thing."

I cross my arms. Andrew notices us and waves, so I smile at him. It *can* be a good thing. I think it could be a great thing.

THIRTY-FIVE

The universe is infamous for playing tricks—and right now, the joke is on me. Not twenty minutes after Flora boosted my maternal confidence, the doorbell rang, and so began a steady stream of messy, rowdy children and their Bermuda-shorts-wearing, mini-van-driving mothers. I'm suddenly one of them, only in four-inch heels and a four-hundred dollar frock. The party has begun.

Flora was right—my heels do sink in the grass. I don't let that discourage me. I pick up napkins that fly off the table with every breeze. I maneuver around toys, discarded plastic cups, and actual small humans.

"I love your dress," one of the mom gushes, her eyes wide. "Is that from the Spring collection?"

"It is, actually," I say, guilty over my obvious surprise.

"Oh, I don't own anything by DVF," she says, "but I follow a few fashion blogs religiously. Just to torment myself."

"Really?" I ask, my interest piqued. "You don't think it's silly?"

"What, fashion? Not at all. A friend of mine and I shop the vintage stores in the area all the time. Once in a while we'll score a rare find like an authentic Gucci clutch. It's better than nothing, which is what my husband lets me have at designer prices."

"You just haven't found your bargaining chip yet."

She tilts her head. "What?"

"No man should have final say over your wardrobe. He can have input at best."

"But it's his money," she says.

"You don't work?"

"Not unless you count raising three children work."

I furrow my eyebrows. "Why wouldn't I? If you're not making a salary for that, then a Gucci bag is the *least* he can do."

"Does that really work?" she asks.

"If it doesn't, calculate back pay on the hours you've worked since your firstborn. That'll light a fire under his ass."

She grins and holds out her hand. "We haven't officially met, but I need to know you. I'm Lynn."

Lynn and I talk fashion a little longer until she's called away by her daughter.

I'm not alone long before another mom takes her place. "I don't think we've met," she says, scanning me from head to toe. "Which one's yours?"

"None," I say. "I'm a friend of the host."

"Andrew?" She blinks. "A friend?"

I nod. "A very good one."

"Oh. I love your dress." Though it's the exact same thing Lynn said, her tone is the opposite of warm and friendly. "It's . . . festive."

I grin, smoothing my hand over the front of it. "It *is* fabulous, isn't it?" I say, as I turn and walk away. Maybe I *can* do this mom thing!

I spot Andrew before he sees me. He's in conversation with a woman—there are a lot of them around—but he keeps looking past her, first at Bell, and then scanning the party. The woman leans in, laughs, and touches his bicep. He crosses his arms, nodding, but he definitely does not look as though he's enjoying himself. When his eyes land on mine, he smiles widely, somehow brightening an already warm, sunny afternoon.

It's all the signal I need. I beeline for him, focusing on the way he tracks my every step, his eyes skimming from my legs to my hips to my breasts and finally, my face. When the woman notices he isn't listening to her, she pauses and follows his line of sight right to me.

"I've been looking for you," he says to me.

"Here I am." I hold out my hand to her. "Amelia."

521

She looks perplexedly at my hand before shaking it. "Kiki. Brynn's mom."

"Nice to meet you, Kiki Brynn's Mom," I say.

"You're Bell's aunt?" she asks.

Andrew lays a heavy arm around my shoulder and brings me into his chest. He kisses the top of my head. "Thankfully not, or that would be weird," he says. "This is my girlfriend."

My heart skips. I'm not used to the new designation, but my surprise is nothing compared to the shock on Kiki's face. Her eyes flare open, and either she doesn't have time to hide her envy or she doesn't know how, because I read it loud and clear. I could teach her a thing or two about composure. "Oh—I . . . I didn't know. When—? I thought—"

"Can you give us a minute, Kiki?" Andrew asks. "I haven't seen Amelia in half an hour, and I'm dying to give her a real kiss."

She scoffs, as if he's affronted her somehow, and takes a step back. "Of course. Why would I mind?" She hurries away. I imagine her casting a glance over her shoulder, but I don't get a chance to look because Andrew spins me so we're face to face. He plants a hard kiss on my mouth. "Mmm. You taste even better than the birthday cake."

I pull back a little. "How would you know? It's still in the kitchen."

"I may have snuck a bite."

"Andrew," I scold, shoving his chest. He stays right where he is, keeping one arm around my shoulders and the other secured to my waist. "That's your daughter's cake. She'll be devastated."

"You think I'm stupid? I was strategic about it. I covered my tracks with icing."

I roll my eyes but hug him back. "Very sneaky."

"It was delicious." He rests his forehead against mine. "You did good."

"Thanks," I murmur. "That woman—have you . . .?"

"What?" he asks. "With *her*?"

I nod. "She seemed really offended."

He shakes his head. "Nah. I don't mess with the other moms. They're rabid. If I were to let one of them into my bed, they'd turn into an even hornier pack of bitches."

I wrinkle my nose. "That many of them are single?"

"No," he says. "Hardly any. Kiki isn't."

"Oh." Understanding dawns. "So they just want to hook up."

"Yeah. The weird thing is, the single moms leave me alone. It's like we understand each other."

I smile a little. "*I* never pretended to understand you."

"Nor I you. You're still a puzzle."

Grinning, I tilt my head up for another kiss just as I hear, "Ugh. I don't know whether to be disgusted or elated."

Without letting go of Andrew, I turn. Sadie holds a plate with a hamburger. Nathan stands next to her with two more. "On the one hand," she says, "I want you both to be happy. On the other . . ." She grimaces. "Ew. You're my *brother*. And my *boss*."

"She's been a bit multiple-personality ever since," Nathan nods at her growing belly, "you know."

Sadie turns to gape at him. "I'm *pregnant*. I'm entitled to indecision and mood swings."

"And foot rubs. And midnight ice cream runs. And three plates of food."

Andrew raises his eyebrows at the burgers and hotdogs. "Those are all for you?"

"As Rachel Green says, 'no uterus, no opinion,'" she bites back before glancing at me. "Do you have anything to add?"

"Only that you're absolutely glowing," I say through a forced smile as I resist asking who Rachel Green is.

"Thank you." She straightens. "I guess I'm just relieved neither of you is as cynical as you pretend, and that you're not failing at hiding it anymore."

Nathan puts an arm around her shoulder as best he can with his hands full. "Come on, babe."

"But—"

"Nope," he says. "We're done here. Let them have their moment."

When they've gone, I shake my head. "Your sister is insane."

Andrew grins. "She'll be your sister too."

I look at him, thinking I've misheard. "What?"

His smile fades. "Christ. Sorry. That was a stupid fucking thing to say."

"She'll be *my* sister?" I repeat. I wonder if it was a slip of the tongue, but the way he swallows uncomfortably makes me realize what he's saying. "You mean if we were to . . . if one day—"

"Don't freak out," he says. "It was dumb. I swear, I don't have a ring in my pocket or anything. I haven't even thought about it. I wouldn't just spring that on you—"

"Hang on," I say, throwing him a lifeline since he's obviously struggling. "Just back up. I'm not freaking out, but what were you trying to say?"

He stops for a moment, squinting behind me, lost in a thought. Finally, he says, "I wouldn't have invited you here if I didn't believe in a future with you. So I guess on some subconscious level, I assume we're in it now. For the long haul." He cringes. "Stage-five clinger status?"

I don't panic. Instead, to my surprise, I laugh. "No. We're not like other couples. We have to think about these things. I'd be more shocked if I hadn't just talked to Flora about being a stepmother."

Andrew's face stills, and for a moment, our roles are reversed, and *I* feel like *I've* gone too far. He clenches his jaw, and the warm blue of his eyes sharpens. "God," he says. "A stepmom. To Bell."

I hold his gaze and point out, "That's the same thing as being Sadie's sister-in-law."

"I know," he says. "I'm not saying it's a bad thing, I just never thought I'd . . . get here. And so quickly."

I rub his back. "It is quick. We have all the time in the world, though. There's no rush."

"Where's Daddy?" Bell calls over the din of the crowd. "I have to blow out the candles *now*."

"Well, maybe a slight rush," I amend, smiling.

"It never ends," he says. "And summer break's around the corner. That's months without a reprieve." I can't tell if it's a complaint or a warning—especially since he's smiling.

Before I can find out, Bell comes running up to us. She stops a few feet away as if she's hit an invisible wall. "Dad?" she asks, uncharacteristically timid.

I go to pull away, but Andrew keeps me where I am. "You're not interrupting," he says. "Come here."

She tiptoes forward, as if she might spook one of us. Her eyes dart between Andrew and me. "We have to, um, eat cake now. So I can open presents."

"Okay," he says. "I'll go get it."

"'K." She turns around, pausing briefly to look at the grass.

"Bell," he says.

She looks back.

"Are you okay?" Andrew shifts so his arm is around my shoulders again, and we're no longer hugging. He holds out his hand to her. "Do you feel confused about this?"

She just stares at us.

"Listen," he says. "Why don't we all go inside and talk about it? We'll answer any questions you have."

After a few seconds, she slumps forward as if he's asked her to call the whole party off. "Do we have to right *now*? I want to open my presents."

He chuckles. "All right then. We'll do it after."

"Whatever. Go cut the cake!" She spins around and runs back to her friends.

Andrew and I exchange a glance. "I was hoping *whatever* wouldn't start for a few more years," he says.

I smile. "Oh, no. *Whatever* is a way of life, honey. It'll only get worse."

He laughs. "Maybe the *whatever* lifestyle is something you can take on. You know, to bond with her."

I purse my lips. "We'll see."

He kisses the top of my head before ruffling it—to annoy me, I'm sure—and walks off toward the kitchen, leaving me alone, frantically trying to smooth down my hair. When it's back to normal, I look around the backyard to see if there's anything I can do and pause when I see one of the women staring at me from across the yard. Another one of Andrew's admirers, I guess, based on the sour look on her face. Even though I've caught her clearly watching us, I'm the one who looks away first.

I find Sadie and Nathan at the picnic table, the only ones left eating, as all the kids have gone back to running around. I take the seat next to Sadie on the bench. "Who's that woman?" I ask.

"Who?" Sadie asks between bites.

"Her." I nod. "By the back gate."

"I wouldn't know," Sadie says without looking, more fascinated by her potato salad. "I don't know any of the moms."

"Oh. I caught her staring at me, and she looked angry."

"Angry?" Nathan repeats. "Why would anyone be angry? It's a kid's party—"

He pauses as he and Sadie meet eyes. They go completely still.

"You don't think . . .?" Sadie asks him.

"I wouldn't put it past her. She has a flare for—"

"Drama," Sadie finishes, nodding. "We should've been on the lookout."

"*Lookout?*" I dart my eyes between them. "What are you two talking about?"

Sadie turns. "Which woman was it?"

I sit a little straighter, searching the crowd. Her back is to us, so I point. "That one with the dark hair talking to Bell."

Sadie drops her fork and starts to stand. "No. Where?"

I stand up too, alarmed. "Why? Who is she?"

"Shana," Sadie and Nathan say together as they spot her.

"She really has some nerve—" Sadie steps out from behind the table.

"Sadie," Nathan says firmly. "Stop. I'll handle this. I don't want you getting worked up—"

"No." I lock my eyes on Shana. My breath comes faster. Adrenaline pulses through me. "Let me."

Nathan holds out a hand. "I don't think—"

Sadie grabs his arm and slowly, she smiles. Sadie has known me long enough to understand bitch-mode on my worst day will trump anyone's on their best. "Let Amelia do it."

I don't even hesitate. In fact, when Shana bends over to get closer to Bell, I quicken my pace. This won't happen. I won't allow it. Bell is distracted by a classmate, who tries to get Bell to go play with her, but Shana won't let her leave. When the girl pulls Bell's arm, Shana reaches out and snatches her back like she's a ragdoll.

My blood boils, my instinct to protect flaring up. "Excuse me," I say when I'm close enough. I grab Shana's forearm and remove her hand from Bell. "Can I help you?"

Slowly, Shana's eyes travel up the length of me, stopping on my face. "Don't touch me."

"Bell," I say, keeping my glare on Shana, "Dad needs your help with the cake. Why don't you go find him?"

"Okay," she says. I'm thankful when she skips off, completely clueless. I quickly check to make sure she's out of earshot. Nathan grabs Bell and pulls her onto his lap before giving me a nod.

I return my attention to Shana. "You weren't invited."

Shana straightens to her full height. She's shorter than me, but if I intimidate her, she doesn't let on. "I don't need to be invited to *my* daughter's birthday."

"You do, actually."

"Look," she glances behind me, presumably to make sure Andrew hasn't spotted us, "I don't know who you are, but that's my daughter. I'm her mother. I love her, and you have no right to pull her away from me."

I tilt my head at her. I work in PR. Bullshit is my business, and I can smell it a mile away. After everything Andrew's told me, this chick's bullshit is pinging off the charts. "I'll walk you out."

She reels back, whipping her eyes back to me. "*Excuse* me? Who the hell do you think you are?"

I cross my arms. "That's irrelevant. You're the one crashing the party."

Her expression closes even more. "You don't have to answer. I know who you are. Another one of Andrew's toys, holding my place on the shelf until I return. Well, guess what, bitch. I'm back. You can go back to whatever hole you crawled out of."

I almost want to laugh, her words are so unnecessarily full of rage. If she believed herself, she'd deliver her blows with class and confidence. But it's clear to me Shana doesn't possess either of those.

I remind myself that she's likely feeling a mix of emotions—including guilt and shame—over how she's behaved in the past and recently. "I understand you're upset," I say calmly but firmly. "I actually would like it if you and I could talk sometime in the future, once Andrew is ready, but this isn't the place."

She looks me up and down, scoff-laughing. "Why would you and I ever talk?"

"Because I'm Andrew's girlfriend, and I'm not going anywhere. If you're back in town, then there's no way around it. We'll have to figure this out."

"Um, no. Sorry to break it to you, but Andrew would never go for you. He doesn't like snobs." She tries to step around me.

I block her path. "Say what you want about me, but I won't let you near Bell without Andrew's permission."

She sighs heavily, rolling her eyes. "Okay. I thought you were joking at first, but seriously? I know Andrew's type, and you're not it. Maybe you've managed to get him into bed—that's no great feat, even Denise pulled it off." She checks my expression.

"I know all about Denise," I say when it's obvious she's waiting for a reaction.

She raises her chin and continues. "But you're deluded if you think it's more than that. He and I have something special. He even admitted it the other night at Timber, when we had a drink, but even if he hadn't, I'd know, because *I know him*. He misses me. He wants our family back together."

Even though her words are meant to sting, they have the opposite effect. I'm relieved. Andrew could've not mentioned talking to Shana at the bar and it wouldn't have been a lie—but he did. And because he did, I'm not blindsided and left questioning our relationship when I should be focused on reeling Shana in.

"You don't know anything about the type of woman I am," I say evenly. "If you did, you'd know manipulation doesn't work on me."

"Well," she shrugs a little, "it does on Andrew, and that's all that matters. He'll be eating out of the palm of my hand in no time."

Behind me, "Happy Birthday" begins, and I pick up Andrew's baritone leading the song. I smile a little, bolstered by the fact that the longer I stay at this party, the less worried I am about a future here. Now, for instance, Shana is giving me even more reason to dig in my heels and *love* Andrew. To protect Bell from getting hurt.

"All right, Shana," I say. "We can battle it out if you want. But for your sake, I suggest you learn how to live in this new reality. Otherwise, it's going to be a painful time for you."

"And I'm sure you're concerned about my life."

"I am," I say. "Very much so. Because you're Bell's mother."

The singing stops, and I turn around just in time to see Bell's eyebrows knit in concentration as she makes her wish. She blows out the candles at the same moment I feel Shana's palms against my chest. I stumble backward but keep my balance, even in four-inch heels, because that's the kind of woman I am.

She looks a little shocked as we stand there, staring at each other. Any urge I might have to retaliate sizzles out. I don't think she meant to do it. A small part of me feels bad for her. I hope I never get to the point where I feel the only way I can make my point is by shoving someone while they're not looking.

"Again," I say, "it's time for you to go."

"You're a terrible person," she says, sounding less angry than miserable. "Trying to swoop in on another woman's family."

"I'm sorry that's how it looks to you, but it's not the case. I love Andrew. And even though I don't know Bell very well yet, I'll love her too. Because she's a part of him."

"Then I feel bad for you," she says with what sounds like all the venom she can muster. "You'll get left behind once we work this out."

"What the hell is going on?" Andrew shouts from behind me as he runs over to us. He gets between us, blocking Shana from my view. "What are you doing here?"

"Andrew, babe," she pleads.

"Nathan said you just pushed Amelia. What the fuck's wrong with you?"

I put a hand on Andrew's back. "It's okay."

He whips his head around, his jaw set. "It—is—*not*—okay."

"I can handle her," I say calmly.

He turns back to Shana. "Leave. Now. I told you already—stay away from Bell. Especially when I'm not around."

"You don't understand," she murmurs so softly, I almost can't hear. "She—*Amelia*—said vile things to me. That I wasn't Bell's mom anymore because *she* is now." Her voice cracks, and anger rises up my chest at the outrageous accusation. "She said I should rot in hell for leaving my child."

"She didn't say that," he says, "and you need to leave."

"Can't we go somewhere and talk alone?" she asks. "Just for a minute?"

"Un-uh. First, it's my baby's birthday. I'm not going to miss any more than I have standing here with you. Second, whatever you want to say, you can say in front of Amelia." Andrew takes my hand, lacing our fingers together. "Don't make me escort you out, Shana. People already have strong feelings about you in this town, and making a scene isn't helping."

She frowns, sliding her thumbnail between her front teeth as she looks behind him at the other guests. They've fallen quiet. I pray someone has taken Bell in the house, but I won't dare turn my back on Shana again. "I'm not going away, Andrew."

"Fine. If what you want is to get to know Bell, I'm not saying no. I'm saying it'll take a lot of time and work before we even get to that part, especially when you pull stunts like this."

She scowls, but I think inside, she must realize what Andrew's offering is generous. I squeeze his hand for reassurance, and he glances at me. It can't be easy to welcome her back into his life, no matter how hard he plans to make it on her.

"We're done here," he says. "Go out the back gate, Shana. When you're ready to be an adult about this, *call me*. Don't just show up."

He pulls me away, leading me over to a table where Bell's surrounded by colorfully wrapped presents.

"I was waiting for you," she says, her lips tinted pink from frosting.

"Oh, yeah?" Andrew asks. "Then why are half of these unwrapped?"

"I left so many," she cries defensively, pointing around the table.

Andrew laughs and leans down to kiss her on the back of her hair. He lingers there a moment, closing his eyes. Our hands are still interlaced, and I drag my thumb over his knuckles. "I'm sorry, baby," he says to her. "Go ahead and open the rest."

As she tears into another one, Sadie comes over. "I asked Bell what that lady said to her. She said she just wished her a happy birthday and was asking about presents."

Andrew straightens up. "Good. I wouldn't put it past Shana to walk right up to her and blurt out the truth."

I shiver at the thought of Bell finding out about her mother that way, and Andrew lets go of my hand to put his arm around me. "Don't worry," he says to me. "We won't let it happen."

Bell opens her next present and squeals, "Look, Dad. Randy got me a pink inflatable pool for the backyard."

"Great," he says. "Randy can set it up, too."

"What'd Shana want?" Sadie asks.

Andrew watches Bell. "What do you think?"

"She can't just waltz back into your lives." Sadie thins her lips. "Not just all of a sudden. Bell's not ready."

"Bell's her daughter," I say. They both look at me, but if I'm going to be part of this family, I have to be able to say what I think. "Yes, Shana's in the wrong. But like she said, she's not going away. Maybe she takes off again, but she'll be back. Won't she?"

Andrew sighs. "Definitely."

"And Bell deserves to know about her mom," I add, "even if it's not an ideal situation."

"We've already started discussing it," Andrew says. "I know she has more questions."

"Shana will have to prove herself," I continue. "Could be years, but that's up to her. When it happens, Bell will know she has all of our support. If Shana hurts her again, we'll be there to make it better."

Sadie sulks. "You guys are making it too easy on her. I didn't even get a chance to bitch her out."

Andrew slowly shakes his head. "If Shana sticks around, she'll give you plenty of opportunities for that."

"But I'm pregnant *now*," Sadie points out. "I won't have an excuse to overreact after the baby comes."

Andrew smiles. "I appreciate the sentiment. But I'm done talking about Shana for the day." He leans over and scoops a chunk of icing with his finger, popping it in his mouth.

"*Andrew,*" Sadie and I scold at the same time.

Bell looks up at us from a pile of shredded wrapping, empty cake plates, and toys. "Is that it?"

Andrew raises his eyebrows. "It is if you don't show a little more gratitude."

She frowns and turns back to the table. "Thank you for the presents," she says to the kids around her, half of whom aren't paying attention. "I love them." Sheepishly, she returns her eyes to Andrew, imploring him.

"I think there might be one more," he says. "Yo! Pico."

Bell puts her hands in her lap, squirming on the bench. "I know what it is," she says. "I just know it."

Pico comes through the back gate wheeling a tricked-out pink metallic bike with tassels hanging from the handles and a white, woven basket on the front.

Bell gasps and maneuvers out from the picnic table to run over to Pico. "A *bicycle*."

Andrew and I walk over hand in hand. "This is a big-girl bike, Bell," Andrew says. "It doesn't have training wheels. We'll have to teach you how to ride it."

She bounces up and down, and then latches onto his leg. "Thank you, Daddy. It's exactly how I wanted."

"I know. It's a custom bike."

Her eyes light up. "Like yours."

"Exactly." He laughs. "Thank Randy and Pico too. They helped build it."

"Thank you," she says to them, then reaches up to Andrew.

He removes his arm from around my shoulder to pick her up. "You're getting too big for this," he says.

"No." She frowns. "Not yet."

"No. Not yet," he agrees. "Give me an Eskimo kiss."

She brushes her nose against his without the slightest concern that all her classmates are watching. She looks at me. "Do you know how to do it, Mila?"

My chest tightens. I'd given my own dad Eskimo kisses as a little girl. A surge of emotion makes my throat thick, so I just shake my head and pretend I don't.

"I'll teach you." She leans over as Andrew supports her. "Come here."

I meet her nose with mine. Her big blue eyes are open, trusting, and innocent, and I know in that moment—I'll do whatever it takes to keep them that way. "Like this?" I ask.

"Yep. Just brush your nose against mine."

I do as she says, and she giggles. "Your nose is a lot smaller than my dad's."

"Hey," Andrew says, knitting his brows. "My nose is a normal size."

"Okay, let me down," she says, suddenly impatient. "I want to sit on the bike."

Andrew puts her down and Pico holds the bike steady as she climbs on. Andrew throws his arm back around my neck and turns me into him. "You're amazing."

"I didn't do anything."

"You did everything. And I've repaid you with a string of bad dates, ending with my ex physically assaulting you."

I smile a little. "Yet I'm still here. That says something."

"It does. I'd go on a hundred bad dates if I knew they'd lead to you."

I flush at the sincere, if slightly left-field, compliment.

He leans in to kiss me, but I pull back. "You've got frosting on your face."

"So? Lick it off. You haven't even tasted the cake yet."

Hesitantly, I lean in and run my tongue along the corner of his mouth. It's barely anything, but I make sure to get it all.

"How's it taste?"

"Like you," I say, "but sweeter."

"Is there any leftover icing?" he asks.

"I think so. Why?"

"It's only fair that I get to taste you too, but sweeter."

I blush when his insinuation occurs to me. "What makes you think I'd let you put sticky, dyed icing on me?"

"You'll let me, because I'll promise to clean off every last bite—with my tongue."

I clench my teeth against the flutter making its way through me. "Are we being inappropriate considering we're at a child's birthday party?"

"Life is about to get very hectic for us. Have to squeeze it in where we can, right?" As he says it, he crushes my front even more tightly to his. "Stay the night. We can teach Bell to ride the bike later."

I bite my bottom lip. How can I say no with his arms wrapped around me, his sweet-frosting mouth on mine, his sugarcoated promises to lick me clean? A month ago, when he wanted to stay with me, I couldn't do it.

Now, I tell him I will.

I can't imagine spending tonight without him.

EPILOGUE

Andrew's head pops up from under the cotton-white, puffy comforter. He makes a show of licking and smacking his lips. "My favorite flavor. Apricot vanilla crème pussy."

I laugh, sated from my first orgasm of the night, third of the day, fiftieth of the trip. Fifty might be an exaggeration, but our vacation feels as though it's been one, long marathon fuck—with some watersports and whale watching in between.

The curtains of the Honeymoon Suite flutter with a breeze from the balcony. We're not married yet—it's on our to-do list—but the hotel doesn't need to know that. This way, we score all the perks . . . like the free champagne we guzzled on night one.

Andrew lifts up onto his arms to hover over me. "I can't believe it's already our last night in paradise. Are you bummed about going home?"

"Do you have to ask?"

"No. I know you're not." He drops a quick kiss on my lips. "Neither am I."

"St. Maarten has been dreamy," I say. "But next time, let's bring the kid."

He grins. "Yeah?"

"She would've loved snorkeling, Andrew. She's going to flip when she sees the underwater photos."

"Speaking of flipping, I'm going to need you to get on your stomach."

I arch an eyebrow at him. "Should I even ask why?"

"So I can spank you. How many times have I asked you *not* to bring up Bell when I'm naked and about to have you? I lost my hard-on."

I shake my head, laughing. I know from experience that one spanking will instantly put him back in the mood. "That's so inappropriate."

"Yeah, well, that's life with an eight-year-old. Messy as fuck."

"Almost nine," I point out. "Can you believe it's been two years since we met?"

"Um, yeah, I can." He rolls his eyes. "I thank my lucky stars all the time that you thought I was a plumber and ripped me a new one."

His tone is sarcastic, so even though I know how grateful he is for me, I smack him on the ass. And then I wince.

"Hurt your hand?" he guesses, reaching around to grab my wrist. He kisses my palm.

I nod. "All that yoga you've been doing."

"Now you're really asking for it," he says. I've been explicitly warned against mentioning yoga—according to Andrew and his friends, it's for chicks only. Except that he started joining me for private classes a year ago. There've been a few arguments during which I was tempted to run to the shop and announce Andrew's new hobby to Pico and Randy. But I don't want him to stop. Yoga has made his body even firmer and leaner, and I enjoy those benefits as often as I can.

I pat his shoulder. "Well, since you're done for the night, I think I'll go to sleep."

He grins wolfishly. With my wrist still in his grip, he lifts my arm over my head and pins it to the mattress. "You know very well I'm not finished. I plan to do this for a lifetime and still not be done."

Andrew lugs our things up the sidewalk to the house, but I lag behind, eyeing my rose bushes. Without even a glance back at me, he calls, "You can inspect them with a magnifying glass later."

He knows me so well. I planted them when I moved in, and I've cared for them meticulously since. I want to make sure the gardeners were good to them during my absence. Bell's almost as diligent as I am about tending to them, but she's still a child. My orange-pink Brothers Grimm roses, which Bell chose just for the name, are my pride and joy. For the first time in my life, I own a piece of the world, something tangible.

To my surprise, the front door hasn't flown open yet. I can imagine Bell must be bursting at the seams to see us. We've spoken on the phone twice a day every day. As eager as she's been for us to return, Andrew and I have made strides getting her to understand we'll always come home. We're not going anywhere. She still gets upset when we leave, but it's not nearly as bad as when Andrew and I started dating.

When Andrew reaches the door, I jog up the walkway to block him from going inside. "I should warn you," I say. "There's a surprise for you in there."

"Yeah?" he asks, furrowing his eyebrows. "How'd you manage that?"

"It wasn't easy," I admit. Considering our history with exes, Andrew and I are completely transparent with each other at all times. This surprise took a lot of secret phone calls and money transfers, but I know without a doubt it'll be worth all the sneaking around. "Come on. You'll see."

As he reaches for the handle, the door swings open. "What'd you bring me?" Bell screams.

So much for her separation anxiety.

"Nothing!" Andrew screams back at her.

Her face falls a mile. "What? Not even a little shell?"

I drop my shoulder bag and open my arms. "*I* brought you presents, baby."

She runs into my embrace. I lift her up and immediately smell her hair. It reminds me she's real. I had no idea I could miss someone as much as I did her—or Andrew for that matter. When I have to go into the city for business, all I want is to come back to him.

"How was your trip?"

I look up. Shana leans in the doorway, her arms crossed. She's wearing her regular get-up of a black halter and dark jeans. I'm not sure I'll ever get used to the cleavage, but somehow, I'm getting used to her.

"Amazing," Andrew says. "And the kid?"

Shana nods. "Thanks for letting me do this. We had fun, didn't we, Bell?"

"Yep." Bell squirms. I put her down. "Shana did fine."

I check Shana's expression. She hates that Bell won't call her *mom*. I've talked to Bell about it, but she gets squirmy. She isn't ready. I haven't mentioned to anyone yet, not even Andrew, that lately, Bell's been calling *me* mom when she's sleepy or emotional. Even if I wanted to share that, I wouldn't be able to without bawling. It's unreal. Special. And for now, it's just between Bell and me.

Shana, almost thirty, has gotten her act together as much as someone like Shana can. She's no angel. She still causes trouble at Timber Tavern and regularly stirs up gossip. She was even arrested a year and a half ago for public intoxication—and promptly called Andrew to bail her out. He didn't. But the last year or so, she's been consistent with Bell, and as long as she continues to prove herself, Andrew and I will cautiously let her into our lives. Under Flora's supervision, along with the help of Pico's new wife, Myra, and of course, her son Sammy—Shana got to spend these last couple weeks taking care of Bell.

She turned out better than Reggie, at least. He hit rock bottom the night he threatened Andrew and me—and kept going. He did his best to hurt us, but no lawyer would take him seriously when Reggie accused Andrew of being a bad father. He had no real evidence, and no charges could be pressed. I later learned that on top of losing his job, he'd invested most of his savings in a failing start-up. Though I can't excuse his behavior, I understand a little better what drove him to my place. Reggie thought I was the one thing he could control that night.

Ultimately, he wouldn't budge on *avec*. I had to let it go. It fell apart soon after I stepped down.

Since I didn't have anything left to fight for, the divorce went through smoothly without Reggie doing too much damage. He tried. He went to the press with the videos he had; but once I stepped down from *avec*, nobody cared enough to run a story about two people in New Jersey who'd once had sex in the privacy of their own home. It was an embarrassing few months while Reggie tried to slander us, but we burrowed ourselves in our home. We used that time to strengthen our unit.

I moved in with Andrew a year later.

Andrew drops our luggage in the living room, and Shana and I move into the kitchen to give him a moment alone with Bell. I'm sorting through a stack of mail on the counter when Shana clears her throat. "I guess I'll take off."

I look up. "Thanks again for helping us out. How'd everything go with the," I lower my voice, "you know?"

She smiles. "Good. Pico and Randy oversaw the entire thing, and I cleaned it this morning. It looks great."

"I can't wait to see his face."

"Um. There's one thing I wanted to ask you," she says, tapping a finger on the tile. "It's not about Bell."

I set down the mail to give her my attention. She looks nervous, which is rare for her, no matter how tense things have gotten between us over the past two years. "It's just—I haven't mentioned it because I wanted to make sure I would follow through. When I graduated from cosmetology school, I started thinking about opening my own salon. Now that I've been hairdressing over a year, I want to pursue my own thing."

"Oh." As much progress as Shana has made, I brace myself. If she asks us for money, I know Andrew won't give it to her. I'm not sure I'd be comfortable with that either, even though she's fierce with enough street smarts to run her own place. I would know.

"I just—I know you're a PR consultant, but Denise said you helped one of her friends restructure her thrift store, and I was hoping maybe we could sit and talk about a business plan. Sometime. When you're free."

I'm relieved. "We can do that," I say. "As long as you're serious."

"I am. It's not exactly easy for me to ask *you* for help," she points out. "I wouldn't if I didn't need it."

"True." I've only ever wanted Shana to do well. She'll always be in Bell's life, and Bell's happiness is as important to me as my own. "How about we sit and talk next month when you pick up Bell for the weekend? You can even stay for dinner."

"That'd be great. I don't have much saved yet—"

"Don't worry about it. You can pay me back when your salon opens by doing my hair." As soon as I say it, we both laugh nervously. I've taken it a step too far. I don't think Shana nor I would ever be comfortable in such an intimate situation. "Let's just stick to business," I suggest. "I'll put next month on my calendar, and I'll make sure Sadie's here too."

Once Sadie had her little girl and *avec* closed its doors, she and I partnered up for PR consulting. We've had small business clients all over the tri-state area, from florists to cafés to a grungy but successful Jersey auto shop—despite its stubborn owner's protests that they were doing fine without "bullshitting people." We've even taken on a couple charities pro bono, something I'd never considered doing with *avec*.

Between my biweekly visits and Andrew's insistence on getting us a hotel in the city one night a month so I don't feel trapped in the suburbs, I haven't even had a chance to miss New York.

We say goodbye to Shana, and as soon as the door closes behind her, Andrew's and my attention goes to Bell. We can't help it—she's nearly vibrating with excitement. "Can we show him now?" she asks me. "Please? I've been *dying* all morning."

I nod my permission, and she grabs his hand, pulling him away.

"Ah." Andrew looks back, lifting one eyebrow. "The big surprise."

"I think we should blindfold him," I say, covering his eyes from behind, sweet revenge for all the times he's blindfolded me.

He groans.

"Maybe gag him too," I whisper in his ear, earning myself a chuckle from him.

We pass through the bedroom to the bathroom. Sensing our location, Andrew says, "If you guys put that goddamn *Little Mermaid* shower curtain in my room when I told you not to—"

I remove my hands and watch his face. He blinks a few times, scanning the bathroom that's double the size it was when he left. "What the . . ."

"Surprise," Bell squeals, jumping up and down. She runs over to the shiny new bathtub and perches on the edge. "For your bubble baths, Daddy!"

He looks from the tub to me. "You did this?"

"They installed it while we were away. Rush job."

He shakes his head, his mouth open. "I can't believe it. This must've been a huge project."

"It'll be worth it." I lower my voice. "I've missed it, taking a bath with you."

"And look," Bell says, lifting a bottle of Glenlivet from inside with both hands. There's a red bow around the neck. "Adult juice."

Andrew grins, taking the whisky from her. He unscrews the cap and raises it in the air for a toast. "To my girls," he says. "I'm the luckiest son of a you-know-what around."

"Bitch," Bell says. "Son of a bitch."

"Language," I say with a defeated sigh. There are years of damage done from growing up around crass men that even *I* can't undo.

Andrew takes a swig, then passes it to me. I do the same, and like every time we settle in with a glass of Glenlivet, the first taste reminds me of our first night together.

Andrew sets the bottle on the counter and puts a heavy arm around my shoulders. "You're the best, you know that?" he murmurs, pulling me into him. He kisses the tip of my nose and whispers, "What better gift could you give me then *more* naked time with you?"

I tilt my face up to his, asking for a real kiss. He gives it to me, sliding his tongue along the seam of my lips and slipping it into my mouth. "Not in lust with you, babe," he says.

"No?" I tease. "Why not?"

"Because I love you."

"Love you too."

We're gazing into each other's eyes when Bell speaks again. "Hmm," she says to herself. "This stuff smells funny."

Andrew and I whip our heads to her. She's picked up the bottle from the counter and is two seconds from taking her first sip of whisky. We lunge at the same moment, yelling in unison, "Don't drink that!"

There's no doubt about it—Andrew and I have our hands full, and that's not changing any time soon.

I wouldn't want it any other way.

TITLES BY
JESSICA HAWKINS

LEARN MORE AT JESSICAHAWKINS.NET/BOOKS

SLIP OF THE TONGUE
THE FIRST TASTE
YOURS TO BARE

THE CITYSCAPE SERIES

COME UNDONE
COME ALIVE
COME TOGETHER

EXPLICITLY YOURS SERIES

POSSESSION
DOMINATION
PROVOCATION
OBSESSION

STRICTLY OFF LIMITS

ACKNOWLEDGMENTS

A special thank you to everyone who helped bring *The First Taste* to life. I'm eternally grateful to my team: my talented editor, Elizabeth London; the cover designer, Shannoff Formats, and photographer, Wander Aguiar; the final pair of eyes, Katie of Underline This Editing; Nina & Jenn with Social Butterfly PR who, along with every blogger out there, I have to thank for getting *The First Taste* in your hands.

To Lisa, Bethany, Amber, Ashley, Tina, Holly, Lea, Amy, Summer, Jennifer, Alexandra, Serena, and the rest of my street team for their encouragement and dedication as they see me through each book and subsequent release.

I'd be remiss not to mention the wonderful author friends I've made over the years, mostly fellow independent authors with whom I have the pleasure of navigating the self-publishing landscape. With pride. And of course, those same authors who continue to write thoughtful, entertaining books to give all of us what we need: the perfect escape, a look inside ourselves, a reminder of what we value, or whatever else it is we're after.

To the readers: none of what I just mentioned would be possible without you. THANK YOU.

CONNECT WITH JESSICA

Stay updated & join the
JESSICA HAWKINS Mailing List
www.JESSICAHAWKINS.net/mailing-list

www.amazon.com/author/jessicahawkins
www.facebook.com/jessicahawkinsauthor
instagram: @jessica_hawkins
twitter: @jess_hawk

ABOUT THE AUTHOR

Jessica Hawkins is an Amazon bestselling author known for her "emotionally gripping" and "off-the-charts hot" romance. Dubbed "queen of angst" by both peers and readers for her smart and provocative work, she's garnered a cult-like following of fans who love to be torn apart...and put back together.

She writes romance both at home in California and around the world, a coffee shop traveler who bounces from café to café with just a laptop, headphones, and coffee cup. She loves to keep in close touch with her readers, mostly via Facebook, Instagram, and her mailing list.